Also by Kim Redford

Smokin' Hot Cowboys

A Cowboy Firefighter for Christmas

Blazing Hot Cowboy

A Very Cowboy Christmas

Hot for a Cowboy

Cowboy Firefighter Christmas Kiss

Cowboy Firefighter Heat

Smokin' Hot COWBOY CHRISTMAS

KIM REDFORD

Published by Sourcebooks Casablanca, an imprint of Sourcebooks
P.O. Box 4410, Naperville, Illinois 60567-4410
(630) 961-3900
sourcebooks.com

Printed and bound in the United States of America.
OPM 10 9 8 7 6 5 4 3 2 1

Chapter 1

"101 Uses for a Bandana—Red, Blue, Yellow, Green, Purple, or White—to Add That Classic Accessory to Your Lulabelle & You Wardrobe." Belle Tarleton cocked her head to one side as she considered the words she'd just typed on her laptop.

Was one hundred and one too many? She'd only come up with nineteen so far. She particularly liked "Fancy Gift Wrap," "Emergency Diaper," and "Trail Marker." Surely she could figure out more uses. She liked the high number, particularly for promotional copy, because it sounded sassy and fun. She was determined to rev up her line of women's Western wear, so she'd come to Wildcat Bluff County to get back to her cowgirl roots.

She balanced her laptop on her knees as she perched on the red-and-white-checked cushion of the swing hanging from the front porch roof of the Lazy Q ranch house, hoping for inspiration. It wasn't that she didn't know ranches. She loved them. It wasn't that she didn't know Texas. She loved the Lone Star State. It was just that she'd been spending most of her time in big cities doing business and she'd grown more comfortable there than in the country. Besides, she was East Texas, born and bred, and that was Southern country compared to the Wild West heritage of North Texas. Piney Woods versus Cross Timbers. They were equally beautiful but equally different.

She looked out over the neatly fenced ranch with Angus cattle, a black herd in one pasture and a red herd in another. By sharp comparison, her front lawn was a disorganized mess. Strewn about were stacks of roof shingles, lumber of all shapes and sizes, lengths of gutter, packages of nails, screws, whatnot, and cans of paint. At least, that's what she recognized by sight. She was clueless about the other stuff piled here and there. All she knew was that the building material was supposed to be on the house and not on the ground. She needed the work completed in time for her make-or-break Christmas party in six weeks to introduce media and buyers to her new Lulabelle & You Ranch.

Unfortunately, there was a big glitch in her plans. Ranch renovations were at a standstill. Was there not a single man or woman in the entire county willing to get the work done? So far the answer appeared to be a resounding negative. She'd had one person after another appear, order stuff she'd paid for, and then, after one excuse or another, disappear never to return. She was actually losing ground instead of gaining it.

She could've called in a team from Dallas to finish her projects, but that wouldn't go over well in the community. She wanted to build a solid, positive foundation with locals to create a good relationship that stretched into the future of the ranch and her business. She particularly wanted to nurture friendships because she had the uneasy feeling, although no one had said anything directly to her, that folks hereabouts didn't much care for the idea of a dude ranch in their midst. They probably thought there'd be extra traffic, which there would be, and a lot of strangers, which there would be, but she planned an upside for the area as well.

She could thank her family for the idea of her taking over the ranch. They'd bought the place to help out friends who'd wanted to retire, but her folks hadn't had time to do much with the land. She'd been at loose ends in a lot of ways...from the breakup of a long-term relationship to the downturn in clothing sales to simply wanting a change in life.

Yes, the ranch was a promotional tool, but she intended it to be so much more. Maybe nobody thought she read emails and messages sent to her at Lulabelle & You, but she read as many as she could snag time for, and her media assistant read all of them. She was particularly attuned to youngsters who wore her clothing line and looked to her as a big sister with answers to their problems. She addressed many of their concerns in her weekly "Belle & You" newsletter, but she wanted to do more for them.

She'd come up with an idea that the ranch could also be used to support the creative arts that were so vital to future generations of clothing designers as well as those aspiring in the other arts. Imagination that translated into creative power was high on her list of important life skills. She also wanted to make available a place that nurtured youngsters living in cityscapes without access to the country, where they could positively interact on tours with farm and ranch animals such as horses, cows, and chickens to experience an agrarian way of life. She wasn't sure yet how she could make it all work, but that was her ultimate goal.

Yet...one step at a time. *First,* she had to get work completed on the house in time for her Christmas party. *Second,* she had to create marketing for Lulabelle & You. *Third,* she had to get local folks to accept and support her goals. A tall order? Yes. But she was a cowgirl, even if she was now on the citified side, and she knew how to get a job done.

She amended that thought as she looked out over the construction-in-progress mess. Normally she knew how to get stuff done. In Wildcat Bluff County, so far she'd met an immobile rock of resistance or ineptitude or something unknown. She just hoped the next cowboy, due to arrive at any moment, would be the silver lining in her stormy sky.

She had high hopes for this guy because he'd been recommended by Hedy Murray, head honcho of Wildcat Bluff Fire-Rescue and owner of Adelia's Delights. When she'd called and talked with him on the phone, he'd said his name was Rowdy, no need for a surname. Why not? It didn't really matter. All that mattered was that he had the ability to arrive on time, carry heavy loads, and drive a nail in straight… maybe he even had a few cowboy firefighter friends who'd help him do the job.

To meet this paragon of construction virtue, or so she hoped, she'd dressed conservatively in a sample of her upcoming line of Western business attire for ladies that was a feminized version of the traditional male Western suit. She was considering a line of bolo ties to accent the shirts and suits, but she needed the right designer to create the look while staying true to its heritage. But that was on down the road. Right now she waited for Rowdy to show up and prove he was just what she wanted and needed to set her life straight.

In her mind, she pictured him as bowlegged from spending life on horseback when he wasn't crabbing his way across rooftops for repair. He'd sport plenty of muscle from wrangling thousand-pound-plus animals even if he might have gone to seed a bit. Looks didn't matter. She'd spent so much time with sleek male and female models on photo shoots for her clothing line that she was immune to physical attributes. All she needed was a man with clever hands and an agile body.

And so she waited. A blue jay took wing from an upper branch of an ancient post oak with spreading branches that had dropped all its leaves. She liked that shade of bird blue and wondered if she could get fabric in the exact same color to be made into a jacket or suit. Maybe it was too bright and brassy for a semi-professional look, although cowgirls did like flashy. She'd keep it in mind for later seasons.

For now, late afternoon in the middle of November was a lovely time of year with the temperature in the mid-seventies. It'd drop into the fifties at night, but that was comfortable weather with a sweater or jacket. She enjoyed being outside now that she was on the ranch. She'd missed the great outdoors with its scent of dry grass riding the air, the sound of wind in the live oaks and cedars, and the natural beauty of the land.

She focused back on Wildcat Road, though it was some distance from the house. Rowdy would come that way, from one direction or the other, turn under the Lazy Q Ranch sign, and follow the gravel road upward. She smiled at a sudden thought. Maybe he wouldn't be in a truck at all. Maybe he'd be riding horseback, jumping fences as he crossed pastures to reach her. She liked the image. Maybe she'd use it in a promotion.

As if she'd conjured him with her thoughts, she saw a battered, faded blue pickup chug up the road with black smoke from its tailpipe proving it was burning oil, turn under the sign, and head her way. She hoped Rowdy was in better shape than his truck because it looked like it was on its last legs. Hedy had said Rowdy was a volunteer cowboy firefighter, so he had to at least be strong enough to lift ladders, tote fire extinguishers, drive fire engines, and handle emergency medical situations.

When the pickup pulled to a stop in front of her on the circular drive, backfiring a few times as the engine died down, she waited with bated breath, hoping against hope that this cowboy was just what she needed to set her Christmas right.

She set her laptop down on a cushion, stood up, and watched as the rusted, dented truck door squeaked open. First one and then another dirt-crusted, scuffed work boot found purchase on the ground. Long, tanned fingers grasped the side of the door, wrestled with it a bit, and then managed to get it shut after several tries.

She caught her breath at the first sight of Rowdy. She was a clotheshorse and appreciated a well-dressed man, so it wasn't his clothes that snagged her attention. He looked like he'd stepped straight out of Hollywood central casting or a modeling agency's book for the hot cowboy who appeared as if he'd been ridden hard and put up wet—yet was still ready, willing, and able to handle any job…or any woman.

He wore stained, ripped, faded Wranglers that showcased long, muscular legs. A washed-to-softness denim shirt with white snaps barely concealed his muscular shoulders, chest, and arms. From underneath a stained, beige-felt cowboy hat, he looked her over with hooded eyes the color of bluebonnets set in a face of high cheekbones, wide jaws, and full lips. He was flat-out beautiful.

He took off his hat and revealed thick, dark blond hair. He placed his hat over his chest...as if sending a message from his heart to her heart. And he smiled, revealing a single, tantalizing dimple in his left cheek accented by a close-cropped beard.

Oh my. She felt a chill race through her body followed by a surge of heat. She wasn't known for strong reactions to good-looking men because she'd seen so many, but this cowboy was under her skin with a single look.

"I'm Rowdy."

"Belle Tarleton." She walked over to him with outstretched hand in business-friendly mode.

When he clasped her fingers in a traditional shake, it was anything but ordinary. She caught his scent of sage and sandalwood. She saw his eyes darken with interest. And she felt the heat and strength of his work-rough palm.

"Hear you need a bit of help with the place."

"Yes." She freed her hand, although he seemed reluctant to let her go, and gestured at the piles of construction material.

He glanced around and then turned back to her with an amused glint in his blue eyes. "I take it you want me to put this stuff where it belongs."

"That'd be good."

"Got a completion date on your mind?"

"I need everything done before Christmas."

He put his hat back on his head. "That's a tall order."

"I'm planning a big party."

"Party." He glanced around again. "Lots of parties going on about that time of year, so folks are busy."

"This particular party is important to my business. Didn't Hedy Murray explain?"

"A bit." He hesitated, as if considering her words.

"I'm the CEO of Lulabelle & You...women's Western wear." She focused on his eyes so he'd understand the importance of what she planned to do. "I'm turning this working ranch into a dude ranch...well, really, it'll continue to be a working ranch, too."

"Is there a lot of interest in that sort of thing?"

"It's mainly to promote my clothing lines." He didn't need to know the extent of her plans to complete the work, so she held back that information.

"You're going to use the ranch to sell clothes?"

"Partly. I want to make the most of this beautiful ranch and share it with others."

He shrugged, appearing skeptical. "It's a lot of work to get done in six weeks or so."

"Do you have friends who might be willing to help?"

"Maybe. But like I said, folks are busy."

"If possible, I want to hire local." She hoped suggesting that she could bring in outside help might motivate him to take on the job.

"Local is good." He pushed the brim of his hat up with one thumb while he gave her a hooded look along with another flash of dimple.

"I think so, too."

"I've got my own ranch to run." He glanced around again. "But I guess I'm willing to take time to help you out here."

"Thank you so much." She felt a surge of relief wash over her. "You won't regret it."

Chapter 2

Bert Two Holloway, alias Rowdy, already regretted it. Still, he was caught between a rock and a hard place, so he had to get out of the chute as fast as possible and hang in there.

He would've recognized Belle Tarleton anywhere because she was the face—and hot body—of Lulabelle & You. He hadn't expected her to pack such a wallop in real life. He'd figured she was all camera angles and retouch in her photos. Not so.

He knew her three brothers, but he'd never met her before, and he wished like hell he could make up for lost time. He couldn't, no matter how much he suddenly lusted after her. Even worse, she'd never forgive him if she ever found out what he was about to do to her...because he'd always be Bad Santa in her personal Wildcat Bluff Christmas.

He wasn't known as the unluckiest cowboy in the county for nothing. He was in a pickle. It was probably the worst of his life, and that was saying something because he'd drawn the short straw. As usual. Now everybody depended on him to stop this crazy dude ranch idea in its tracks. No doubt about it now, his bad luck was holding course like a compass pointing due north...and that particular arrow targeted Belle Tarleton.

She had it all. Hair the exact tint of ripe wheat. Eyes the

color of spring green with an outer ring of golden brown. Skin the shade of rich cream. She wore a Western shirt of emerald green with white piping and black jeans that set off her curves and long legs. She also wore cowgirl boots, but not just any boots. They were a snazzy red-and-gray, tooled, inlay boot with a snip toe.

She looked real fine in that I've-got-it-all-together way a woman who knew her worth could pull off without a second glance. For him, she was worth several glances... and his palm still burned from the single touch of her soft hand. He hadn't counted on wanting her, and it complicated matters, but he was a man on a mission, and his goal had to come first.

If he was luckier, particularly with the fair sex, he wouldn't be here to save Wildcat Bluff County from Belle Tarleton's wild ideas. He'd be comfortably sitting on the veranda of Holloway Farm & Ranch and sipping sweet tea while making Christmas plans with Bert One, his dad, and Hedy Murray, his dad's ladylove. They'd probably be talking about putting the finishing touches on the new Wildcat Bluff Fire-Rescue fund-raiser calendar since the department was all-volunteer and self-funded with Hedy in charge of the station.

Heaven help all the local cowboy firefighters when this calendar was released in time for Christmas sales because Sydney Steele, head wrangler of the venture, was calling it "Wet and Wild Cowboy Firefighters." She'd snagged photographs from the dunking booth at Wild West Days over Labor Day weekend, and they were all definitely wet with their clothes clinging to their bodies. They'd also been wild at the time...wild to get away from the dunking booth and the cowgirls who were taking the opportunity to get payback for real or imagined slights in the past.

He bet the calendar would bring in a fresh batch of city gals looking for their own personal cowboy firefighter like the last calendars had done. They'd almost caused a riot at the fire station. Sydney was still kidding the cowboys about it. Guys who were footloose and fancy-free might have taken an opportunity or two, but the cowgirls of Wildcat Bluff County weren't much for sharing, so trouble was brewing with the publication of this calendar.

No doubt about it, he wouldn't be sitting on the veranda sipping tea this year because he'd be riding herd on Belle and her shenanigans. He didn't mind the riding herd part. What gave him pause was the possibility of earning her undying enmity and the fact that her brothers were no lightweights and protective of their little sister. He'd just have to make sure she never found out the truth. When she gave up on her dude ranch, he'd slip back into his own life, and nobody outside of the county would ever be the wiser… and he'd never see her again.

"Uh…do you want me to show you around the place?" Belle gestured at the ranch house as she gave him a querying look.

"Good idea." He realized he'd been staring at her too long while not saying a word. Truth of the matter, she was inspiring him. On his better days, he was a poet. Not that anybody much cared or that there was much money in it, but cowboy poems were an old tradition like cowboy music, and he descended from a long line of Texans who put words to paper and words to music. Bottom line, they were all storytellers.

"How soon can you start work?"

He wanted to say, "Never," but that wasn't an acceptable answer. "Why don't you show me around the place? I'd like to get an idea of what we're looking at here."

"But when can you start the job?"

"Pretty quick." He realized he was actually going to do this for the county, even if he didn't want to do it. "By the way, this is volunteer work on my part."

"What do you mean?"

"I'd like you to donate whatever you think is right to Wildcat Bluff Fire-Rescue."

"What if I don't think it's worth much?"

"That's for you to decide. Like I said, I'm volunteering my services to benefit our local fire department."

"That's good of you." She gave him a high-watt smile. "I'll be happy to make a very nice donation to the cause."

"Thanks."

"Now…how quick can you get started here?"

He could see she was a woman who liked to get her ducks in a row before she started a project. He was with her on that one…normally. He'd hate being left with the mess in her yard, but it was only going to get worse. He held back a sigh. He was the cowboy slated to make her life even more miserable. At least he wasn't going to charge her for it. Nobody in the county wanted to see her or the ranch hurt, but they did want the construction process drawn out long enough and be complicated enough that she lost interest in the whole project and went back to the city.

"Today? Tomorrow? Next week?" She stepped closer to him. "We're quickly running out of time before Christmas."

"Today." He forced the word out, regretting it even as he said it.

"Wonderful!"

"Yeah." If she only knew how badly folks wanted her dude ranch to hit a dead end, she'd give up and go home now.

"It needs a new roof." She pointed up toward the roof and then down at stacks of plastic-wrapped dark shingles on wooden pallets and rolls of black tarpaper where they'd been unloaded from a truck onto the grass on the outside curve of her circular cement driveway.

"How old is the roof? Are there two layers or one?"

She looked at him in total puzzlement and then shrugged in defeat. "No idea."

"Did somebody say you needed a new roof?"

"Yes. That's why we ordered the shingles."

"I see." He didn't see, not exactly, but she needed to trust him, so he must appear confident. He didn't know who-all had been out here checking the place and making decisions, but he wished he'd been in on it from the beginning so he had a better idea of what was going on. An even stronger urge was to do exactly what she thought he was here to do. He liked construction. He liked seeing homes made safe and sound and beautiful for happy families. And he liked creating furniture out of cedar and cherry and oak in his spare time. He really was the perfect person for this project, if he'd been in a different position.

"We simply must get these shingles off the ground and onto the roof before my party. Imagine if they were still here? What a mess."

He nodded, thinking the shingles might very well be

the perfect item to make her give up and go home. They were heavy, bulky, and smelly. They got hot and soft in the summer and cold and hard in the winter. They were best moved in bulk with a forklift. And they were an eyesore besides being in the way of guests or visitors.

"You can shingle a house, can't you?"

He nodded again, deciding shingles were the last thing he was going to deal with because they were absolutely perfect for the Belle Tarleton removal plan. She should've checked out Wildcat Bluff County before she decided to change it to her satisfaction and found out hereabouts its residents were big on tradition.

"Good. That's a relief."

"I can imagine." He gave her a reassuring smile. "You want the place looking nice for your Christmas party."

"Nice!" She gestured around her again. "I want more than nice. I want perfection. I want updates and upgrades. I want vintage with a wow."

"I got you." He crossed his fingers behind his back. "You can put your faith in me. I'm totally behind Wildcat Bluff County and anything that benefits its residents."

"Perfect." And she returned his smile. "Now let me give you a tour of the Lazy Q that I'm renaming Lulabelle & You Ranch."

"Catchy." Maybe she didn't realize it, but the ranch would always be known locally as the Lazy Q. That's just the way it worked in the country. Houses, ranches, farms, and property were forever known by the original owner's name or the name they'd given the property. Of course, Lazy Q probably couldn't be marketed nearly as well as Lulabelle & You, but her plan was never going to get that far, so it didn't much matter what she called the place.

"I think so, too." She gave him another smile. "Please come this way."

He followed her…or at least the sway of her hips. He wondered if her underwear matched the red shoes or the white blouse or the blue suit. He hoped it was red. He hoped it was sheer and lacy. He hoped he'd get to see it someday.

And he stopped his thoughts right there. He was here to cause trouble, and if she ever found out, she'd hate him for life. He didn't stand a chance in hell of ever seeing her lingerie, no matter if it was red, white, or blue. At the idea of those colors, he felt a swell of patriotism despite the fact that it was well past the Fourth of July. He'd probably always think of her when July 4 rolled around, and that'd be better than remembering the Christmas he'd played Scrooge.

"First of all," Belle said as she pointed at the front of the house, "the place screams eighties."

"That's when it was built. The old farmhouse was just too much to repair, so the Simpsons replaced it."

"Really." She stopped on the cement walkway and cocked her head to one side as she looked at the house. "I wish they'd saved the old one. Wouldn't that have been fun to restore?"

"The family didn't think so."

"I guess when you're running a ranch you're kind of busy."

"Yeah."

"I wish the house was bigger, too, but at least there's a fairly large closet and bath for each of the four bedrooms."

"It was considered real nice when they built it." He supposed one person's palace was another person's camper.

"Yes, I can see it would've been wonderful for their family. But—"

"Not fancy enough for Lulabelle & You."

"I'd like to update and upgrade everything."

"By Christmas?" He almost choked at the ridiculous idea—as if anything could be done that fast, even if he was actually working at it.

"I guess that's too much to ask."

"For one person, there's no doubt about it."

She stomped her foot. "We'd be so much further along if anybody in all this time had completed even one item on my to-do list."

"Folks get busy with their own lives."

"But couldn't they be professional?"

"It's different in the country."

"I know that, but I also know stuff gets done."

"That's why I'm here. What's your priority?"

"Everything!" She gestured in a circle to include the house and all the debris distributed around it.

He couldn't blame her for being frustrated, even angry, because folks had done a good job of holding her up. Everybody's main concern now was that she'd bring in a sharp team from Dallas and get it straightened out lickety-split. Fortunately, she was trying to work with locals and stay on their good side, so she was letting them run on a long lead before she hauled back, and so far she hadn't done it. Too bad she didn't realize she ought to go ahead and get plenty of outside professional help...but he wasn't the one to tell her.

It was a pretty ranch house made of peach brick with white trim. Traditional in that it was long with a garage on one end but not low since it had a peaked roof to accommodate a second floor. Double front doors opened onto a covered front porch with six square pillars set in the cement floor. An old, stained, pale-gray roof looked in need of replacement before it started leaking inside. Two chimneys rose above the roof, announcing that the fireplaces inside would be cozy round about Christmas.

Architecture from the 1980s suited him just fine. It was a good, solid construction period. He never cared to see a building taken out of its time with a bunch of stuck-on new stuff that kept the structure from being one thing or the other. He was glad nothing had been done that couldn't be undone.

He also liked the old red barn in back that wasn't used except for storage since they'd built the big, modern barn farther away. This barn had a steep peaked roof and center breezeway that separated the two halves of the building so that hay could be kept on one side and horse or cow stables on the other. It could use a new coat of paint and a touch-up of white trim.

He realized that he was getting into the project, beginning to imagine how he could restore the place to its former glory. If he wasn't careful, Belle Tarleton was going to lure him into all sorts of bad ideas.

"What do you think?"

"Looks like it could use a new roof."

"We've got one." She pointed at the shingle stacks. "We just need to get it off the ground and onto the house."

He walked up to the house and checked the lower edge of the roof. "Looks like you've got two layers of shingles."

"Does it matter?"

"Yes, it makes a big difference. We're talking about extra time and effort." He realized she knew nothing about construction so she was on a steep learning curve. In this case, it was to his benefit since she wouldn't know what was going on. "If there are two layers, the bottom layer will be old and crumbly."

"So?"

"When I take it off, it'll break up into small pieces if it doesn't disintegrate entirely, and there'll be a lot of debris—along with a lot of nails—that'll fall to the ground no matter how careful I am when I shovel off the shingles. After that, I'll have to check for damage. I may need to replace part of the deck here and there. Hopefully, there won't be much of that, but you never know until you remove the shingles."

"Oh my…that sounds like a lot of complicated and time-consuming work."

"That's not all. Once deck repairs are made, I'll lay down tarpaper over the entire structure. After that, I'll use my gun to nail the shingles onto the roof."

"Gun?"

"Nail gun."

"Right." She walked over to a shingle stack and patted the plastic cover with the flat of her hand. "I suppose it'd better be shingles first. The last thing I want is for these to be on the ground and not on my roof when it's time for the party."

"I hear you."

"Could you put together a team to get the work done faster?"

"I'll see about it."

"Perfect." She headed toward the front door. "Let me show you inside."

And he followed her again, wondering not so much about the shingles as about the underwear that might match her fancy boots.

Chapter 3

Belle was a pretty good judge of character. She had to be in her business. Right now she couldn't put her finger on it, but there was something not quite right about Rowdy's story. She just hoped he could and would do the job. Whatever else was going on with him didn't matter… at least she hoped it wouldn't affect her one way or another. He could be having personal problems or ranch problems or any number of other problems. That was life. She just needed him, and as many of his cowboy friends as he could corral, to get her place beautified by Christmas.

She thrust open the double front doors made of what appeared to be hand-stained and oil-rubbed cedar with big brass handles. Fortunately, she liked the doors, although the beige trim around them was not her personal choice. If there was time, she could easily remedy that issue with a pop of color. Anyway, that was for later after more urgent matters were completed to her satisfaction.

She stepped inside onto the glossy oak floor of the entry and heard Rowdy right behind her.

"You okay with the front doors?" he asked in his deep, sexy voice so typical of Texas men.

"Yes." She turned to look at him, getting that odd vibe again. "I wouldn't change a thing. They're perfect."

"Good." He grinned, flashing white teeth and dimple as his eyes lit up in pleasure.

She took a step back from the wattage, feeling it drill deep. What was it about this guy? He was just another hunky cowboy slated to be a blip on her radar of life.

"Thanks."

"Thanks?"

"My work."

"You *made* the doors?"

"Yeah. Woodworking is a hobby of mine."

She gazed at him a little harder, feeling that uneasiness ratchet up a notch. Who was he? If she had friends in the area, she could've asked somebody and found out why a cowboy with so much talent, looks, and strength appeared to be living life on the edge. She didn't like things that made her ponder their significance because they might come back to bite her at the worst possible moment.

He raised his arms to reveal thick, muscular wrists topped by broad-palmed, long-fingered hands that looked like they could make anything come alive, be it wood or... she stopped her thoughts right there.

She swallowed hard. "You do nice work."

"I like it." He smiled again. "Morning Glory carries a few of my smaller pieces in her store."

"Morning Glory?" She could only wonder if that was a person's real name or an alias. In this neck of the woods, it was surely an alias.

"She sells local artisan creations in Morning's Glory. It's located in Old Town."

"Sounds interesting." She did think it sounded like a good place to shop. She loved talent of all kinds, and she liked to support it. Maybe she'd even see something that would work into her line or fit into the house.

"MG makes perfumes and bath salts and creams and such stuff. I think you'd enjoy her place. Most out-of-towners do."

"I'm not an out-of-towner." She felt a little deflated at the idea that he considered her an outsider just when she was trying to be part of the community...particularly the local creative community.

"Right." He gave her a little quizzical look that said volumes about what he really thought her status to be.

"Exactly." She wouldn't let his opinion matter. She was now a Wildcat Bluff resident who intended to make a positive difference.

"You want to show me the house?"

"Yes, of course." She tugged her mind back on track. Why did she keep letting him throw her off-kilter?

"You can tell me what you have in mind to change."

"If there was time, I'd say pretty much everything."

"I wish you'd start thinking in terms of the original time period when this house was created to be the best of the best."

"But that was the eighties."

"Think about it." He took off his hat, appearing thoughtful as he turned it around and around in his hands. "You can't go back in time and change how this house was constructed, so why don't you visualize instead how you can enhance what you've got with color and texture and upgrades that fit the time period?"

She just stood there, thinking like he'd told her to do as she felt the house around her. There'd been a lot of love here. And pride, too. Maybe she needed to respect it. Had she been running so hard and fast for so long, always trying to catch the next wave of style, that she'd lost track of what was most important? A house wasn't just a house. It was a home. And if it was filled with love, it was the best of all possible worlds.

She took a good look at Rowdy. He was thoughtful. He was sensitive. He was making sense. And he was doing it in such a way that she listened to him. She wanted to know him better. She wanted to know what made him tick...and why he set off her inner alarm system that nothing was as it appeared to be with him. She felt a little shiver run through her, as if her body was giving her information about him that her mind had yet to process.

She must get her head in the game. She finally had somebody here who seemed to know what he was doing and was willing to do it. She couldn't let the opportunity slip through her fingers by questioning each and every little thing about him. She was a professional, and she'd better start acting like one or she'd never have the place ready for Christmas.

"All right," she finally agreed. "We don't really have time for me to do anything else, do we?"

"It's more than about time."

"I understand what you're saying, but we still don't have much time."

"Did they leave it in a mess?"

"No." She stepped into the foyer and motioned him forward. "At least, I'd say mostly no. See for yourself."

"The hardwood floors look in good condition."

"I agree. And we don't have to replace carpet, so that's a plus."

"Isn't there carpet in the upstairs bedrooms?"

"Yes. I don't mind it up there. At least for now. And it's been cleaned, so it looks fresh."

"Good. There's no time to replace flooring."

She led him past a staircase with a wood railing that led upstairs. She walked into the living room with its beamed ceiling and slate-wood walls set at an angle around the brick fireplace that reached from floor to ceiling. She touched a light switch on the wall and flicked on the amber light globes that hung from two ceiling fans with wooden blades to illuminate a large, open area with a leather sofa, love seat, and two recliners that she had selected for the room.

She took a step up to a large alcove that had once served as a formal dining room. She thought it would make a terrific area to set up catering tables where guests could pick up drinks and food as they walked around the living room or stood in groups to chat about Lulabelle & You. Unfortunately, the area had been decorated with floral wallpaper in gold and rust with rust-tinted wainscot beneath. At least it was still in good shape.

She opened a side door and stepped into the kitchen that had an eat-in section framed by several bay windows to accommodate a table and chairs for cozy family meals. She paused as she looked at the kitchen itself. Lots of dark-wood cabinets and almond laminate countertops with an almond porcelain sink.

"I suppose you'd like chrome appliances with quartz or granite countertops," he said as he glanced around the area.

"It's really dated, isn't it?"

"Yeah. Still, everything works, doesn't it?"

"True." She sighed. "It's just that…well, there's not even a microwave. And no bar."

"There's plenty of room to turn this kitchen into what you'd like and still keep it period."

"But not by Christmas."

"We could try, but I'd hate to leave it in a mess."

"That'd be worse than outdated."

"I agree."

"Come on. I want to show you my favorite room in the house."

"I bet I know what it is." He chuckled as he followed her. "I always liked it best, too."

She walked back down the hall off the entry, past the living room, opened an interior door, and stepped onto the terra-cotta tile of a long garden room. A bank of windows with a single door at one end stretched across one side of the room and gave a beautiful view of pastureland and a small barn in back. Beyond that was a newer, bigger barn along with outbuildings and corrals.

"What do you think?" She glanced over at him as she walked to a window and looked across the ranch stretching into the distance.

"It'll be great for your party."

"I think folks will love it out here in this room more than anywhere else. If the weather is good, I could even throw open all the windows."

"I wonder," he said thoughtfully as he walked over and looked outside. "You've got nothing but grass out there. This room might not be large enough to accommodate all your guests."

"That's true."

"What would you think about installing a flagstone patio that stretched outside down the length of the windows? We could even get fancy and put in an outdoor kitchen or at least a grill. A firepit for winter would work well, too. We could match the brick of the house out there."

She glanced over at him in surprise. She hadn't expected him to be so creative. "I love it."

"Really?" He smiled at her with a hint of dimple.

"Would it be terribly difficult to do? Would there be time before Christmas? Would you need help?"

He glanced away from her, appearing thoughtful, and then he looked back with a smile on his face. "We could give it a try, although I'm not sure if there's time."

"I hope we can do it." She felt more lighthearted about the house and party than she had in quite some time. Rowdy was turning out to be better than she could ever have imagined him to be. She definitely wanted to do something nice for Hedy Murray since she'd recommended him.

"What about the old pool room?"

"I turned it into my office since it's a large area." She quickly turned, walked across the tile, and opened a door into another room with beamed ceilings, a wood floor, and a brick fireplace between two large windows. A built-in bookcase with lower cabinets and a desk made of dark wood stretched across one end. She wasn't fond of the beige wallpaper, though she did like the line of running horses above the dark-wood wainscot.

"Perfect place for an office," he said.

"I'm still getting set up, but you're right, there's lots of room here."

"Do you want to make changes?"

"Yes. But we don't have time now, do we?" She didn't have space in her calendar to make decisions for the room anyway, but someday she wanted to make it all her own by featuring designs from Lulabelle & You on the walls.

"There's nothing really wrong with it."

"Except the decor."

"Wallpaper and colors can be easily changed when you get the chance," he said.

"I'm all for it."

"I'd like to take a look upstairs."

"Let's go."

She quickly led the way up the stairs where she opened the double doors into the large master bedroom, bath, and closet. Rose and white were the primary colors with ecru-tinted Country French cabinetry in the bathroom and a huge, outdated whirlpool tub with gold faucets and towel bars.

"What do you think?" he asked.

"I can live with it for now."

"Good. We could replace the tub with a smaller one and add a shower beside it."

"I'd like that a lot."

"But there's not time before—"

"Christmas."

"Right."

She just shook her head as she headed back into the bedroom with the sliding-glass door that led out to a small balcony. She could actually imagine sitting there watching horses and cattle in the distance. She glanced over at Rowdy. He looked at her about the same time. Something zinged between them, as if this was their bedroom on their ranch and if there had been a bed in the room it would have been perfectly naturally for them to settle on it...and into each other's arms.

Surprised at her vision, she quickly glanced away from him, cleared her throat, and walked out of the room. She heard him follow her, but she didn't look back. She didn't want to see the expression on his face because she didn't want to know if he'd read her thoughts or if he'd had the same ones. Professional. She must maintain that level of relationship with him.

"I'm afraid from here on out we're mostly pink." She threw open a door to reveal a pink bedroom.

"Three daughters." He chuckled as he peeked into the room. "At one time, they were all about pink."

"Lots of girls are at a young age." She joined his laughter. "I should know since I design some of their clothes."

He gave her an admiring look. "That must be interesting and satisfying."

"Thanks." She could tell he meant it. "It is that, but it's also hard work, and sometimes I just don't get it exactly right."

"That's the thing with creativity, isn't it?"

"What do you mean?"

"People don't always get your vision, but when they do, it's the greatest feeling in the world, isn't it?"

She felt her breath catch in her throat. He was exactly right. But how did he know? Maybe his woodworking was like that. Otherwise…who was this man who could so easily understand her desire to reach others through her creativity?

"Come on. I want to see the polka-dot room again."

She smiled, knowing just the room. She walked down the hall, threw open another door, and stepped inside. The bedroom was painted aqua with large pink polka dots here and there on the walls and a thick pink carpet on the floor. What she really liked was the deep window seat with a cushion that could serve as a small bed. There was even a light above it and drawers underneath. The bathroom had reverse colors, pink walls with aqua polka dots.

"You like this room, don't you?" he asked.

"I'm not sure I'd ever change it since it's so original and fun."

"It totally suited that particular daughter. She's all grown up now and lives in Dallas, but she put her mark on Wildcat Bluff before she left for the bright lights of the big city."

"From the looks of this room, I can just imagine."

"So, what do you think?" He glanced over at her. "Do we need to do anything upstairs?"

"Once I get furniture up here, I think we're good to go."

"Then let's focus on downstairs."

"And outside."

"Right."

She hesitated as she saw that look in his eyes again that gave her pause. "You do want the job, don't you?"

"Sure." He placed one hand over a big polka dot. "I'm here to make sure everything goes exactly right…for Wildcat Bluff County."

Chapter 4

Bert Two trailed Belle down the staircase, wishing he was anywhere else. No, he didn't mean it. He wished he was here to really help her turn the Lazy Q into the Lulabelle & You Ranch. He liked her idea, except not to update and upgrade till the house was a shadow of its former self. He'd like to see the creative center she was developing here bring new excitement to the county…if she wasn't going to dude ranch the whole thing into a mockery of normal life.

He tried not to sigh as he watched the sway of her hips. Christmas couldn't come soon enough. Between lying and lusting, it was going to be six weeks of hell for a cowboy who just wanted a simple life.

When they reached the entry, he hesitated…still watching her as she sauntered outside, put her hands on her hips, and surveyed the area. Yeah, Christmas was going to be a long time coming.

She turned back and cocked her head to one side. "Rowdy, where do you want to start?"

Without thinking about it, he looked over his shoulder for Rowdy. Not good. He'd better start remembering that was his new name or he'd never be able to answer to it. For that matter, folks in the county ought to get used to it, too. Now that it was too late, he should've thought of the ramifications before he came up with a new name. It could go bad fast.

"Rowdy?"

"Yeah. That's me."

"I know." She gave him a puzzled stare.

He didn't want her to consider the possibility that he might be using an alias, so he had to be quicker and sharper about it in the future.

"Well?"

"Right." He wrenched his thoughts back to the matter at hand. He had to pretend to make some sort of headway... or at least do something that looked like progress to her. "Maybe I'd better have a look at the material out front and get it in some sort of order so we know what we have and what we need."

"Good idea." She smiled, appearing happy. "All that stuff makes little sense to me. Plus I'd be grateful if it was stacked and organized in such a way that it wasn't underfoot with us coming and going through the front doors."

"That's doable." He said the word, but it didn't mean much since he'd gotten fixated on her being grateful to him. How grateful? If he took care of her needs, would she take care of his needs? He squashed the idea. He was taking care of nothing for her. Christmas was shaping up to be a lump of coal in his stocking while everyone else received goodies. Unlucky didn't begin to describe his situation.

Maybe his new name would change his luck. If he looked on the bright side, it might be time he moved beyond his dad's mantle, not only in name but in purpose. Not that he didn't admire his dad and not that they didn't work well together on their ranch and all, but his dad spent a lot of time with Hedy now, so they didn't hang out as much. Maybe it was time he pursued something of his own more diligently...like his cowboy poetry. He could even write as Rowdy the Cowboy. He chuckled at the idea. Maybe Belle and the whole cockamamie dude ranch were a blessing in disguise because they got him thinking in new ways.

He followed her outside, stopped, and glanced up at the blue sky dotted by fluffy white clouds. It was dry and fairly warm, so it was a nice day, all in all. As a volunteer firefighter, he kept an eye on the sky, always scanning for a telltale sign of smoke that would give him an early warning sign that trouble was brewing in the county. Sometimes he'd smell smoke, but usually a visual alert worked best to save lives and property.

"It's so pretty here." She walked over to him. "In East Texas you don't see far for all the trees and hills. Here, it's like you can see forever."

"That's flat plains and prairies for you." He caught her scent, tantalizing orange-and-clove. "Do you like it here?"

"Yes." She took a deep breath. "I wish I'd come to the ranch sooner."

"No point in should've or could've. You're here now." He looked away from her and scanned the horizon again. The sun was in an early-afternoon position, so the heat of the day was coming on strong even in November.

"True. And I'm glad to be here now." She gestured around the lawn. "Guess I'd better let you get to work. If you need anything, I'll be in the office."

"I'll call your cell if I have any questions."

"You can just come find me, too. If you need water, there are cold bottles of it in the refrigerator."

"Thanks."

"Will you be here tomorrow?"

"Eight okay?"

"Perfect. I'll have coffee on if you want some." She smiled, and it lit up her bright eyes.

He smiled back, catching her happiness. She looked as if the weight of the world had just lifted off her. He wished like hell he was worthy of that smile and trust. If only...but her happiness wasn't his goal.

He turned away and glanced across Wildcat Road to get his mind off her. He thought he saw smoke spiraling upward from the dry grass. He blinked several times to make sure he wasn't imagining fire. Nope. It was there all right. He felt his body stiffen in response.

"What is it?" she asked.

He didn't want to alarm her, but he had to drop everything like all the volunteers did when they needed to fight a fire.

She stepped closer to him. "What do you see out there?"

"Looks like the beginning of a brush fire beside the road."

"I see it now." She put a hand protectively over her chest. "Let's get the fire extinguishers in my kitchen."

"Wait." He pulled his cell phone out of his pocket and hit speed dial for the fire station.

"Wildcat Bluff Fire-Rescue," Hedy answered in her no-nonsense voice. "Bert Two, what's going on?"

"It's Rowdy."

"Right...uh, Rowdy," Hedy said.

"I'm at the Lazy Q. I see smoke on the other side of Wildcat Road."

"Class A fire?"

"Right. Looks like it's just getting started, but it'll spread fast."

"You know it. I'll send you a booster."

"Thanks. I've got gear in my truck. I'll try to get the blaze under control before it spreads too far."

"Don't put yourself in danger. Help will be there soon. And I'm calling Sheriff Calhoun right now."

"Appreciate it." He clicked off and shoved his phone back in his pocket. Good thing she was sending a rig just in case they needed backup. They had a dandy new red booster truck with a three-hundred-GPM pump capacity and a 250-gallon water tank. It could easily handle small fires that didn't require the big engine.

"What do you want me to do?" Belle asked.

"Best stay safe here. The fire would have to jump the road to get to you. We'll have it contained before then." He liked the fact that she didn't panic and offered assistance, but he didn't want her anywhere near trouble.

"Let me help. I can fight a fire. Maybe not as well as you, but I know the basics."

"You've had training?"

"Everyone in my family is trained to handle whatever might come up on a ranch, and that includes brush fires."

He liked her better all the time. She was definitely more than a pretty face. "You might ruin your clothes and boots."

"There's more where they came from."

"Okay then. Let's see what we can do. But I want you to stay back where it's safe."

"Hah." She stepped forward, hesitated, and then looked back at the house. "Let me run and get towels and fire extinguishers."

"Good idea. We'll use up my two cans pretty quick."

"Won't take a moment."

He watched her jog into the house before he checked the smoke that was rapidly spiraling into the air. He hoped they could contain it now so they'd limit danger to livestock and wild critters. Birds most likely had already flown from the area.

He jerked open the back door of his truck and checked to see if he had extra turnout gear to share. He didn't, so they'd make do with the single yellow reflective vest. He usually carried more equipment, but he'd taken it out to clean it and hadn't put it back in the truck yet. Shortsighted on his part, but nothing he could do about that right now. His cowboy boots would do to protect his feet and ankles.

"I've got them," she called as she came running and holding a stack of blue towels with two canisters balanced on top.

"Thanks." He set the towels and cans on the seat, grabbed his gear, and shut the door. "I know this is too big for you, but I'd like you to wear it." He held out the vest, wanting to protect her as much as possible.

"What about you?"

"I'm used to fighting fires."

"I don't want to take your stuff."

"We're running out of time. Please put on the vest so I don't worry about you."

She gave him a quick assessing look and then nodded in agreement and slipped into the vest.

"Let's do it," he said.

He swung into the truck on one side, and she did the same on the other side. No doubt about it. She knew pickups. She must have won her spurs driving them long ago. He gunned the engine and tore off down the lane toward the smoke.

At the bottom of the hill, he hit the brakes, made a quick turn, and parked on the side of the road across from the fire. Red-orange flames ate up the dry grass, leaving black stubble behind as they sent up plumes of smoke. Fortunately, the fire hadn't spread too far, and there wasn't much of a breeze to fan the blaze, but it was still spreading quickly. If they stood a chance of controlling it, they needed to act fast.

"I'll take the towels while you use my cans. One is pressurized water, and the other is ABC dry chemical. Both will work in this situation. Your canisters will do as backup."

"Okay."

"We need to get out ahead of the fire before it leaps the fence and gets into that pasture with the Angus herd." He also worried about small ground critters that couldn't fly away like toads and snakes and rabbits, which could easily get caught in a fast-moving blaze and not be able to escape.

"I'm willing to do whatever it takes to stop this fire."

"Thanks." He saw her set her jaw in determination...and he liked her even more. "Help is coming, so if it gets out of hand, we back off."

"Right." She opened her door and stepped down.

As soon as he left his truck, he felt the searing heat and smelled the stench of burned grass. He couldn't tell for sure, but ground zero appeared to be at the base of a "No Hunting" sign. There wasn't a way to know yet what had started the fire, but they'd do their best to figure it out later.

He jerked open the back door, pulled out his fire extinguishers, and handed them to her. She slipped a strap over each shoulder so the cans hung by her sides. He could tell she was strong enough to handle the weight, so she really was a cowgirl dusting the city off her boots. He felt a little zing of pleasure at the knowledge. She was turning out to be his kind of woman.

He grabbed the towels, shook them out, and clutched two in each hand. They were thick and a first-rate choice to beat out the blaze. As he headed toward the far side of the fire, she fell in beside him. Closer to the blaze, the heat hit him harder. Smoke stung his nose and burned his eyes.

"Why don't you work on an outer area of containment?" he said. "It should slow the fire if not outright stop it."

"Okay."

As a slight breeze sent the flames south, he watched as she moved into position. She set down one canister before she wielded the nozzle of the other extinguisher like a pro. She sprayed fine yellow powder across the red-orange blaze, and it caused an immediate pullback to leave a blackened area.

Satisfaction that she knew what she was doing and wasn't in danger set him free to use the towels. He raised them over his head and whipped down hard, smothering the flames, beating them back. He followed up by walking farther into the fire, feeling the heat, breathing the stench, but all the while hitting harder and harder as the blaze escaped, strengthened, and tried to claw its way up his leg like a wild animal. He stomped on it with his thick, leather cowboy boot soles and drove the fire into the ground as he continued to beat it out with the towels. Soon he had a rhythm going—*slap, lift, slap, lift, slap, lift*—and with each slap a little bit of the blaze gave way.

He glanced up. Belle was making good progress just like him, although the fire was still trying to grow. She must have felt him looking at her because she glanced up and caught his eye. She gave him a big grin and then tossed down her first can and started spraying with the other.

And he'd thought the flames were hot. Her cocky cowgirl attitude totally set him ablaze. He couldn't look away till he felt the hem of his Wranglers catch fire...and then he was beating out the blaze with a towel and laughing at his reaction to her. Maybe he'd better add snow to his Christmas list and hope it came soon.

When he heard the sound of a siren in the distance, he gave a big sigh of relief...not only would the rig stop the conflagration in its tracks, but it'd take his mind off a too-hot cowgirl who was getting under his skin worse than any fire.

Chapter 5

Belle heard a siren as she finished off the last of her fire extinguishers. She couldn't have been happier to hear that sound because they needed help. They'd managed to keep the fire in check, but it threatened to break out at any moment...particularly since she'd emptied her canisters. She hooked the can's strap over one shoulder and then grabbed the other empty one.

She glanced up as a red booster—four-wheel-drive truck with flatbed that carried water tank, pump, and automatic coiled hose—pulled off Wildcat Road and came to an abrupt stop.

As she stepped back from the blaze, two cowboy firefighters leaped from the rig and jogged over. They wore yellow fire jackets, green fire pants, black leather boots, and cherry-red helmets that served as hard hats. They'd stuffed fire-resistant, thick leather gloves into their pockets.

Rowdy shook their hands. "Slade. Cole. Good to see you."

"Let's pump and roll," Slade said. "We'll get this fire knocked out pretty quick."

"Just what we want to hear." Rowdy stepped back to give them room. "If you need any help, just holler."

"Thanks," Cole said. "We'll take it from here."

Slade grabbed the nozzle while Cole played out the hose. Soon Slade sent a powerful stream of water over the fire while smoke spiraled upward to the sound of hissing, spitting, and snarling. Sparks flew into the air as the fire fought back, trying to regain territory even as it dwindled in size and scope and ferocity.

Belle breathed a sigh of relief at the sight. When she glanced at Rowdy, he gave her a thumbs-up while holding her burned and blackened towels.

By the time Cole turned off the water and rolled up the hose, all that was left of the fire was a large scorched patch of what had been dry grass.

Rowdy turned to Belle. "This is Slade Steele. He runs Steele Trap II."

She nodded at the big, tall, blond-haired, blue-eyed firefighter. "We're really glad to see you."

"Anytime," Slade said with a smile.

"This is Belle Tarleton. She's taken over the Lazy Q."

"Lazy Q?" Slade's eyes turned from blue sky to gray steel. "If you've got a moment—"

"Not now," Rowdy cut in, gesturing toward the other guy. "This is Cole Murphy. He manages the county dump."

She only had a split second to wonder about Slade's sudden freeze before she focused on the other man. He was about thirty years old and six feet tall with a whipcord body that suggested great strength with little bulk. All muscle. Whatever he did at the dump, he must ride horses, too. He had a strong face—tanned skin, high cheekbones, straight nose—with short, dark hair and five-o'clock shadow. Sharp, penetrating brown eyes didn't miss much.

"Pleased to meet you," Cole said in a deep, melodic voice. "Looks like you did excellent work before we got here."

"Thanks." She liked Cole, if Slade not so much. "We

were early on the scene, and that helped a lot." Her burned towels were definitely going into the trash...maybe ending up in the county dump. She hadn't thought much about where throwaways went around here, but it could be more of a challenge in the country than in the city. With all the construction she hoped would be going on at the Lazy Q, they'd probably need the dump's services.

Rowdy walked over and scuffed at the edge of the soot with the toe of his boot, shaking his head as he glanced around the area.

"What do you suppose started the fire?" she asked.

"Don't know," he said. "On the side of the road like this, it could've been a cigarette butt not completely pinched out before being tossed through an open window."

"Let's take a look and see what we can see," Cole said.

Belle watched as Slade walked along the road in one direction while Cole went in the other. She stepped up to the "No Hunting" sign, where they'd seen the worst of the fire when they'd arrived at the scene. Now that the blaze was out, she could see a broken bottle at the base of the sign.

"Rowdy, come look here. Maybe this means something."

Slade glanced up. "Rowdy?"

"I'm coming," Rowdy called as he tossed a hard look at Slade.

She wondered about the look. Maybe they weren't as good of friends as she thought at first. Of course, she was the new kid on the block, so she didn't know family or friend or foe connections in Wildcat Bluff County. When Rowdy reached her side, she pointed at the glass.

He gave a quick nod and then glanced at the firefighters. "Hey, get over here. I think this is our culprit right here."

When Slade and Cole joined them, they all took a moment to examine the shattered glass. Rowdy glanced up at the sign.

"Are you thinking what we're thinking?" Slade asked.

"Yep," Rowdy said. "Looks like a broken mason jar to me."

"Yep," Cole agreed.

"Yep," Slade said.

"Do you suppose late last night or another night a couple or more cowboys were cruising around, drinking white lightning, and looking for trouble?" Rowdy asked.

"Saw the 'No Hunting' sign, got mad, and threw the jar," Slade said.

"It hit the sign, fell to the cement pavement, broke up, and scattered across the grass," Cole completed the thought.

"A mouse could've made a nest of dried grass or other debris collected under that piece of the glass." Rowdy pointed at a larger piece. "At the peak of heat during the day, sunlight could've struck a convex shape of fragment that narrowed and focused the light to a pinpoint…and started the fire in highly flammable material."

"Are you sure?" Belle asked. "That seems sort of far-fetched to me."

"Did you ever start a fire with a magnifying glass?" Slade bent down and took a closer look.

"No," Belle said.

"Same thing." Cole knelt down beside him.

As she considered the possibility, she heard a vehicle coming toward them on Wildcat Road. She glanced over to see a blue pickup slowing down and then stopping on the side of the road. She'd expected to see a deputy from the sheriff's department, but maybe they were all busy in other parts of the county.

Instead, both doors opened about the same time. A tall, blond-haired woman stepped down from the driver's side. A girl who looked to be eight years of age with wild ginger hair wearing boots, jeans, and a pink sweatshirt that read "Fernando the Wonder Bull" leaped out the other side and made a beeline toward them.

The girl stopped in front of Belle, put her hands on her hips, and stuck out her chin. "I recognize you from your website. Give Daisy Sue back or you're in big trouble."

Belle didn't know what to say, so she looked at all the guys who had stopped what they were doing to stare at the two of them. She had no clue what was going on. Mistaken identity despite the website reference? She couldn't think of anything else that made sense.

"Fernando's sick at heart. He's off his feed. And it's all your fault."

"That's my sister, Sydney, and my niece, Storm." Slade stalked over to stand beside his kinfolk...and face Belle.

She felt as if she'd somehow landed in the middle of an Old West shootout with her wearing the black cowboy hat as the villain. It made no sense...although she'd heard about a bull named Fernando in the news. But what did he have to do with her? And who could Daisy Sue possibly be?

She glanced over at Rowdy and shrugged her shoulders. Maybe he could make sense out of the drama. In the meantime, she focused on the family who looked so much alike from their tall blondness to their narrowed eyes. They were sincerely upset. With her.

"Sydney, Storm, I'd like you to meet Belle Tarleton,"

Rowdy said. "She's just taken over the ranch. I doubt if she knows much about what is going on there yet."

"I'm working on the house." She hoped that would ease the situation.

"What about the animals?" Storm leaned forward.

"Kemp Lander, the foreman, and the ranch cowboys are taking care of them. I have a deadline to meet," she said.

"But is Daisy Sue okay?" Storm stomped a foot. "Fernando needs to know."

"Who is Daisy Sue?" Belle felt more confused by the moment.

"The Lazy Q shares a property line with Steele Trap Ranch," Slade said. "Fernando is friends with Daisy Sue."

"Are you telling me Daisy Sue is part of the Lazy Q herd?" Belle asked.

"Yes." Sydney put both hands on her daughter's shoulders. "One day she was no longer in the pasture. Kemp is being cagey on the subject."

Belle simply shook her head, feeling relieved now that things were becoming clear. "Is that all?"

"All?" Storm clenched her small fists. "She's the love of Fernando's life. Maybe there's a baby. She needs to come home."

"We'll be happy to buy her," Sydney said. "You do understand that Fernando is a famous and beloved bull. We want him to be happy."

"He's the bull that made his way home for Christmas last year, isn't he?" Things were finally beginning to make more sense to Belle.

"Yes," Storm said. "We'll pay whatever you want us to pay…if you'll just bring Daisy Sue home to Fernando."

"I wish I could help you." Belle pasted a smile on her face in hopes they wouldn't be so upset with her. "But I don't know a thing about Daisy Sue."

"We contacted your office," Slade said. "Nobody responded to our inquiries about her."

"Of course not." Belle glanced around the group. "No one there knows much about the ranch or cattle or missing cows."

"Did you get our messages?" Storm asked.

"I've been in transit from city to country, and everything is in disarray until I get settled in at Lulabelle & You Ranch."

"What ranch?" Sydney asked.

"I'm renaming the Lazy Q."

"But it's always been the Lazy Q." Storm looked more put out than ever. "My whole life it's been the Lazy Q."

"Things change," Belle said, trying to be sensitive but at the same time realizing she wasn't getting very far with this group. "I need to make the change to help my business."

"It is a lovely line of Western wear." Sydney smiled, but it didn't reach her blue eyes. "Do you think you could find out about Daisy Sue? It'd mean a lot to Storm and Fernando."

"Yes, of course…surely a cow doesn't go missing for no good reason," Belle said.

"Cattle rustlers got Fernando right before last Christmas." Storm shook her head. "We're worried it happened to Daisy Sue."

"I hope not," Belle said. "But if so, we should alert the authorities so they can find her."

"Will you ask Kemp and let us know?" Slade asked.

"Belle, I can go with you to talk to him." Rowdy glanced around the group. "I'll be working on your house anyway.

I could let these folks know what we find out so a little girl doesn't worry her pretty head any longer."

"Yes. That works for me." Belle smiled at Storm. "I regret that you've been worried. I'm sure there's some reasonable answer. Maybe she's in a different pasture."

"She's not," Storm said.

"How do you know?" Belle asked.

"Fernando says so."

"Oh yes, well...it's hard to argue with a big bull." Belle's attempt at humor fell flat. "We'll ask Kemp."

"She's gone," Storm said. "We want her back for Fernando before he gets sick from missing her so much."

"It's okay." Slade hugged his niece. "The lady says she'll ask about Daisy Sue, so we just need to be patient. Okay?"

"I promise I'll do my best to find her." Belle felt worse about the situation all the time. She wished she could wave a magic wand and produce Daisy Sue. She was reminded of how much she wanted to help youngsters through her newsletter and the ranch. If she couldn't find one missing cow, she wasn't doing much of a job of reaching out.

"Thanks," Cole said. "I know they'll all appreciate your effort. Storm's had the entire county worried about Fernando's lost love, so any news will help."

"The entire county?" Belle couldn't believe so many people could care about one little girl's happiness...or one bull out of hundreds. Maybe she needed to rethink Wildcat Bluff County.

"Yes, indeed," Cole agreed. "Fernando is everyone's favorite bull. And I don't mean just in Wildcat Bluff County."

"That's right." Storm raised her chin again. "I've been keeping fans updated on his loss of Daisy Sue.

Everyone—thousands, at least—are waiting to find out if the Lazy Q, or Lulabelle & You Ranch, brings her home to him."

Belle felt a chill run through her. Storm had just tossed a publicity nightmare right into her lap, intentional or not. She had to find that cow. But what could have happened to her?

"Belle will do her best," Rowdy said. "And I'll help."

"Thanks…uh, Rowdy." Storm gave him a sly smile. "We're all still waiting for your cowboy poem about them. 'Ode to the Love of Fernando and Daisy Sue.' Right?"

"I'm not sure what I'm going to call it yet." Rowdy smiled back at her. "I'm waiting for inspiration."

"Don't wait too long," Storm said. "Christmas is coming up, and it's our gift to Fernando's fans. They're waiting for it."

"I won't let you down," Rowdy said.

"We just need to get Daisy Sue home for Christmas." Sydney placed a soft kiss on her daughter's cheek.

"Fernando made it home in time for Christmas last year. Daisy Sue will do the same." Storm nodded at Belle. "Right?"

"I'll do my best." Belle just hoped she could make this girl and the entire county happy by bringing Daisy Sue home in time for Christmas…as well as avoid a Lulabelle & You publicity meltdown.

She glanced at Rowdy and saw sympathy in his eyes. She suddenly felt as if he was the single friendly and familiar face in the whole group…and she'd only just met him. Still, there was something about him that inspired so much trust and confidence.

Chapter 6

Rowdy didn't just like Belle, he felt sympathy for her. She was unknowingly dealing with a community that wanted her and her ideas gone. Add to that the fact that she'd accidentally stepped into the entire Fernando phenomenon without a clue. And it'd come down on her shoulders. Daisy Sue had to be in a barn or pasture on some ranch, since a feedlot didn't make sense for her. Any rancher worth his salt could tell with one glance she was a high-dollar cow from a good bloodline. She had to be protected by somebody somewhere. But where was she? And why was it a secret, even from the owner herself?

At least they'd put out the brush fire. He liked things that were controllable in his life...except for his poetry and woodworking, which gave him an outlet for his creativity. Besides, he was high-energy and always needed more to do. He'd like to spend some of that time and energy with a cowgirl who shared his interests, but so far it hadn't worked out...at least not in the long run. Maybe it was bad luck. Maybe he expected too much. Maybe he lost interest. At thirty-three, enough water had run under the bridge that he realized it'd take an exceptional woman to team up with him.

He liked women. He liked their sweet scent, soft hair, curvaceous bodies, and view of life. He liked to laugh with them over the absurdities that always found their way into whatever was going on. And he liked their companionship...along with the sex, of course, but they couldn't spend all day and night in bed, no matter how much he might like to do it.

All in all, Belle Tarleton appeared to be the right fit at the wrong time in the worst possible place. He wasn't even going to let his mind go there, or at least he was going to try to keep it from going there. She wasn't for him—no two ways about it.

And here they were, all standing around with the fire out and waiting for Sheriff Calhoun or one of his deputies to show up. Not much to say about the blaze except accidents happen. The sheriff's department, along with the fire department, would still want a record of it.

Fortunately, the grass fire wasn't an issue anymore, but there was palpable tension between Steele Trap Ranch and the newly named Lulabelle & You Ranch. Storm was giving no ground, not that the strong-willed little girl ever did for any reason, particularly not if it involved Fernando. Belle kept looking up toward her house as if it was high ground in rising water. She wanted to escape the situation. Rowdy didn't blame her. Storm wouldn't rest easy until all was well for her beloved bull, and Belle was now responsible for that to happen.

He glanced toward Wildcat Road and was glad to see a Texas Highway Patrol SUV repurposed for the Wildcat Bluff County sheriff's department since it was the best they could afford on limited funds...and they were grateful for the upgrade even at 300,000 plus miles on the odometer.

When the vehicle eased to a stop near them, Sheriff Calhoun stepped out. He was a tall, broad-shouldered man who wore a tan police uniform with a holstered revolver on his right hip, black cowboy boots, and a beige Stetson. He walked right over to them.

"Everybody okay?" Sheriff Calhoun glanced around the group, sharp brown eyes missing nothing.

"We're fine." Rowdy took charge since he had been first on the scene. He pointed toward the "No Hunting" sign. "Looks like somebody threw a mason jar against the sign. It broke. We figure sunlight hitting the glass started the fire. Simple accident. Still, it's your call."

Sheriff Calhoun walked over, knelt down, and nodded as he perused the burned area. "Looks about right. We're lucky you caught it in time." He stood up, pulled out his phone, and snapped a few photographs. "I'll write up a report."

"Thanks," Rowdy said.

Sheriff Calhoun rubbed his chin. "Wouldn't be a bit surprised if the Everett brothers weren't out riding around the county, like they do, looking for trouble at night or to make mischief from sheer orneriness or boredom or pick your reason. They particularly don't like to be kept from hunting, or poaching in their case, whenever and wherever they want to do it. They've been a continual problem since they were teenagers."

"Yeah. Don't we all know it." Slade stepped forward and shook the sheriff's hand.

"I've had to run them off the dump when they took to taking potshots at the raccoons," Cole said, shaking his head. "I doubt they've ever been gainfully employed."

"Doubt it, too." Sheriff Calhoun looked off down the road as if he could see the brothers. "Still, their family's been in the county for generations, so they're here to stay on that ragtag acreage that's seen better days."

"It's not bad land," Slade said.

"Right." Cole nodded in agreement. "There's just no maintenance on it."

"Maybe one day they'll pull their lives together. For now, all's well that ends well." Sheriff Calhoun tipped his hat to Storm and Sydney. "Ladies, always a pleasure."

Storm pointed at Belle. "She's calling the Lazy Q by a new name."

"Is she now?" Sheriff Calhoun quirked an eyebrow.

"Lulabelle & You." Storm flicked back a long strand of hair in disdain at the name. "It's after her business."

Belle stepped forward, holding out her hand. "I'm Belle Tarleton, new owner of the Lazy Q. And yes, I'm renaming the ranch as a promotional vehicle for my line of women's Western wear."

"Pleased to meet you." Sheriff Calhoun shook her hand. "I'd heard you were in the county. If I can be of assistance, please let me know."

"Thank you. Right now Rowdy is helping me update and upgrade the ranch house."

"Rowdy?" Sheriff Calhoun appeared confused at her words.

"That's right." Rowdy gave a big smile, hoping to ease the moment. "I'm at her beck and call for a bit."

"Oh yeah." Sheriff Calhoun grinned as he took off his hat and glanced down at it. "Right. Construction."

"Exactly," Belle said. "And if we aren't needed here anymore, I'd like for us to get back to work."

"Sure thing." Sheriff Calhoun appeared amused as he put his hat back on his head. "I need to be on my way, too. Thanks for the help."

Storm stepped close to the sheriff. "Any word about Daisy Sue?"

He knelt so they were at eye level. "Not yet. But we're on it."

"Thank you." Storm pointed at Belle. "She's going to help, too. After all, Daisy Sue belongs to her, and you'd think she'd know where she put her own cow."

Sheriff Calhoun stood up. "Don't worry. We'll find Daisy Sue."

"Just you wait and see," Storm said. "She'll be home in time for Christmas like Fernando last year."

"I don't doubt it. If I learn her whereabouts, I'll be in touch." Sheriff Calhoun gave a nod all around and then walked over to his vehicle, got inside, and drove off.

"Well, that's that." Belle glanced around at everyone with a pleasant look on her face. "It's been a pleasure to meet all my new neighbors...and put out a fire."

"Glad you caught the fire when you did." Slade gestured toward the burned section of pasture. "Guess we'll be seeing you around, since we share a property line."

"Certainly," Belle said, maintaining her pleasant expression.

"And you'll let us know about Daisy Sue?" Storm stepped forward. "Do you have Mom's phone number?"

"I have it, and I'll give it to her," Rowdy said.

"Thank you." Sydney grasped her daughter's hand. "We'll be off then."

"We'd better get back to the station," Slade said. "Hedy will be waiting for us."

"And you never know when we'll need the booster again, so it's best we be on our way." Cole nodded at Belle. "Nice to meet you."

"You, too."

Rowdy stood beside Belle as the others loaded up, headed out, and drove off. He couldn't help but have noticed the stilted language so unlike the norm in their county. Belle wouldn't be winning any popularity contests anytime soon.

"They don't like me, do they?" Belle said in a matter-of-fact tone.

He didn't know how to respond. He hated to be the one left to pick up the pieces of the Daisy Sue problem.

"And how would I know about one missing cow?"

"Fernando is pretty famous...and now Daisy Sue is, too."

"I understand about promotion...and narrative. But a bull and a cow? I don't get it."

"He's a hero. He saved Storm's life. Folks far and wide like his story, and they enjoy sharing bits and pieces of his life." Rowdy didn't know how else to explain the situation. It just was what it was.

"And Daisy Sue?"

"She's part of Fernando's life now."

"What if I can't find her?"

"You will."

"How?"

"She can't have disappeared into thin air."

"Nevertheless that seems to be the case."

"We'll ask Kemp Lander."

"He'd better know and produce her pronto." Belle put her hands on her hips and looked off into the distance. "Otherwise, Lulabelle & You is right in the middle of a marketing nightmare."

"It'll be okay." He wished he believed his own words,

but he had no idea about anything that was going on at the ranch…except his part in the slowdown. "Come on. Let's get back up to the house."

"And talk with Kemp."

"Is he at the main barn?" Rowdy headed for his truck with her right beside him.

"I have no idea."

"No?"

"I've been focused on the house and my business."

"The ranch is now your business, too."

"Guess so. I just hadn't thought of that aspect of it before all this came to light."

He opened the door to his pickup and made sure she'd stepped up and sat down safely inside. As he walked around the front, he realized he'd become protective of her. She might know ranches, pickups, cattle, and all, but she still seemed to be too trusting with strangers. Maybe it was him. Maybe it was her nature. Maybe it was something else distracting her. For now, he'd better keep an eye on what was going on at the ranch beyond the house. He didn't need the aggravation or the worry, but she appeared so alone and yet so independent and determined to succeed. He wished things were simpler between them.

He sat down inside his truck, started the engine, and glanced over at her. With the determined set to her jaw, she reminded him of Storm. Nobody needed two strong-willed cowgirls butting heads. Maybe he needed to take on the job of finding Daisy Sue so at least that wasn't part of the boondoggle.

"Want to get something to eat?" Food always eased situations, so he gave it a try.

"No."

"Guess you're not in a mind to chow down at the Chuckwagon." He crossed Wildcat Road and headed toward the house.

"Why not?" She gave him a puzzled look and then turned to stare forward again.

"It's owned and run by the Steele family."

"I don't know why you or anyone else would think I had anything against them. I'm simply trying to get up to speed here. One cow was not on my agenda."

"Is it now?"

"Of course it is." She stiffened her shoulders. "I told you it could be a marketing nightmare."

"What about the cow...and Storm?"

"I'm sympathetic. I don't like to see a little girl upset or a beloved cow go missing."

"That's what I figured." He was glad to know she wouldn't solve the issue strictly because it'd hurt her business. He wanted to believe she had a big heart. Still, Daisy Sue could be a helpful distraction in addition to what he'd be doing at the house, so the longer she had to look for the cow, the better for the county.

He maneuvered up the drive and parked in front. He wanted no part of the upcoming business, but Wildcat Bluff County came first. And he'd agreed.

She released her seat belt, turned toward him, and placed a hand on his right bicep.

He felt her touch like a torch through the cotton of his shirt and blaze all the way to his gut—hot as fire. When she released him, he felt the loss like a chill. Not good. And yet he had to see this to the end—and that meant running her out of the county.

"Look, I'm a straight shooter. I like you. You've been honest and kind to me. I need it here where I feel as if the world is against me. And I don't know why."

"It's just—"

"I'm not local. I get it. But I have plans to help."

"Plans?" He didn't like the sound of that at all, and nobody else would either. Had she bought something else in the county that she was going to transform, too?

"I don't want to talk about my plans just yet, but please believe me when I say I'm not here to harm the county or anyone in it."

"What plans?"

"That'll come later." She touched his arm again, but with only her fingertips this time.

He felt her touch go deep. She was revving him up like nobody's business. He had to get a handle on his reaction to her, or he'd never be able to stay on course.

She opened her door. "Let's see what we can find out about Daisy Sue."

He just sat there a moment, feeling as if Belle Tarleton was going to change his life...and the natural order in Wildcat Bluff County.

Chapter 7

Belle stalked toward the front door with Rowdy right behind her. She shouldn't have touched him—not his arm, not anywhere. But oh, that bicep was rock-hard, exciting, enticing, tempting. And she hadn't touched him only once, she'd done it twice. Something about Rowdy just set her off. Where it came from, she didn't know, didn't care, didn't need. She had to get back in control…or maybe she was tired of being totally in control with nothing but work on her agenda. Was that true? If so, she didn't have time for it, not with so much on the line.

As if her attraction to Rowdy wasn't bad enough or her sudden need for a getaway even worse, there was this entire Daisy Sue business to cause trouble. She wasn't sure if any of the Steele Trap folks believed her. She had to admit that losing a high-dollar cow didn't make much sense from a rancher's viewpoint, but she hadn't been here when it'd happened, so she couldn't possibly know about it. Now she needed to get information.

She'd start with Kemp Lander. She hadn't seen him or heard from him since he'd set out for a pasture that morning. She'd been so busy with the house and her business that she hadn't paid enough attention to the ranch, and she still didn't have time to do it. She depended on Kemp, even though she hadn't known him long. But where was he? She should've heard from him by now.

She stopped abruptly in her tracks and felt Rowdy plow into her back. He grabbed her shoulders to keep from knocking her over and pulled her against his muscular chest. She froze. He froze. She heard his breath ratchet up, caught his scent, felt his heat…and neither of them moved, maybe couldn't for the power of the energy zinging between them.

Finally, he cleared his throat, lightly squeezed her shoulders, and dropped his hands. "Sorry. I didn't mean to run into you. Are you okay?"

"My fault. I stopped in front of you."

She didn't look back at him. She couldn't. She feared what he would see in her eyes. Lust. Pure, unadulterated lust. Red and pink and purple lust. She went from hot to cold and back again. She felt her fingers tingle and itch with the need to stroke him all over, every single bit of him. And still she didn't look at him. She stared at the double front doors in front of her, unable or unwilling to move away from him. He didn't move either. They weren't touching now, but they might as well have been because that energy still bound them…as if it were a rope meant to capture, tie, and hold forever.

She took a deep breath. This was powerful stuff—so sudden, so all-encompassing. Instant attraction. That was it. Hormones. Plus she'd been working extra hard, so she was off-balance. She was in a strange place. He was helpful and attentive. Nothing more.

"Maybe we ought to find Kemp and ask about Daisy Sue." Rowdy's voice had gone deep and mellow and a little rough around the edges.

She felt that roughness twine around her, binding her even tighter to him. She focused on breathing in and out, rebuilding her strength of will. This passion wouldn't do... at least not right now with so much on the line.

Finally, she stepped forward and opened both doors, feeling as if she were leaving part of herself behind with him. Imagination. She was getting way too imaginative—in the wrong direction—out here on the ranch. She stepped into the foyer and heard him follow her. She wished she didn't need him. She wished there was somebody else to help her. She wished she wasn't backed into a corner.

"Kemp?" He shut the doors behind them.

"Right. Guess I'd better contact him."

"Yeah."

"Do you know him?"

"Not really. Far as I know, folks around here just know him enough to say hello when they meet him at the feed store or someplace in Wildcat Bluff."

"Kemp hasn't been around this area long, has he?" She glanced up, unable to resist looking at Rowdy again, even though just the sight of him upped her heart rate.

"No. When your family bought the Lazy Q, they hired him."

"Maybe he worked at our Tarleton ranch."

"Could be. He's got an East Texas accent."

"Like me?" She chuckled at the amusing idea, since folks did notice it. Of the five Texas accents, East Texas was the one most Southern, probably because it bordered Louisiana as a gateway into the Deep South.

"Yeah." He grinned, revealing the dimple in his left cheek. "Real pretty."

"Thanks. Yours isn't bad either."

"More Western, isn't it?"

"Right." And then she realized that they were kind of flirting and it felt good, almost like coming home after a long absence. "Uh, I'll call him."

"Okay."

And yet she simply stood there looking at Rowdy while he looked at her. And it hit her. He had it as bad as she did. She felt a little thrill of excitement.

Finally, he turned away and walked into the living room, as if to give her privacy for the call.

She slipped the phone out of her pocket and hit speed dial for Kemp. Nothing. He didn't pick up. She tried again. Still nothing. She followed Rowdy to the fireplace. A big blaze would be cozy and colorful for the Christmas party.

"No answer?"

"None."

"If he's out in a pasture, he probably doesn't have cell coverage."

"I suppose I need to know more about this ranch."

"If it wasn't for Daisy Sue, would you just let it rock along until after Christmas?" he asked.

"I really don't have time to get up to speed right now."

"Do you trust Kemp and the cowboys hired to work here?"

"My brothers would've made sure all was in order before ever turning the ranch over to me."

"That's a good start," he said. "Maybe your assistant could follow up on Daisy Sue."

"Won't help a bit. A ranch isn't my office's area of expertise. At least not yet. We're all focused on the Christmas party and the launch of Lulabelle & You Ranch."

"Is there anything I can do?"

"I need you for the house and grounds."

"I'm here," he said.

"Once I get hold of Kemp, we'll have this Daisy Sue mystery solved, and all will be well on that front."

"Hope so."

"It will." But she wasn't quite so sure now that she thought about it because so far things weren't going according to plan in Wildcat Bluff County. Yet surely now that Rowdy was on the job things would turn around in her favor.

"Why don't I go outside and see about organizing what's there."

"Good idea." She walked with him to the front door. "I'll keep trying to get Kemp."

As he stepped outside, a dark-blue boat of a Buick—nineties Park Avenue model—stopped on her driveway.

She followed him, wondering who could be coming to call, particularly since she hardly knew anybody. As she stood with him in the covered entry, all four doors of the huge car popped open, and four women stepped out. They had short silver or white hair topped with felt hats in a variety of designs and colors decorated with feathers. They wore colorful sweaters, knee-length skirts, and low-heeled shoes. They carried large leather handbags on the crooks of their left arms.

Belle blinked to make sure she was seeing correctly because their style had probably reached its peak in the fifties. Still, it suited their trim bodies with erect posture, as if they'd practiced walking with a book on their heads at a young age and never lost the knack.

"Best be on your toes," Rowdy whispered. "They're

known as the Buick Brigade, since they drive matching vehicles and you rarely see one without the others. They're close to ninety if they're a day, and they know everything—absolutely everything—that goes on in Wildcat Bluff County. They've been friends all their lives, and they've outlived one or more husbands."

"Why are they here?"

"They'll let you know. They attend weddings, baby showers, graduations, and funerals. They make love matches. They comfort the sick. They feed the hungry—or at least provide food at most occasions."

"I'm impressed."

"If you've got their approval, you're good to go. If you don't, you'd best mend your ways."

"Really?"

"They're the matriarchs—mothers, grandmothers, and great-grandmothers of at least half the county. Everybody loves them, but—"

"Yes?"

"They're tough. Meet-you-at-the-door-with-a-shotgun-cradled-in-their-arms kind of tough. But fair. Kind. Smart. And they love Wildcat Bluff County with the kind of devotion and protection that a mother gives her children."

"Should I be worried that they showed up on my doorstep?"

"They must have heard about you."

"And come to call or make sure I'm not a troublemaker?"

"A bit of both, most likely."

"Guess I'd better be prepared for them. Anything else I ought to know?" She watched as one of the ladies leaned inside the Buick and pulled out a large plate wrapped in silver foil.

"They live in a small town named Destiny above the Red

River. It was never much more than four Victorian mansions built side by side across the street from a row of clapboard businesses and smaller homes. Story is that four businessmen came from back East with plenty of money and a need to watch each other from their front porches. Maybe they were foes in the beginning, but they're friends now."

"That's an odd tale."

"Maybe it's true. Maybe it's not. If the Buick Brigade knows, they've never told."

"And nobody asked, I bet."

"It'd be flat-out rude to ask."

"Everyone would like to know the truth, right?"

"Yeah…but good luck with that one."

Rowdy stepped forward to greet the ladies as they moved up the walk with one carrying the covered plate ahead of her friends.

"Hello," Belle called as she joined him.

"Good day to you. I'm Blondel." She held out the plate. "And these are my friends Doris, Louise, and Ada." She pointed to each one in turn.

"Pleased to meet you. I'm Belle Tarleton." She accepted the plate with both hands, careful not to drop it. "Thank you so much."

"Yes, we know who you are, dear," Blondel said. "That's why we've come to see you."

"You came because I'm Belle Tarleton?"

"We're here because of Lulabelle & You." Ada tittered behind her hand, appearing mischievous. "We want to discuss fashion with you."

Belle smiled around the group, feeling relieved that they were here for a happy reason. "Please come inside."

"Rowdy, dearest." Blondel pinned him with a sharp look. "Do get on with your work. This is lady business."

"Okay," he said. "But first, I want to know if those are cowboy cookies."

"Oh yes." Ada pointed at the plate. "And the whiskey I added to the sugar cookies is quite aged as Great-granddaddy made it in his own still."

"Just what I hoped you'd say. If I'm promised cowboy cookies later, I'll get back to work."

Ada shook her finger at him. "Now that's for the lady of the house to say since these cookies are our gift to her."

"I'll make coffee," Belle said. "And I'll be happy to share cookies."

"Thanks." He gave her a big grin, tipped his hat to the women, and walked away.

"Please come inside." Belle gestured at the open front doors.

"Thank you," Blondel said. "You are too kind."

"Please have a seat in the living room." Belle stood back as the women walked inside, moving almost as one instead of four. She quickly followed them, watching as they sat down without their backs touching the furniture.

"Lovely home," Doris said. "I remember when it was built back in the eighties."

"I plan to refresh the place." Belle smiled around the group, not about to mention updates or upgrades because she didn't figure her ideas would be appreciated by them. "Let me take these cookies to the kitchen. Would you like coffee, tea, or water?"

"Thank you, dear, but nothing for us," Blondel said.

Belle quickly walked into the kitchen, set the

plate—which turned out to be glass that would need to be returned—on the countertop, and went back to take a seat near them.

"Excellent," Louise said. "Now, as you can imagine, we've come on a mission."

"You mentioned my clothing line," Belle said. "Is that it?"

"That was simply a ruse," Ada said with a smile.

"The dude ranch?" Belle asked, wondering if they would like the idea and hoping they'd be supportive.

"No, dear," Doris said.

"Daisy Sue?"

"Oh, dear, no," Blondel said.

"What then?" Belle was clueless. "You'd like a donation to some worthy cause?"

"Thank you, but not at this time," Ada said.

"I really thought you wanted to talk fashion." Belle looked from one smiling face to the other, wondering how to persuade them to get to the point.

"You design beautiful clothes for cowgirls and ranchers," Ada said. "That's not our style, but we do appreciate it."

"It's a little closer to home than that," Louise said.

"I'm afraid I don't follow you." Belle clasped her hands in her lap, deciding she just needed to wait for them even though she was used to getting right down to business.

"Rowdy." Louise gave her a broad smile with mischief in her eyes. "Did you realize he's known as the unluckiest cowboy in the county?"

"No." Belle was surprised by the news.

"It's true," Blondel said. "And he is particularly unlucky in love."

Belle was even more surprised at that announcement. "But he's so…so attractive."

"We think so, too," Ada said.

"I guess there must be some reason, maybe a deep, dark secret." Belle hated to learn that Rowdy wasn't all he appeared to be.

"No," Blondel said. "He's simply unlucky."

"Christmas is coming up," Ada said.

"And it's time his luck changed," Louise said.

Doris pointed at Belle. "We've decided that you, Belle Tarleton, are going to single-handedly change Rowdy's luck from bad to good."

Belle felt her breath lodge in her throat, as if caught in some fairy tale where four wise women pronounced someone's fate…and it always came true. She stared at them wide-eyed, unable to say a word.

All four ladies stood up in unison, smiling happily about their pronouncement.

Belle joined them, returning their smiles although not so happily, since she felt uneasy about the entire visit.

"You'll be receiving little messages from us…" Blondel said.

"And if you faithfully follow each one…" Doris said.

"Rowdy and the entire county will celebrate…" Ada said.

"You as the star atop everyone's Christmas tree," Louise said.

Belle gave them all a bigger smile, deciding to treat the entire visit as something to be chalked up to quaint country customs. After all, it could've been just a visit, but they'd elevated it to a fairy tale. She really had to appreciate their creativity.

All four turned as one, gracefully walked to the front

door, and then turned and smiled at her with twinkling winks.

She joined them outside, shepherding them to their big Buick and waving them away as they drove down the hill toward Wildcat Road.

Rowdy dropped a two-by-four and walked over to her. "What'd they want?"

"Are you really the unluckiest cowboy in the county?"

"Yeah. What of it?"

"The Buick Brigade has decided to change your luck."

"That's thoughtful of them." He cocked his head. "What do you have to do with it?"

"I'm going to be careful not to prick my finger on a spinning wheel."

"What?"

"I don't want to sleep for a hundred years. I have a party to plan."

"Maybe you need a nap. It's been a long day."

"How much whiskey do you think is in those cookies?"

"Let's find out."

Chapter 8

"I WISH ADA HAD BROUGHT A BOTTLE OF HER FAMILY'S famous whiskey instead of cookies made with whiskey. Not that her cookies aren't great, but I've always thought they were a waste of good whiskey, no matter how tasty." Rowdy sat at the bar in Belle's kitchen and watched her pour coffee into two Lulabelle & You promotional mugs in the shape of cowboy boots. He appreciated her marketing creativity.

"It's been that kind of day." She set the mugs beside Ada's pink pressed-glass, vintage plate.

He chuckled as he picked up a mug, eyeing the plate's contents. "Cookies look drunk, don't they?"

She laughed, too. "They do look like they ingested a bit too much whiskey and they're a little out of shape." She picked up one and bit into it, still smiling. "Delicious, though."

"They're supposed to be in shapes like stars, boots, and the state of Texas. She has special cookie cutters for them." He selected a cookie, took a big bite, drank coffee, and chuckled again.

"They taste like sugar cookies, so aren't they drop cookies?"

"Right." He finished off the cookie. "Sometimes she'll just drop the dough onto a cookie sheet and press it with the bottom of a glass dipped in sugar."

"That sounds about right."

"But she usually likes to get creative with her cookie cutters...not that it ever works out real well. We've been known to take bets on what the shapes are meant to be. I think she has a cow head with longhorns, and that one is always iffy. Plus she changes them every once in a while—probably finds cookie cutters to buy online."

Belle pointed at the plate. "Fat boot maybe. Plump cloud?"

"Could be." He chuckled as he picked up another cookie. "I'm guessing the Lone Star State on this one, but it looks more like Louisiana."

"You'd think she'd figure out a way to make them come out right."

"Perversity knows no bounds with some folks."

Belle laughed as she selected another cookie. "You mean she likes to keep everybody in the county guessing at her cookie shapes?"

"Beats making it real clear, doesn't it?"

"Maybe so."

He picked up another cookie as he looked into Belle's hazel eyes that shone with humor. He felt the moment coalesce into something that went way beyond sweet cookies...something that connected them at a deep level so personal, so intimate, so raw that she glanced away from him, shielding her gaze. But he'd seen enough. Heaven help them both. She was into him. And he was her worst nightmare.

She ate another cookie and drank more coffee, all while looking out a window.

"Help?" he asked.

"Yeah. Food usually does help. Like you said, it's been a long day...between the brush fire, the lost Daisy Sue, and the Buick Brigade. I'm about ready to put my feet up till tomorrow."

"You forgot to mention Kemp Lander."

"Oh yeah." She pulled her phone out of her pocket, hit speed dial, and shook her head when she received no answer.

"He's probably out in some back pasture."

"Maybe he went home for the day."

"Where does he live?"

"No idea. We don't have a bunkhouse. Kemp told me the cowboys live at their own homes."

"That works." He took a deep breath, wanting to say plenty but knowing it wasn't his place to interfere with her ranch or her business.

"You don't have to say anything. I know how that sounds. Like I said earlier, I haven't had time to come up to speed, and it hasn't been a priority."

"I get that, but still—"

"This ranch has been doing well enough without me, so I figure it can keep going the same way for a couple more months."

He took another breath, trying to slow himself down because he was beginning to want to wade into the deep end for her, and that'd be nothing but trouble on top of trouble. He'd only just met Belle—and he was already caring way too much.

"Don't you agree?"

"No." He watched as she absentmindedly slid the tip of one long finger with a peach-tinted nail around and around the top edge of her mug. Sensuous…no other word for it. It made him hungry for a lot more than cookies and coffee.

"No?"

"If you don't keep control of the reins, you can have a runaway ranch in no time."

"That's Kemp's job."

He knew he should let well enough alone. He was here to make trouble, not solve it. But still… "Daisy Sue is missing, isn't she?"

"I doubt if she's missing. She's just in another pasture."

"She's missing."

"Oh, all right. She's missing, maybe." Belle picked up a cookie and played with it. "As soon as I get hold of Kemp, we'll know where she is right now."

"You've got a missing cow. Now you've got a missing foreman."

"I doubt they're related events. And I doubt they're even missing."

"Okay." He set down his ceramic cowboy boot. The coffee was good, but the mug was a pain to drink out of. He stood up, not about to get more involved in persuading her to take a closer look at her problems. If she had any kind of trouble, that was all to the good. He just wished he could get himself to believe it.

"Are you going back to work?"

"I'd better get to it. We're burning daylight."

"If you need anything or have any questions, let me know."

"Will do."

"And I'll let you know when I reach Kemp."

"Right."

He walked away without a backward glance because he could feel her looking at him, evaluating him, wondering about him...about what it'd be like with nothing but bare skin between them...just like he was wondering about the same thing with her. And yet he already knew. It'd be dynamite. They had so much chemistry they could start their own lab—and burn it down with the heat they generated with their friction.

He kept right on walking, one foot in front of the other, forcing his body to go where it didn't want to go. He'd like nothing better than to turn back, take the coffee mug out of her hands, push the cookies to one side, left her up on top of the bar, spread her legs, and go deep. He turned white-hot at the image.

He jerked open the front door and slammed it shut behind him. Cool air helped ease his heated flesh. He desperately needed something—anything—to take his mind off Belle Tarleton.

When he gazed around, there was plenty to take his mind off her. He wasn't sure where to start. Maybe he could simply move piles of stuff around so that they were in different places to make it appear like he'd been working.

Material had been delivered for a new roof, as in shingle stacks, tar paper rolls, nail rolls for nail guns, ribbon boards, metal drip edges, and rolls of thin metal flashing. The shingle stacks on wooden flat crates had been delivered and placed by tractor on the grass beyond the outer edge of the driveway. They were too heavy to move by hand except in individual packages, so he'd leave them alone. He picked up a roll of flashing and carried it to an empty area near the shingles. After he set it down, he moved another roll and then another until he had all the flashing organized near the shingles. He saw a guttering system, so he stacked the lengths near the shingles so the roof material was in one place.

That's when he realized he was doing the exact opposite of what he was supposed to do—instinct had taken over, and he was getting done what should be done, not what he was there to do. Still, he couldn't bring himself to change it. In fact, he kept on going, telling himself a little organization wouldn't hurt his primary slowdown job. After a bit, he stepped back and liked how he'd removed some of the chaos.

Anyway, he figured the roof was perfect for his goal because it could really use a crew of at least two people to get the old shingles off and the new shingles up. There were two layers of old roof, so the time was more than doubled to get them scraped off with a shovel. He walked over and checked the edge of the roof in front again. Two layers. The bottom layer would be original to the house, so by now heat and age would have turned it to dust, crumbly bits, and loose nails when it came down on a tarp. If there was deck damage, it could be replaced and repaired to make a strong base for the new layer of shingles. Bottom line, the roof would look real fine when it was complete.

He glanced around again, assessing the material. She must've requested that the outside be repaired and repainted because he saw five-gallon containers of paint along with wood boards for corner trim, window trim, fascia, and tubes of caulk. All in all, it wasn't that big a job. She basically wanted the outside redone except for the brick. It could be completed by Christmas…except it wouldn't ever get that far. He felt a pang of regret at what could be—and what wouldn't be, even though he'd like doing it. He sighed. Why did he always have to get the short straw? Unlucky didn't begin to describe his life, particularly now that he'd met Belle.

He decided he might as well organize all the material. It'd look like he was doing something, and he would be. It'd make him feel better about the entire situation. Still, pretty quick he'd have to invent a problem that would take time to resolve while the clock ran out.

For now, he'd organize the material and think about how he'd go about completing her job even if he was never going to do it. He wondered what colors she'd chosen for her house. She could do a lot better than white trim and pale gray roof, although the current shingles had probably faded in sunlight and once were a darker gray that contrasted with the pale brick.

He liked the idea of helping restore her house. It felt good to do something positive for her...kind of like, well, what a husband would do. He froze with one hand on top of the paint container. Husband? How had he gotten so fast from "Hello, good to meet you" to "Let's get married"? If it was summertime, he could explain that he'd been too long in the sun. He had no excuse, not now...except she just did something to him that he wanted long term. Now that he'd met her, he couldn't imagine life without her. Women didn't fall that fast. Men knew instantly, one way or another. And he knew now—deep down in his bones. But she wouldn't know—not yet.

It wasn't smart, any which way he looked at it. He had obligations to his community. She had obligations to her business. They were set on a collision course. And still, he could feel a poem building inside him. Maybe it'd be about forbidden love because he had a big secret that stood between them. And if it ever came to more and she ever found out about his true intentions, the poem would be all about loss. He'd be a fool to go anywhere near that kind of pain, and yet—

"Rowdy!" Belle called.

He glanced up. She stood framed in the entrance, arms outstretched with a hand clasping the edge of each open door. She sort of shimmered in the shadow of the porch, or maybe that's the way he saw her now as not completely of this earth. She took his breath away.

"I got hold of Kemp. He's on his way."

Rowdy tried to wrestle his mind back to business, but his thoughts skittered away to her image, her sheer presence that could inspire a man to create poetry in her honor.

"Rowdy, did you hear me?"

"Yeah." He finally got the word out, but his mind lagged behind because he was thinking, *A cowgirl dressed in gossamer dreams. Daytime. Nighttime. Anytime.*

"He'll be here in a moment and tell us about Daisy Sue."

Rowdy hated to leave the poem unfinished, but reality most often trumped fantasy. "He couldn't tell you on the phone?"

"He didn't...wouldn't...or couldn't."

"Odd, don't you think?"

"Is it? He's the foreman, so he does what he thinks is best for the ranch. Isn't that why he was hired by my family?"

Rowdy nodded, not agreeing or disagreeing, as he glanced down at the smear of paint on top of a container. Blue-green or deep turquoise. It'd be a vibrant contrast with the peach brick. She was definitely going to change the place to suit her own personal taste. Creative…how he loved creative women because they could surprise you and awaken you to all sorts of new possibilities.

And his mind slipped back to his poem. *A cowgirl blessed with soaring wings. Daytime. Nighttime. Anytime.*

"Here he comes!" Belle pointed at a four-wheeler coming around the side of the house.

Rowdy felt his hackles rise at the sight of another man entering his territory. *His* territory? No, not his turf…not at all. He was getting way too protective of the whole situation. As foreman, Lander belonged on this ranch. Rowdy was the interloper—here today, gone tomorrow.

And yet he didn't feel that way. He'd gone on high alert. Lander needed to be watched in case he was taking advantage of his position without previous supervision and now with Belle here alone. Besides, she was too distracted with the upcoming party to spend any time or effort learning about this ranch and how it was handled by Kemp. He didn't blame her. He understood priorities. She was doing what she considered best for her situation.

She didn't need to know it, but he was going to watch her back.

Chapter 9

Belle had this uneasy feeling in the pit of her stomach that all wasn't going exactly—or maybe anywhere near—as planned. Folks kept turning up on her doorstep like the Buick Brigade, but they weren't there to help her. They were looking out for Wildcat Bluff County folk like the so-called unlucky Rowdy.

She wasn't one of them. That fact was only too clear. And yet…she suddenly wished she was exactly that special person who belonged here because it felt like home in a way no place ever had before, even her family's ranch.

Of course, she was Belle Tarleton of Lulabelle & You as well as part of the Tarleton family of East Texas. That wasn't small potatoes. But still she felt a strong yearning tug at her heart to belong here. And with that tug came renewed determination to make everyone proud of what she did with her special ranch. Maybe then—and only then—would she really be welcome in the county.

First she had to deal with her ranch foreman. Rowdy was right that she needed to get in control of the situation, but first she had to focus her time and energy on getting ready for Christmas. Lulabelle & You Ranch could do so much good for so many youngsters and others that she shouldn't dilute her focus. And yet she couldn't let a problem creep up on her either.

She wished Rowdy was her foreman because she

instinctively trusted him. She looked over at him standing there so strong and steady, as if he were rooted deep in the ground, making it possible to pull up vital earth energy and help her achieve her goals. She sighed, knowing she was getting fanciful and he had his own life but also knowing it was simply the way he affected her.

When she heard the whine of a four-wheeler's engine, she turned in the direction of that sound.

Kemp Lander rounded the corner of the house, stopped near her, and stepped off his ATV.

Rowdy took long, purposeful strides and joined them.

Kemp raised his beige-felt cowboy hat with a smile on his face.

"Thanks for joining us." She took a good look at her foreman. He was tall and muscular with the self-confidence she appreciated in those who worked for her. He wore a green-plaid Western shirt that emphasized the green of his eyes and set off the darkness of his thick hair worn a little long. Faded, ripped Wranglers emphasized the length of his legs. He'd broken in his dusty, scuffed cowboy boots a long time ago. Unlike Rowdy, she got no zing from him, but it didn't mean other women wouldn't find him attractive.

"You wanted to talk with me, so I'm here." Kemp set his hat back on his head.

"It's about Daisy Sue," she said.

"Right. You left a message."

"Storm of Steele Trap Ranch is concerned about the cow since she's not in her former pasture."

Kemp lifted one corner of his full lips in a wiry smile. "That bull of hers has a way with gates."

"Fernando." She felt as if she was missing something

here, but she couldn't imagine what. "I'd prefer not to create friction between ranches."

Kemp stiffened and spread his feet farther apart as if preparing for battle.

"She's wondering about the location of the cow," Rowdy said.

"That's right." She noticed Rowdy move in just behind and to one side of her. His action felt protective, but she must be wrong. She never needed protection…or she hadn't before coming to this county.

"That bull wouldn't leave your cow alone," Kemp said. "The Steele family didn't control him, so I took action."

"This situation is much more than a bull and a cow," she said. "Fernando is famous…and Storm has made Daisy Sue famous, too."

"I've been doing my best to protect the livestock," Kemp said.

"If not handled properly, it could turn into a promotional nightmare."

"I get it." Kemp took off his hat and ran a hand through his thick, dark hair. "Guess we've got a problem then."

"Problem?" Rowdy asked.

"Problem?" she echoed, feeling Rowdy's body heat as he moved closer to her.

"You can't have a thing like that going on with a prize cow like Daisy Sue," Kemp said.

"Do you mean making her a star?" she asked.

"No." Kemp put his hat back on his head. "Pregnant."

"Oh." Belle felt her world coalesce into a tiny pinpoint.

"That'd be one fine calf," Rowdy said.

"Do you mean to say Daisy Sue is pregnant?"

"I don't know for sure, but I'd guess so. And from my angle, it looks like a whole lot of trouble." Kemp glanced toward Steele Trap Ranch. "Think they wouldn't do everything in their power to get that calf?"

"No doubt," Rowdy said.

"But it wouldn't be theirs to get." Kemp looked from one to the other. "Fernando was trespassing on your ranch, so that calf, if there is one, will belong to you. Keep in mind that I've had your best interests at heart."

Belle felt a sinking sensation in the pit of her stomach. "Where is Daisy Sue?"

"Well, that's the rub," Kemp said.

"Rub?" Rowdy's voice came out tight.

"Well…yeah." Kemp pulled his collar away from his neck as if it was constricting him. "Remember, I was protecting the Tarleton cow."

"And?" Belle felt a little sicker.

"I didn't want any of your family involved because of Fernando's notoriety. Besides, he's an Angus bull, and you always keep your eye on bulls. They're unpredictable."

"That's not Fernando," Rowdy said. "He's a smart, gentle bull…with Storm."

"Right." Kemp nodded in agreement. "He's okay with one little girl, but—"

"That's enough." Rowdy leaned forward, brushing his bicep against Belle's arm. "You know it as well as I know it. Animals have different personalities."

"True," Kemp said. "But I don't take chances. I wanted Daisy Sue safely out of the way."

"Okay." Belle looked from one man to the other. "That's fine. But where is she? And when can we bring her home?"

Kemp appeared even more uncomfortable.

"This is not a guessing game," Rowdy said.

Kemp gave him a hard stare. "Who are you on this ranch? I'm the foreman."

Belle quickly stepped between the two men, not about to let the situation get out of hand. "Rowdy has kindly agreed to help me with house renovations."

"Rowdy?" Kemp laughed, shaking his head. "Belle Tarleton, you've got a lot to learn about Wildcat Bluff County."

"What does that mean?" she asked.

"They take care of their own," Kemp said.

"Just tell me when Daisy Sue will be back in her pasture."

"No can do," Kemp said.

"What?" Belle felt as if she'd stepped into some alternate reality.

"Like I said, my main goal has been to protect Tarleton livestock. I asked my cousin Lester to pick up Daisy Sue, haul to her to a safer location, and take care of her."

"Couldn't you have simply moved her to a different pasture?" Belle felt more uneasy all the time.

"That Fernando is one persistent bull. I wanted plenty of space between them."

"Okay," she said, trying to stay reasonable. "Now that I'm here and in charge, please bring her home."

"Can't."

"Say that again."

"Well, after I got your message, I tried to get Lester on his cell phone. No answer. I figure he might've tied one on and be sleeping it off…or he's decided to get back on the rodeo circuit. Sooner or later, he's got to pick up."

"Please tell me he didn't sell Daisy Sue." She glanced at Rowdy, and he gave her a sympathetic look.

"Far as I know, he didn't, but if Lester was short of cash...no, even if he is *that* cousin, he wouldn't go so far."

"You're not making me feel better about Daisy Sue." She looked at Kemp more closely. "Have you ever even been a ranch foreman before now?"

"Sure." He put his hands on his hips to either side of a big, shiny, colorful rodeo belt buckle. "But I never had to deal with a bull like Fernando. Famous? Website? Fans?" He shook his head. "That's one pampered bull."

"He's a hero to a young girl as well as to his many fans." Belle leaned forward. "We must get Daisy Sue home by Christmas."

Kemp adjusted his cowboy hat, as if to give himself time to think. "My cousin...well, Lester is usually good about taking care of animals. I'm pretty sure he wouldn't have sold her to pay rodeo entry fees if he decided to go back on the circuit."

"Pretty sure?" Belle felt more alarmed than ever.

"No matter what happened, she can be traced by the tattoo on the inside of her lip," Rowdy said. "If she was sold, there will be a record of it with the American Angus Association."

Belle felt a little reassured, but then she had a horrible idea. "Black market sale. Maybe out of the country?"

"It's possible, but I doubt it. That's a lot of trouble," Rowdy said.

"One way or another, we must get Daisy Sue back." Belle took a deep breath. "If not, Storm will be devastated, a pregnant cow may be in danger, and I'll look like the most inept ranch owner in Texas…not to mention the whole marketing problem."

"If it helps, I'm right sorry," Kemp said. "I thought I was doing the best thing for everybody, but I should've known better than to trust Lester with something this important."

"Kemp, your primary goal now is to find that cow and bring her safely home by Christmas. Use any resources. Go anywhere." Belle looked straight into his green eyes to make her point clear.

"Okay." Kemp put his hat back on his head, adjusted it, and straightened his broad shoulders.

"What's going on with the ranch?" Rowdy asked. "Any problems? Anybody you trust to take over your job till you get back?"

Kemp gave him a long perusal, looked speculatively at Belle, and glanced back. "You hunting for another job… Rowdy?"

"No. I just happened to be on hand when the matter of Daisy Sue's disappearance came up."

"If the cowboys all know their jobs, we should be fine through the holidays." Belle took control of the situation. "Right?"

"Sure." Kemp nodded in agreement. "I doubt it could take till Christmas to find out what happened to Daisy Sue. It's not like Lester's a real crackerjack out to conquer the world one cow at a time."

"Good." She felt a little bit better about the situation, even though it wasn't near resolution. "I'll reimburse your expenses, so keep your receipts. And stay in touch."

"Will do. " Kemp gave an encouraging smile, hopped on his four-wheeler, and took off.

"Don't that beat all," Rowdy said.

"It sure does." She turned to look at him. "Do you think any of what he said is true? If he stole Daisy Sue in the first place, I may have just given him the opportunity to hide his crime and cover his tracks."

"He'd be a fool to jeopardize a good job and reputation for one cow."

"It's such an unlikely story that I'm going with it as the truth. I just hope I didn't make a mistake."

"I'm with you on this one. You need to give the guy a chance to make it right. If he doesn't, then you can try something else."

"In the meantime, Daisy Sue is in the wind and—"

"You'll have to buck up and explain the situation to Storm—"

"Who will want to tell the world why the love of Fernando's life is still gone."

"That's about it," Rowdy said.

"I can't do it. Not yet. Somehow I must buy Kemp time to come up with Daisy Sue. Any ideas?"

"Hide out? Leave Texas? It might be a little cold in Alaska, but there are warmer climates in the South Seas."

"Not funny." Belle paced away from him and then turned back. "How long do you think I have before Storm comes for me?"

"She's pretty impatient, like all the Steele clan, but I figure a few days, maybe longer, before they're at your door."

"Hopefully Kemp will find his cousin by then."

"It's possible."

"Okay. Let's table that issue and get back to the matter at

hand." She had to get on with her goals or she'd never get it all done by Christmas.

"That'd be?"

"For you, renovations. For me, I need to check in with marketing at my office. I only hope Lulabelle & You isn't tracking with the Fernando and Daisy Sue story."

"And if it is?"

"Damage control. Somehow I'll deal with it in my weekly newsletter."

"Do you think it might be best to simply leave it alone?"

"Do you mean ignore the situation—or at least pretend I know nothing?"

"Maybe that's where you're at right now."

"Perhaps I am." She paused and gave him a long look. "Are you sure you don't have a part-time job as a ranch manager or marketing consultant or something along those lines?"

He stepped back, shaking his head. "Me? I'm just agreeing with you. None of those are my ideas. I'd better get back to work."

She watched him walk away, wondering again about him. Something just didn't add up. Perhaps he'd fallen on rough times or spent all his hard-earned money on buying his dream land, no matter how risky or uncertain. What was his background that he could be so knowledgeable and savvy?

No matter. She didn't have time to wonder about him. He just needed to do what she'd brought him onboard to do.

Chapter 10

"I'm falling down on the job," Rowdy admitted a few days later in the front bar of legendary Wildcat Hall. He tried not to look sheepish before the committees for Christmas in the Country, Christmas at the Sure-Shot Drive-In, and Wildcat Hall's Honky-Tonk Christmas. He sat at the head of the tables they'd pushed together so they could sit side by side and make plans.

"That's not an encouraging way to start this meeting," Hedy Murray said, drumming her fingertips on the armrests of her power wheelchair before she flicked her long silver braid over one shoulder.

He took her words to heart since she was Wildcat Bluff Fire-Rescue's head honcho and proprietor of Adelia's Delights mercantile in Old Town…besides being his dad's fiancée.

"Uh, Rowdy…what's going on?" Bert Holloway cocked his head with its silver-streaked dark hair to one side. "Are you taking too much time to write cowboy poetry?"

"You're not sweet on that Belle Tarleton, are you?" Morning Glory leaned forward in her chair to give him a sharp-eyed look as she played with the long chains around her neck.

Rowdy took MG's words seriously, too, because she was the heart and soul of the county's creative community through promoting their wares at Morning's Glory, her eclectic gift store in Old Town.

"Now, darling, I do believe you've got sweet on your mind." Mac McKenzie, the new owner of Wildflower Ranch, gave MG a wink.

Morning Glory gave him a coy look in return, tossing back a long lock of ginger hair. "If I do, it's all your fault."

"I'm happy to take credit where credit is due."

Rowdy cleared his throat, not about to let the meeting get completely off track, particularly not along the lines of love where he did not want his mind to wander. On the other hand, he didn't want them talking about his job either.

"Let's cut to the chase." Craig Thorne put an arm around Fern Bryant's shoulders and pulled her close. "We've got our Honky-Tonk Christmas mostly under control here at the Hall with bands lined up, food ordered, and drinks arriving daily."

"Of course, there could be last-minute glitches," Fern said in her smooth singer's voice. "Maybe a band has to cancel or a particular brew doesn't get here, but we can fill in and make do."

"Excellent." Hedy gave them a warm smile. "If something comes up and you need our help, just holler."

"Will do." Fern gave the group a warm smile that lit up her sparkling green eyes.

"So far so good. We have everything as ready as possible in Sure-Shot for the parade, the antique car show, and arts and crafts at the drive-in." Bert glanced at Rowdy. "Are we okay as far as vintage Christmas movies to show at the drive-in?"

"Yeah." Rowdy was glad he'd been asked about something he'd handled before and knew how to make come out right.

"What about the snack shed?" Bert asked. "You're in charge of eats and drinks besides the movies."

"I'm on top of all that. It's easy compared to—"

"Belle's ranch?" Hedy leaned toward him. "Bert Two, spill it."

"Rowdy," he said automatically and was rewarded with laughter around the table. "Better get used to my new alias. It's my name till Christmas...and maybe I'll keep it afterward."

"We're trying to remember your new name, but it's not easy after a lifetime of calling you Bert Two." Morning Glory twined a chain around one fingertip.

"Couldn't you have picked something a little more...a little less—" Bert said.

"I wasn't going for dignified." Rowdy frowned around the group. "I was going for cowboy."

"Good choice." Slade Steele nodded at Ivy Bryant, who sat close to him. "It goes real fine with cowboy poetry."

"Fact of the matter," Fern said. "Craig and I were thinking you might be interested in hosting a cowboy poetry reading night here at the Hall during the Christmas festivities."

"Great idea." Hedy gave Rowdy an encouraging grin. "Cowboy music. Cowboy poetry. Cowboy cookies. We've got a great Christmas theme going here."

"I bet Erin and Wildcat Jack would be happy to broadcast poetry reading on live radio at KWCB," Morning Glory said.

"Do you have Christmas poetry?" Fern asked. "If you give credit, maybe you could read some Louis L'Amour poetry. It's wonderful."

"Not a bad idea," Rowdy said, warming to the idea. "I

don't know if there's time or interest, but we could invite cowboy poets from around Texas to join us. Original poetry is best."

"I like it." Slade drummed his fingertips on the tabletop. "But we may have left it too late to fit into our schedules."

"I don't see why we couldn't find a couple of hours for it somewhere during our festivals," Craig said. "If not here at the Hall, then maybe at the gazebo in Old Town Park."

"I'm making a note of the idea." Hedy inputted information on her tablet. "I'll let everyone know if we're good to go with that idea."

"I like it, but now that I think about it a little more, I don't know how it would pan out. Most folks will already have made Christmas plans." Rowdy didn't want to get involved with something else that could turn problematic.

"Let me check our schedules, and I'll get back to you," Hedy said. "I bet you're right about poets. If it's too late for poetry, then we'll give it a try another time."

"Even if we can fit readings into the schedules, I'm pretty busy at the ranch to follow up on it...well, not exactly busy but pretending to be busy. I've got to tell you that looking busy while not being busy is hard work." Rowdy just rolled his eyes at the laughter that followed his words. He couldn't win at this Belle thing, coming or going.

"You'd best bring us up-to-date." Bert gave his son a sympathetic look. "How are things at the newly minted Lulabelle & You Ranch?"

"I know what I agreed to do," Rowdy said. "But I get there and I look around and I try not to do anything, but—"

"What'd you do?" Hedy asked.

"I started caulking and painting the trim." He hated

to admit his failure, but it was true. "I won't do the roof, but she'd picked a pretty color for the trim, and I was just messing around with it while she was inside doing business. Anyway, somehow or the other, I started to do real work."

"I suppose your training is overcoming what you're meant to do there," Bert said.

"Guess so. I'm used to working hard and getting lots accomplished at our place. That's what I like, too."

"You know we're not being mean about this slowdown, don't you?" Morning Glory gave him a gentle smile. "We open up our county to others during our festivals several times a year, but that's not nearly the same thing as extra traffic and disturbances and hordes of folks all the time."

"I know." He knew they knew he knew, but it didn't help matters. "Belle's nice. And she wants to do good for the community...at least that's what she says."

"She comes from nice folks," Bert said. "We've known the family for years. We like them. Still, she should've stayed in East Texas where they already have plenty of land and opportunities. I don't know why they wanted to expand over here and then turn the ranch over to her."

"I think she wanted a change." Rowdy realized he was defending her and the whole cockamamie idea, but he'd come to see her position. And he just flat-out liked her.

"Change can be good or bad," Craig said. "Hopefully, we can get her to alter her mind so that it's good for everybody."

"There's another thing going on here." Slade looked around the group with a purposeful gleam in his blue eyes. "Daisy Sue."

Rowdy groaned, along with everyone else.

"Belle is either stalling for some reason or something bad

has happened to Daisy Sue." Slade leaned toward Rowdy. "Do you know anything? Storm is getting more and more agitated since she can't get a straight answer."

"If I knew the location of Daisy Sue, I'd tell you." Rowdy stared at the scarred-wood tabletop, wishing he could solve the disappearance.

"Do you think Daisy Sue is still alive?" Slade asked, pushing his point. "It's Storm's greatest concern."

"As far as I know, the cow is well," Rowdy said.

"But where is she, and why is it a secret?" Slade asked.

"I'm just the help. I'm not told everything," Rowdy said, stalling as best he could in the situation because he felt he owed it to Belle and Kemp to avoid making them appear inept as ranchers. Besides, he didn't know enough to even hazard a guess as to Daisy Sue's whereabouts.

"If you learn anything about her location, you'll let us know, won't you?" Slade asked.

"Right."

"And you'll slow that paint job down," Bert said.

"Right."

"If you run into trouble, you'll call us, won't you?" Hedy asked in a gentle voice.

"Right." Rowdy glanced around the group. "It's just… Belle is okay. She's got big plans and a big heart. I'm getting to where I hate to stall, even when I know it's what we decided to do."

"Are you writing poetry about her?" Morning Glory asked in a tone as gentle as Hedy's.

He hesitated, wanting to lie and not knowing if he could do it or if they'd hear it in his voice. Besides, it was embarrassing to admit.

"She won't be here long," Bert said in a sympathetic tone. "If you get involved, it'll be another case of—"

"Bad luck." Rowdy completed the thought he knew was on all their minds. "I'm the unluckiest cowboy in the county, and this just goes to prove my luck is never changing from bad to good."

"I wouldn't go that far," Morning Glory said. "But I guess we should've thought twice before putting you in a position to...well, get inspired enough to write poetry."

"Maybe her bad luck in moving here will cancel out his bad luck in living here." Hedy gave the group a tentative smile.

"You mean Rowdy's luck will change when Belle's gone?" Morning Glory asked.

"It's a thought," Hedy said.

"Look, there's no getting around my luck—or lack of it." Rowdy didn't want to talk about it anymore because there was no way out of the unending circle. "Let's table it. I'll keep my word on the slowdown. Anything else is nobody's business but my own."

"You're right," Morning Glory said. "Sometimes we're just busybodies in this town, and you deserve your privacy."

"Reminds me." Rowdy couldn't keep from chuckling at the thought. "Guess who turned up to see Belle last week?"

"Do you mean she actually has a friend in Wildcat Bluff County?" Slade asked.

"I haven't seen friends visit her at the ranch, but she might meet someone in town or elsewhere," Rowdy said.

"Then who came to see her?" Hedy asked.

Rowdy chuckled again, knowing how his words would affect the group. "The Buick Brigade."

After a long moment of stunned silence, everyone at the table leaned toward him.

"All four ladies?" Morning Glory asked.

"Yep." Rowdy grinned at the group. "And Ada brought cowboy cookies."

"That's serious," Hedy said. "Did Belle eat the cookies and return the plate?"

"I ate quite a few of the cookies. Good as usual." Rowdy smiled as he remembered sharing them with Belle in her kitchen.

"Did you figure out the shapes?" Craig asked.

"No more than usual. Belle seemed to have a better eye for them, but who can ever tell for sure," Rowdy said.

"What do you suppose they wanted with Belle?" Hedy looked at Mac. "Nobody wants to get on the bad side of those powerful women."

"Right," Morning Glory agreed. "It'd be bad mojo at the very least."

"What did they say to Belle?" Slade asked. "I can't think this development in the county can be good…at least for us."

"I didn't hear," Rowdy said. "They got rid of me pretty quick so they could have a nice, cozy, private chat with Belle."

"That's really not good news," Hedy said. "If they've taken her under their wing, they won't take kindly to us getting her out of the county."

"But why would they do it?" Morning Glory asked. "They don't know her. How'd they even hear about her?"

"The Buick Brigade knows everything and everybody." Slade nodded at the group. "They're up to something…and you never know how something they've instigated will turn out."

"That's the truth," Hedy agreed.

"I'd better let my family know about it," Slade said. "Granny knows them best of all of us, but she's got no sway with them. Nobody does."

"True," Morning Glory agreed. "They're a law unto themselves."

"But what could they want with Belle? That's the question," Hedy said.

"I don't know." Rowdy shrugged his shoulders. "I'm just reporting that they came to call, but not on me."

"Okay," Hedy said. "This adds a new wrinkle to the entire situation."

"It surely does." Morning Glory clutched her necklaces. "Bert Two, you'd better—"

"Rowdy."

"Yeah," Morning Glory said. "You'd better report anything that goes on between the Buick Brigade and Belle Tarleton."

"I doubt I'll know much more than you do."

"You're on the spot," Hedy said. "If Belle hasn't returned that plate, figure out a way to go with her to deliver it to Ada in her home. You might learn something useful."

"If I'm even allowed into Ada's house," Rowdy said.

"There's always that." Morning Glory nodded. "Give it your best shot and report back to us."

"One thing for sure," Hedy said. "This Christmas is shaping up to be one to remember."

"Like last year?" Slade asked. "We worried about Fernando making it safely home. This year, Daisy Sue is out there somewhere, and we're waiting for her to get home by Christmas."

"Maybe the Buick Brigade knows something about Daisy Sue," Bert said.

"Could be." Morning Glory reached out to Mac and squeezed his hand. "You didn't know there'd be so much going on in the county when you moved here, did you?"

Mac chuckled. "At least there's never a dull moment."

"Never that," Morning Glory said.

"I guess the bottom line here is for Rowdy to keep slowing Belle's project, keep an eye on the Buick Brigade, and get a lead on Daisy Sue." Hedy made more notes.

"And we'll get on with Christmas plans for Wildcat Bluff County," Morning Glory said.

"Could we change jobs?" Rowdy rubbed his jaw in frustration. "I'm not sure I'm up to Belle, the Brigade, and Daisy Sue. It's just too many females all together...and that can only spell trouble."

Chapter 11

"BIKINI!" BELLE LAUGHED AT THE FUN IDEA AS SHE added it to her growing list. "101 Uses for a Bandana" was definitely picking up steam.

She typed the word into her laptop and then picked up her coffee mug where she'd set it on top of a turquoise metal table she'd found in the garage. It'd been dusty and dirty, looking more fifties than eighties, and left behind by the original owners. She'd cleaned it off, along with four matching folding chairs, and brought the set out to the back of the house where she wanted Rowdy to build her a stone patio. She liked the whimsical touch to her new home.

Could she make "101 Uses..." a theme for her Christmas party? It'd be different as well as ranch-related. Traditional red and green colors would work in this setting. Red bandanas would be easy to get, and green ones, too. She could even create a scavenger hunt around the idea. Yes, she liked where she was going with this party. She could even tie it to her summer line that utilized bandana designs in the fabric. It was a good way to achieve optimum product placement along with introducing Lulabelle & You Ranch.

She gave a satisfied sigh. Everything was coming right along...except for the house. Rowdy was working long hours, but he didn't appear to be accomplishing that much. Even so, she'd made a donation to Wildcat Bluff Fire-Rescue because the department deserved the support no matter how little or how much happened at her ranch. He'd assured her there was a lot of prep work to do first, so she was waiting to see more finished product. She liked the color she'd chosen for the trim since at least he was getting some paint up on the house.

She checked her list again. She drummed her fingertips on the tabletop. She looked up at the blue sky. She needed something a little different that wasn't wearable. She thought a bit more. And then she got it. *Wall hanging.* That'd work. She typed it down, feeling really good about the day.

She glanced back at the sky for inspiration. A bird caught her attention because it appeared to be heading straight toward her. She expected it to veer away and land in a treetop or on an eave of the barn, but it kept coming and coming...as if she were the bullseye on a landing pad.

As the bird grew closer, she could see it was a pretty pigeon with bright feathers gleaming in the sunlight. She liked birds, particularly pretty birds in town like sparrows, pigeons, and grackles. Yet she hadn't expected to see a pigeon flying alone on her ranch.

She watched the bird in fascination as it changed course and flew in a circle above her house and then came lower and lower and lower. Finally, it gracefully floated down, made a perfect landing in the center of her table, and folded back its long wings until the feathers made a smooth finish from the dark gray head to iridescent green neck to plump gray breast.

She felt rooted to the spot, not wanting to move for fear of spooking the beautiful bird. And yet...a pigeon on her table?

It took a few steps toward her, long claws clicking against

the tabletop. It stopped, turned its head, looked at her with one round, bright eye before it turned its head and looked at her with the other eye, as if to confirm she was really who she was supposed to be.

"Nice to meet you," she said because it seemed like they needed an introduction. "I'm Belle Tarleton. And you are?"

The pigeon bobbed its head before putting a pink, clawed foot forward.

That's when she saw the small capsule attached to a tight band on the bird's skinny lower left leg. "Homing pigeon?"

The bird held its position, as if patiently waiting for her.

She glanced around, trying to see if someone was playing a joke and watching her. Nope…nobody but her and the bird here. Surely folks didn't send messages by pigeon anymore. Did they? She knew they were used in World War II for communications, and nowadays racing pigeon clubs sent birds cross-country. Could the pigeon be lost?

Maybe it was the Christmas season or maybe it was simply Wildcat Bluff County, but there was something magical going on around here. For a fact, normally birds didn't just land on your table. Neither did four wise women arrive on your doorstep with cookies and omens. And how did one bull named Fernando and the love of his life become media sensations?

She just shook her head. With all the mojo in this place affecting everything and everyone, her products ought to fly off the shelves during the holidays, and her party should be one for the century. At least she hoped a bit of the magic fairy dust sprinkled down on her…or maybe all she needed to do was reach out and claim it for her own.

She leaned forward and slowly held out her hand. The

pigeon remained still and calm as if used to being near people. She reached for the capsule and felt the warm softness of breast feathers as she slowly, carefully slid a small, rolled piece of paper out of the capsule.

"Thank you." She smiled at the bird in appreciation.

The pigeon gave a soft, fluttery coo and then launched into the air, flew several circles overhead, landed on the roof of the red barn, and disappeared from sight under an eave. Well, she hadn't expected that, but she hadn't expected a bird in the first place, so it kind of fit with the entire scenario.

Curious, she unrolled the piece of paper, stretched it out flat on top of the table, and held it open with a fingertip on each end. She read the first line out loud, "Pigeon-Gram." Well, that was to the point...and oh so curious.

She glanced around again, but everything appeared normal, even if more homing pigeons might be on the wing. She turned her attention back to the handwritten note and read aloud again, "Saturday night next requires your presence at Wildcat Hall with escort Rowdy. And Homer is home."

"Homer?" She glanced toward the barn. Did the note mean the pigeon's name was Homer? Okay, maybe. But who could have sent her the message? And why?

She was struck by a sudden memory. Doris, of the four wise women, had said, "We've decided that you, Belle Tarleton, are going to single-handedly change Rowdy's luck from bad to good."

She remembered the Buick Brigade's other words. "You'll be receiving little messages from us. And if you faithfully follow each one, Rowdy and the entire county will celebrate you as the star atop everyone's Christmas tree."

Belle didn't want to be anyone's star. She just wanted to throw the best Christmas party ever. But it looked like this could well be the start of the Buick Brigade's Rowdy campaign...and they were involving her whether she wanted it or not. She could ignore the message. She could refuse to go along with any of their plans. She could easily be too busy. Yet she wanted to be accepted by the community, so causing trouble with the wise women wouldn't be helpful in that regard. But even more important, she realized that she'd like to see Rowdy's bad luck turn good.

Saturday night at Wildcat Hall. She supposed there'd be food and drink and music and dance. She hadn't been out in the county for fun. In fact, she hadn't been much of anywhere for fun in a long time. And it sounded like a date. She hadn't been out with a guy in a long time. She really didn't do either...not anymore. Business was one thing. Fun was quite another.

It probably wasn't a good idea to even consider going along with the Buick Brigade's plan. She really didn't have time. She really, really wasn't ready to reach out to the community. And she really, really, really didn't want to get involved with a guy. All in all, this situation wasn't optimal.

She crumpled up the small note. And immediately felt guilty. Had she become so hard-hearted while completely focused on her business? She hadn't thought so, since she helped others through Lulabelle & You and that was part of the reason she was here. And yet when confronted with an in-your-face situation, she didn't want to go there. She wanted to stay safely behind her work and away from emotional entanglements. What did that say about her?

She straightened out the message, pressed the strip of

paper against the tabletop, and tapped it with her fingertip. She supposed she could meet Rowdy at Wildcat Hall so as to avoid any possibility of it being considered a date. There'd be loud music, so not much of an opportunity to chat with local folks at the honky-tonk. And she wouldn't stay long. All in all, she could help Rowdy and the Buick Brigade without getting too involved in their lives.

Of course, if she went along with it, she'd need to show Rowdy the note and make plans with him. How would he react? No way to know. Dealing with another person could be unpredictable when she liked everything to be predictable. He might not like the entire situation. He might want to back out of working with her to avoid trouble. He might... What if he *liked* the idea? That gave her a chill. Maybe the safest thing would be not to tell him about the note. Maybe the best thing would be to forget about it. Maybe she simply needed to get back to work on her newsletter...and not second-guess what she was doing in Wildcat Bluff County.

As she looked at the message, considering her options, her phone alerted her to an incoming call. She checked the screen. Kemp Lander.

"Kemp, please tell me you have good news," she answered, feeling a little breathless with excitement.

"You wouldn't believe what I've been through to find one cow," Kemp said in a bit of a growl.

"I regret to hear it's been so much trouble, but—"

"Trouble? You don't know the half of it." He coughed. "I never could get Lester on the phone. He wasn't at the last ranch where he'd been working as a cowboy. Finally, I bit the bullet and went to his mom's ranch—that'd be my Aunt Dotty. Boy howdy, is she a talker...makes good pie, though."

"But what about—"

"You got to hear my sad story because I'm doing it all for you."

"Go ahead." She tried to relax in her chair, knowing she wasn't going to get out of this conversation easily. She had to let him say his piece, tell his story, in the way that cowboys were wont to do.

"First off, she had to bake me that pie. Apple, if you're interested. While it baked, she had to show me the latest family photos and tell me the latest news and try to get me married to some gal down the road. We're talking three hours and I'm getting nowhere fast."

"But was your cousin there?"

"No. Did I forget to mention it? He'd left to go rodeo."

"What about Daisy Sue?"

"Second off, Aunt Dotty didn't know about the cow, but she figured Daisy Sue might be on the ranch somewhere, if Lester had put her in with the herds."

"Oh my..."

"Right. Third off, I was burning daylight riding around on an old bag of bones that was slower than molasses."

"And?"

"Fourth off, I had to spend the night because I didn't get through all the pastures. And that meant Aunt Dotty had to go and drag out all the old family albums, and with those came all the old stories about total strangers. About that time a big glass of dry Texas whiskey would have gone down easy...but she's a teetotaler. At least I got some good coffee the next morning along with eggs, bacon, and biscuits. She can sure cook."

"What about Daisy Sue?"

"I'm coming to that. You're only having to hear the story. I had to live it."

Belle didn't say another word. He was right. It sounded like his aunt was a lonely woman who enjoyed his company, but he was on a mission and time was short, so he'd been impatient.

"After I tromped across another field or two, I gave up."

"Daisy Sue wasn't there."

"No. But I've got Lester's phone now."

"You can call him?"

"No." Kemp gave a loud sigh. "Right before he left, he dropped his own cell in a cow patty—of all things—and it was mighty fresh, so it totaled the phone. Aunt Dotty bought a new one online and had it sent to her, and now I'm supposed to give it to my cousin as soon as I find him."

"But how can you reach him?"

"Oh yeah, he's got a burner phone, and I've got the number...but so far he's not answering it, not for his mom or me."

"And this is what...your favorite cousin?" She tried to keep from laughing despite everything because this was just the sort of trouble that Texans so liked to tell on themselves.

"I told you before. He's *that* cousin. Everybody's got at least one of them, so you know what I mean."

She finally did laugh. "I think I've been *that* cousin a time or two."

"You and me both." He chuckled, too.

"So where does this leave us?"

"Bottom line, Lester dropped his phone—wouldn't you just know—while he was roping a cow to take to auction to pay for rodeo."

"Not Daisy Sue, surely?"

"I hope not. He couldn't be that—"

"Remember, he's *that* cousin."

"Yeah. I'm going to the auction house next, but it's a bit of a drive, so give me time to see what I can see. I doubt I'll get there before it closes for the day."

"Okay. I'll keep my fingers crossed."

"Toes, too. Bye."

She clicked off and sat there, shaking her head. Daisy Sue was still in the wind. If she'd been sold, Kemp could trace her to a ranch and retrieve her, no matter the price.

In the meantime, she might as well get back to the business at hand. At least she'd had an update from Kemp. Bandanas. Maybe a red one could be tied around Daisy Sue's tail as a cow fashion statement.

Chapter 12

As she sat at the table, she heard Rowdy's rust bucket of a pickup sputter to a stop out front. He was home. No, she meant he'd come back to work after going to some sort of county meeting in town to make plans for the upcoming holidays. He didn't seem the type to go to meetings, but she'd already learned that they took Christmas festivities very seriously around here.

She heard his footsteps before she saw him rounding the corner of the house. He looked good, just like he always did in his boots, jeans, shirt, and hat. None of it was stylish or the way she thought of clothing styles, but it was all quality, if a little worn and faded around the edges. Clothes might not make the man, but they surely sent a message about his life.

She quickly slipped the pigeon-gram under her laptop, not sure if she'd show it to him or not.

"What's up?" He strode toward her with his usual self-confidence that radiated outward from his body like a sunray.

She felt her own body respond, as if relaxing in the warmth of a sun-drenched afternoon. He did have an effect on her that made her want more…more of his attention, more of his smile, more of the heat they generated between them. And yet she was more used to being practical.

"Getting some work done?"

"Yes." She motioned to a chair across the table from her. "I heard from Kemp."

"Great. Did he find Daisy Sue?"

"Not yet."

"Why not?"

"He's still trying to track down his cousin."

Rowdy shook his head. "Not good."

"No...but Kemp is trying hard, so I'm giving him plenty of rope to run with."

"Best you can do."

"Yeah. That's about the size of it." She sighed. "Why don't we discuss where we are and where we need to go from here?"

"Sure." He pulled out the chair, but he stopped in mid-motion as the flutter of wings made him look upward.

She glanced up, too, knowing what she'd see but still a little surprised at the grayish streak of feathers that slowed with a flap of wings before Homer gently dropped to Rowdy's shoulder and nestled there.

Rowdy grinned at her.

"Friend of yours?" She wondered when she'd stopped being shocked by anything that happened with this man. He was just full of surprises, much like the whole county.

He looked at the bird on his shoulder, and the pigeon looked back. Then they both looked at her. "Sure. I see you met Homer."

"Yes, indeed."

"Get a message?"

She nodded, feeling a bit wary.

"Buick Brigade?"

"I think so."

"Sounds about right," he said.

"Do they keep pigeons?"

"Yes, they do."

"Homing pigeons seem a bit antiquated, don't they?"

"They work." He smiled with a mischievous glint in his eyes.

"True. Still, what about phones, texts, emails, or letters?"

"We're talking the Buick Brigade. They do things their own way."

She looked at Homer again, feeling even more puzzled about the bird. "Why didn't he deliver the message and go home?"

"He is home now."

"When I moved here, he wasn't here, so I don't see how this can be his home."

"He's a homing pigeon. Homer was in another location. When he was released, he flew straight home. That's here."

"Do you mean the Buick Brigade held him captive?" She didn't know whether to laugh at the ridiculousness of the idea or feel sympathy for the pigeon.

"No." Rowdy shook his head, still smiling.

"Please tell me those four women don't go around the countryside stealing pigeons and holding them for ransom or something."

"Well, I do admit folks love their pigeons, so they might be willing to pay ransom, but in this case it's more like a pigeon rescue service."

"Rescue?" She felt more curious all the time. "What do you say, Homer, did you break out of jail?"

Homer cooed in response and then snuggled closer to Rowdy's neck.

That kind of did it for her. She'd always trusted the instincts of animals, and this bird surely did trust Rowdy. Maybe she should rely on her own instinct to trust him, too.

"Guess you ought to know a bit about Homer's history seeing as how he's moved in with you," Rowdy said.

"If anything, he moved into the barn."

"Right."

She looked a little closer at the pretty, plump bird. "What does he eat?"

"Now you're getting into the spirit." Rowdy stroked the top of Homer's head with a fingertip. "I'll buy some feed and grit, take it to the small barn, and put it in a bin so you can scoop out of it."

"That sounds pretty permanent. I wasn't counting on birds, particularly not when I have so many other items on my agenda."

"They're easy—not a lot of time involved at all."

She sighed as she looked in the direction of Steele Trap Ranch. "Do you suppose the Steele family would accept Homer in place of Daisy Sue, as in lose a cow but gain a bird?"

Rowdy laughed, shoulders shaking and causing Homer to ruffle his feathers before he resettled again. "I doubt they're exchangeable."

"I figured as much. Still—"

"Here's the deal with Homer. The prior owners of this ranch raised pigeons. There's a dovecote in the loft of the barn out back. It's designed so the birds can come and go because they love to fly unless you decide to lock the outer window so they stay inside. I helped out with the pigeons when I was younger, so the birds know me. When they sold out to the Tarleton family, they decided to protect their birds by giving them to the Buick Brigade because their families have always kept homing pigeons."

"I don't understand how the process works with pigeons."

Rowdy gently stroked the top of Homer's head again. "A homing pigeon's home is where he grew up. If he's moved to another location, when he's set free, he'll return to his original home. For Homer and the other pigeons raised with him, this is home."

"Can that instinct be changed?"

"Yes. They can be trained in other ways, but this is most natural to them."

She cocked her head to one side in contemplation. "Maybe Homer living at Lulabelle & You Ranch isn't such a bad idea. It has all kinds of marketing possibilities besides being an additional attraction and educational opportunity for those who come to the ranch."

"Great idea. Lots of folks enjoy homing pigeons, so reaching a wider audience would work out well."

"When I get time, I'll give it more thought," she said. "Homer is a very pretty bird."

"He is that."

"He looks clean, too."

"Birds are very clean if they aren't confined in dirty cages. You'll see them cleaning often, as in stroking down their feathers with their beaks, because that's critical for their safety in flight."

She nodded thoughtfully. "Will he be okay here?"

"Inside the barn, he's fine. Outside can be dangerous. Hawks and merlins will take on a pigeon."

"Oh no."

"But a pigeon is fast and strong and can defeat a hawk… if he's in the air. On the other hand, if he's caught perching on a fence or pole or someplace where he doesn't have time to lift off, then he's vulnerable."

"I'm getting more concerned for him. I've seen hawks flying around here."

"That's natural."

"If I accept that Homer is my responsibility right now…"

Rowdy leaned forward and clasped her hand. "Homer will be okay in the barn. I'll check to make sure the original coop is still viable and he's safe there."

"Okay." She squeezed his fingers, letting him know she appreciated his support with Homer, as well as everything else, and reluctantly let go of his hand.

"Let's get back to the note. What does it say?"

"I believe I've been caught up in Buick Brigade drama."

"Weren't you expecting it?"

"Not exactly…and certainly not by homing pigeon."

He chuckled, nodding. "I figure most folks in the county have been caught up in their drama at one time or another. Take it as a compliment and a welcome to the community."

"It's just that this involves you, and—"

"You were trying to keep me out of the drama?"

"Pretty much." She smiled at him with a slight shrug of her shoulders.

"There's not much point. Once those ladies get something in their mind, you might as well go with it if you want to keep them happy."

"I'll read the note to you."

"Okay." He leaned toward her.

"Saturday night next requires your presence at Wildcat Hall with escort Rowdy. And Homer is home."

Rowdy chuckled, leaning back in his chair. "Sounds like they want me to take you dancing. Right?"

"I could just meet you there. We don't have to dance."

"You do dance, don't you?"

"Of course."

"Line dance? Two-step?" he asked.

"You bet."

"We've been working hard. We could use a night on the town."

"You're making it sound like a—"

"Date?"

"Right." She still wasn't sure if this was the right way to go or not. "We could just meet at the Hall, grab a drink, and that'd fulfill the requirement. Everybody ends up happy."

"Not me."

"No?"

"I want the date. Besides, the Buick Brigade will know exactly what we do down to the last detail."

"They'll have somebody watching us?"

"Nothing happens in this county that they don't know about—gossip is alive and well here."

"You know, we don't have to make them happy."

"I know. But folks around here have figured out that what makes the Brigade happy eventually makes us happy. They have a knack for happiness."

She sat very still, looking at him as she contemplated his words. "I'm beginning to think they really are fairy godmothers."

"I don't know about that, but let's give their message a chance and go to Wildcat Hall Saturday night."

"I suppose—"

"Have you been there yet?"

"No time."

"There will be a live band. You'll like the music. And it'll be a good chance to get out and let folks meet you."

"I'm not sure I'm ready."

"Sure you are." He glanced at Homer again. "Did you return that cookie plate yet?"

"No. I should've, but for the past week I've been so busy making plans that it slipped my mind. Besides, I don't know where Ada lives."

"I do." He glanced at the house and then back at Belle. "We could go right now."

"Now?"

"The plate was an invitation to visit them."

"Even so...what about Homer?"

"He's home, so he knows his way around here. Besides, like I said, he's okay in the barn."

"But why go now or any time?"

"What do you think?"

She didn't say it, but she realized he was making her think in new ways. If she was going to be part of the community, if she was going to make friends, if she was going to garner support for her ideas, she couldn't isolate herself on the ranch. She didn't really have the time to take off work, but she gave him a little nod of agreement.

"Let's go."

Chapter 13

Belle sat in the front seat of Rowdy's pickup, feeling every bump in the road from the worn-out shocks and listening to the engine hit and miss as it struggled to climb the cliff to Destiny.

She kicked crumpled Chuckwagon Café take-out sacks to one side, although they kept sliding back on top of her feet. Fortunately, she'd pulled on simple black cowgirl boots, so any mess on them wouldn't be seen and could be cleaned later. She wore last season's jeans because they were broken in just right, and she'd paired them with a rust-colored sweater. She'd tied a blue bandana around her neck to keep her mind in the "101 Uses…" groove.

She'd also made a point of fitting with Rowdy's down-on-his-luck look so they didn't appear too far out of sync. Maybe nobody else would've noticed it, but she had an eye for how a couple fit together. That thought stopped her in her tracks. They weren't a couple. They were occupying a vehicle together. They were paying a visit…just as friends or some such.

"We should've taken my SUV like I told you." She couldn't keep the words to herself any longer, mainly said out loud to distract her from thoughts of that couple business. He was just too hot for her to be alone with in an enclosed space like the cab of a pickup, particularly when the testosterone level was rising rapidly and making her feel a little giddy. She hoped they reached Destiny soon, or she might finally flat-out tackle him.

"You don't know the way."

"You could've directed me."

"It wouldn't have been proper."

"Proper? What does that have to do with anything?"

"The Buick Brigade knows the difference between proper and improper."

"In this day and age, I didn't think 'proper' existed any longer." She sounded testy and knew it, but she blamed it on his pheromones agitating her. He sounded a little testy, too, so maybe the enclosed space was getting to them both.

"It does in Destiny."

She clutched the pink-glass cookie plate in her lap. She shouldn't have let him talk her into this road trip because that's what it was beginning to feel like...although it probably hadn't been more than thirty minutes since they'd left the ranch. Still, the drive felt like going from one world to another, so the length of time kept spiraling outward.

"A man drives a woman to an engagement."

"What?" She turned to look at him in surprise. Was he some type of throwback romantic? And then she remembered his cowboy poetry, his sensitivity to animals, his regard for the Buick Brigade. Perhaps his concern for others came before matters like a new pickup or the season's latest clothes. In her dog-eat-dog world, she could hardly fathom his viewpoint. And yet he was luring her there.

"I mean, that's what is expected in Destiny."

She continued to gaze at him, as if she could get inside his mind and understand him. How could he be the unluckiest cowboy in the county...unless he answered to his own set of values—honor and integrity—that sometimes set him at odds with the world around him? *A romantic.* He believed in the goodness of life. She felt a little thrill of excitement at this sudden flash of knowledge. She'd charted her own path in life, too. It wasn't always easy, but she couldn't live any other way, even if often it was a lonely life without a like-minded partner.

"Of course, it's not really necessary." He gave a little twitch of one shoulder as if to belie his statement or reveal that he didn't expect her to understand his actions because nobody ever did.

"What is Destiny like?" She wanted to reassure him that she did understand, or at least she was beginning to understand, but she didn't even know how to go there yet.

"Beautiful…and kind of haunting, too."

"What do you mean?"

"We've got a lot of history around here. We're proud of it. People come to see Old Town in Wildcat Bluff or go to Sure-Shot for a touch of the Old West."

"Is Destiny like those towns?" She placed a hand on the dashboard to steady herself from the rough ride…and the rough realizations.

"No. It's got its own beauty, and it holds its own against all comers."

"What do you mean?"

"Hard to explain. Let's just say it doesn't increase or decrease. It always stays the same." He reached over and clasped her fingers. "I think you'll like it. You have a thing for beauty."

She had to admit he was right. She did have a thing for beauty—his face, his body, his spirit.

He gave her a little smile, winking his dimple, and then squeezed her hand and let go.

She felt hot and tingly all over. She hadn't thought a simple ride in a pickup could affect her this much, but it was turning out to be not so simple. She lowered her window and took deep breaths of cool air until she felt more stable. He'd ignited a spark in her the moment she'd set eyes on him. And he was fanning that spark into a blaze that was growing bigger by the moment. Cool air wasn't going to do the trick. She closed the window.

"Too cold for you?" he asked, concern lacing his voice.

"Just wanted a quick breath of fresh air."

"Nice time of the year."

"Yeah."

As the pickup crested a rise and chugged to a stop on top of the cliff, she looked down at the muddy Red River below where it made its way toward Louisiana and eventually arrived via the Mississippi River at the Gulf of Mexico. To the west, buildings rose above the flat-topped mesa.

"Made it." He patted the dashboard as if in appreciation of the truck's service like he would a stalwart horse.

"Thanks." She patted the dashboard, too.

"For background, there wasn't a ferry at Destiny like there was at Wildcat Bluff."

"Why not?"

"It's too high above the river. You'll notice there aren't many trees…at least not since the first settlers arrived and created the town."

"They didn't like trees?"

"They built their homes out of the lumber. And I'd say they wanted a clear view from every direction."

"For the pretty vista?" She looked across the river at the tree-lined, red-tinted earth of Oklahoma, once known as Indian Territory.

"Doubt it, although it is pretty. I suppose they didn't want anybody to be able to sneak up on them, and so they created a clear field to return fire if necessary."

"Defensive, then?"

"That's the prevalent wisdom, but now I suppose it's anybody's guess."

"And the Buick Brigade?"

"So far, mum's the word."

"Well, it is interesting."

"You'll notice the road up here doesn't end in the town." He turned his truck west and followed the two-lane road. "That's probably defensive, too."

"Guess they were protective of their privacy and—"

"Safety."

"Did they have outlaw shootouts here like in Wildcat Bluff?"

"And Sure-Shot." He pointed toward the town. "Far as we know, it's always been quiet—genteel even—in Destiny."

"But it's like they were expecting trouble."

"Yeah."

"But it never came."

"Far as we know."

"That's good."

"Right." He rolled into town and eased his truck to the side of the street so she could see it all. "Here's Destiny."

"Oh, wow. It is lovely…like out of an oil painting from the 1890s. Those houses are definitely Queen Victoria era." She feasted her eyes on the beautiful sight.

Four three-story Victorian homes stood side by side on large lots situated on the south side of Main Street. A single-story carriage house and former stable had been built behind each home.

The painted ladies came in four colors with accent trim. The first on the block was pale yellow with gold. The second was fuchsia with purple. The third was white with navy. The third was aqua with green. They all had wraparound porches, octagonal turret rooms, multi-peaked roofs, distinctive ornamental trims, and wide-entry staircases with elaborately carved handrails. Each home had a unique whimsical design from a steamboat with keyhole windows to gingerbread fantasyland to multicolored stained glass to jewel-cut fascia.

On the other side of the street, five single-story buildings with Western false fronts promoted businesses on hand-carved, hand-painted signs that hung above the continuous boardwalk under a connecting portico. Destiny Books and Coffee Parlor. Destiny Sweetheart Café. Destiny Mercantile. Destiny Feed and Fashion Emporium. Destiny Junk and Antiques.

On either side of the businesses, twelve small, single-story farmhouses with peaked roofs spread out, six to each side. Each house had been painted a different pastel color and gleamed like a long rainbow in the late afternoon sunlight. All had matching gray-slate roofs. And the front lawns were enclosed with white picket fences. Not a single vehicle was in sight, although there appeared to be horizontal parking spaces in front of the business buildings.

"Oh wow," she said again. "I see what you mean about this town being special. It's as if time forgot it."

"Beautiful, right?"

"Oh yes! And so perfectly maintained you'd never know the buildings were well over a hundred years old."

"Do you want to look in any of the shops before we see Doris?"

"I have to admit that Feed and Fashion Emporium certainly caught my attention. That's an unusual combination, but I've noticed in small towns that the stores frequently carry a wider assortment of merchandise than in big cities. I wonder if they carry my line of Western wear."

He glanced at the storefront. "Could be. Want to go there?"

"Not today. Let's stay focused. When I get back to the ranch, I'll check my store list. If they aren't on it, I'll definitely be talking with them."

"Okay." He looked at her. "Which of the four houses do you think belongs to Doris?"

She glanced down the row and then started to chuckle.

"What's so funny?"

"No doubt, it's the fuchsia one."

"How did you guess?"

She laughed harder. "I do believe that's Doris standing at the top of her purple staircase waving to us."

He jerked around to look and then joined her laughter.

"Did you let her know we were coming to town?"

"No."

"How could she have guessed?"

"Maybe Homer let her know," he said.

"By now I guess it's safe to say anything is possible in Wildcat Bluff County."

"I wouldn't bet against it."

He drove down Main Street, made a U-turn, and parked in front of Doris's house.

"What is that little building?" She looked more closely at the small structure that resembled Doris's house in color and design except that it had been built on wooden pillars.

"Dovecote."

"Do you mean it's a pigeon house?"

"Right. Every one of the Buick Brigade's houses had a dovecote originally built beside it. They still use the dovecotes because they raise pigeons like their ancestors."

"That's a surprise."

"Pigeons and doves have always been a part of country life since they're popular and useful in communities. There are some beautiful dovecotes in Europe at the old castles."

"I'd like to see them."

"I'm sure we can find some photos online."

"Good." Belle held the empty plate to her chest. "Any last words of wisdom before we see Doris?"

"Wherever she's going, just don't get in her way." He gave Belle a sharp-eyed look. "And please let me open all the doors."

"I take it Doris expects a man to act like a gentleman."

"In Destiny, the old ways hold sway."

"Suits me." She laughed as she hugged the plate harder. "I've never been one to stand in the way of progress reversal."

"Good. The Buick Brigade can't help but love you."

"Suits me even better. I bet I'm going to end up loving them just like everybody else does."

He gave her a quick grin before he stepped out of his truck, walked around the front of it, and opened her door.

She returned his grin as she let him help her down to the

ground from the high cab. She could easily imagine in days gone by that the physical restrictions of corset, petticoats, heavy gowns, and heels might have made help from a gentleman much appreciated by a woman. She'd probably have enjoyed fainting couches, too, if she'd lost her breath due to a tight corset.

All in all, she liked the look of the Victorian house, but she wouldn't have wanted to live during that time period... unless she could have been living it up freely in the Wild West like sharpshooter Annie Oakley and other far-ranging cowgirls.

Rowdy placed his hand across his waist and extended his elbow to her with a wink and a nod.

She got the message and tucked her fingers around the crook of his arm while holding the plate with her other hand. As they walked up the sidewalk toward the house, she didn't mind being this close one little bit. She liked the heat of him and the feel of his strong muscles under her palm. In fact, she could very possibly get used to this kind of pampering and attention—if she wasn't normally in such a hurry. Maybe those Victorian ladies had something on the ball after all and the time to enjoy it.

Doris stood on the porch, or maybe portico was a better term for the wide expanse of floor under a purple, gingerbread-laced edge of roof. She wore a sweater and knee-length skirt in a rich lapis shade of blue to accent her pretty pale blue eyes and the shiny silver of her short hair. She also wore a triple strand of luminous white pearls. She extended her hands out to either side in a welcoming gesture.

Belle walked up the stairs with Rowdy until they reached the porch and then held out the plate.

"Thank you so much, my dear. I'll return Ada's plate to her later." Doris accepted the plate, stepped back, and gestured toward a section of the porch with a white wicker love seat and two matching chairs. A small table had been positioned in between and held a tray with a violet-flower patterned delicate china teapot and three matching teacups with saucers. A plate was stacked high with misshapen cowboy cookies.

"Thank you for the cookies. They were delicious," Belle said.

"Please join me for tea."

"We'd be happy to join you." Rowdy gently clasped the back of Belle's arm to steer her forward.

"And, please, both of you sit there." Doris indicated the love seat.

Belle had been headed for a chair, but she quickly sat down on a soft purple cushion on one end of the small settee. When Rowdy joined her, his thigh nestled against her own because there was simply no other room. She wondered if their hostess had planned it that way.

Doris sat down in the chair across from them, set Ada's plate beside the tray, picked up the teapot, and poured liquid into three cups. "Now I want to hear all about your plans for Saturday night."

Chapter 14

Rowdy caught Belle's reaction to Doris's question by the way she carefully accepted the cup and saucer so as not to drop it. He wasn't much better when she gave him china that felt so fragile and delicate in his big hand. He was lucky he didn't lose his grip, but he was particularly cautious since he'd been at this rodeo a time or two.

When Belle lifted her cup to her lips instead of responding to the question, he knew he had to step in and make sure everything went okay, or at least as okay as he could make it.

"Saturday night?" Doris sipped tea, watching them over the rim of her cup.

"Homer only arrived a little bit ago." He was stalling, and she realized it, but he also knew politeness would prevail.

"Pretty bird." Belle appeared to take his hint about stalling the direction of the conversation.

"I thought it was time he went home," Doris said.

"He might want to come back here." Belle took a sip of tea.

"Oh no." Doris shook her head in disagreement. "He's home now, and he'll want to stay there."

"She's not prepared to board pigeons." He picked up a cookie, always willing to eat them even if he didn't want to hazard the tea.

"Everything he needs is either still in the barn or was delivered this afternoon." Doris gave them a sweet smile.

"Everything?" he asked, feeling Belle stiffen beside him.

"Absolutely."

"I know nothing about pigeons." Belle set her cup in her saucer with a definite click.

"Do you like cows better?" Doris asked.

Rowdy snatched another cookie and stuffed half of it into his mouth. He hoped this wasn't a lead-in from Doris about the missing Daisy Sue.

"Yes, I know and like cattle." Belle set her cup and saucer down on the table, as if to free her hands for whatever was to come. "Pigeons might be a good addition to the ranch, but I'm not sure if—"

"Belle will be fine with the pigeons." He quickly stepped in to soothe matters. "I'll help her. There's not much to it. And she'll enjoy the company."

Belle gave him a sidelong glance but said nothing to dispute him.

"That's what my friends and I think, too." Doris smiled benignly at them. "Homing pigeons are a wonderful addition to any ranch...particularly one with a missing cow."

"If you're wondering about the location of Daisy Sue, I don't know." Belle appeared ready to rise but held herself steady on the love seat.

"That's a shame," Doris said. "If my friends and I may be of assistance, please let us know."

"I appreciate the offer," Belle said. "And thanks for Homer. I'm sure he'll fit in well at the ranch since he lived there before. If you ever need him back—"

"We'll let you know, but it's doubtful."

"Thanks." Rowdy was ready to leave now that the cow and pigeon issues were settled. He started to stand up, but

Doris held out the plate of cookies to stop him. He selected one and eased back on the love seat close to Belle's warmth.

Doris leaned forward with a pleased expression that lit her face with happiness. "Now about Saturday night—"

"We haven't had time to make plans," he said around a mouthful of cookie that had looked a little like the Lone Star State, but as always, it was hard to tell just what the original intent might have been.

"I've discussed it with my friends." Doris sent a big grin their way. "For such an important occasion, we've decided you should borrow Blondel's granddaddy's Packard."

Rowdy almost spit cookie crumbs all over Doris. He swallowed hard, now being the one who wanted to escape.

"Packard?" Belle asked, looking interested at the idea.

"No!" he said. "That's a Packard Six Fourth Series Model 426 Runabout. 1927. Peach and cream. Plenty of chrome. Whitewall tires. That roadster is irreplaceable. It shouldn't ever leave its garage. Personally, I wouldn't touch it, much less drive it and park it at a honky-tonk."

"Oh dear, I can see you feel strongly about that old Packard." Doris shook her head, appearing disappointed at his reaction. "And we had our hearts set on you two arriving in style."

"I'll borrow a pickup, if that'll satisfy you."

"And we have flapper clothes to go with it." Doris fluffed her silver hair. "Our ladies have always had an eye to style."

"Oh my." Belle inhaled sharply. "Flapper clothes? What a fascinating era for women. They cut and crimped their hair. They shortened their skirts. They danced to their hearts' content. And, oh, they had such unique style."

"Yes, indeed," Doris said. "Just think of the beautiful, feminine fabrics, the long necklaces, the matching shoes.

And the men dressed up to go with them. We have those clothes, too."

Belle leaned back against the love seat with a disappointed expression on her face. "I doubt the clothes would fit us nowadays. Ladies and gentlemen were so much smaller back then."

"Not our families. We've always been on the tall side." Doris focused on Belle. "I'd say the clothes would almost fit you or could be altered to fit. Rowdy, too."

"How very intriguing. I'm thinking of a photo shoot already." Belle leaned forward, eyes gleaming with excitement.

"No!" Rowdy stood up. "No classic Packard. No vintage clothes. I hate even to think what you'd want to dress me in."

"Something quite nice." Doris gave him a long, slow appraisal, making a point of his current scruffiness.

"I'm not a mannequin."

"Oh, but you could so easily be one in a photo shoot." Belle tapped her fingertips on the knee of her jeans. "Honestly, I'm thinking of how I could incorporate vintage—from the flapper era—into my new line."

"Good idea." Doris grinned even bigger.

"I don't suppose they wore bandanas?" Belle asked.

Doris glanced at the bandana around her neck. "Perhaps long strings of pearls were more the thing, but someone somewhere would have worn bandanas, too…for sure right here in Wildcat Bluff County."

Belle fingered the blue fabric around her neck. "I'm writing a promo piece about '101 Uses for a Bandana.' If you have any ideas you'd like to share, please let me know."

"Oh, what fun!" Doris clapped her hands together. "I'll

tell the others, and we'll put our heads together. That's quite a few uses, but I'm sure it's doable."

"That's what I think, too."

Rowdy took a step back. Women and fashion. This mutual admiration society was getting completely out of hand. He hadn't meant for them to become friends. It might mean more offers of the Packard and flapper or other vintage clothes in his future. He wished he'd never pulled that short straw.

Doris glanced at him. "You know, Rowdy dear, I do believe she's a keeper."

"We've got to go." He held out a hand to Belle as he took another step backward. "Homer needs to get settled in. Saturday night's coming up. And there's the work on the house to be completed in time for Belle's party."

"Party?" Doris asked, eyes shining in anticipation.

"Christmas party." He wished he'd never said the word *party*. It could only mean more trouble for him.

"Yes, indeed." Belle stood up. "You and the…the other ladies must come and join us."

"How exciting!" Doris leaped to her feet. "Theme. Decorations. Costumes. Food. Drink."

"Exactly…although I hadn't had costumes in mind. I keep trying to make plans, but something always gets in my way." Belle gave Doris a suspicious look and then shook her head as if tossing away an idea. "I'm sure it'll all come together in time for Christmas."

"We'll give your party some serious thought, and we'll let you know what we believe will be suitable. Our families used to throw the best of the best parties in Destiny. Now that I think of it, I don't know why we stopped doing it. I guess life just dwindled down here until there were only the four of us. But that shouldn't preclude fun and games, now should it?"

"No, it shouldn't." Belle edged toward the staircase. "But really, it's more of a promotion for introducing Lulabelle & You Ranch to select media and buyers."

"You've come to the right place. My friends and I know exactly how to plan effective campaigns."

"Wonderful," Belle said.

Rowdy resisted a groan, thinking of former county campaigns. If the Buick Brigade was moving from local to global, he wasn't sure the world was ready for them. But he wasn't about to be the one to get in their way when they were on a mission. He had his own mission to accomplish. At least he'd averted the Packard and clothes debacle. He had to be grateful for small favors. Now was the time to get out while the getting was good. He gently touched Belle's elbow to let her know they should be on their way right that very moment.

"Thank you so much for the tea and conversation." Belle smiled as she turned and grasped his arm.

"Delighted to have you here. I can't wait to share your good news. My bosom buddies will certainly want to help out with a party."

At the top of the staircase, he nodded at Doris. "Please give my best to our friends."

"I certainly will." Doris followed them. "And we'll be in touch. This Christmas will be a magical time for all."

"Thank you for everything," Belle said.

He quickly led her down the sidewalk, opened the pickup door, and helped her inside. He rounded the front grill in record time, threw himself inside, and started the engine. He took off with only a belch of smoke.

"What a delightful lady." Belle lowered her window and waved goodbye to Doris, who waved back from the porch.

"That Packard and clothes were a near-miss."

"I'd like very much to see that car and those dresses."

"I have a sinking sensation in the pit of my stomach that you will."

"Do you mean they might come to my party in the Packard and flapper dresses?" She turned toward him with excitement shining in her eyes.

"Maybe...maybe not."

"They'd be a huge hit. Talk about beauty. Talk about style. Talk about class. Think of the photos!"

"Magazine worthy, I'd guess."

"I bet we'd be all over the internet. You can't buy that type of promotion." She squeezed his arm. "Thank you so much for bringing me here."

"Please don't be disappointed if none of this comes to pass. The Buick Brigade does what they want when they want."

"If nothing comes of this, I won't blame you, and I'll be okay with it."

"Good."

She leaned back in her seat. "It's just that there's so much creativity in this county, so many interesting people...and I've only scratched the surface."

He said nothing, absolutely nothing, as he felt his gut clench. She liked it here. He was supposed to make sure she didn't like it here. How unlucky did he have to be to make one mistake after another with her?

He needed to regroup. He needed to get his head on straight. He could hardly think, straight or otherwise, with her anywhere near him. She was sweet. She was funny. She was clever. She was tough. She was kind. She was beautiful, in so many different ways. She had to be the answer to every man's prayers...or the single item on their Christmas wish list.

He felt like banging his forehead against the steering wheel, but that'd probably send them over the cliff into the muddy Red River. The Buick Brigade would never forgive him if he let anything happen to their latest favorite. If it wasn't for Homer, they wouldn't even be here. Why did he ever get involved with homing pigeons in the first place? But that was years ago. Who knew it'd come to introducing Belle to Destiny...and everything that might eventually entail? He had to think past this debacle.

Maybe he could undo his bad luck on Saturday. If he set his mind to it, he bet he could make her miserable. When they danced, he could step on her feet so they hurt. When they ate, he could drop food on her clothes so she looked like a slob. When they drank, he could spill beer on her shirt so she stunk. She'd be so unhappy she'd insist he take her straight home. Now there was another good idea...he could fix the truck so they had trouble about halfway home and they had to walk the rest of the way.

All in all, he felt better about Saturday night...almost lighthearted, in fact. Nobody could ever accuse him of being unlucky after he gave Belle the worst night of her life. She might even leave straightaway, not bothering with the party or redoing the house or charming the Buick Brigade. He'd be crowned the luckiest cowboy in the county for his actions. He grinned, feeling quite sure this plan would finally change his luck from bad to good.

"About Saturday night—"

"Not to worry," he said. "I've got everything under control."

Chapter 15

A few days after the trip to Destiny, Belle sat at her patio table in late afternoon with her laptop in front of her. She enjoyed the warmth of the sun and the vision of squirrels scampering up and down and around the trees in her backyard. She also kept an eye on the sky...just in case there was a new message from the Buick Brigade. So far she'd heard nothing from them since her visit to Doris, but she was ever mindful of their presence.

After being on the phone and internet with her corporate headquarters through the week and into the weekend, solving problems and delegating duties, she enjoyed simply sitting there and thinking up ideas for her growing list of "101 Uses for a Bandana." Besides, it took her mind off that evening, when Rowdy planned to take her to Wildcat Hall. She hoped it was still a good idea.

She hadn't even seen him since he'd dropped her off after Destiny, explaining that he had pressing matters at his ranch that took precedence over her ranch. Life in the country. Most folks had more than one job or a job and a ranch and...who knew how many irons in the fire.

She glanced over her shoulder at the house and had an uneasy feeling things still weren't going well with the renovations. How did she hurry Rowdy? She had no idea. So far, he was her best bet for getting anything done, but when he disappeared for days, she became concerned about the situation. She really needed the roof repaired at least. She'd already begun downsizing her original goals, accepting that stuff might not get done. If it came to it, she was practical enough to realize that she might have to go with whatever was completed by the time of her party...either that or give up the idea entirely, and she wasn't willing to admit defeat at this stage of the game.

She might be able to make the party work if she scrapped indoors and went for outdoors. She might not get her patio constructed by that time, but the grass was dry—if it didn't rain—and could be cut short. Surely she could locate wooden picnic tables and square bales of hay harvested last summer. Both would do for her Western bandana theme and be eye candy, too. She could count on that simplicity being workable...at least she hoped so.

With that alternative solution in mind, she turned her thoughts back to bandana uses. She needed more ideas. She thrummed her fingertips on the tabletop. Wait...that was the ticket. Napkins and placemats. They could be coordinated in matching colors or mismatched colors for more oomph. And they'd be perfect for her outdoor Christmas party, if that was the way she ended up having to go.

She typed in the two words and then leaned back and stretched her back. Actually, she wouldn't mind a bit of dancing to ease out the kinks of the week. She was so focused on the upcoming holidays that she wasn't getting enough exercise. She could use a bit of horseback riding, too. All in all, she was beginning to ease back into country mode...and realizing that she'd missed it.

If she was going to get the local community behind her ranch and other ideas, she needed to reach out to them. The honky-tonk would go a long way toward that process. She wished she had Daisy Sue in tow because that would put her in a good position to make friends with the Steele-Duval family.

She scratched her head in irritation. No Daisy Sue. No Kemp. How hard could it be to find one registered Angus cow in Texas or even farther afield in other states? If her ramrod didn't check in again soon, she was going to have to send out a search party for a man and a cow.

That'd be bad enough, but she'd have to admit to her family that she'd lost her ranch foreman and a prize cow. Oh, how they'd laugh, but in the end, they'd help her. If she could avoid it, she didn't want to go through the embarrassment. After all, she was CEO of Lulabelle & You, so she was known to be on the ball within the industry as well as with her family. Something about Wildcat Bluff County was making her edge toward feeling out of control…and she needed to reverse that trend.

When her phone rang, she grabbed it, as always hoping it'd be Kemp saying he'd found Daisy Sue. And this time it was Kemp calling…

"Okay," he said. "I've got good news and bad news. Which do you want first?"

"Good. Tell me you found her."

"Nope."

"Then what's the good news?"

"Daisy Sue wasn't auctioned off, at least not from the closest place to Aunt Dotty's ranch."

"And he'd go there?"

"Lester always likes easy, and that's the easiest place for him to sell a cow."

"Okay. She wasn't sold. Now what?"

"The bad news," he said. "I called Lester's burner phone and finally somebody answered...but it wasn't my cousin. A cowgirl he'd hooked up with at a rodeo—about like I'd thought—said he'd left in a hurry for the next rodeo and forgot his phone."

"That's some cousin."

"Tell me about it."

"Do you have any clue to his whereabouts?"

"I got the name of the next rodeo where he's supposed to be," Kemp said.

"You can meet up with him?"

"If he actually goes there, I'll find him."

"What if he doesn't?"

"I'll start calling his friends and making the rodeo circuit. He has to turn up somewhere."

"But what has he done with Daisy Sue?"

"It's the burning question, isn't it?" Kemp sighed into the phone. "If I thought it'd do a bit of good, I'd apologize again. I am right sorry. Now all I can do is stay on the trail of Lester—"

"*That* cousin."

"I'm beginning to wonder if we're kin at all." And Kemp clicked off.

Belle took a deep breath. If Kemp's story wasn't so ridiculous, she'd think he was making it up. Still, she'd heard stranger things, so she might as well believe it. And hope he caught up with his cousin soon.

About that time she heard Rowdy's rackety old pickup pull up out front. Maybe he'd get a little more painting done on the house before dark...and their sort-of date-that-wasn't-a-date. She needed to decide what to wear. For sure, it'd be something from her new line because she always had promotion in mind, no matter the circumstance.

"Howdy." Rowdy tipped his cowboy hat as he rounded the corner of the house.

She just sort of froze at the sight. He looked good—way too good, if she wanted to admit the truth of the matter—in Wranglers with ripped knees. A leather belt with a big, shiny rodeo buckle emphasized his narrow hips. He must have gotten hot or something because he'd unbuttoned his denim shirt a time or two, revealing a line of dark blond hair that drew her eyes to a broad expanse of muscle that just begged to be fondled, caressed, licked...she stopped her thoughts right there.

She crossed her legs and then uncrossed them as she tried to ease the heat, the tightness that always came at the sight of him. If he ever touched her or she touched him, she knew the heat would blaze into a wildfire that might consume them both. She wished she didn't want it, but she did, and it'd been a long time coming...a man who flat-out set her on fire. She really shouldn't go out with him tonight because she just didn't trust herself—or him, from all indications of his interest—to keep their minds on the business at hand.

"How's your day going?" He gave her a hint of a smile with a touch of dimple.

"Fine." She gestured toward the chair on the other side of the small table so he'd feel free to join her. "Kemp just called in a report."

"From the look on your face, I take it he still hasn't found Daisy Sue."

"Not yet…first he has to find the cousin."

"Twisting in the wind." Rowdy shook his head as he sat down. "Ready for tonight?"

"No. I mean, I will be, but not yet."

"Me, too."

"I'm getting a little concerned about the pace of our renovation."

"I don't blame you. I'm doing my best." He looked down and then back up at her. "You know…you could put off your Christmas party and introduce your ranch next year. Spring is a pretty time."

"Spring!" She sounded horrified because that was the way she felt about the idea. "That's way too late."

"Just an idea." He shrugged. "Are you sure you like the idea of Lulabelle & You Ranch anyway? Daisy Sue is still missing. That sets Storm Steele and her entire family on edge."

"I know. I've been reading about how Fernando is pining away on his website and hoping the love of his life will be home in time for Christmas."

"Well, that's about the size of it."

"There's still time. If I don't hear from Kemp soon, I'll take action."

"What kind?"

"I could get my family involved in it. They know lots of cattle folks around the country."

"Your family?"

"Yeah. I've got three Tarleton brothers, and one's about as cocky as the other. Nobody messes with them." She noticed Rowdy turn a little pale, so maybe she'd described the trio in the wrong way. "I mean, they're kindhearted but a little protective of their only little sister."

He nodded, cutting his blue gaze to the side. "I wouldn't involve them yet. Like you said, there's plenty of time."

She drummed her fingertips on top of the table. "I'd just as soon not involve my family at all."

"Good idea. Let's cut Kemp some slack. Sometimes things just spin out of control and it takes a while to get them back on track."

"I've had it happen in my business, but still…this is just one cow."

"You're right. She's an important one, but still a single cow."

"Do you think I should talk with Storm and the Steele family and explain the situation?" she asked.

"Tell them the truth?"

"It's embarrassing, I know, but I don't want a little girl to be worried all the time."

"She'd probably put out a BOLO online for Daisy Sue."

"Would that be so bad?"

"I don't know. It's your business that could be affected because it's your ranch."

"I'm just not sure what to do because it's gone on so long now." She looked away from him, realizing she was discussing personal and professional business with him. She usually discussed such matters with family or trusted business associates. When had she come to trust him so much? Maybe it was because he was on the scene and he understood the players in a way no one else possibly could. And then there was the fact that he had a soothing effect on her, as if he'd been there, done that, and come out ahead of the game…or maybe it was because he had that cattleman's ability to calm wildness in animals so that they came to trust him, too.

"Tell you what." He eased back in his chair, as if relaxing into the moment. "Folks will turn up at Wildcat Hall tonight. Even if it's a Saturday night, it's always family night in the tradition of the old dance halls."

"How do you mean?"

"The halls originated as community centers where families gathered to discuss crops, animals, kids, and the weather. All ages came, from toddlers on up. Of course, there was no day care back then, so they congregated as one big happy family."

"Are you saying you think Storm might be there tonight?"

"Can't say for sure, but it's likely the Steele family could show up."

"Okay. Maybe I'll get a chance to talk with them in person." She took a deep breath, fortifying herself for what was to come. She just needed to get on this horse and ride it to the finish line. She'd faced worse before, and hiding out never solved a single thing.

"Good." He gave her a nod of agreement. "Hear anything from the Buick Brigade?"

"Not a peep. I'm not sure if that's good or bad."

"No way to know." He glanced toward the barn. "Homer settle in okay?"

She smiled, feeling happy at now sharing her place with the pigeon. "Thanks for the help getting him situated in the barn. All is well...so far."

"You'll enjoy him."

"I think so, too."

"Well, I'd better see what I can get done with the little time left today." He stood up. "Let me know if there's something specific you want me to fix."

"I will." She had such a long list that she didn't even bother to mention it, particularly now that she had a secondary plan in mind.

After he rounded the corner, she looked back at her laptop. She needed another bandana use.

"Belle!" Rowdy called from the front of the house. "You'd better come here."

She jumped up, feeling her heart rate pick up. What now? She quickly walked around the house and saw him standing with his hands on his hips.

He pointed at the shingle stacks. "Did you hear anything last night?"

"Like what?"

"Pickup. One-ton. Vehicle lights. Voices. Loud sounds."

"No. I sleep in back…although I did wake up at one point, but I didn't notice anything except the sound of dogs barking in the distance."

"Maybe you need a dog."

"Why?"

"He'd alert you to trouble on your property."

"Trouble?" She felt more uneasy than ever at his words.

He pointed down at an empty wooden pallet. "You had a stack of shingles there, didn't you?"

She glanced at the other shingle stacks that were still on wooden pallets and then looked back. "Are you telling me that somebody came right up onto my front lawn and stole my shingles?"

"Not somebody. Shingles are heavy. It'd take several strong men to load up that many shingles in the back of a truck."

"That's not good."

"No, it isn't. I didn't think anybody would be that bold, but—"

"If we're missing shingles, we'll never get the roof completed in time for my party." She felt a little sick to her stomach at the bad luck and the fact that strangers had been up to her front door in the middle of the night while she was in a deep sleep.

"We can order more."

"If this happened in Dallas, I'd—"

"You need to call Sheriff Calhoun and let him know. Other construction sites may be losing equipment or material, too."

"Okay. I guess you're right." But she didn't want to waste what little time she had left for house renovations on making a police report.

Rowdy pulled out his phone again. "Want me to call?"

"Go ahead." She leaned against a stack of shingles, thinking how this might impact their plans for the night. "See if the sheriff can come out right away."

He gave her a tight smile.

She returned his smile even though she didn't feel like it. At this rate, she might need to make even more adjustments to her Christmas party plans…and she wasn't sure she had much leeway left.

Chapter 16

"If you'll make a report, I'll file it with the department and a deputy will look into it." Sheriff Calhoun handed Belle an official form and a ballpoint pen.

Rowdy watched as she set the form on top of a shingle stack and then glanced back at the sheriff.

"What should I say?"

"Just put it in your own words. Write down the last time you saw the shingles, what time you noticed them missing from your front yard, and the approximately value," Sheriff Calhoun said.

"Value is probably about a thousand, give or take." Rowdy really regretted the bad luck, but if he was honest with himself, he had to admit it tied perfectly into the whole slowdown.

"What are the chances of catching the thieves?" Belle asked as she started writing on the questionnaire.

"I'd like to say we'll nab them in a few days, but we've had a rash of small burglaries all over the county, and they've kept us running here and there."

"Any luck catching them?" Rowdy asked.

"No. They're monitoring our radios, so we've gone to using our cell phones."

"Sounds either organized or clever or opportunistic," Rowdy said.

"Most likely all of them." Sheriff Calhoun took several

photographs of the crime scene, and then he examined the entire front lawn.

"Inside or outside houses?" Rowdy asked.

"Both. That's not good, but none of it is."

"It sure isn't." Rowdy couldn't help but think about Belle living alone. What if the burglars forced entry? He needed to discuss her security system with her and get it ramped up pronto.

Sheriff Calhoun glanced at the house. "My major concern is your safety. You don't have surveillance cameras that would've captured video of the thieves, do you?"

"No. It never even entered my mind," Belle said.

"They didn't get all the shingles." Sheriff Calhoun gave her a direct look with a lot of meaning behind it.

"Do you think they might come back?" she asked.

"Shingles are expensive. The thieves probably think if they lucked out one time they might again," Sheriff Calhoun said.

"I wish I didn't agree, but I do." Rowdy glanced around, considering the house and grounds from a security standpoint.

Sheriff Calhoun pointed at the roofline above the front door. "You could install a simple camera up there. Even a dummy camera would be better than nothing since it'd make thieves think twice before bothering your property."

"When I moved in here, there wasn't a surveillance camera, so it didn't even enter my mind to get one installed on the house." Belle looked up at the front eave, too. "Anyway, I thought everything was perfectly safe here."

"For the most part, it is," Sheriff Calhoun said. "But there are always a few troublemakers."

"I can install a motion-sensor camera in the next few days. A light that comes on when it detects motion would be a good idea, too." Rowdy glanced at Belle to make sure she wanted him involved in her security.

"Good idea," Sheriff Calhoun said. "I wish we had photos of the thieves right now. That way we'd stand a better chance of catching them, although they could be from out of the county and not known to us. Yet."

"I wish you had photos, too." Belle stopped filling out the form to look up. "I've been so busy trying to put the place in order that a camera didn't even reach my to-do list."

"I'd say it'd be a good idea to get it on your list now." Sheriff Calhoun patted the top of a stack of shingles. "You've got plenty of expensive construction material. You may not have seen the last of the thieves."

"I think we ought to move everything out here to the barn, no matter how much trouble and time," Rowdy said. "These shingle stacks would require a lift to move them in bulk, so they'll have to wait."

"Do what you can do." Sheriff Calhoun nodded in agreement.

"I'll help move stuff." Belle walked over and handed the sheriff her completed form and his pen. "I hope this helps catch them."

"It's a start," Sheriff Calhoun said. "If you have any more trouble, call me. And stay safe."

Rowdy watched the sheriff walk to his cruiser, get in, and drive back toward Wildcat Road.

"What a mess," Belle said. "Can't anything go right on this project?"

"I'm about to finish painting the trim."

"And it looks good. Thank you." She pointed at the five-gallon containers of paint and other assorted supplies. "I can carry the smaller items to the barn, but I can't lift those paint cans."

"I'll do it. I'll get the gutters, too." He glanced toward the small, red barn and back again. It wasn't close by any means. "I bet there's a wheelbarrow in there that'll help cut down on time."

"Good. Anything that'll help us move stuff as fast as possible. We still need to get ready for Wildcat Hall."

"Yeah." He walked over to the long stack of gutter material. "If I'd been in control from the first, I'd never have left all of this out here."

"It's not your fault. Anyway, nobody thought it'd take so long to do this job. The other guys came and went until it all just piled up. I should have realized sooner that something needed to be done with it."

"There's no point in laying blame on anybody...except the thieves. We are where we are. Let's deal with it."

"I agree."

He looked out toward Wildcat Road. "Another thing...I hate to bring it up, but we ought to consider it."

"What?"

"You're not near the road. For burglars to know you had material and supplies in front of your house, I'd guess they needed to use binoculars."

"What!" She whirled toward Wildcat Road. "I don't want to think that, but you're right, or they know who is buying what and where it's being delivered in the county."

"Good point. I'll make sure Sheriff Calhoun follows up on that idea, if he isn't already on it."

"Thanks."

"In the meantime—"

"We move as much of this stuff as we can."

"And if you like, I'll get cameras installed tomorrow."

"I'd very much like it and appreciate it."

"Okay." He turned toward the barn. "I'll go get the wheelbarrow."

"While you do that, I'll gather up the smaller items."

As he got up to leave, his phone rang, alerting him to possible trouble because it was the special ringtone for the fire department. He went on instant alert as he clicked to answer the call.

"Where are you?" Hedy asked in the no-nonsense voice she used when she handled firefighters.

"I'm at Belle's place."

"Good. I need you to check out a situation."

"What? Where?"

"Got a call from a guy who said he thought he'd seen sparks by the side of the road down the highway from the Lazy Q Ranch."

"That's not much to go on."

"I know, but somebody needs to check it out."

"Do you think it's a prank call?"

"Could be." Hedy hesitated. "I've got a gut feeling about it."

"What do you mean?"

"Sometimes folks have nothing better to do than stir up trouble."

"Tell me about it," he said.

"Anyhow, will you drive down and take a look around that area?"

"I'm on it."

"I'm happy to send out a rig, but not unless there's real need."

"You don't need to explain it to me. We're all volunteers, and the last thing we want to do is waste our time," he said.

"Right."

"I'll let you know what I find out."

"Thanks."

He clicked off and glanced over at Belle.

"Fire?"

"Maybe."

"Around here?" she asked.

"Maybe."

"What does that mean?"

"It means I'm going to drive down to Wildcat Road and see what I can see. If there's trouble, I'll let you and Hedy know."

"Do you need me to do anything?"

"Not yet."

He hurried around the side of the house, got in his pickup, and raced down to Wildcat Road. He drove slowly along the highway, checking out the short, dry grass on the downward slope. He looked for a wisp of curling smoke, a red-orange blaze, or even a tiny spark that glinted in the sunlight. Nothing. He kept going, mile after mile, even when he didn't see anything that registered as danger.

Finally, he decided there was nothing in that direction, so he made a U-turn and headed back the other direction. He drove even slower, watching closely for something that would trigger his instincts, but again, he didn't see anything that set off alarm bells. He passed the entrance to Belle's ranch and kept going. He wasn't about to let any possible fire slip past him. He drove for miles before he turned back and headed down the other side of the highway, staying on high alert as he scanned the side of the road. Still nothing. He ought to have felt glad, but it irritated him that somebody with nothing better to do was playing a prank to cause trouble.

He didn't want to think it, but he had to wonder if the thieves had set them up by making the call to confuse matters at the house. He hoped not. Still, either way, it was good that he hadn't found a fire.

He turned off the road, passed under the Lulabelle & You Ranch sign, and stopped in the middle of the narrow lane. He picked up his phone and hit speed dial for the fire station.

"What'd you find?" Hedy asked.

"Nothing."

"That's good. Prank call. I had a feeling about it."

"Guess so. Still, I don't like it so close to Belle's house."

"Best keep an eye out."

"Will do."

"Later." And Hedy was gone.

He tucked his phone back in his pocket, feeling uneasy about the false alarm, but there was nothing he could do about it. He drove on up to the house, parked, and got out. He looked at the mess on the front lawn and shook his head. Plenty to take care of here.

He walked to the back of the house, but he didn't see Belle, so he pulled out his cell and called her.

"Is everything okay?" she asked as she answered her phone.

"No fire."

"Good."

"I'll get back to what I was doing. First thing I'll check out the barn and make room for the supplies."

"Do you need help?"

"Not yet."

"I'll join you in a moment. I'm inside getting another canvas bag since I already filled up one."

"Okay."

As he passed the back of the house, he glanced over at her table and chairs. She wanted a fancy patio for her party. It'd require heavy physical labor to dig up the sod, put down sand, and position the heavy stones, but it'd be worth it to see her eyes light up with pleasure. As far as an outdoor kitchen and a firepit, he'd like to install those for her, too.

He forced his gaze back to the barn, pushing helpful thoughts down into the abyss of all he wasn't supposed to be doing here. No doubt about it, he wanted to please her. He wanted her to be happy. He wanted her to see him as capable, not as a guy who couldn't get anything done. Of course, that wasn't happening. Now he was the one who'd been overseeing the job when her shingles were stolen, so it'd cost her more in the long run.

Still, how she saw him, one way or another, didn't matter…not so long as she was safe.

He opened the barn door and stepped into the shadowy interior. What a mess. It obviously hadn't been used for anything but storage in a long time…not that anything was worth all that much, but ranchers and farmers always kept extra material just in case they needed it.

He flipped on an interior light, looked around, and saw a wheelbarrow under a pile of odds and ends of lumber with rolls of electrical wire, baling wire, gauge field wire, and barbed wire piled on top of it. He'd have to move everything to get to the wheelbarrow, and there was no good place to put the stuff when he moved it because he needed all the available floor space for the gutter material, paint cans, and everything else. Maybe the best thing to do was for her to go ahead and hand-carry small items while he moved the big pieces.

As he turned to leave, she walked inside carrying a canvas grocery bag that she'd filled up.

"I decided the wheelbarrow was a lost cause."

She glanced at the situation and nodded in agreement. "Where do you want me to put this stuff?"

"Over in that corner. I need the floor space for your gutter system."

"Okay." She started taking material out of the bag and stacking it neatly against a wall.

As he moved a couple of two-by-fours to make more room, he heard the flutter of wings. He glanced up and saw Homer descending from the square-cut hole in the ceiling that led by a staircase to the loft above. He landed on Rowdy's shoulder and nestled against his neck.

Belle emptied her bag and looked at them. "Hey, Homer. How are you doing?"

Homer cooed in response.

"I bet he's getting lonely." Rowdy stroked soft breast feathers. "Pigeons are social, and he's used to being part of a community."

"Do we need to take him back to Doris?"

"Not yet." He didn't say because he wasn't sure, but he figured the Buick Brigade would send more pigeons Belle's way sooner rather than later.

"If we get time, maybe we should come out and see him."

"That's a good idea."

"Do they bond with people?"

"Absolutely."

She set down her bag, walked over, and raised her hand. "Do you think he'll let me pet him?"

"I don't see why not."

She tentatively placed the first fingertip of her right hand on Homer's head and stroked down about an inch.

Homer cooed what sounded like encouragement.

"You can stroke down his back and belly. He'll like it."

"He won't bite me?"

"No." Rowdy smiled, feeling tender toward her at the hesitancy.

He realized she would be fine with a big animal like a horse or cow, even a dog or cat. Folks not used to smaller birds could think them delicate, but they were strong and swift. And wary. In this case, Homer obviously liked and trusted Belle, and that went a long way toward developing a relationship. He was happy for them because neither needed to be alone when they could share life with another.

That thought brought him up short. He was just as alone, even with his father and friends, as these two were now. He held back a sigh. He wanted more in life. He wanted her to be stroking him like she was the oh-so-lucky Homer. But he was the guy set to make her life miserable while the bird made her happy. Sometimes life just wasn't fair.

When she stroked down to Homer's wing, he turned his head and gently nipped her with his pointed beak. She jerked back, eyes wide open.

"Oh, no. Did I hurt him?"

Homer ruffled his feathers and leaned into Rowdy's neck.

"He was just showing you affection. If he'd meant to warn you off, he'd have pinched your skin." Rowdy chuckled in remembrance. "I can tell you right now it can hurt. For his size, he has powerful muscles and can apply a lot of pressure."

"Okay." She stepped closer and reached up to stroke down Homer's head to his back and down to his tail. "His feathers are so soft."

But Rowdy had ceased to think about birds or feathers because as she stroked over and over she was also touching his neck...so light and airy as to be almost imperceptible but with such an impact that he felt his body tingle and tighten and harden in response. Bare skin to bare skin. Not much. Hardly there. And yet enough to give him an idea of just how strong their reaction would be if they ever really touched each other.

He could hardly stand still. He wanted to wrap her in his arms. He wanted to find the nearest bales of hay. He wanted to take this feeling to its completion, joining them so closely that there could never be a coming apart.

"You're so handsome," she said in a singsong voice. "I could just kiss you."

Rowdy wanted her to talk to him like she was talking to Homer.

"You're my very own good boy, aren't you?"

Rowdy wanted very much to show her what a very good boy like him could do for her.

"I'd like to hold you and cuddle you so very close and tight."

Rowdy wanted her to say those words to him…needed it in the most fundamental way possible.

And then more of his poem came full-blown into his mind. *A cowgirl clothed in red bandana. Daytime. Nighttime. Anytime.*

"Do you think Homer would let me hold him?" she asked, still stroking down his feathers.

"I think he'd like it." Rowdy didn't add that he'd like it, too, because he could feel her fingers touching his neck with each stroke, building up heat and desire and want of a kind he'd never experienced before. If not for his subterfuge, he might've felt like the luckiest guy in the world. As it was, he simply picked up Homer, careful to hold his wings to his sides, and set him on Belle's shoulder.

Homer cooed in contentment, snuggled up against her neck, rubbed the tip of his beak against her cheek, and then gave Rowdy a look from a big, round eye of one male to another when he'd just won the prize of love.

Rowdy had to admit he'd lost this round to a bird…a very handsome bird, but still a bird.

Chapter 17

Wildcat Hall Park, the famous North Texas historic dance hall and cowboy cabins, was a jumping place on Saturday night.

While Rowdy drove around the large, concrete parking lot full of pickups and one-ton or two-ton trucks searching for a place to park, Belle studied the area. She was impressed with the cowboy cabins that were lit by carriage lamps on tall poles under green live oak trees.

The five rental cabins appeared to be made of recycled materials from deconstructed old houses and barns as well as items from junk stores and reclaimed materials. The cabins had rusty corrugated tin for roofs, weathered barn wood for siding, and natural stone for entry stairs leading up to porches. All the windows and doors looked repurposed since they were different shapes, sizes, and colors.

She could easily imagine staying in one of the iconic cabins and enjoying every minute of it. Wildcat Bluff County impressed her more all the time with its historic buildings and creative residents. She was glad the Buick Brigade had encouraged her to spend an evening at the Hall.

Rowdy nosed his pickup into a narrow place fairly near the entrance and glanced over at her in triumph. She wasn't only appreciative of his parking place. He'd shown up in a fancy new truck all dark blue with loads of chrome and a big cowcatcher in place of the front grill. He must have borrowed the vehicle from a friend, and she appreciated his effort on their behalf.

The honky-tonk had a side garden with twinkling lights in the trees above a dozen or so wooden tables with benches. Folks sat, stood, sauntered, chatted, and nibbled on goodies and drank from to-go cups. Big barrels that served as outdoor firepits had been placed strategically here and there to add light and warmth to the evening.

"What do you think?" Rowdy glanced at her as he turned off the engine of the truck.

"So far, I'm really, truly impressed. It's just lovely here."

"I'm glad you like it. Folks have been coming here since 1884, well over a hundred years now."

She looked more closely at the honky-tonk itself. She loved the style of horizontal wood slats painted white with a Western false front, a high-pitched tin roof, and side flaps for open-air dancing. The double front doors and tall windows allowed plenty of circulation with screens that had black-painted slats. A side door led to the outdoor garden.

"Reminds me of Gruene Hall in the Hill Country. I always enjoyed going there to listen to country bands."

"And dance?"

"Right."

"Wildcat Hall can't compare to fancy honky-tonks like Billy Bob's Texas in the Fort Worth stockyards with 100,000 square feet of boot-scooting space, but we're pretty content with our own 4,000 square feet."

"That's not shabby at all."

"Fern Bryant and Craig Thorne own Wildcat Hall now. They're both musicians, and they love the place. They're working to make our honky-tonk a major destination attraction and music venue like Gruene Hall."

"That's exciting. How's it coming along?"

"They're slowly building a bigger audience with promotion and entertainment from up-and-coming as well as established artists."

"That's wonderful." She clapped her hands together in excitement. "Do you know what I'm thinking?"

"You want to dance...eat...drink?"

"Well, yes, all of those, but I could promote Wildcat Hall in my Lulabelle & You newsletter."

"That'd be really helpful."

"Beyond that, I'm thinking it'd be a fabulous location shoot for my summer line. Do you think they might agree?"

"I can't imagine why not. It's the kind of cross-promotion that ought to work well. At least, I'd think so."

"I think so, too." She took a deep breath to settle her excitement. She hadn't thought to reach out to the community in this way. It was just the kind of real-life situation she'd hoped for but never dreamed of actually getting without creating it all on her lonesome. Wildcat Bluff County was turning out to be a blessing in disguise. She felt so lucky.

"Uh, I ought to say..." Rowdy glanced over at her, appearing a little concerned about something.

"What is it?"

"Well, you being a stranger and all...folks might be a little standoffish at first...I mean, just until they get to know you better."

"Do you mean they won't all be like the Buick Brigade?"

"Those four are in a world of their own."

"Oh." Belle felt her enthusiasm deflate. She knew small

towns and communities could be clannish, but she'd been so welcomed by Doris and the others that she'd felt she could easily become part of this special world.

"Don't get me wrong… It's not that they won't like you…it's just that—"

"It's okay." She squared her shoulders. "I have no intention of pushing myself on anybody. I won't mention the photo shoot. I won't mention the party. I won't even mention Daisy Sue."

"That's not what I meant." He reached over and squeezed her hand.

She felt his comfort go straight to her heart and ease the sudden ache of rejection before she'd even had a chance to make her case with local folks.

He threaded their fingers together. "Don't you dare be anybody but you. They'll love you. How could they not? I… I mean, I… I'll help you."

"That's not what you started to say."

"Let's leave it at that." He squeezed her hand again and then let go. "You're Belle Tarleton. You're Lulabelle & You. You could be the best thing that ever happened to this county."

"Thanks." She clasped her hands together, feeling cold now that he was no longer touching her. "I don't want to be a problem for you, but I appreciate all you're doing for me."

He stiffened beside her. "Let's go inside and see what's what and who's who."

"Okay."

Mindful that the Buick Brigade might have eyes on them, she waited for Rowdy to walk around the front of his truck, open the door, and help her down. He shut the door but kept hold of her hand, as if it was the most natural thing in the world to do. And it felt that way. He was coming to mean a lot to her. Good or bad, she wasn't sure, but she wanted the feeling, wanted the companionship...simply wanted him. She thought he felt the same way, and yet there was a barrier he kept between them, and she didn't know why. Maybe tonight on neutral ground it'd finally come down.

As they walked toward the entry, she glanced at him. He'd cleaned up real good. He wore a fine Western-cut suit in dark blue with a pale-blue, pearl-snap shirt and a turquoise bolo tie. He'd put on classy ostrich cowboy boots and wore them as if they'd been made to order special for him. Tonight he fit with the pickup, the clothes, the attitude as if he'd been born to them...not borrowed for the evening.

She'd dressed up, too. She'd chosen a flirty little knee-length skirt in blue denim that would whirl around her body when she danced to something fast. She'd paired it with crimson tights and blue cowgirl boots. For a top, she'd gone a little sexy with a form-fitting sweater that had a ribbed bottom that hugged her. And she'd chosen it in bright crimson to go with her tights.

All in all, she and Rowdy fit as a couple...in looks, in clothes, even in closeness. And it was the first time she'd felt that total natural convergence between them. She liked it. She wanted more of it, and she was willing to put a lot on the line to get it. But then she was used to taking chances. Rowdy just might be worth taking a big chance with her heart.

She clasped his hand when they walked into the front bar, and he squeezed her fingers in return. She could tell right away that this room was the heart and soul of Wildcat

Hall. It had a long wooden bar with a black cast-iron foot-rail, a pressed-tin ceiling accented by ceiling fans with schoolhouse lights, and floor-to-ceiling windows in front. A big, red, professional-size fire extinguisher lay on its side, as if ready for instant use, across one end of the wooden bar.

The decor was minimal. Rusty metal beer advertisement signs had been tacked around the walls along with sepia-toned photographs of cowboys on horseback and country music legends. A framed Lone Star State flag hung in back of the bar, while a rack of deer antlers loomed above the front doors. A flat-screen monitor above the bar was the only contemporary touch, but it could mostly be ignored if it wasn't turned on. Hand-hewn, scarred-wood tables with high-back chairs filled the area.

Folks sat in the chairs and stood several deep at the bar. Laughter and talk and music filled the air along with the scent of coffee and cookies, beer and pretzels, sarsaparilla and peanuts.

She simply stood still for a long moment, savoring the atmosphere and imagining how beautiful and evocative this room would be as a backdrop in a photo shoot with her clothing designs worn by models who would fit perfectly into the honky-tonk.

"Come this way to the dance hall," Rowdy whispered in her ear and then led her through the throng to a short hall and turned left.

She stepped with him through an open doorway into a large room with rows of long, narrow, hand-hewn wood tables with matching benches placed on each side of the dance floor in front of a wall of screened windows that were open to let in the cool night air. Revelers filled the benches or stood on the sidelines while others danced to the sounds of a country band. It was a scene in a riot of color and scent and sound that excited all the senses.

Once more, she could imagine the dance hall as a backdrop to a photo shoot. It was simply a marvelous visual to accentuate the beauty of her clothing line. She squeezed Rowdy's hand in appreciation that he'd brought her here. He threaded their fingers together and gave her a slow smile.

She looked to the right where a band played on an old-fashioned, recessed, raised stage with a hand-painted backdrop of crimson curtains trimmed with gold pulled open to reveal a pastoral scene of cowboys herding longhorns. She glanced up at the high ceiling with exposed wood rafters that held black ceiling fans, hanging light bulbs, a sprinkler system, and a row of stage lights.

Again, she was enthralled by the sheer perfection of the setting and wished she could take photographs of it right that moment. When she returned to the ranch, she'd be able to consider lighting and angles that would work best for a photo shoot. But she was getting way ahead of herself. She was here to enjoy the evening, not make business plans.

She glanced from the stage to the other end of the dance floor at the long bar that served drinks and munchies. Two open windows allowed bartenders to serve customers on the dance hall side and on the front bar side at the same time. She liked the practical setup just like everything else about Wildcat Hall.

She looked once more toward the stage, where a beautiful singer with ash-blond hair and vivid green eyes strummed an acoustic guitar and sang with a pure, sweet voice to the accompaniment of a man playing bass guitar beside her. He wore his long chestnut hair to his shoulders and looked at the singer with adoration in his hazel eyes. They both wore fancy, colorful Western wear of shirts, jeans, and boots.

Rowdy leaned down close to her ear. "That's Fern Bryant and Craig Thorne."

"They're the owners?"

He nodded in agreement.

"Wait. Isn't she that famous chanteuse who was involved in helping to save Storm Steele from her kidnapper last Labor Day? It was on all the news."

"She's the one...but Fernando was the real hero who saved Storm."

"That's what I heard." She smiled up at him. "I'm beginning to think there's never a dull moment in this county."

"Not so you'd notice." He nodded toward the dance floor. "Do you want to dance?"

"Yes, let's do."

As he led her toward the dance floor, the music ended, and people faded away, leaving them almost alone at center stage.

Craig grinned as he leaned toward his mic. "Folks, we already told you that we'd be starting a poetry night right here in Wildcat Hall."

People clapped and whistled in appreciation.

"Well, I've got good news for you." Craig pointed at Rowdy. "Our very own local cowboy poet named Rowdy is right here."

More clapping and whistling filled the dance hall.

"That's right," Craig said. "Let's let Rowdy start our poetry off on the right foot...right here and right now."

Belle looked around in surprise as the dance hall

erupted in more clapping and calls for Rowdy to step up and perform.

"Sorry. I didn't expect this tonight," he said.

"It's okay. Do you need to go up there?"

"Yeah...I'm thinking so."

"Come on, Rowdy." Craig gestured for him to approach. "One poem. That's all we're asking of you tonight."

Rowdy gave Belle a quick smile and then turned away.

She watched as he walked up to the stage, mounted the steps, and leaned into the mic on a stand as the room went completely quiet in anticipation. She'd had no idea he had this type of reputation in the community.

"Folks, you caught me by surprise," Rowdy said in his deep, melodic voice. "I don't have anything in particular planned, but I've been writing a special poem. If you want to hear it..."

Again, the room erupted in clapping and cheers of encouragement.

Rowdy looked right at Belle as he spoke into the microphone.

"A cowgirl dressed in gossamer dreams.
Daytime. Nighttime. Anytime.
A cowgirl blessed with soaring wings.
Daytime. Nighttime. Anytime.
A cowgirl clothed in red bandana.
Daytime. Nighttime. Anytime.
A cowgirl showered with love forever.
Daytime. Nighttime. Anytime."

And Belle felt his words go straight to her heart.

Chapter 18

Belle simply stood there, caught in Rowdy's spell...not just his love poem but the look in his eyes as he continued to hold her gaze while the dance hall remained silent around them, for everyone had been captured by the power of his words.

She wasn't the only one inspired by Wildcat Bluff County or the coming of Christmas. Magic filled the air. Rowdy was living proof of it as a cowboy poet. He was good, really good. And if she was the recipient of his words or the inspiration behind them, then she felt truly blessed.

She'd never dreamed coming here could change her life as much as it already had in such a short time. Rowdy. The Buick Brigade. Homer. And even Daisy Sue. Maybe Belle had been ready for a change...perhaps needed a change to bring back inspiration and challenge in her life. She'd like to give back, if possible, to this incredible community.

Rowdy stepped down from the stage and walked toward her with a determined stride, never looking right or left, never deviating from the path that led directly to her.

She waited for him, feeling the rest of the world fade away until there were only the two of them...and nothing else mattered in this moment outside of time and space.

When he reached her, he stopped—never breaking eye contact—and held out his right hand.

As she placed her fingers against his rough palm, the

band started up, and Fern's sweet voice floated over the dance hall as she sang Dolly Parton's "I Will Always Love You."

And then Belle was in Rowdy's strong arms, her hands on his broad shoulders, his warmth radiating around her. He gently led her in a slow dance that bound them tighter and tighter as he drew her closer and closer until she could feel the beat of his heart against her chest and the warmth of his breath in her hair. She felt softness unfurl deep inside her, as if she'd been waiting a lifetime for this man of all men to take her in his arms and hold her close...promising... promising she wasn't sure what, but she wanted that promise as much as she wanted him.

"I tried to resist you," he whispered near her ear. "I tried to be professional."

She felt him press a gentle kiss to the whorl of her upper ear, and she shivered in response.

"I can't do it." He trailed the kiss down the edge of her ear and lightly nipped the lobe. "You're everything."

She shivered harder, clutching his shoulders to keep upright because his words and actions were making her weak in the knees.

"Tell me I'm not alone."

She wanted to tell him something, anything, but her words were frozen somewhere in her mind, and all she could do was twine her hands around his neck and thrust her fingers into the thickness of his hair.

He pulled her closer, hardly moving as he held their bodies tightly together while other dancers whirled around and around the dance floor, making them the center of a multi-petal flower unfurled into glorious bloom.

Still she knew—knew only too well—that they weren't close enough, not nearly close enough, to satisfy the promise that shimmered between them, growing stronger with every beat of their hearts, every touch of their hands, every whisper of their breaths.

"Tell me, please." He gently pressed his temple to hers, as if by doing so he could read her mind and know the true extent of her feelings.

She tried to take a deep breath and answer him, but her chest felt constricted with so much emotion that she could hardly breath, much less speak.

And then the moment fell away as the music slowly faded into nothingness that left an empty place where soaring emotion had once filled the dance hall.

Rowdy let his hands slip to his sides. "You aren't going to answer me?"

She put a hand to her heart as she caught her breath, caught by the intensity of his gaze, caught in the magic of the moment. "You're not…alone."

He gently placed his hands on her shoulders, leaned down, and kissed her lips. "That's a promise to us."

"Promise?" She touched her lower lip with a fingertip in wonder, feeling almost as if she'd never been kissed before this man in this place at this time. Could a person truly start over, letting past disappointments, past pain fall away as if they had never existed at all?

"Yes, promise." He clasped both her hands. "I'm not my own man right now."

"No?"

"I'm under obligations."

"Obligations?"

"There's so much I want to tell you...so much I can't tell you, but please believe you can trust me."

She felt a little chill work its way up her spine. When people asked you to trust them, it usually meant you shouldn't. She wished he hadn't used that word. She wished he'd stopped with promise. She wished they could go back to the dance when she did trust him...with her heart. Now she took a deep, steadying breath to fortify herself against what might come.

And yet...trust was the basis of every relationship. If she couldn't trust him, she couldn't go forward with him, and she wanted that so very much. Maybe too much. And yet, from the very beginning, it'd been there between them, that special closeness, that special oomph, that special spark. Did she dismiss it all just because he'd asked her to trust him? She either did or she didn't. If she didn't, then this was it. But could his poem be meaningless? Surely not. He'd touched her and everyone with his words. Did she believe his poem, or did she believe her past experience? Did she trust her heart, or did she trust her mind?

She looked into his eyes as the band began to play another song.

He lifted his hand to her.

She glanced at his work-worn fingers, holding out such promise.

He smiled, revealing that little dimple in his cheek.

She returned his smile. Heart or mind? And then she knew she was going to take a chance on him. She'd known, even if she hadn't admitted it, since the first moment he'd stepped down from his truck and sauntered over to her. She was going with her heart...and so she clasped his hand.

He leaned down and put his lips near her ear. "Let's go. Nothing else suits me here anymore. You're all I want."

She felt a little thrill halfway between excitement of the present and fear of the future. He was all she wanted now, too.

Hand in hand, they left the dance floor and walked through an open doorway that led into the outdoor garden. It was a cool, crisp night with stars tossed like bright jewels across the dark sky. Heat and light blazed from the open fires in three metal barrels. Folks gathered at tables or in groups or warmed their hands over a fire as they chatted with friends.

Belle thought it was a lovely place to spend time, but on this night she simply wanted to be with Rowdy back at her house. As he led her around the side of the building, she heard footsteps running up fast behind them.

"Belle Tarleton, wait up!" a little girl called out.

She turned to see Storm Steele wearing a pink sweater, Wranglers, a crystal-encrusted belt with a huge buckle, and a pair of pink cowgirl boots. Sydney Steele and her fiancé, Dune Barrett, were right behind her, both looking concerned about the girl.

Storm came to a quick stop in front of Belle, put her hands on her hips, and leaned forward. "I've only got one word for you. Daisy Sue."

Belle felt Rowdy squeeze her hand in encouragement before he let her go and stepped back.

"Please..." Storm said in a sad voice. "Can't you just bring her home?"

Belle went down on her heels, feeling her heart go out to this child who loved animals so much that she'd created a world that starred Fernando the Wonder Bull and the love of his life, Daisy Sue.

"Fernando is sad."

"I'm so sorry." She held her hands up in helplessness. "I can't locate Daisy Sue."

"What!" Storm appeared horrified at the news.

Belle glanced up at Sydney and Dune. "I'm trying to find her. I sent my foreman Kemp to bring her home."

"It doesn't make a lot of sense," Sydney said.

"Trust me, I know." Belle looked back at Storm. "As soon as I can find Daisy Sue, I'll let you know. Trust me." And she realized she was asking to be trusted just like Rowdy had asked her…sometimes belief was all you had to offer someone.

Storm glanced down, shaking her head. "I'll let fans know we're searching for her."

"I'd appreciate it if you let them know it's not Lulabelle & You Ranch's fault. This happened before I took ownership."

"We understand." Sydney stepped forward and squeezed Belle's shoulder in a comforting way. "Things happen."

"I'm doing all I can do." Belle stood up.

Storm cocked her head to one side. "If you really want to do something—"

"What?" Belle asked.

"I believe it'd comfort Fernando if you came out and told him about the situation. It's not far. We're neighbors," Storm said. "And you kind of owe us."

"Uh…the bull?" Belle glanced around the group to see if they were taking Storm's words seriously. They were.

"If you like, we could record the meet and greet." Storm nodded in satisfaction. "Cross-promotion is never a bad idea."

Belle looked at Storm a little more closely, realizing she was glimpsing herself in the past. She'd developed a passion for business early in life, too. She grinned, respecting this savvy little girl for her concern and her smarts.

"We could put the video up on both our websites," Storm said. "I like your newsletter. You could mention Fernando and Daisy Sue there, too...if you want."

"What else?" Belle wasn't about to get in the way of this fascinating impromptu brainstorming session.

"You could always hire me as a fashion consultant," Storm said. "I have great taste in clothes. Ask anybody."

"Do you think my clothing lines need help?"

"Once Daisy Sue disappeared and you showed up, I did a little research on Lulabelle & You."

"Really."

"Yeah. Always do your groundwork."

"I've said that myself many a time."

"Never hurts to hear it again."

"I've said that, too."

Storm gave Belle a closer look. "Maybe you have a little bit on the ball."

"I've been known to get things right once in a while."

"Me, too." Storm grinned, giving Belle an approving nod.

Belle grinned back, returning the nod.

"You started that line of kids' clothes."

"Right." Belle crouched down in front of Storm, getting into the discussion. "I decided it was an underrepresented area of Western wear."

"Good idea." Storm leaned closer. "Trouble is, you're appealing to parents and grandparents."

"They're the buyers."

"Past tense." Storm rolled her eyes. "Kids get money. Kids get whiney. Kids get what they want."

"Point taken. Solution?"

"Take girls…more pink, more rhinestones, more glitter. And this may surprise you, more accessories to give a feeling of rich detail."

"How do you feel about bandanas?"

"Use them to style up or down?"

"Either/or." Belle leaned forward this time. "I'm working up a list. '101 Uses for a Bandana.' What do you think?"

"Promo?"

"Absolutely."

"How's it going?"

"I'm getting there."

"Do you really think anybody will take the time to read that many uses?"

Belle sat back on her heels, suddenly wide awake. "I thought it was a catchy number. Do you think it's too many?"

"Well, yeah…unless you're going to break it up over a series of newsletters. Maybe you ought to ask your readers to write in with their suggestions." Storm pursed her lips thoughtfully. "Interaction is always better on social media, don't you think?"

"Yes, of course."

"I rest my case."

"It's a good one."

"Okay. That's solved." Storm gave Belle a sharp-eyed look. "Now…about Fernando."

"Cross-promotion is a good idea, particularly since we're neighbors." Belle stood up again. "Great graphics are a must. I have a home office. You could come over."

"I have a home office, too. When you come to see Fernando, we could convene there." Storm's hazel eyes turned crafty. "Fernando T-shirts have been selling well. You might want to consider a Fernando or Fernando and Daisy Sue Western wear line."

"Oh my." Belle absolutely loved Storm's cocky attitude. "I'd need to see the numbers."

"I'd need to see the designs."

They stopped, looked at each other, and laughed together.

Sydney held up her mobile phone. "Why don't we get a picture of the three of you?"

"Right!" Storm grabbed Belle's hand and then Rowdy's hand and grinned at the camera.

"Belle, you might just make a good addition to the county," Sydney said.

"I'm always on the lookout for talent. It's one of the reasons I took over the ranch."

"Really?"

"I thought it'd be a good place to support the arts in all their many forms, but particularly for youngsters just developing their creative talents."

"How would you do it?" Sydney asked.

"I'm not sure yet. I want the ranch to be accessible to city kids who don't have a chance to interact with animals or develop their creative talents in a country setting."

"That's a tall order," Sydney said.

"And I want to support the local arts, too."

"That's something we need right now," Dune said. "Our high school had its funding for the arts cut. We've been trying to figure out how to go forward from here."

"I had no idea," Belle said. "I'm glad you told me."

"We're thinking about a fund-raiser during the holiday." Sydney shrugged, shaking her head. "But with so much going on already, we just haven't put it together yet."

"It wouldn't be enough anyway," Dune said. "It'd be stopgap, and we need something more permanent."

"I won the Fernando jackpot last Christmas when folks donated in the contest to guess what time Fernando made it home after being snatched by cattle rustlers. I donated my winnings to the school program," Rowdy said. "But it didn't last long."

"Like I said, we need something more permanent." Sydney glanced around the group. "Hopefully, somebody will come up with something soon."

"Right," Rowdy agreed.

"For now, you're welcome to come over and see Fernando any time," Sydney said.

"Thank you. I'll stop by."

"About that fashion consultant business," Storm said.

"Yes?"

"I work cheap."

"How cheap?"

"Clothes."

"Samples?"

"Done." Storm looked thoughtful. "But if I model, that'll cost you."

Everyone broke out in laughter except Storm, who looked serious...and Belle, who gave the young entrepreneur a knowing wink.

Life was definitely looking up in Wildcat Bluff County.

Chapter 19

When Rowdy turned under the shiny, new sign for Lulabelle & You Ranch and drove over the cattle guard, he felt relieved on several accounts. First, nobody had slipped up and called him Bert Two at Wildcat Hall. Mostly they hadn't called him anything, which suited him fine. Second, Belle had made friends, or maybe "business acquaintances" was more accurate, with Storm and Sydney. Maybe now they could become allies in the hunt for Daisy Sue. Third, he'd given it up with Belle—and this should have been number one—so she knew exactly how he felt about her. She'd responded even better than he'd ever imagined in his lust-filled fantasies. Maybe it had been the poem, the song, or the dance. It didn't matter. All that mattered now was that she was in his pickup, and he was taking her home, and he was going inside, and he hoped against hope he'd get to see her bed. Unmade.

But that dream was cut short when his headlights swept across a one-ton, eight-foot-wide truck that had been backed up to the front of Belle's house. Its tailgate was down, and two muscular guys in T-shirts, jeans, and boots were grabbing heavy packages of shingles and tossing them into the bed of the truck.

"They're back." Belle pulled her phone out of her purse. "I'm calling Sheriff Calhoun."

"No way can he get here in time. Big county."

"Maybe he or a deputy is nearby."

"Doubtful. Go ahead and call, but I'm not waiting around."

She punched the sheriff's phone number on speed dial.

"Those guys aren't taking any more of your shingles." He hit the brakes, stopped his pickup, reached under his front seat, pulled out his Sig P320, and set the .38 with its safety engaged in his lap.

"Sheriff Calhoun, this is Belle Tarleton. Those shingle thieves are back. We're headed up to the house right now."

Rowdy gave her a quick glance before he gunned the engine. He was so ready to nail those guys...and he'd like to use a power nail gun to do it.

"I sincerely doubt Rowdy is going to wait for you. Me either." She listened to the sheriff's response. "Thank you." She set her phone back in her purse. "He'll be here as soon as he can make it."

"You might be in danger. Will you get down in front of the seat and stay out of sight?"

She looked at him with a raised eyebrow. "Got another one of those Sigs?"

He grinned, chuckling at her response. "You're already dangerous. I'm not sure I can handle you armed *and* dangerous."

"You're not the one who needs to be worried. Those thieves are the ones in my line of sight." She sat up straighter. "I'm tired of playing nice in this county. It's not getting me anywhere."

"Did you just join the Buick Brigade?"

"Now that you mention it, I'd like to be driving a big ole boat of a car right now. I think it could do some serious damage. Those guys would think twice before they ever stole shingles again."

Rowdy grinned even bigger… If he'd thought she was hot before, now she was positively on fire. And he was ready to burn up her bed.

He sped up the long drive, but the guys had seen him. One leaped into the driver's seat while the other jumped into the bed of the pickup on top of the shingles, ran across the stacks, and grabbed the headache rack with one hand as his partner tore out across the lawn.

Rowdy left the driveway to head off the thieves, but they cut a wide swath around him through the grass, dodging trees, plowing through shrubs as they headed for Wildcat Road. He followed them, gunning his engine, tearing up the lawn, staying right on their tail end that was illuminated by the row of red lights across the top of the cab and the red running lights that outlined the sides. The guy in the bed of the truck held tight to the horizontal, steel-bar headache rack across the cab's back window to keep from being thrown over the side. He made a dark silhouette in the pickup's headlights.

Rowdy hit his bright lights, hoping to blind the driver so he'd slow down or stop and give up, but the guy gunned his engine, plowed through the front fence, and landed on the highway going as fast as he could control his vehicle.

Not about to give up at this point, Rowdy stayed near the truck's back bumper even as the thieves upped their speed. They rocketed down the road, head to tail like two railroad cars shackled together.

"It's not worth endangering us." Belle slipped the Sig from his lap and held it with both hands. "I bet they've got a record, so they'll do whatever it takes not to get caught."

"I won't let them get away." He gritted his teeth as he gripped the steering wheel with both hands and kept the pedal to the metal.

"If a deer leaps into the road...or even an armadillo or a raccoon or a cow wanders out of a pasture...we'd be in a world of hurt."

"I know, but still..."

And then he could hardly believe his eyes because the guy in the bed of the truck reached down with one hand while clinging to the headache rack with the other and ripped the plastic open on a bundle of shingles. He pulled a long shingle free and slung it outward like a Frisbee. The sharp edge of the cold shingle—much like a hard tile—hit the pickup's windshield with a loud crack. A zigzag pattern moved outward from the hit to obscure Rowdy's vision. Soon he could hardly see through the spreading cracks in the glass, but he kept right up with the truck. He wasn't about to let the thieves get away.

Another shingle came flying out of the back of the vehicle, cleaved through the air, and caught under Rowdy's windshield wiper. Now he had to lean to one side and look between the cracks and the shingle to see the road at all. But he stayed steady, keeping up his speed as he bird-dogged the truck.

The thief kept jerking shingles out of the package, slinging them outward, and hitting the pickup with one blow after another. Rowdy dodged the flying missiles as best he could, jerking his steering wheel back and forth, so most of the shingles hit the cowcatcher, bounced to the side of the road, and cartwheeled onto the grass. But enough hit dead center in front of his view, again and again, until the windshield finally cracked hard enough to spew shattered glass.

He ducked his head and hit the brakes as the sharp shards covered him like sugar crystals. He stopped the pickup on the side of the road, glanced down, saw his clothes were covered in bits of glass, and shook his head in disgust.

"Are you okay?" He flipped on the overhead light and glanced at Belle.

"I'm fine. You're the one covered in glass. Are you hurt?"

"Not much. Just mad as hell."

"You're sure?"

"Yeah." He looked through the open windshield and caught the scent of diesel as the thieves roared down the road. They'd bought enough time with their shingle stunt to get ahead. He turned off the overhead light and hit the gas again, determined to catch up.

"Please, just let them go. It's not worth the danger to us." Belle leaned toward him, concern lacing her voice.

"If we let them get away, we'll never catch them again."

"It's not that much money involved in the theft."

"It's the principle." He glanced at her again and then back at the road. "And the fact it's you."

"Me?"

"No guy should ever think he has the right to drive up to your house, steal your things, and endanger you. It's not right… I won't allow it."

"Allow it?"

"Yeah."

He caught up to the truck again, thankful he was driving his own pickup with its satisfying big engine instead of the rattletrap that would have conked out on him from the get-go.

"Do you want me to shoot out their tires?"

"Can you do it?"

"Maybe...but it'd be chancy with that guy back there. I don't want to send shingle thieves to the hospital."

"It'd be a lot of paperwork."

"And I don't have time for it."

"Okay. Let's see if I can sideswipe them and push them off the road."

"You'll damage your paint. It'll be a more expensive repair than the shingles are worth."

"It's personal now."

He roared up to the back of the truck, checked to see that the road was clear ahead, and angled to pull up beside them. He didn't get far when the guy in back reached down, ripped open another package, jerked out a shingle, and let it fly. It hit the cowcatcher and fell harmlessly to the side.

"Please let them go," Belle said. "Next time you may not be so lucky. I'm worried about you. He can hit your face now. If he does, it'll feel like the hard edge of a clay tile... and could do serious damage to you."

"Hate to let them go, but you're right." Rowdy eased off the accelerator and watched the truck roar away.

"Thank you."

He pulled off to the side of the road and stopped his pickup. He left his headlights on, opened his door, jumped down, and shook the glass off the front of his clothes as he watched the thieves get away.

"Guess that's that." Belle leaned over the seat and looked out the open door at him.

He gave a big, long sigh. "One thing, I doubt we'll ever see their mangy hides again."

"True." She glanced down at the Sig. "We didn't remember to get their license plate number."

"No point. It was covered in mud."

"They've been at this rodeo a time or two before, haven't they?"

"Sure looks that way."

He jerked the shingle from under his windshield wiper and tossed it in the back of his pickup. Maybe tomorrow in daylight they could salvage some of the others that had landed beside the road. At least they got one back for sure, if it wasn't too damaged to use on the house. As he walked toward his open door, he heard the growl of an engine coming from the direction the thieves had disappeared into the night. He stopped to watch because he thought it might be Sheriff Calhoun or one of his deputies, although it sounded like a one-ton, not an SUV or cruiser.

"Do you want me to contact the sheriff again?" Belle called from inside the cab.

"I'm waiting to see if this could be him coming to us now."

"Okay." She slid the Sig under her seat and then leaned forward to peer out the front window.

He realized it wasn't the sheriff a little bit late because the now-too-familiar truck roared up, slowed down, and slid across the road. The driver's window came down, and a hand flung out a jar with a burning bandana sticking out of it before the truck roared off into the distance again. The bottle hit the cement highway with force and broke into small pieces. A red-orange blaze leaped up like an angry animal, spreading fast across the dry grass and toward Rowdy.

He stepped back, but his jeans were almost instantly engulfed in flames. He slapped at his lower legs with his hands, feeling the heat and the burning but knowing he couldn't allow the fire to spread over his body. Fortunately he was wearing jeans made of thick fabric that helped protect his legs.

"Rowdy!" Belle yelled as she opened her door, jumped down, and ran around to him. She stomped the fire out of the burning bandana with the soles of her boots.

"Get the fire extinguisher off the back floorboard."

"Will do...but can you believe it? That's another use for a bandana. Molotov cocktail!" She wrenched open the back door and grabbed the canister.

"Not funny." He slapped at his clothes with his bare hands to put out the fire and stomped on the ground to keep the flames from spreading to his pickup.

"Yeah." She turned toward him. "What now?"

"Pull the pin and spray me."

She jerked out the pin, aimed the nozzle, and sprayed chemical over his legs and the ground around him.

He felt immediate relief, although he knew he'd been burned but not how badly. "Use the whole can. Make sure the fire's completely out."

"I'm doing it." She kicked a shard of glass to one side. "Looks like a mason jar. Do you suppose it's the same guys who started that other fire?"

"No way to know for sure, but I bet that was moonshine—maybe one hundred proof—because it burned hot and fast." He grabbed a flashlight out of the back floorboard and felt pain stab his palms. He ignored it as he turned on the light and checked the area while she continued to spray.

"I think the blaze is out."

"Looks good." He examined the area one more time before he was satisfied they weren't leaving any dangerous embers.

She emptied the can and then set it on the back floorboard.

"Let's go."

"Shouldn't we wait for Sheriff Calhoun?"

"No. We can see this easier in the morning." He tossed the flashlight on the back seat and shut the door. "I want us out of here right now."

"Why?"

"They might come back to see how much damage they caused, and if it's not enough—"

"Let's go." She hurried around and got into the pickup.

He took one more look around before he sat down beside her and started the engine. He felt better with them inside for the protection. Still, he didn't like being out here. Even worse, what if the thieves had gone back to her house and waited for them there? Those two guys had gone way beyond stealing a few shingles. He supposed he'd made them mad by not just rolling over and letting them take whatever they wanted at her home. Wasn't going to happen…not now, not ever.

"Belle, would you call the sheriff?"

"Sure."

"Tell him there's been an uptick in the situation."

"Okay." She glanced at him. "What aren't you telling me?"

"I want you safe." He turned his pickup around and headed back.

"I am now."

"Just call the sheriff."

She hit speed dial again and then speakerphone. "Sheriff Calhoun, it's Belle Tarleton again. Rowdy is here, too."

"Sorry it took me so long. I'm getting to your place right now."

"Good," Rowdy said. "Are you on Wildcat Road?"

"I'm turning off it as we speak."

"Be on the lookout for a red truck with a black cow-catcher," Rowdy said.

"Up by the house?" Sheriff Calhoun's voice ratcheted up a notch in timbre.

"Yes. It's probably not there, but just in case."

"I take it you've had a little more trouble," Sheriff Calhoun said.

"Yeah."

"We'll see you in a moment. And thanks." Belle slipped her phone back into her purse.

Rowdy made a sharp turn off Wildcat Road and headed toward the house. He could see the sheriff pulling to a stop in front. He was glad to see the new motion-sensor light had come on over the front doors so there was illumination across the front lawn in addition to his headlights. He parked behind the sheriff's SUV.

She quickly opened her door, stepped down, and headed to where Sheriff Calhoun was exiting his cruiser.

Rowdy got out, but he took his time walking over to them so he could get a good look around the area. He didn't see anything suspicious beyond the fact that more shingles were missing, but it was obvious the thieves had been disturbed in the act since they hadn't taken an entire stack this time.

"Sheriff, we chased those thieves down the road, but they got away." Belle pointed toward Wildcat Road.

"You chased them?" Sheriff Calhoun looked from one to the other. "You think that was wise?"

"We caught them in the act," Rowdy said. "We were in my pickup, so I just took out after them. I thought maybe they'd stop if we caught up to them."

"There was a guy in back who threw shingles at us." She sounded incensed at the idea. "My shingles, no less."

Sheriff Calhoun shook his head. "You could've been hurt."

"Just the pickup." Rowdy gestured toward his ruined windshield.

"That's replaceable," Sheriff Calhoun said. "Your lives are not."

"You're right." Rowdy shrugged. "I hate to say it, but I let my anger take over."

"It happens to the best of us." Sheriff Calhoun shook his head, as if remembering his own past behavior.

"I'm sorry, but we didn't get a license plate number," Belle said. "They'd spread mud over the numbers."

"We stopped by the side of the road." Rowdy picked up the story. "They came back and threw a jar at us. They'd stuffed a bandana in a flammable liquid—most likely white lightning because of the way it burned—and set it on fire."

"Any injuries…besides your pickup?" Sheriff Calhoun looked at Rowdy in concern.

"Let me check." He walked over and held his palms out to catch the strong illumination of the headlights so he could evaluate his medical condition. Fortunately he was an EMT as well as a firefighter. He noted red skin like sunburn on his palms and a few small blisters on the sides of his hands where the skin was thinner and more sensitive, so he had limited second-degree burns, too.

"Rowdy?" Belle asked, motioning toward his hands.

"Do you need to go to the clinic?" Sheriff Calhoun asked.

"No. I'm okay. Superficial burns." He turned to look at them. "Mostly first-degree."

"Good," Sheriff Calhoun said.

"Anyway, I have an EMT kit it in my truck."

"I'll take care of him." Belle leaned into Rowdy and tucked her hand in the crook of his arm.

He smiled down at her and then turned his mind back to the business at hand. "Somebody from the fire department ought to check the scene and write up a report tomorrow," Rowdy said. "I can do it."

"Don't trouble yourself. I'll see to it." Sheriff Calhoun glanced toward the shingle stacks. "I'll take a written statement from you two then."

"Okay," Belle said. "I'm ready to do anything to help catch the thieves."

"You two were lucky tonight." Sheriff Calhoun looked from one to the other. "Those guys are escalating, and I don't like it. I'll be on the lookout for them. And you two be more careful."

"We will," Belle said.

Rowdy watched Sheriff Calhoun get in his cruiser and drive away. The sheriff was right. He should be more careful, particularly when Belle was with him. But he'd been so mad...and then they'd taunted him. Still, safety should come first, and as a first responder, he knew that fact only too well. He'd just gotten so protective of her that reason had flown out the window.

He hesitated, not wanting to push too far, too fast, but reason had already fled, so he plunged ahead. "I don't want to leave you alone tonight."

She gave him a soft smile. "Come inside. I'll take care of you."

Chapter 20

Belle sat beside Rowdy at the kitchen table. They were so close together she could feel the heat of his body and smell the smoke on the fabric of his singed jeans. He'd placed both hands on the tabletop with palms turned upward. They were red with only a few small blisters along the edges. He was quiet, his breathing easy as she gently cleansed dirt and debris away with a soft cloth.

She felt tenderness well up in her, a softening of her heart and her entire being. She'd felt desire before…strong and willful when her body tried to overpower her mind, but this with him was so much more than passion. She didn't understand quite how it had happened. Sometimes she felt as if it'd been instant attraction, but other times she felt as if she'd been coming to him for her entire life.

Now that they were alone in her house with everything and everybody that could distract them outside, she felt almost shy in his presence. It was so unlike her. Still, he brought out aspects of her that usually remained hidden or dormant or out of reach. He simply had a profound impact on her. Perhaps because he had so many facets, as if he were a stone that had been cut and buffed into a precious gem that glittered no matter which way she turned it and yet at its heart remained its original solid, indestructible core.

Trust. She'd come to trust him, as she had no one else but her family. When she thought about it, he felt like family…

her very own family. She couldn't imagine ever being apart from him.

Love. Had love snuck up on her or arrived full-blown? Was this what it felt like to not just want to be with someone but to *need* to be with them to feel complete and happy? At the thought of love, that tenderness in her heart bloomed like a flower unfolding its petals in the warmth of the sun.

Life. She wasn't sure she'd ever felt as alive as she did with him…each moment to be savored like fine wine. Every little twinkle in his eyes when he looked at her with so much happiness. Every little smile that was just for her and revealed the delightful dimple in his cheek. Every little moment when he appeared to be on the edge of offering so much more to her.

And yet she actually knew little about him, even as she felt she knew everything she needed to know about him. She might be wrong. She might be wearing her heart on her sleeve. She might be putting her trust in the wrong man. But for tonight, she wasn't going to back away. She'd take a chance. And so she turned her mind back to the current situation.

"Do you want me to put anything on your hands?"

"Check in the EMT kit for the blue tube of antimicrobial ointment."

"Okay." She opened the kit, found the tube, and squeezed out the soft, white cream. She gently rubbed it over his palms and the sides of his hands, watching his skin quickly absorb it. "How does that feel?"

"Good. Thanks."

She put the tube back and then looked him over. "Are you in pain?"

"My palms sting, but not too bad."

She checked the EMT kit again and found a bottle of over-the-counter pain medication. "You ought to take a couple of these pills."

"Okay." He smiled at her. "You're the EMT in charge tonight."

"That's exactly right." She gave him a teasing glance before she walked over to the sink, filled a glass with water, came back, and set the glass before him.

He downed the pills and then the entire contents of the glass before handing it back to her.

"Good. I'm feeling better about your injuries." She looked him over again. "But what about your shins?"

"They're okay, I think. They need to be cleaned, too, but that'd require—"

"A shower."

"I suppose I better head home and get one."

"Didn't I promise to take care of you?"

"You're getting into above and beyond the call of duty."

"Do you have a change of clothes, or at least jeans, in the truck? I'd guess you don't since you borrowed it."

"I'm a volunteer firefighter. I always carry extra clothes, EMT kit, and at least one fire extinguisher wherever I go."

"That's good."

"You just never know when disaster might strike."

She nodded in understanding as she set aside the used cloth. "Why don't you take a shower while I run out to the truck and get your clothes?"

"Are you sure?"

"I don't think you should go home where you'll be alone. You might develop a fever or something that needs immediate care later in the night."

"I want to stay here, but I don't want to be a bother or impose or—"

"You're staying." She leaned forward and placed a soft kiss on his lips. "Let me take care of you like you've taken care of my home."

He smiled, revealing his dimple. "There's a small duffel bag behind the front seat."

She stood up. "You know the layout of my home as well as I do. Why don't you use the shower off my bedroom, since it's the biggest one?"

"Okay."

"Towels are in the cabinet. You'll find everything you need there."

"Thanks."

She stood up. "Is your pickup unlocked?"

"Here." He reached into his pocket and pulled out a set of keys with an attached remote control.

She held out her hand, but he didn't drop them into her palm. Instead, he set them there and then slowly slid his fingers away, leaving a trail of heat behind him. She felt that heat all the way to her core. She stepped back, thinking she needed to get to his pickup and back as quickly as possible...but the heat stayed with her in the warmth of his keys.

He stood up, too, giving her a long, hot look. "If you need me, I'll be in your shower."

Oh, she needed him, all right, but first things first. She got out of there as quickly as possible, wanting him more than she could've imagined possible.

Once outside, she gratefully inhaled the cool night air. Mind over matter. She was glad for the bright porch light. She glanced around to make sure those shingle-stealing guys weren't lurking in their truck someplace nearby. She hoped they had the sense never to darken her doorstep again. She didn't see anything amiss, so she figured maybe they were gone for good.

She hurried over to Rowdy's borrowed pickup, hit the remote control, and heard the lock click. She opened the back door, and the inside light came on, but she didn't see a duffel, only firefighting equipment, a few towels, and a blanket. Frustrated, she slammed the door and then opened the front passenger door. She looked in the floorboard but didn't see a duffel there either.

She stepped inside and sat down, trying to think where he might have put the bag. She leaned over to peer under the seat and hit her head on the console, knocking open the glove compartment. A piece of paper fluttered to the floor. She grabbed it, recognizing an auto insurance form. He definitely didn't need to lose that important piece of information.

She picked it up, intending to set it right back, when she noticed the name on it. *Bertram Holloway.* So that was who had loaned Rowdy the truck. Nice guy. And then something dawned on her. The name was familiar. Bert Two was friends with her brothers. They'd talked about taking firefighting classes with him. She'd never met him, but she probably would soon since he and his dad owned Holloway Farm and Ranch someplace near her new ranch. She supposed the pickup could belong to Bert Two's dad, since they had the same name, but she doubted it. Rowdy was about the same age as Bert Two, so they were probably closer friends. All in all, it was a small world...and a good one.

She slipped the form back into the glove compartment

and snapped the lid shut. She looked under the seat and found the duffel. It was smaller than she'd expected, but then Rowdy was a man and probably had nothing more in there than shirt, shorts, socks, and jeans. She grinned at the very idea of such a limited wardrobe. Maybe she should consider a line of Western wear for men, but she doubted she could interest them in much more than what they already considered basic and essential.

She grabbed the duffel, stepped down to the ground, and locked the door. She hoped the fancy pickup didn't get any more damaged while Rowdy borrowed it, particularly when it was parked on her front lawn. She'd definitely pay for the repairs.

She walked back to the house and then shut and locked the front doors behind her. She'd locked the exit door to Homer's loft earlier in the evening, so she knew he was all settled inside, too. She felt satisfied that all was safe and secure for the night.

She heard the shower running, so she followed the sound to her bedroom, where she knew Rowdy stood naked behind a closed door. She set his keys on top of her chest of drawers and then just stopped and listened, imagining how it'd be to come home to him as a natural part of her day. Of course, he must already have a house, but maybe he'd be willing to spend time here beyond the work on her home. That reminded her. She needed to make another donation on his behalf to Wildcat Bluff Fire-Rescue, but that was for another day. Tonight it was all about needs...her needs, his needs, their needs.

She set his duffel beside the chest and glanced around the room, considering her options with the sound of running water in the background. She needed a shower, too. Could she be so bold? Was she ready to go from zero to one hundred in an instant? No, it wouldn't be like that. They'd been together in so many other ways that this would simply be an extension of what they'd already built between them.

She tossed back the turquoise-silk comforter on her king-size bed with the hand-carved cedar headboard, scattering throw pillows in shades of pink and purple here and there, to reveal silky aqua sheets. She'd decorated her bedroom in a Western motif with the cedar set that included a dresser, chest, and nightstands. An antique fainting couch with purple silk upholstery was one of her favorite places to relax after a long day. A delicate rosewood Queen Anne table beside it was stacked with books that were marked with sticky notes for future reference. But tonight she wasn't in the mood for research. She had something very different in mind.

She sat down on the edge of the bed, tugged off her boots, and flung them into a corner where they thudded and sent up a cloud of dust. She quickly pulled off her jeans and her sweater before she tossed them on top of her boots. She selected a bright-red lipstick from the collection in the crystal dish on her dresser and painted her lips with it. Now she wore nothing but her crimson bra, thong...and smile.

She opened the bathroom door and then shut it behind her. Steam clouded the closed door of the shower...and she smiled a little more. She leaned back against the bathroom door and locked it. No interruptions, not this night.

He'd stripped and flung his clothes at a countertop where they'd half spilled onto the floor underneath, leaving a mess that simply enlarged her smile because it spoke of his comfortableness in her home. He'd pulled off his boots and dropped them to the floor, leaving one lying on its side while the other stood upright as if awaiting his return.

She padded barefoot across the eighties-era blue tile to the shower. She splayed her hand on the warm glass, imagining her fingers caressing Rowdy's bare chest just a moment before she clicked open the door…not far, just enough to let him know he had company.

"Belle?" he asked.

"I thought you might need help. Your hands. Your legs."

He chuckled, a husky sound that vibrated deep in his chest. "It's not my legs and hands that need help."

"Really?" She widened the door a bit more, but still not enough for either of them to see each other.

"Yeah." He curled his long fingers around the edge of the door, but he didn't open it either. "Do you need to take a shower, too?"

"I got dirty outside." She was tantalized by that little glimpse of tanned skin that promised so much more exposed flesh.

"How dirty?"

"Dirty enough I may need help getting clean."

"Help?" His fingers tightened around the edge of the door, as if already taking on the task…or holding back a sudden need.

"Yes."

He pushed the door open a bit more, letting out steam that smelled of lavender soap and aroused male.

She shivered as the soft warmth and hard scent hit her.

"Join me?"

"I'm still dressed, sort of."

"How much dressed?" His fingers tightened even more on the door.

"Well...just a little bit."

"Are you toying with me?"

"Well...maybe just a little bit."

"That sounds like trouble." He edged open the door, and more steam and scent flowed across her.

"Well...maybe...just a little bit, but we already had trouble tonight."

"We got rid of that trouble."

"Perhaps we don't want any more."

"This is a whole different kind of trouble."

"You think?"

"Yeah." And he opened the door...completely.

She felt her breath catch in her throat at the sight of him with not a stitch of clothing anywhere. He looked wet and on the edge of wild. Soap suds drifted down the hard muscles of his chest before tangling in short, dark blond hair and flowing down his six-pack abs. She let her gaze drift lower. Oh, he was definitely ready for trouble...

Chapter 21

Rowdy felt the sting of hot water in back and the hotter sting of Belle in front. He didn't move...couldn't. He simply stared at enticing crimson, from her lips to her breasts to her triangle. *His* Belle. He felt a surge of male desire not only to join with her but to entice, soothe, protect. It'd been a long evening, maybe too long to indulge fantasies. Maybe a simple shower would be best, but he honestly didn't know if he could stop there.

She stepped inside and pulled the door shut behind her, taking any type of decision away from him.

"Trouble?" She leaned back against the shower wall and let water spray over her, wetting her red accents until the sheer fabric molded her curves.

"Trouble in red." He made no attempt not to feast his eyes. How could he do anything else? He saw her lips pucker in the form of a kiss. He saw her nipples poke at the material of her bra. He saw her firm thighs wedge the wisp of fabric between them.

"Do you like red?"

"I adore red...on you."

"Are you in pain?"

"Absolutely...more every moment."

"Do you need to go to the clinic?"

"No. I need to go to you."

She stroked her bottom lip with the tip of her tongue. "Do you think it's wise, in your condition?"

"If you mean the burns, I don't feel them at all."

"But still—"

"I need help with my other condition."

She smiled, letting the pleasure travel from her eyes to her lips and back again. She reached out and slowly stroked the tip of one finger down his long, hard length, gazing into his eyes the entire time.

He took a deep breath. "I thought trouble, but I changed my mind."

"Did you?" She put that fingertip to her mouth and sucked it inside.

"Siren."

"Really?" She spoke around her finger with mischief dancing in her hazel eyes.

"I've fallen under your spell."

She removed her damp finger and stroked down the center of his chest. "Which spell is that?"

He covered her hand with his own strong fingers, feeling her softness and warmth over his heart. "Love…it can only be a love spell."

"Do you think we could share the spell?" Mischief slipped from her eyes to reveal tenderness.

"Nothing could make me happier." And he was all done with talk. Now was the time for action.

As water gently sprayed over them, he lifted her hand and placed it on the back of his neck while he leaned forward, gently kissed her red lips and then toyed with her lower lip with his tongue, his teeth until he plunged deep inside, drawing her body closer…not yet completely against his own but close enough to feel her heat. He was in no hurry. He'd waited so long for this moment that he meant to savor every last bit of pleasure...and give it to her in return.

She moaned, a raw, ragged sound, as she returned his kiss—deep and moist and hot—while she ran her fingers into his thick hair and tugged his face closer as she tucked her body into him, demanding, commanding, suggesting.

And that was it. He was totally into red. He knew he'd smeared her lipstick across his mouth. Now he went for the straps of her bra and gently lowered them until he slowly revealed the upper slopes of her breasts, all wet from the water and pink from the heat. And then she helped him by reaching behind her back with both hands, unhooking her bra, and letting the red fabric dangle down until she dropped it to the floor.

He feasted again, letting his gaze caress the rosy-tipped mounds before he reached out and cupped her breasts, feeling the tips harden. He hissed under his breath, part pleasure and part pain, as he stroked her bare flesh with the sensitized palms of his hands.

Still there was more red to tantalize him as he roamed downward, pausing at her navel to toy with the indentation before he reached her thong. It was nothing more than a stretch of lace around her hips, so he tore the edges, slipped the last bit of red from her, and dropped it to the bra. Now she was as he had often imagined...only so much more in living, breathing, tantalizing naked flesh.

As he reached for her, she reached for him, clasping his shoulders and drawing him close. He pressed between her legs, feeling her hot and wet and ready for him, while he grasped her bottom with both hands and pulled her to him. Finally, they were body to body with nothing between them that could stop or slow their coming bliss.

And then he remembered protection...and gently set her from him.

"Rowdy?"

"Condom in the pocket of my jeans."

"How could I forget?"

"Heat of the moment. I almost forgot, too."

"Wait...do you always carry a condom in your jeans?" She stepped back, crossing her arms over her breasts. "That sounds, well—"

"Only since I met you."

"You've been that sure of yourself?"

"I've been that hopeful." He opened the shower door. "Let me get it."

"I don't know now. It seems so—"

"I'll be right back."

She gave him a narrow-eyed look and then picked up a washcloth and soaped it. "While you're gone, I'll just take my shower."

"I'm only walking across the bathroom."

"Take your time." She ran the washcloth across her breasts, leaving them covered in soap bubbles.

He groaned at the sight. "You're toying with me again, aren't you?"

"I thought you said you wanted trouble." She washed each leg, letting soapy water run down them.

"Changed my mind." He wasn't about to step out of the shower, not with this show going on. "I prefer siren now."

She glanced up at him and grinned, looking mischievous. "Go get it."

"Not unless you promise not to move an inch while I'm gone."

"Go." She balled up her washcloth and tossed it at him.

He caught it, dropped it, and stepped out of the shower, never taking his eyes off her to make sure she didn't do something else he didn't want to miss.

She stood still, watching him as she let the water cascade over her, washing away the soapy residue.

He finally turned away, walked across the room, and picked up his jeans. About the time he put his hand in the pocket, he heard the shower turn off. When he looked back, she'd stepped out, grabbed a towel, and headed for the door.

"Not so fast." But he was slow, caught trying to dislodge the condom while watching her sashay across the room.

She unlocked the door, cast him an amused smile, and stepped from the room, leaving behind only a soft trill of laughter.

He couldn't help but chuckle, knowing he was well and truly bound to this beautiful siren. No wonder she inspired him. She was poetry in motion.

He got hold of the condom, left the bath, and found her lying supine across the aqua sheets of her big bed...damp towel cast aside on the floor. She'd gone from hot red to cool blue in the time it took to cross a room. But he knew how to heat her up again.

She raised a hand and beckoned him closer, giving him a smile that was almost shy and in contrast to the sultriness of her body.

He hesitated, not exactly sure how to approach her because he didn't want to do anything to mar this special time. With the heat of the moment left behind in the shower, maybe what they had now was a tenderness born of love that connected them not only on a physical level but on a deeper one as well.

And then he realized he was waxing poetic. How did he know if he was even right? Yet every thought, every word, every touch to this point had felt so very perfect that he couldn't deny it. He ripped open the condom wrapper. She waited for him to set her body on fire. Did anything else really matter now?

He sat down on the side of the bed, slipped on the condom, and turned to her. "If I told you I loved you, would you think it too soon?"

She reached out, leaving her palm turned up and empty, as if waiting for him to claim her. "Is there a correct time and place, or even people, for love?"

He clasped her hand and threaded their fingers together. "Sometimes it's just right, isn't it?"

She squeezed his hand in reply.

And then he was struck anew by the big lie that stood between them like an insurmountable mountain. She didn't know he wasn't really Rowdy, although the name had now become like a second skin. He wanted that name to be him. He was done with the Bert Two business. She'd been instrumental in bringing him into his own skin, his own place, his own reality. Now he knew why he'd been unlucky in love—and every other thing in life. He'd been missing her, the magical siren with the power to set his world right.

He held her gaze and felt his heart open to her, a sensation he'd never experienced before this moment. Strength, born of love, rose in him. To keep her close, to bond with her, to nurture their budding commitment, he could never let her know he'd picked the short straw that had set him on the path to destroying her most cherished dream.

"Come here." She gave him a lazy smile. "I'd almost think you were hesitant."

"It's that love thing."

"Do you need me to say the words to you?"

"Yes."

"I can, but I'm not completely sure." She squeezed his hand again.

"Sure isn't necessary. It'll come in time."

"Do you really think so?"

"Yes."

"All right...I think I love you."

"That's not good enough."

"Do you really need to have it all right now?"

"Yes."

She pursed her lips together thoughtfully, as if giving the matter great thought.

"Come on."

"Are you telling me that we can't have sex without love?"

He wondered if that were true. How had it come to this? It'd never happened before. Sex was good, any which way you got it. But this was different. If they came together without love, would they stay together, or would they drift apart?

"Tell me."

"I don't want to lose you."

"I'm here." She gave him a slow, tender smile so full of love that it said more than any amount of words could ever say.

And he was satisfied...at least for the moment.

He leaned forward, cupped her face with both hands, and then gently pressed a kiss to her lips, now rosy and swollen from their earlier kisses. He leaned back to see her expression and was rewarded with a satisfied smile on her face. She hadn't forgotten what they'd started in the shower any more than he'd forgotten. Maybe there wasn't any need to rev up when they were both already ready to sprint to the finish line.

She scooted over to make room for him and then patted the bed, all silky and soft, that would appeal to a woman and simply be useful to a man.

Useful was more than enough for him. Comfy was icing on the cake. Belle was the cherry on top.

He wrapped her smooth body in his arms, feeling her hands slide up and down his shoulders as if memorizing him or cherishing him or something that felt so sensual it practically put him over the top without any need for more...and he intended for there to be much more this night.

He reluctantly left her lips to trail kisses down her throat, between her breasts, across her navel to reach the triangle between her legs where he lingered, basking in the scent that was hers alone. He followed his mouth with his hands, learning every peak and valley, every sensuous curve, every little sensitive spot that made her squirm and dig her fingers into his hair, arching up against him. She was every delight he could ever imagine.

But setting her on fire was setting him on fire. He didn't know how much longer he could last without being inside her.

"Rowdy," she whispered, voice gone hoarse. "I can't wait. Please, don't make me wait any longer."

"I want this to be good for you."

"Trust me. It already is very, very good."

He cringed at the word "trust" because it was the last thing he wanted on his mind right now. He wanted nothing but the two of them together without anything in the outside world impinging on them.

"Rowdy?"

He spread her legs with both hands, rubbing up and down the inside of her thighs, feeling the roughness and sensitivity of his palms against the smoothness of her velvety skin.

"Yes," she said on a soft hiss of air.

And he couldn't wait a moment longer. He lifted her legs, placed them over his shoulders, and nestled between her thighs, slowly, gently, carefully pushing into her hot, wet, tight center. She rewarded him with another moan and clutched him inside, outside until he joined her moan with a groan of his own while plunging harder and faster and deeper, riding the wave with her, seeking the ultimate oneness with her...until finally they reached their peak together and rode the crest outward, upward, inward to complete their circle of love.

In the aftermath, he rolled to his side and gently tucked her head against his chest so he could keep her near his heart.

"I'll never let you go." As soon as he said it, he knew the words would never do, not in this day and age. And yet he meant them.

"Did I say I wanted to go?" She rose up on one elbow and pressed a soft kiss to his lips. "You're home now. Neither of us is going anywhere."

And he felt a satisfied smile curl his lips.

Chapter 22

A WEEK LATER, BELLE FELT CAUGHT BETWEEN HEAVEN and hell. On one hand, Rowdy gave her everything she could dream of in a romance, but on the other hand, she was frustrated and discouraged at the lack of progress on her house. He did fine work…when he did it, but he frequently couldn't spare the time. She'd begun to rethink bringing in a team from Dallas, but she knew if she did it wouldn't go over well in the county and it could cause her more harm than good in the long run.

She stood in front of her house with both hands on her hips, looking upward. The new paint was wonderful because it added colorful sass to the house. She was also glad to have cameras and lights in front and back and on the nearby barn, so she felt more secure. Rowdy had done all that and done a good job. Only the shingle stacks were left as an eyesore on the front lawn. And yet she had to be grateful they were still there. Fortunately, the thieves hadn't returned, but they hadn't been caught either.

She'd hoped to have a patio installed in back outside the long row of windows in time for her party, but she'd begun to think she might simply have to go with the short grass. All in all, maybe the party wasn't even a good idea. She didn't have to do it. She hadn't sent out invitations. She might already be too late because people made holiday plans well in advance.

As she walked around the side of the house, she decided she'd been too distracted to make the best decisions in life. She had her regular business to maintain that required so much of her. She'd added her love affair with Rowdy. And she was trying to turn Lulabelle & You Ranch into something for everyone.

Maybe she'd taken on too much by coming here. Maybe she should go back to the city. Maybe...but how could she leave Rowdy or Homer or the Buick Brigade? Daisy Sue was still missing, but Kemp was good about calling in to update her. He seemed to be on a wild goose chase, picking up his cousin's trail from one rodeo to one friend to one honky-tonk. Surely he'd catch up with Lester soon. And that brought her to Storm Steele. She'd like to mentor the huge potential in that little girl if allowed to do so by Storm or her family.

She stopped beside the table and chairs in back. When had she become so involved with the folks of Wildcat Bluff County? By comparison, she suspected big cities might start to seem tame—maybe even on the boring side—after living here. How could she give up finding out how everything turned out? And even if not for all of that, how could she walk away from Rowdy and all he was coming to mean to her?

She plopped down in a chair, put her elbows on the tabletop, and dropped her face into the palms of her hands. Life in this county was not the straightforward path she'd intended when she'd moved here, but it was certainly interesting on so many levels. Not the least of which was Rowdy. Just the thought of him made her turn hot with a need that only he could meet. She'd never intended to get involved with a guy. She had no idea where their relationship was going. Still, she had no intention of turning back at this point. She was enjoying him way too much to alter course.

She needed to get her mind back on business, but it wasn't easy with so much else going on. At least she could think about something positive like bandanas. Storm had been exactly right. She'd thrown "101 Uses for a Bandana" out on social media and in her newsletter, and she'd gotten back lots of excited responses with creative uses. Readers were still having fun with suggestions. Not that she would ever mention it, but nobody could possibly match the thieves' fiery use…and she didn't want to go there again.

She had to admit that life in Wildcat Bluff County was good if challenging on several fronts, so she really shouldn't complain if work was slow going her on her house, even though it still left her in limbo for the Christmas party. She had to make a decision about how to handle it soon or miss any chance of it coming together for promotional use.

As she sat there, she pushed her fingers back into her hair as she contemplated her next move and heard the whirl of wings overhead. She glanced up in time to see Homer land in front of her on top of the table. He walked over, claws clicking against metal, and stopped in front of her. Oddly enough, he had a capsule attached to his leg.

"Homer?" she asked, wondering how he'd gone to Destiny, picked up a note, and returned to her. But no, that's not the way they'd told her it worked for homing pigeons. Once home, they stayed home.

This pigeon cocked his head to one side, looking at her

with a round eye before turning his head to look at her with the other eye.

"Maybe you're not Homer." She smiled at the idea that the Buick Brigade might have sent her another pigeon-gram. That'd certainly add fun to the day.

She slowly put out her hand to see how he would react to her. Like Homer, he remained calm as if used to being with people. She reached for the capsule and felt the warm softness of breast feathers as she carefully slid a small, rolled piece of paper out of the capsule.

"Thank you."

The pigeon gave a soft, fluttery coo, ruffled his feathers, and launched into the air. He flew straight to the barn and disappeared inside.

She guessed Homer now had a companion and that would make him happy. Fortunately, there was plenty of room in the loft for other pigeons. She turned her mind back to the matter at hand. She unrolled the piece of paper, stretched it out flat on top of the table, and held it open with a fingertip on each end. She read the first line. "Pigeon-Gram." Okay...here we go again.

She read out loud. "Now is the time to visit the famous bull. Rowdy will escort you. Aristotle is home."

She'd put off going to Steele Trap Ranch to see Fernando, mainly because she'd been hoping to take Daisy Sue with her when she set foot over there. It didn't look like that was going to happen just yet, so she supposed there was no real reason to wait until the cow's return. But why would the Buick Brigade think it was important to go now...if by now, they meant that very afternoon?

She let the note roll up on its own and then tucked it

into the pocket of her jeans. Tomorrow or the next day would serve just as well. Right now, she needed to get her thoughts in order...particularly about the party.

But she didn't give it much thought because she heard Rowdy's pickup pull up out front. She'd thought he was gone for the afternoon, but here he was back again. She supposed she'd better tell him about the pigeon-gram, although he probably didn't have time to escort her to see Fernando. She turned in her chair to watch for him.

Soon he rounded the corner and gave her a big grin and then a bigger kiss when he stopped by her side.

"What brings you back?"

"Aren't you glad to see me?" He plopped down in the chair across from her.

"I'm always glad." And she definitely enjoyed the eye candy as well as the other side benefits. "I just didn't expect to see you till evening."

He rubbed his jaw. "I got a call."

She noticed then that he was better dressed than his usual attire. He looked more like he had when they'd gone to Wildcat Hall. He just had on shirt, jeans, and boots, but they were excellent quality. Maybe he just usually wore work clothes that might have smears of paint or caulk.

"Not interested in my call?"

"Of course I am, but first I think you'll be interested that I received another pigeon-gram."

He smiled, chuckling under his breath. "And the pigeon's name is—"

"Aristotle."

He grinned even bigger. "Fine pigeon."

"And friends with Homer?"

"Siblings."

"Good. He flew off to the barn."

"Homer will be happier now." He leaned toward her. "What did the note say?"

She pulled it out of her pocket and read, "Now is the time to visit the famous bull. Rowdy will escort you. Aristotle is home."

Rowdy nodded, leaning back in his chair. "That's about the same as my call from Blondel…except for the Aristotle part."

"Do they actually expect us to drop everything and go right over there?"

"Pretty much. I'm here, aren't I?"

"Maybe it doesn't mean anything to folks around these parts, but I do have a business to run."

"It's all about priorities."

"Right. Theirs. Not mine."

"Sometimes priorities dovetail."

"I can't imagine how that can be the case here."

"Nobody can…not until the Buick Brigade reveal their last card."

"So, I'm to assume this somehow helps me."

"And others."

"Okay." She stood up. "I'm not going to fight this pigeon stuff. Let me grab my jean jacket and purse."

"I'll wait for you in the truck."

"Shouldn't I call Steele Trap first?"

"No point. Somehow, I do believe they'll be expecting us."

"Buick Brigade, I take it."

"Yeah."

She went into the house and slipped her jacket over her green sweater and blue jeans before she grabbed her phone and tucked it in her purse. She locked the back door before she hurried into the kitchen. She rummaged through her purse, selected a tangerine lipstick since the color would go well with green, applied it, and was good to go.

She stepped outside, locked the front door, checked it twice to make sure it couldn't be opened while she was away, and then walked over to Rowdy's rusty pickup with the passenger door wide open. She stepped up and sat down, setting her purse on the floor by her feet.

"One thing."

"Yeah?" She glanced over at him, wishing they could be alone instead of heading out. She'd bought a little something at Morning's Glory that she wanted to try with him… but it would have to wait for another day or, better yet, evening.

"You'll need to be extra sensitive with Fernando."

"How so?"

"He's been down in the dumps ever since Daisy Sue went missing."

"I won't even mention her name unless it comes up."

"That's wise, but it's still bound to come up for discussion."

"I'll let Storm lead the way."

"Good." He put the pickup in gear and headed out.

Once they were on Wildcat Road, they didn't have far to go since she shared a property line with the other ranch. Pretty quickly he turned off and drove under a sign of black metal with a cutout that read Steele Trap Ranch. A clear blue sky shone through the open letters, and a red-suited, white-bearded Santa Claus perched on one corner slowly waving at passersby with his battery-operated, animated arm. She smiled at the sight and waved back.

Rowdy followed a winding lane upward to a hill that overlooked the Red River. At the top where the road split, he stopped his truck. On the left rose a big, new metal barn, an older wooden barn, several corrals, an open-sided shop, and a multi-vehicle garage.

"It's pretty here," Belle said.

"Let's take a look around. The Steeles won't mind, particularly since you're neighbors. They've added a couple of houses over the years as their family grew bigger."

He turned and slowly drove past a redbrick ranch house with a red metal roof that had brick arches enclosing a shady portico with cedar chairs. For Christmas, they'd outlined the arches with long ropes of red and green lights to match the bright wreaths in every window. They'd also positioned a multipiece, hand-carved, hand-painted wooden Nativity scene under the spreading limbs of a green live oak.

"What a comfortable, cozy-looking home," Belle said in appreciation.

"Next is the original farmhouse. Bet you'll like it even better."

"Oh, I do."

She loved the wide front porch with a hanging swing that set off the farmhouse painted white with aqua trim and a high-peaked, gray-shingled roof. A large crimson-and-gold Christmas wreath added a dash of holiday color to the natural-wood entry door.

"Slade built that last house when he came back from the

rodeo circuit. It's modular, so it doesn't quite fit with the other buildings, but it was quick and easy."

"Nice, too."

He turned around in front of the structure with lots of glass windows and doors, wood-looking siding, and all the modern conveniences plunked down on the edge of an old pecan grove. A hand-painted wooden cutout of Santa in his sleigh pulled by five prancing wildcats dominated the lawn.

"We'd best get on up to the barn. Storm will want to see you right away, if I'm any judge of character."

"I bet. It'll be good to see her again, too."

He followed the road back to the split and drove up to the barns. He stopped his pickup near several people who were congregated near the corrals. He opened his door, glanced over at Belle, and gave her a thumbs-up.

She took a deep breath, ready for whatever would come next, pushed open her door, and stepped down to the ground.

A pint-size ball of energy with wild ginger hair and big hazel eyes wearing boots, jeans, and a T-shirt with "Fernando the Wonder Bull" emblazoned on it in rhinestones hurtled toward them.

Storm stopped in a cloud of dust and pointed toward a corral where a big, black bull watched them. "Hurry! Fernando is waiting for you."

Chapter 23

Belle straightened her back and put a smile on her face. She felt as if she were about to be introduced to the king or CEO of Steele Trap Ranch. She needed to put her best foot forward…and then she remembered Fernando was a bull, maybe a famous one but still an ordinary—or perhaps not so ordinary—black Angus bull. And Daisy Sue was a cow of the same breed.

She didn't know when it had gotten so confused, but it was well before her time here. She simply needed to make sure nothing got out of hand now that she was on the case, so to speak, because it had all, somehow or other, become entwined with Lulabelle & You Ranch…and that meant her business.

A group of people clustered in front of the corral attached to a barn made of red metal with a shiny, silver roof. She recognized the Wildcat Hall Park owners, Fern Bryant with Craig Thorne, each holding an acoustic guitar. Sydney Steele stood beside them, looking like a grown-up version of her daughter. Beside them, leaning an elbow on the top rung of the corral, was a leathery-skinned, bowlegged cowboy who appeared a little frayed around the edges but with bred-in-the-bone toughness. Every one of the group wore traditional ranch clothes of cowboy shirts, jeans, boots, and hats in various colors. An Aussie cow dog, wearing a red bandana around his neck, prowled back and forth in front of the folks.

Belle couldn't help but think that she ought to add "Dog Western Wear" to her list of "101 Uses for a Bandana." It'd be popular with dog lovers everywhere. Bandanas would look good on cats, too, particularly a large one like a Maine Coon, if it could be persuaded to tolerate one. But that was for later. She needed to stay focused on her current situation.

She looked at Rowdy. He looked at her. Maybe there was something in her expression or the situation, but he placed his hand over his flat stomach and extended his elbow to her like a knight of old times would do to support his lady. She hesitated as she stood there with everyone watching her because Rowdy's action made the introduction appear even more formal, as if a lady from a neighboring estate had arrived with her entourage to greet the reigning monarch.

She took a quick reading of the group, but nobody blinked an eye. She'd attended less formal board meetings. This was serious stuff, at least to Fernando lovers... and she supposed she was about to become one of them. She wrapped her fingers around Rowdy's elbow, actually feeling a little glad of the support, although it totally belied her normal in-charge self. Everything about Wildcat Bluff County was beginning to make her feel uneasy, as if she was never going to be able to gain control over anything that occurred here.

Storm hurried ahead, barely containing her abundant energy, and knelt beside the dog, patting his head while his pink tongue lolled out of his mouth in a big grin that revealed his happiness.

Belle followed with Rowdy as her escort. When they neared the corrals, she caught the scent of fresh hay and fresh manure, both familiar—and somehow comforting—smells from growing-up days on her family's sprawling ranch in East Texas. She stopped and glanced around the group with what she hoped was a pleasant smile on her lips.

"Good afternoon." Sydney smiled in return. "Welcome to Steele Trap Ranch."

"Thank you. I'm glad to be here."

"Took you long enough." Storm rose to her feet, keeping a hand on the dog's head. "This is Tater, best cow dog in the county and Fernando's friend."

"Good to meet you," Belle said formally. "Tater, that's a lovely bandana."

"Thought you'd like it." Storm gestured toward the cowboy leaning against the corral. "This here's Oscar Leathers."

Oscar tipped his cowboy hat to reveal a bald head before he set the hat firmly back in place.

"He's the best ranch foreman in the county…and he's never lost a cow in his life."

"For a fact…cattle get stolen," Oscar said.

"But not lost." Storm gave Belle a narrow-eyed look.

"In a storm, could be…or a downed fence," Oscar said. "It happens."

"But not to the love of Fernando's life." Storm threw a glare at Oscar.

"Risky business, I'd say." Oscar looked directly at Belle with a grin.

She resisted a sigh and instead settled on holding Rowdy's arm a little harder. She felt his muscles tense under her fingertips.

"Any news?" Sydney asked.

"Kemp is still on the hunt." Belle glanced around the

group. “I realize this is an unusual situation, but Daisy Sue will be found in due time.”

“That’s the thing,” Oscar said. “We need to know when Daisy Sue is due and get her safely back here for the big event.”

“I’m trying to get her home.” Belle might have been offended, or even surprised, at Oscar’s language, but she’d grown up on a ranch, so she knew exactly what he meant by those words.

“You’d better meet Fernando and explain yourself.” Storm motioned Belle over to the corral as the others stepped aside.

Belle caught her breath at the first glimpse of Fernando. He was huge…at least two thousand pounds of pure muscle with a short, sleek black coat. Handsome. And smart. He looked at her with big, dark eyes as if evaluating her backbone to get a job done right. In this case, the job was to bring Daisy Sue home. So far, she was failing miserably. And he knew it.

She let go of Rowdy’s arm and stepped close to the corral. She realized quite well that if Fernando had a mind to do it, he was strong enough to plow through any enclosure. He stayed where he was by his choice alone. She didn’t want to arouse his anger…not in any way.

Storm walked up. “Fernando, I’d like you to meet Belle Tarleton. Daisy Sue was living on her ranch.”

Fernando looked from Storm to Belle, cocking his massive head to one side as he considered her with thoughtful brown eyes.

“Daisy Sue was gone before I got here,” Belle said. “I’m doing my best to find her.” She realized she’d explained herself and her business to a lot of powerful people but never to a bull with a lonely heart. It gave her pause, making her consider what was more important—love or money?

Fernando lowered his head, rubbed at an itch on his leg with his jaw, and then looked toward Lulabelle & You Ranch.

"He watches your ranch all the time," Storm said. "He'll know when his love returns. Nobody will need to tell him."

Belle felt bad about the situation. She was just discovering for herself the amazing power and importance of love between like-minded souls. She glanced at Rowdy and then back at Fernando. How had she come to be in this impossible position, not only in her personal life but in this family's life as well? All she could do was blame it on love...the glue that held everything of importance together.

She had to put her own concerns aside and focus on Fernando. He was the reason she was here. Anybody who knew animals could tell he was really down and out. Now that she'd met him and seen his loneliness, more than ever she wanted to do something to fix his situation...and do it now. Yet her hands were still tied by the missing Daisy Sue.

"Craig and I came over to play music for Fernando," Fern said. "It soothes him so much."

"I heard music could do that with animals." Belle looked a little more closely at Fern and Craig. She hadn't thought about musicians at her party, but of course, a country band or even singers with guitars like the two standing before her would add a great deal to her event...if they were still available at this late date. Of course, it was just one more possibility to consider in a county overflowing with creative possibilities.

"Why don't you play for Fernando?" Storm said. "He's met Belle now, so he knows the truth for a fact. She doesn't have Daisy Sue hidden somewhere…otherwise he could smell her."

"It's been a pleasure to meet you." Belle focused on Fernando, hoping he'd sense her sincerity.

He gave her another long, considering look and then turned his attention to the musicians.

"So far Fernando's favorite number is 'The Lonely Bull,'" Craig said.

"It was a big instrumental hit in the sixties by Herb Alpert and the Tijuana Brass." Fern adjusted the strap of her guitar on her shoulder. "Let's see if this will soothe him today after his meeting with you."

"He's disappointed," Storm said. "He was hoping that somehow Belle would bring Daisy Sue back to him."

"If I could, I'd do it this instant." Belle stepped back from the fence, realizing that Rowdy had moved up beside her. She tucked her hand in the crook of his arm, feeling his warmth and strength as an antidote to the shifting sands around her.

Fern started out humming the original trumpet part of "The Lonely Bull," and Craig added more depth to the number with his guitar.

Belle watched Fernando to gauge his reaction to the music. He lifted his head and looked at Fern with big, luminous eyes, and a peaceful calm radiated out from him. Belle could almost see a smile settle across his face.

Craig added his deeper voice to Fern's soprano as they looped the song, adding their own variations to keep it going since the music obviously had a soothing effect on their own lonely bull.

As they played, Fernando stretched out his neck toward Storm. She slipped between the bars of the corral. He lowered his massive head and gently bumped her small chest until she wrapped her arms around his neck. He blew air out his nose in a deep sigh and laid his head on her shoulder for a hug.

Belle experienced such emotion at the sight that she grew teary. If you were open to it, love knew no bounds. She felt Rowdy's rough palm cover her hand and press her fingers against his arm. She glanced up at him, saw tenderness in his gaze, and felt an answering response. She had no doubt everyone right there, right now felt the same outpouring of love.

And then her sentimentality ended as the sound of an approaching vehicle's engine cut through the music. She glanced around and saw a big, dark-blue Buick headed up the lane toward them.

"Oh my," she said under her breath. "It's the Buick Brigade."

"I bet they planned this meeting down to the exact second," Rowdy whispered in her ear.

She nodded in agreement because by now, she could well believe it.

Fern and Craig turned toward the sound, glanced at each other, and slowly finished their song until only silence hung in the air.

"Fernando knew they were coming." Storm broke the silence. "He likes them."

"He likes their cowboy cookies," Sydney said.

"That, too." Storm slipped out of the corral to stand beside her mother. "But he knows they always get the job done, no matter what."

"That's true. They do." Sydney put an arm around Storm and drew her close.

Everyone stood quietly, almost at attention, as they waited…with only a snort from Fernando to indicate any type of impatience.

The Buick came to a sharp stop in a cloud of dust, and then all four doors popped open. Four women of ageless beauty stepped out. They wore elegant felt hats over short, silver hair, colorful sweaters, knee-length skirts, and low-heeled pumps. They focused sharp eyes on the group around Fernando.

"How is our lonely bull today?" Ada carried a plate of cookies in both hands as she led the group to the corral.

Fernando snorted again and edged closer to the railing.

"I'm glad you brought cookies." Storm reached out and accepted the plate. "He's had a disappointing afternoon."

All four women looked directly at Belle, as if waiting for an explanation.

"Still no Daisy Sue," Belle said. "I'm doing my best."

"We know." Louise gave her a warm smile.

"Things are taking an interesting turn." Blondel walked over to Craig and looked him up and down.

"Can I do something to help? I mean, besides the music." Craig smiled, but he appeared uneasy.

"How is Thorne Horse Ranch?" Doris moved over near him.

"Good. We've got the barn rebuilt…something like the new one they rebuilt here," Craig said.

"Excellent." Doris joined her friends.

"We needed it after the last one burned down."

"Understandable." Louise completed the group surrounding Craig.

"A fire can leave..." Doris said.

"Open wounds..." Blondel said.

"That in time..." Louise said.

"Must be healed," Ada said.

Craig backed up a step, looking from one woman to the other. "Everything's fine at the ranch. No wounds or anything else to heal."

"Christmas is a time of healing and renewal," Louise said.

"Trust me, everything's fine." Craig backed up another step.

"Perhaps you need to look a little farther afield," Blondel said.

"Nope." Craig attempted another smile.

Fern stepped forward, holding her guitar at her side. "You're talking about that one-room schoolhouse, aren't you?"

"You mean the memorial grove?" Craig asked.

All four of the Buick Brigade nodded in unison.

"We've been meaning to follow up on that mystery, but we haven't had time," Fern said. "Do you know something about it?"

"We know everything, dear, but not all stories are ours to tell." Louise gave a little wink.

"Exactly," Blondel said.

Ada turned toward Belle and pointed a long finger. "She has answers, too."

Belle shook her head in the negative. "At this point, I have more questions than answers."

"Oh yes." Doris turned toward Craig. "We believe it's time for you to give Belle and Rowdy the key to the schoolhouse. Let them take it from there."

“The key?” Craig asked. “But why would they want it? That place is locked up tight.”

“We didn’t want to disturb it,” Fern said.

Blondel gave her a gentle smile. “Remember, it’s Christmastime, and presents come in different forms.”

“It’s best not to look gift horses in the mouth…not when there’s magic in the air,” Louise said.

“This Christmas,” Blondel said. “Belle Tarleton is Wildcat Bluff County’s gift horse.”

All four wise women turned to smile at Belle, bright eyes shining in the sunlight.

Chapter 24

Rowdy stood beside Belle as he watched the Buick Brigade disappear in a cloud of dust onto Wildcat Road. He was quiet, along with everybody else, because the four wise women usually left a stunned silence in their wake. This time was no different, except they appeared to be upping the ante this Christmas.

"Does anybody know what they were talking about?" Belle asked, glancing around the group. "It seems like it has something to do with me, but I can't imagine why. I have a lot going on, and I don't need anything else on my plate."

"I'm not so sure it's you, or at least not completely," Craig said.

"I don't know. Belle appears to be some sort of catalyst in their minds." Fern adjusted her guitar.

"Nobody ever knows their ultimate goal till they tie up all the loose ends in a neat little bow for us." Rowdy rubbed the side of his neck, feeling decidedly uneasy since Belle appeared to be their target.

"They're bossy," Storm said. "They think they can just go around telling folks what to do."

"They usually get their way." Sydney glanced at her daughter. "And they're not the only bossy-pants around here."

"Yeah. Somebody is getting her way ramrodding that new calendar. Do you really have to call it 'Wet & Wild Cowboy Firefighters'?" Rowdy gave Sydney a hard look.

"Yes, I do. Hot bodies sell. Anyway, I just do what needs to be done," Sydney said. "Wildcat Bluff Fire-Rescue needs the benefit to meet upcoming bills."

"Daisy Sue comes first of all." Storm put her hands on her hips and a frown on her face. "I'm not real wild about schoolhouses anyway. That kind of thing can get in the way of more important business."

Rowdy chuckled along with everyone else.

"It's not funny," Storm said. "Fernando is important business."

"Yes, he is, but there are a lot of other things going on at Christmas, too." Sydney smiled at her daughter.

"Daisy Sue." Storm leaned against Sydney. "You know, right?"

"We'll get her home somehow," Belle said.

"You bet we will." Oscar patted Tater on the head. "If Kemp don't get his act together, we'll find that beauty of a cow ourselves."

"Thanks," Storm said.

"I guess you'd better hear our story about the one-room schoolhouse." Craig lifted his cowboy hat, ran a hand through his hair in agitation, and then replaced the hat. "I wouldn't get into it at all with so much else going on this time of year, but once the Buick Brigade set their minds on something, it's usually easier to go along with them…at least a little bit of the way."

"I don't remember anybody mentioning a one-room schoolhouse around here," Rowdy said.

"We stumbled onto it by accident last Labor Day." Craig gave Fern a quick kiss on her cheek.

"That's right." Fern took up the story. "We were hoping

another dance hall survived from the Wild West days, so we were driving around looking for one from a copy of this old map Morning Glory gave us."

"I've never heard anything about this before now," Sydney said. "Why have y'all been holding out on us? It sounds interesting."

"Not to me." Storm moved back over to the corral and held out her hand to Fernando.

"Well, it is, but it's sad, too," Fern said.

"Sad?" Belle asked.

"Yeah," Craig said. "To back up, I'd bought this little piece of property, sight unseen, just because it bordered my horse ranch near Sure-Shot. We ended up there."

"What did you find?" Belle asked.

"The schoolhouse, but—" Fern said.

"There'd been a fire," Craig continued the story.

"Oh no." Rowdy hated to hear that news because it probably didn't have a good ending.

"The blaze didn't burn down the building, but there was obvious smoke damage from the fireplace," Craig said.

"And there were children inside because we found small hats." Fern shook her head. "We hope they got out alive, but we don't know who they were or what happened to them."

"Far as we know the story about the fire didn't survive down through our families or even in county lore," Craig said.

"That's odd," Sydney said. "Something like that ought to have been important enough to record and remember."

"I think it was on purpose," Craig said.

"Right." Fern clasped his hand. "The building is surrounded by a grove of trees like a memorial. It was pretty much impenetrable till Craig hacked through the undergrowth."

"Do you mean it was hidden on purpose?" Belle asked.

"We think so," Craig said. "It looked like they didn't want anyone to disturb the tranquility of the place."

"It's a beautiful building." Fern nodded at Belle and Sydney. "You'd like the Victorian architecture."

"Maybe it should be left in peace," Belle said.

"That's what we've done until we could learn more about it," Fern said.

"But nobody so far knows a thing," Craig said.

"Sounds like the Buick Brigade might know something." Rowdy had an uneasy feeling about the entire matter.

"Right," Craig said. "And it also sounds like they want you and Belle to go see the place."

"But why?" Belle asked. "What could we possibly have to do with it?"

"I don't know...but they talked about healing, and that place felt so forlorn, so empty," Fern said. "I wish...well, I wish we could make it right."

"How long ago do you think it caught fire?" Rowdy asked.

"I don't know," Craig said, "but it might have been at least a hundred years ago."

"I never heard about it." Oscar adjusted Tater's bandana and then looked at the group. "If anybody'd know, it'd be Arn of the Crazy Eight. He's about that old. He's ornery as all get-out, but he might know, and he might tell or he might not, depending on his mood."

"Is he still on that horse ranch near Sure-Shot?" Craig asked.

"Yeah," Oscar said. "That cantankerous granddaughter of his runs it now."

"Samantha?" Craig grinned. "I remember her. Tall redhead. She could ride like the wind."

"She's back home," Oscar said. "She won't know nothing, but Arn might."

Rowdy glanced at Belle and caught her eye. Wherever this was going, he didn't want to get involved in it. He knew she really wouldn't want to get involved in it either. He had no idea why the Buick Brigade was trying to draw them into some drama that happened a hundred or so years ago. They had enough to do to get ready for Christmas.

"Truth of the matter," Fern said. "When we were driving around looking for an old dance hall, I was kind of hoping we'd find a building we could turn into a community creative center...something like that since the funding for the arts in the high school was cut."

"Arts?" Belle's head snapped up. "I was thinking along the same lines."

"Really?" Fern focused on Belle. "Drama? Painting? Writing? Music?"

"Clothing design, too." Belle nodded in satisfaction.

"Business," Storm said. "Creative arts applied to business. My Fernando T-shirts are selling better than ever."

"Don't try to get me involved," Oscar said. "Ranching is my one and only game. Tater here, too."

"It makes life simpler." Rowdy thought about his own creative interests and how they complicated life, but on the other hand, he couldn't imagine living without them.

"Poetry." Belle smiled at Rowdy.

He smiled back, knowing she was thinking about the poem he'd written and recited for her.

"Do you think—" Belle said.

"It's small." Fern shook her head.

"That's why we keep guys like Rowdy around who can build stuff," Sydney said.

"I'm already overextended." Rowdy wasn't about to get involved in any more construction projects, or non-construction, as was currently his project.

"It's okay," Fern said. "I sincerely doubt it'll come to anything. We don't have the funds to upgrade or build or anything. It was just sort of a pipe dream of mine."

"You're right," Sydney agreed. "We've got too much on our plates this Christmas already."

"Daisy Sue comes first," Storm said.

"Right." Belle nodded in agreement. "And I'm busy at my new ranch. It's just kind of a fun idea."

"Tell you what." Craig pulled his key ring out of his pocket. "To stay on the good side of the Buick Brigade, why don't y'all run over to Sure-Shot one afternoon and see the schoolhouse? It wouldn't take long, and that'd be that."

"You might stop by the Crazy Eight on the same trip," Fern said. "We don't have time right now to do it ourselves what with Wildcat Hall Christmas preparations, but I'd really like to know what he has to say, if anything."

"Here's the padlock key." Craig selected a key on his ring, slipped it off, and tossed it.

Rowdy caught the key even though he didn't want it. "We don't have time to get involved in this right now either."

"Just a quick look," Sydney said. "Then we'll all be off the hook."

"I guess we could take a few hours." Belle shrugged as she glanced around the group.

"We'll see, but I'm not promising anything." Rowdy

pocketed the key where it felt like it was burning a hole in his pocket. The old schoolhouse was interesting, but lots of things were interesting. Just because he had a key didn't mean he had to investigate the mystery.

"Daisy Sue first." Storm glanced down at the plate of cookies she held in both hands. "Nobody cares anything about what happened a million years ago. Fernando cares about his love, and she's missing right now."

"I do understand," Belle said. "And I haven't forgotten about discussing cross-promotion with you either."

"Yeah." Storm nodded in agreement. "Now that you've met Fernando and he's accepted you, we can move forward with our plans."

"I didn't know this was an audition." Belle chuckled as she walked over to the corral.

"Fernando has very discerning taste." Storm leaned against the railing beside her. "He likes you."

"He's certainly handsome," Belle said. "I like him, too."

Rowdy glanced around the group, and they all smiled at each other at the bonding taking place. Storm was the one with discerning taste, and if she liked somebody, they were considered solid gold, not gold-plated. Belle might have had a rocky start in the county, but she was covering ground fast. At this rate, maybe he'd be let out of his slow-walking her construction job...at least he could hope so.

"Fernando," Belle said. "It's been lovely meeting you."

He gave her a long look with his big, brown eyes, and then he focused on the cookies Storm held in her hands.

Belle selected a cookie, balanced it on her flat palm, and held it out to him.

Fernando gently took the cookie into his mouth.

"He got hooked on these when he was a baby," Storm said.

"They're good," Belle said.

"He's so smart he probably even recognizes the shapes," Storm said.

"Could be." Belle glanced back at Rowdy. "I guess we better be on our way. We've taken up enough of y'all's time today."

"It's time well spent," Storm said. "You'll find Daisy Sue now. I just know it."

"Yes, I will...and I'll let you know when I hear something about her."

"We appreciate you stopping by to meet Fernando," Sydney said.

"And Tater." Oscar chuckled as he patted the dog's head.

"Right." Belle walked over and fingered the bandana around Tater's neck. "Fine-looking accessory."

"He's got them in all colors," Oscar said. "But red's his favorite."

"It looks good on him." Belle glanced around the group. "I'd just like to say...I'm really enjoying living in Wildcat Bluff County. I hope I can make a positive contribution to the area."

"We're glad you're here," Fern said. "My sister, Ivy, and I came here from Houston, big-city folks, so we know how it is to find your own niche in the country."

"Thanks." Belle glanced at Rowdy again.

He moved to her side, feeling proud of the way she was handling the situation but also knowing it was time to move on.

"Now, don't be a stranger," Sydney said.

"Right." Storm walked up to Belle. "Give that Fernando and Daisy Sue line some thought, why don't you?"

Belle grinned at her. "I will. And let's stay in touch."

"You bet." Storm grinned back.

"Let us know if you follow up on the schoolhouse," Fern said.

"We will. See you later." Belle waved and then headed for Rowdy's pickup.

Rowdy nodded to his friends before he followed Belle, opened the door, made sure she was safely inside, and shut the door. He rounded the cowcatcher and sat down beside her.

"Are you okay?" He started the engine and then set off down the lane before anybody else could arrive and hold them up.

"Yes." Belle leaned her head back against the seat. "Quite a group of folks you've got in this county."

"Tell me about it." He reached over and squeezed her hand. "You did great. They all like you."

"That's good...I think."

He chuckled at her comment. "I get it. The more they like you, the more they can think of for you to do."

She joined his laughter. "One-room schoolhouse? Arn of the Crazy Eight?"

"We don't have to put that on a front burner."

"No, we don't, but it is intriguing, isn't it?"

"Yeah. But right now I'm taking you home where you can catch your breath."

"Will there be cowboy cookies?"

"No." He crossed over the cattle guard and then glanced at her. "But there'll be a cowboy."

"Oh my." She fanned her face as if he was too hot to handle. "Does this cowboy have a name?"

"He'll answer to whatever you want to call him."

"Bad boy?"

"Yep."

She reached over and lightly stroked his arm with long fingers. "Fernando. Daisy Sue. Storm. The Buick Brigade. And now my very own 'bad boy.' Life is certainly interesting in this county."

"Let's see how interesting we can make it once we get you home."

"Without drunken cowboy cookies?"

"We won't even need the whiskey."

And then he turned off Wildcat Road and roared up to the front of her house with all the shingle stacks glistening in the sunlight.

Chapter 25

A few days later, Rowdy knew for a fact that he was doomed, doomed, doomed to lose the love of his life… kind of like Fernando. Belle. Daisy Sue. How had they come to this point?

He glanced over at Belle where she sat beside him in his ratty pickup, looking just as pleased as punch. She'd gotten her way, so she ought to be happy, but she didn't have all the facts, or she wouldn't have come anywhere near where he was taking her now.

Up ahead, he saw the entry that proclaimed to folks who knew about it to take the next turnoff. He slowed down, noting that the silver double gates with HF&R in the center that usually stayed closed were wide open for him. On either side of the cattle guard rose a four-sided column with Holloway Farm & Ranch engraved into the pale sandstone. Blue-and-silver rope light wound around each column with a large, blue bow on each flat top, representing holiday packages waiting to be unwrapped on Christmas morning.

He turned off Wildcat Road, crossed the cattle guard, and headed up the well-maintained black asphalt road. Red Angus cattle stood in clusters under the spreading limbs of green-leafed live oaks or grazed on what was left of summer grass now turned golden in the winter. Sunlight glinted on a large pond with green lily pads floating across its blue surface while a weeping willow cast a dark shadow across one corner of the water. In the distance, a large red barn and numerous outbuildings rose above the gently rolling prairie land.

All Rowdy could think was home-not-so-sweet-home now that he was bringing Belle to his family ranch.

"This is beautiful." Belle pointed out her side window. "I don't know why you were so reluctant to bring me here."

"I don't like to intrude. The Holloways haven't been much for parties or visitors since Bert lost his wife and Bert Two his mother."

"That's tough. I hope they're doing better now."

"Yes, they are. Now that Bert is seeing Hedy, everybody in the family is happier." He felt like a fool referring to his dad and himself as if he didn't know them well. If Belle ever found out...it didn't bear thinking on.

As the lane wound upward, higher and higher, they passed a pasture that held white-face Herefords with deep-red bodies. They weren't as popular as they'd once been on ranches, although he still preferred the breed for looks and temperament. Black or red Angus was the current favorite among North American ranchers due to economics because Angus cattle matured quickly and easily put on weight.

"Big spread, isn't?" Belle said.

"Thousands of acres. It's been in the Holloway family for generations like most of the big ranches around here."

"That's the way it is with my family, too. We were lucky to get the Lazy Q in this area."

"Yep." He could've said a lot more, but he was trying to keep his mind in the right groove. He'd phoned ahead so they were expecting him and knew to continue playing the stupid game. He hoped they could stop it soon, but then what would he tell Belle? He pushed it from his mind and drove on up to the house that dominated a rise on the ranch.

"I hadn't expected to see such a lovely Southern mansion." Belle glanced at him and then back at the house. "If my brothers hadn't insisted I stop by to pay my respects to the Holloway family, since they're friends, I wouldn't be here now, and I'd have missed seeing this beauty."

"The Holloways were originally from the South like a lot of folks who settled in Texas. I know their house looks unusual here on a ranch instead of perched on a cliff overlooking the Mississippi River or on a rise above the Gulf Coast. I guess you know the style is Colonial Revival from the antebellum period."

"I do indeed, since I'm from East Texas. It reminds me of Jefferson, the riverboat town that used to be the gateway from the South to the West. Beautiful homes there, too."

He parked in front and waited so she could get a good look. He didn't normally notice the architecture much since he lived there with his dad. He was always just running in and out to take care of business. Anyway, he was away from home more than usual now that he and Belle were… doomed, doomed, doomed if this didn't go well today.

He tried to see his home with fresh eyes. It was a large white two-story house with black shutters on the floor-to-ceiling windows that were overshadowed by the covered portico that ran the length of the front with tall columns holding up the roof. Redbrick chimneys rose on each end from the ground to high above the roofline. A redbrick path meandered from the lane up to the house through a golden, manicured lawn with neatly trimmed bushes and ancient, leafless oak trees.

As he turned off the pickup's engine, the double front doors opened, and Bert and Hedy in her motorized wheelchair came outside. His dad wore his usual rancher suit, cowboy boots, and Stetson, while Hedy looked good in shirt, jeans, and boots.

"They're such an adorable couple," Belle said thoughtfully.

"Kind of like us?" He couldn't resist saying it, hoping the words would ward off any bad mojo coming their way.

She glanced over at him with a smile that lit up her hazel eyes. "Just like us."

"Good." He reached over and clasped her hand, clinging for a moment before he let go. "If anything happens...I mean if something was said...it's just that no matter what...I love you."

"You're really uneasy about this, aren't you?" She gave him another sweet smile. "There's absolutely no reason to be intimidated by this fancy house or thousands of acres just because you've only got...well, I don't know what you've got, but judging by your clothes and vehicle...I don't mean to say you have less since I really don't know. I'm not doing this well at all." She took a deep breath and looked at him with love. "It doesn't matter to me what you have or don't have. What matters to me is the person you are right this moment. You're honest, trustworthy, kind, considerate, loving in a world that needs more of your type of person."

He didn't move a muscle because he felt sick to his stomach. Every one of her words was a knife thrust to his lying, cheating heart. He wasn't honest or trustworthy. Maybe he had been, but not since meeting her and accepting his assignment. If she ever found out…no, she couldn't find out. He'd come up with some reasonable excuse when the time came to kick his actions into the dustbin of history with all the other nefarious doings of humans.

"I've embarrassed you, haven't I?" She leaned over and pressed a kiss to his cheek.

"No. It's just…well, I do want you to see my place, and today is—"

"The day for me to make friends with the Holloways. It's important to my brothers. I wonder if Bert Two will be here."

Rowdy rolled his eyes, but not so she could see it. "I think he's out of state."

"Really?"

"He hunts with bow and arrow, so he might be up in the mountains of Southeast Oklahoma."

"That's interesting."

"Not really." He didn't want any more discussion of Bert Two or he wasn't going to be able to keep it together. "Let's go say hello."

He got out, walked around to her side of his truck, and opened the door. He was getting into the Buick Brigade gentlemanly conduct, and it seemed appropriate here and now. Belle stepped down, clasping his hand and smiling at him in encouragement. If she'd been any sweeter about the situation, he'd have a toothache. As it was, he just had to buck up and bear it.

He held her hand as they walked up the redbrick path, stopped, and waited for Bert and Hedy to come down the ramp to join them.

"Belle Tarleton, it's a pleasure to meet you." Bert held out his hand, but when she reached out to shake, he gave her a big bear hug. "That's to let you know I consider you part of our family while you're here in Wildcat Bluff County."

"Thank you." Belle stepped back with a big smile as she turned to give Hedy a quick hug. "I'm so glad to be here."

"Rowdy," Bert said with a grin and roll of his eyes, "thanks for bringing Belle to see us."

"My pleasure." Rowdy gave his dad a narrow-eyed look that should warn him off laying it on too thick.

"I regret Bert Two is out of pocket today," Bert said.

"That's okay. I've been meaning to come over, but I've just been so busy getting my new home ready for the holidays," Belle said.

"We understand perfectly, my dear." Hedy gave her a warm smile. "Plus I know Rowdy here has been keeping busy at your house."

Rowdy rolled his eyes at her behind Belle's back. If he didn't watch out, they were both going to get him into hot water. Trouble was they were enjoying the situation at his expense.

"I promised Hedy I'd show you my bluebird collection," Bert said. "She sold me the entire collection over several years. It was my best excuse for seeing her, since she wouldn't go out with me. I shamelessly took advantage of the fact that I could find her at Adelia's Delights and spend time with her."

"He's such a romantic." Hedy smiled up at him. "And persistent."

"You've always held my heart," Bert said. "And my bluebird house is my way of showing it."

"It's impressive. Right this way." Rowdy gestured ahead at the redbrick path.

"I'm anxious to see it." Belle took the path that ran alongside the house.

Hedy went next in her wheelchair. She was followed by Bert. Rowdy brought up the rear. He always enjoyed seeing the bluebird collection from the perspective of someone who had never viewed it.

Soon they came to an extensive back garden with stone benches, gurgling fountains, trimmed hedges and rosebushes, a manicured lawn, a flagstone patio with blue-and-white-striped cushions on redwood furniture, and an infinity swimming pool and hot tub. Blue-and-silver rope lights outlined the house's roofline, while crimson poinsettias in large green ceramic containers adorned the patio.

And yet all of that beauty paled in comparison to Bert's bluebird house. In the center of the garden, a glass-walled gazebo in a hexagonal shape rose as a delicate work of art into the sky, glowing blue fire where the brilliant rays of the sun struck the multitude of bluebirds inside.

"Oh, my," Belle said. "That's absolutely stunningly gorgeous."

"Thank you." Bert opened the glass door to the gazebo. "Please go inside."

Belle went in first, followed by the others. She turned around in a complete circle as she took in the bluebirds... eyes bright with wonder.

Rowdy gazed at the sky-blue glass bluebirds in a variety of sizes from small to large but all in the same smooth bird shape. Bert had placed them on clear glass shelves around the walls to better catch the rays of the sun. And for Christmas, he'd added decorations in the form of silver tinsel scarves around necks or gold-foil hats on heads or red-and-white candy canes at beaks.

"I absolutely adore this gazebo." Belle turned to look at Bert and Hedy. "Thank you so much for sharing it with me. It's an inspiration...a lovely testimony to love."

"Bert taught me all about love. And it's never too late to learn and share it." Hedy smiled at her and then glanced up at Rowdy.

He took her meaning to heart because she was right. It's just that he was between a rock and a hard place.

"I agree." Belle clasped Rowdy's hand, giving him a soft smile.

"Why don't we take a closer look at the garden?" Rowdy gestured toward the open door, and the women went outside.

Bert hung back. "You weren't supposed to get involved, were you?"

"Dad, she's the one."

"Are you sure?"

"Yes."

"You're definitely a chip off the old block. Love hits Holloway men hard." Bert sighed. "You're in a pickle, aren't you?"

"She trusts me. If she finds out I'm there to sabotage her plans, she'll never forgive me."

"Son, love does conquer all."

"That's easy for you to say. You and Hedy—"

"What do you want me to do?"

"Get me out of this mess."

"That's not so easy."

"Look, I've been with her enough to know she has good intentions toward the county. She's not going bring in a lot of riffraff and trouble. She's sincere."

"That's what I'm starting to hear about her."

"If it means anything, Fernando likes her...along with Storm, Sydney, Fern, and Craig."

"That means a lot. Besides, she comes from a good family. That means something important, too." Bert glanced from his son to the women and back again. "I'll talk with Hedy and the others."

"Thank you. I want out of this job in the worst way."

"In the meantime, why don't you go ahead and make a little progress on the house?"

"I already painted the trim."

"Did it make her happy?"

"Yes. She's been really patient."

"That reveals good character."

"Yeah." Rowdy glanced toward the back garden. "Something else."

"What?"

"The Buick Brigade have taken a liking to her."

"Really? Now that's another plus in her favor."

"You know how they are."

"What do they want her to do?" Bert asked.

"I'm not exactly sure, but they're involving me."

"What are you going to do about it?"

"So far, nothing."

"That won't work." Bert stroked one of the bluebirds. "It's Christmastime. If you want a miracle with Belle—and it's beginning to look like you'll need one—you'd better reconsider what the wise women told you to do."

Rowdy sighed. "I was afraid that's exactly what you would say."

Chapter 26

"I'm not so sure this is a good idea." Belle sat stiffly in the front seat of Rowdy's truck...or rather Bert Two's pickup, since Rowdy had borrowed it again. Really, it was a relief because it was so much more comfortable and safer on the road than his old rattletrap. Maybe someday soon she'd get to meet Bert Two because he seemed like a real nice and generous guy.

"We already talked about it." Rowdy threw a glance her way and then focused back on the road. "And we decided to do it."

"I'm having second thoughts."

"We're almost at Sure-Shot."

"I don't care. It's not that far back to Wildcat Bluff."

"Okay." He slowed down. "What's really eating at you?"

"It's my Christmas party."

"I got the trim painted on your house, and it looks good."

"True. But shingle stacks are still on the front lawn."

"At least they're there and not stolen."

"But Sheriff Calhoun hasn't caught the thieves."

"He's working on it," Rowdy said.

"It's just...just—"

"Go ahead. Spill it."

"I'm disappointed I didn't get to send out invitations. I thought folks would enjoy my party along with Christmas in the County in Wildcat Bluff, Christmas at the Sure-Shot Drive-In, and Wildcat Hall's Honky-Tonk Christmas."

He glanced at her with wide eyes and then quickly looked back at the road. "It's a good thing you didn't do it. That weekend is already packed with stuff, and everybody is overworked making it come off without a hitch."

"It would've been a fine way to showcase the community and let folks see the creative, vibrant world that is now home to Lulabelle & You."

"We're only three weeks out now. Invitations would've had to go out ages ago."

"I know, but still it's a disappointment." She tapped her fingernails on the dashboard. "And now I'm heading off into the wilds of horse country—"

"It's not wild. It's Sure-Shot and environs."

"Anyway..."

He pulled off to the side of the road and turned to look at her. "Is it my fault you couldn't throw your party?"

"Well, you are a pretty big distraction."

He grinned, shaking his head. "I meant about the house."

"It's not all you. Remember how it looked when you got there. Lots of people before you let me down. At least you made progress."

"I'm sorry for the delay."

"Thanks."

"One good thing."

"What?"

"You don't have to worry about making plans or getting the house fixed up or anything else. You can simply enjoy all the local Christmas festivities."

"That's true." She put her hands in her lap, looked at them, and realized she needed a manicure. She couldn't seem to get enough done. "It's just that it would've been good for business."

"Are you sure?"

"What do you mean? I intended to use the party to introduce and showcase the ranch."

"Wouldn't spring be a better time when everything is green and you've had an opportunity to get the ranch in order?"

"Do you think I was rushing it?"

"Do you?" he asked.

"Maybe so."

"Right now everybody is hurrying around to finish up stuff and attend parties so they can take time off during the holidays and enjoy Christmas. Maybe the last thing they needed was another party invitation."

"Good point. Sometimes you sound like an entrepreneur." She cocked her head to one side, looking at him and trying to figure him out. Somehow or the other all the pieces just never quite fit together. Who was this man who'd become such a vital part of her life?

"I'm a practical guy, that's all."

"I guess there's no point in crying over spilled milk."

"Not one bit."

"This way I can focus on more pressing matters at the ranch as well as my business. And maybe Kemp will soon find a way to bring Daisy Sue home." She felt as if a weight lifted off her shoulders, even if she was disappointed not to use the bandanas or the hay bales or...just do something fun. Of course, it didn't mean she couldn't use the great ideas when she finally did throw her welcome to Wildcat Bluff County and Lulabelle & You Ranch party.

"For now, do you want to go back or go on?"

"When you put it that way, I never like to go back. That's

part of my problem with the party. I just kept plunging forward no matter the obstacles or the time of year or anything. You're right about spring being better all the way around."

"Stay or go."

"Well—"

"It'll give you something else to think about."

She rolled her eyes at him. "Sometimes you make too much sense. Let's do it."

"Okay." He pulled back onto the highway.

"I've got the map. You've got the key. Do you think we can find the schoolhouse?"

"Yes. I know a little about the area."

"Do you come over here often?"

"Well...I like the Sure-Shot Drive-In Theater," he said.

"That sounds like fun."

"It is. I'll take you there sometime, if you like."

"I'd like it a lot. Maybe we can make out in the back seat."

"Anytime." He glanced over at her with that special light in his eyes that told her exactly what he was thinking about doing in the back seat.

"You're on." She grinned at him, suddenly feeling happier about her non-party. With love in the air, how could she possibly be down about anything?

"We'll turn off before we get to Sure-Shot."

"Do you need me to navigate?"

"I studied the map, and I know my way around the area, so I'm good to go."

"If you need it, I have the map right here." She clutched Craig's crude drawing in her hand, but she wasn't sure she could make sense of it because she didn't know this horse country at all.

He turned off the highway before he reached Sure-Shot and headed down a road that was little more than washboard ruts that bounced the truck with every turn of the wheels. Pretty soon that played out into nothing but a tall stand of horse-belly-high dry grass. He stopped the pickup.

"Can this be right?" All she saw ahead was a thick section of old-growth vegetation that rose out of nowhere.

She'd researched the area enough to know that the Cross Timbers once stretched from Kansas to Central Texas, cutting a wide swath between East Texas and West Texas. Each side of the plains was densely bordered by sturdy post oak, flowering cedar elm, hard-as-nails bois d'arc, blossoming dogwood, Virginia creeper, and thorny blackberry.

It had originally been part of the Comanche empire that had stretched from central Kansas to Mexico. In the old days, there had been a brush fire every year, and the tree line that made up the border of the Cross Timbers would grow back too dense to penetrate. Comanche warriors had used the prairie between the two tree lines as a secret passage so enemies couldn't see or attack them.

Lots of folks in Wildcat Bluff County were descendants of the Comanche and still protected thousands of those acres, but they kept the wildfires under control so the thicket line didn't grow back as dense.

"You know about the Cross Timbers, don't you?" Rowdy asked.

"Yes. We're in the center of it, aren't we?"

"Pretty much. What's odd is that section doesn't grow north-south. It grows east-west. That's all wrong." He pointed at the thicket line. "And that's really out of place."

"What do you mean?"

"Look at it. Hundred-plus-year-old post oaks do not grow in a circle, or semi-circle from what I can see from here, with a pretty dogwood tree set in between each trunk. It's not natural. And those dogwoods shouldn't even still be alive. Eighty years is about their limit. They'd need really rich soil to live this long."

"Maybe the oaks are younger than you think."

"Could be. It's all entwined with blackberry vines that would shred most anything trying to get through on foot or hoof." He glanced over at her. "It's like Craig told us. At some point way back in time a grove was planted here... looks like to keep somebody in or somebody out."

"That's a chilling thought."

"You know it. And why right here near Sure-Shot in the middle of ranch land? It makes no sense."

"I guess it's up to us to try to make sense of it."

"Let's find that gap Craig left between a post oak and a dogwood."

"And see what we can see."

"Right."

She picked up two flashlights from the floorboard, stepped out, and joined him in front of the pickup. She was dressed for an excursion into the woods in a jean jacket, a thick sweater, Wranglers, and work boots. She'd also brought leather gloves. He was dressed in similar warm, tough clothes. She handed him one of the lights and then glanced around the area.

"It seems too quiet here, doesn't it?"

"We made enough noise driving up and getting out that we probably disturbed everything."

"Yeah."

"Once we get inside the grove, we shouldn't find much vegetation because there won't be enough sunlight filtering through the oaks."

She walked with him to the row of trees where Virginia creeper, blackberry, and poison ivy grew in a thick mass along with the twisted and thorny branches of bois d'arc.

"Don't touch any of that growth." He pulled on his leather gloves. "Most of it can shred skin and poison you."

"Don't worry. I'm not touching it. I'm just looking for the opening Craig said he'd left here." As she slipped on her gloves, she watched Rowdy walk along the thick growth, stopping and checking to see if any of the vegetation was loose.

"Here we go." He grabbed hold of a section and tugged on it, jerking hard, and it gave way to reveal an opening large enough to go through without getting tangled up in briars. He glanced over and grinned at her.

"Perfect."

"Why don't you do the honors and go first?"

She carefully stepped into a quiet glade with him right behind her. Dappled sunlight through thick branches of the surrounding trees cast long shadows across ground covered with dry leaves that hadn't been disturbed since they'd fallen last autumn.

She felt as if she'd stepped back in time to another era captured in the perfection of a small Victorian building with gingerbread trim around the peaked roof and the railing around the front porch with a crawl space underneath. It even had a fancy bell tower. After a hundred years or so, it still looked beautiful. The white paint had faded or eroded to almost nothing except bare wood, and pieces of gingerbread hung haphazardly from the eaves, but overall it looked remarkably well preserved for its age.

"It's lovely here, isn't it?" She spoke softly so as not to disturb the tranquility.

"Yes." He gestured around the area. "You can see the trees were planted in a perfect circle around the schoolhouse. Next to white oaks, post oaks are the hardest, longest-lasting oak. And dogwoods have spiritual meaning to people."

"It's very special. I wish I knew why this was done...and who did it."

"I think that's why we're here."

"Let's take a closer look."

As they drew nearer, she could see that things didn't appear quite as good as they had from a distance. Blackberry vines twined up the railings and across the floor of the porch, creating a gray, thorny barrier.

"It's obvious there was trouble here." He clasped her hand, giving an encouraging smile.

"And sad."

She walked with him to the side of the house where a single window had been boarded up.

"As a firefighter, I hate to see so few exits," he said.

"Maybe there's a rear door."

When they reached the back of the house, he pointed toward the lower half of the building, where dark stains tarnished the wood and stroked upward toward a brick chimney that was blackened with soot and had partially crumbled to the ground.

"No back door," he said. "The blaze must have started in the fireplace or the chimney. At first, smoke would have been more problem than fire. There's only one small, high window on this side and probably the same on the other side."

"You're thinking there aren't enough exits, aren't you?"

"Right. I wish I'd been here to help them. Back then, they couldn't have called volunteer firefighters."

"No. They would have been on their own, but they were resourceful." She squeezed his fingers to comfort them both.

"True. They may all have made it out alive."

"I don't know what we'll find inside, but let's go see."

"Okay."

She walked with him to the front door, dreading going inside and yet feeling it was her responsibility...after all these years.

"I'll go first. I want to make sure the wood isn't rotten or termite-eaten."

"Be careful."

She watched as he edged up the stairs leading to the front door, crushing blackberry vines under his boots. When he got to the porch, he turned and beckoned her forward. She carefully stepped where he'd stepped until she reached the landing and stopped beside him in front of a beautiful hand-carved door that matched the Victorian architecture.

He pulled a key out of his pocket. "Craig replaced the missing doorknob, so it's easier for us to enter now. It'd been boarded up."

"And no one else has been here, as far as we know, in all these years except Craig and Fern...and now us."

"That's right. Are you ready?"

"Yes."

"Remember, a firefighter is here to help...at last."

Chapter 27

Rowdy took a deep breath before he inserted the key, turned the lock, and pushed open the door. He switched on his flashlight, stepped into the schoolhouse, and swept the single room with light. No rodents, raccoons, or other small animals were in evidence, although cobwebs hung from the ceiling in the corners. He caught the scent of dust, decay, and smoke that was trapped inside because the building had been shut up for so long…and if he wasn't mistaken, a touch of sadness still lingered in the air.

"It's safe." He glanced back at Belle. He was well aware he'd been overly cautious and protective since they'd arrived at the grove, but everything about the place set him on alert. He couldn't tolerate even the thought of something negative happening to her. He well knew that she was having enough trouble dealing with her bust of a Christmas party primarily because folks in the county had decided they didn't want her to succeed before they'd even met her. And he'd let them suck him into their scheme, so what did that say about him? Or them? He didn't feel good about it, that was for sure…and by now his friends probably didn't either.

The Buick Brigade was right on the money as usual. They'd reached out to Belle first and welcomed her with cookies. Nobody else had. What if Belle found out about the hoax that had been played on her? And left? It'd be a major loss to the community—not to mention how it would break his heart.

Maybe this schoolhouse mystery could somehow heal not only an old wound but this new one as well because the situation with Belle was turning out to be a festering sore for them all. They'd made a mistake, but surely they could find a way to right it.

She sneezed as she followed him inside...footsteps causing the old wooden floorboards to moan and groan and squeak, disrupting the stillness of the room and sending dust flying.

He slowly and carefully cast an arc of light around the inside. It wasn't big here. It wasn't fancy. It was utilitarian. From the outside, he'd expected Victorian gewgaws, but no. Wooden walls. Wooden ceiling. Wooden floors. And wooden benches that had seats and backs made of single boards with circular saw marks that indicated the time period of construction because that type of saw hadn't been used in a long time.

Most of the benches had been knocked over and lay on their sides. A single, straight-back chair with charred rungs had been tossed on its back near the fireplace, where the floor was scorched and blackened from the fire.

None of that surprised or shocked him because he'd seen a lot of fire damage and the resulting chaos over the years. Hats. It was the hats that did it. He felt his gut twist and turn at the sight. It'd been winter because there'd been a blaze in the fireplace. They'd have worn woolen hats and coats to school. On one side of the fireplace, three round hats still hung on the rows of pegs that had been pounded into the wooden wall. All the other hats lay on the floor near the fireplace in various stages of decay from completely burned to partially burned to twisted and crumpled and stomped on.

Belle stopped beside him and put a hand on his arm. "They used the hats to put out the fire, didn't they?"

"It was a good idea to smother the blaze."

"Do you suppose they didn't think they'd ever need the hats again because they weren't going to make it?"

"No. I'd say the hats were just handy and somebody was smart enough and quick enough to think of using them."

"I hope that's it." She leaned down and looked closer. "They're all small, you know."

"I know."

"Little kids."

"I know."

"Do you suppose they got out in time?"

"Smoke would have been their biggest danger, because the fire didn't spread and burn down the building."

"Somebody stopped it."

"And that somebody probably had a coat or blanket or something bigger to completely smother the fire."

"But was it in time?"

"I don't know."

"I hope so."

"Me, too," he said.

"I wish this memorial grove made me feel better about the final outcome."

"Yeah. It's like nobody escaped. They only had the one exit, and if that door was stuck or the kids were too little to reach the knob or—"

"What about the teacher? She'd have been tall enough,

aware enough, determined enough to make sure they all got out alive. Wouldn't she?"

"Yes...if she wasn't overcome by smoke inhalation," he said.

"And so they closed the building on their deep sorrow and planted a memorial grove in honor of their loved ones."

"We don't know that for a fact. Maybe they all got out, but no one wanted to use the building again. Bad luck is bad luck." He knew all about trying to ward off bad luck, for all the good it did.

"And the memorial grove?"

"It kept folks away from taking a chance on the schoolhouse."

"I don't know...I just don't know," she said. "Maybe they put a sacred memory to rest, and now we've disturbed it."

"No. I don't think so...or maybe...but the Buick Brigade sent us on this quest, so they want something to happen, something good, I'd wager."

"It's almost Christmas." She squeezed his arm. "Do you suppose that's the time of year when the fire got out of control?"

He felt chilled at the thought. She wasn't the only one growing cold despite their warm clothing. How cold had it been that fateful day? No doubt it'd been cold enough to warrant a blaze in the fireplace...and afterward, there'd been no Christmas cheer for anyone.

He played his light across the walls around the fireplace and then focused the beam on the floor in front of them. A single book...splayed open on its back with broken spine and charred pages...lay there forlorn and alone.

"If their kids got out alive, they'd never have trusted them here again, would they?"

"No."

"They'd have taken them to town for their educations."

"Yes."

"One thing," she said. "There's tragedy here, I know, but there's also love...of learning, of community, of friendship, of a dedicated teacher."

"That's a good way to look at it."

"And now, after a hundred years, it's been placed in our hands." She turned to stare at him with wide eyes. "Why?"

"I can't answer that question. I wish I could, but I can't."

She turned away from him, splashing light across the walls, the floor, the benches, and back to the fireplace.

"Do you want to go? We've seen it. I don't know what else we can do here."

She turned back to him, dropping her hand to her side so that her flashlight illuminated uncharred words on the splayed book.

He didn't say anything while she stood there, shoulders down in an attitude of contemplation, and her focus stayed on the lighted book.

After a while she straightened her shoulders, as if coming to a decision. She reached down and picked up the book. It crumbled to dust in her hands. She glanced at him...and gave a sweet, sad smile.

He didn't know what to say, so he simply stood there, waiting, watching, wondering. He felt as if the impetus had moved from the Buick Brigade to Belle Tarleton. Some type of Christmas magic, maybe.

"I don't want to leave this schoolhouse like we found it."

She walked to the front door, looked outside, and turned back. "It's beautiful here. Special."

"It's that, if not for—"

"I want to set the benches upright. Do you think that'd be okay?"

"I don't know. It's not our place." He rubbed his jaw, not really wanting to get more involved here. They'd said they'd come see it. They'd done it. They could move on…except now Belle had a gleam in her eyes as she looked around the room. Perhaps that was good. He hoped so.

"This was a place of learning before the fire." She walked around, light flashing before her, picking out a bench here, a hat there, a book tossed in a corner. "Why can't it be that way again?"

"Craig owns it. I guess he can do whatever he wants with it."

"He doesn't love it."

"Well, no. He's got his horse ranch and Wildcat Hall. And Fern."

"I already love it."

"You just got here."

She walked directly to the fireplace and placed the flat of her palm against the blackened brickwork. "I want to heal it. I want it to live again. I want it to be what it was always meant to be."

This was so much more than he'd counted on, but then again, he'd already thought about healing old and new wounds. Maybe she was trying to replace the loss of her Christmas party with the schoolhouse.

"I came to Wildcat Bluff County for several reasons. Business, yes. But I also want to help others…in particular, youngsters."

"That's a noble cause."

"I don't know about noble, but I think it's important. Kids reach out to me at Lulabelle & You like I have all the answers. I don't. Sometimes, maybe...but I'm only one person. This county is special, and it's full of folks who could share their love, knowledge, and expertise in all matters creative as well as just life experience."

"There are a lot of good folks here." He was beginning to think he might have to fess up soon before she gave them all undeserved halos.

"I thought I'd build my outreach center at the new ranch, but what about beginning here?" She twirled the light around the room, illuminating everything so that it appeared as if it were suddenly coming alive.

"It's not that I'm against the idea, but this schoolhouse belongs to Craig."

"Fern was already thinking along these lines."

"And then there's the time, energy, and money that'd need to be invested to bring the place up to current standards...and just to make it usable."

"It looks like it's in good shape." She crisscrossed the room, as if examining it for flaws or problems.

"I'd need to check the structure, but it appears basically sound. Still, there isn't any electricity, running water, air-conditioning, heating. We're talking none of our modern conveniences."

"I didn't think of all that." She stopped, looking down, shoulders slumping again.

"I'm not saying it couldn't be done...if somebody wanted to take on the project and they had permission, at least a rental contract, from the owner. I'm saying it's a big expenditure of time, labor, and money."

"You're right." She stopped beside the chair in front of the fireplace. She tried to place it upright, but it kept tipping over because the legs were so badly damaged by the fire. She finally gave up. Next, she knelt to pick up a hat and then stopped and glanced at him.

"You want to set everything right here, don't you?"

"Yes." She stood up. "It just seems like it should be done. I want to take back what was lost and offer it to others."

"Like I said, it's a noble idea."

"But?"

"We still don't know what happened here. Is there a good reason to leave the past in the past?"

"You mean the schoolhouse and grove should remain as they've been for so many years?"

"I don't think we have enough information to make any type of decision right now. We haven't talked with Arn yet." He didn't want her to be disappointed later if her idea wasn't workable.

"That's true." She patted the fireplace and then stepped back. "I believe this one-room schoolhouse wants to be loved and used again."

"Maybe so, but—"

"That won't happen today."

"No, it won't." He glanced around the room, wanting to find a way to help her. "I guess what we mainly need first is information."

"That'd help."

He checked the watch on his wrist. "It's about four. Arn sometimes plays checkers at the Bluebonnet Café along about this time."

"Is that in Sure-Shot?"

"Yes. We aren't far away. Do you want to see if he's there and will tell us something?"

"That'd be great. And it'd be quicker than going to his ranch another day."

"Sure would be...if we could even find time later."

"Let's do it."

"Better head out."

"Okay." She took a deep breath, as if drawing strength from her surroundings. "Now that I've been here, I'll never forget this place. And I want it to know that I'll be back when the time is right."

"Maybe after Christmas, when we have more space to take on new projects, would be a better time to think about it."

"Maybe." She gave him a little smile. "I wonder what the Buick Brigade would think about waiting until the new year dawns."

"I can't hazard a guess." He walked over to the front door, wanting her to have what she wanted but not knowing if it was feasible. Arn might have some helpful insights if he'd be willing share his knowledge.

She followed him to the door. "I don't really want to leave just yet, but I suppose it's time."

"We'll return."

She looked back into the room and gave a little wave before she turned, walked out the front door, and headed down the stairs.

Oddly enough, the schoolhouse didn't feel nearly as forlorn as when they'd first set foot inside. He shut and locked the door behind him.

Chapter 28

Belle sat quietly in the front seat as Rowdy drove away from the grove, slowly, carefully making his way down the deep ruts. He was a big, solid presence beside her, comforting in her moment of disorientation. She felt as if she'd just returned from a fairy tale where magic conceals what's real and only truth can set it free. But what was the truth… and could she find it now that she was back in the regular world?

She glanced behind and saw nothing more than the impenetrable barrier to the grove and schoolhouse. If she hadn't known what lay beyond, she'd never have guessed its existence. How had it stayed hidden all these years? She had many more questions than she had answers. Maybe Arn of the Crazy Eight Ranch could set her on the path to enlightenment.

"You haven't been to Sure-Shot before, have you?" Rowdy asked.

"No. I heard about it. It's a small Western town, isn't it?"

"Sure-Shot was named for Annie Oakley, the famous sharpshooter and exhibition shooter who was called 'Little Miss Sure-Shot' on the Wild West show circuit."

"Really? I wonder if she ever lived in the town."

"Doubt it. She was a celebrity in her day, so everybody knew her name." He turned west on Highway 82. "We'll be there pretty quick."

She noticed that the fence lines that stretched along both sides of the road were white round pipe or four-slat wooden enclosures instead of barbwire, so she knew they'd moved from cattle country to horse country. One ranch after another flashed by, announcing their names—from whimsical to practical—in black sheet-metal cutouts or burned into wood arches that towered over entryways.

Thoroughbred horses with rich coats in a variety of shades grazed in some pastures, while in others, brown-and-white-painted ponies sought shelter from the sun under the spreading limbs of green live oaks. Crimson barns and metal corrals, along with houses ranging from redbrick, single-story fifties ranch-style to two-story contemporaries in cream-colored stone, had been built well back from the road for privacy and convenience.

Soon Rowdy turned south at a sign with Western-style letters that read SURE AS SHOOTIN' YOU'RE IN SURE-SHOT! under the black-and-white silhouette of a smoking Colt .45 revolver.

She pointed at the sign, chuckling. "That's fun."

"Yeah. And it gets the point across to anybody who might be wondering about the town's name."

"No doubt."

"Sure-Shot originally catered to cowboys on their cattle drives from Texas to Kansas and back again. There were dance halls and saloons, along with other businesses like mercantile, café, blacksmith, livery stable, bathhouse, bank, and freight depot."

"Busy place."

"It was a lot like Wildcat Bluff, except not as fancy." He followed the asphalt two-lane road that turned into Main Street.

"Oh my, it looks like the set of an Old West film. Please slow down so I can see it better."

Sure-Shot had a classic wooden false-front commercial district. A line of single-story businesses connected by a boardwalk, covered porticos, and tall facade parapets extending above the roofs were individually painted in green, blue, or yellow with white trim. Small clapboard houses with wide front porches and fancy double-wides fanned out around the downtown area. A few pickups and Jeeps were parked in front of the businesses, but a couple of saddle horses with their reins wrapped around the hitching post in front of the Bluebonnet Café switched their tails.

When Rowdy kept driving, she turned to look at him. "Aren't we going to the Bluebonnet Café?"

"Yeah. There's not much more, but I thought you'd like to see the rest of downtown."

"Thanks."

"Folks enjoy getting together at the park on Sunday afternoons for the Summer Music of Sure-Shot as well as other stuff." He slowed in front of the park where a white Victorian-style bandstand dominated the short, golden grass and leafless trees.

"What a great gathering place." She glanced at him. "I can see why you like it here."

"The beauty shop was repurposed from an old Sinclair gas station that was originally used as a livery for horses and mules."

"Something else fun here. I like it, too." She saw that the Sure-Shot Beauty Station was located in a building with the same tall, flat, wooden false front as the other structures. All the turquoise beauty chairs inside were filled with women. "Looks like it's doing a big business."

"Popular, alright."

He made a U-turn in front of the beauty salon before he started back down Main Street. He parked in front of the Bluebonnet Café, switched off the engine, and turned to look at her.

"Arn might not be here. If he is, he might not talk to us."

"That's okay. All we can do is try to see him." She gave Rowdy an encouraging smile even as she wished she was better dressed for the occasion. Clothes might not make the woman, but stylish never hurt. Then again, maybe she was so caught up in clothes that it never entered her mind not to consider their importance.

When he opened her door, she hopped down and took his hand. He smiled at her, giving an encouraging nod. They stepped up on the boardwalk, where a couple of cowboys sat on a long, wooden bench outside the café eating ice cream from waffle cones.

"Howdy." Rowdy smiled as he opened the front door.

Both men nodded in reply but kept eating their ice cream.

Belle stepped inside and immediately loved the café's interior. It appeared to have been updated and upgraded in the fifties with no changes since that time. The interior was all chrome, red-vinyl booths and barstools, gray-linoleum floor, and rough-wood walls decorated with framed photos of veterans and rodeo winners.

A few folks sat at several of the chrome-framed tables with laminate surfaces and matching chrome chairs with red-vinyl seats. A glossy black-and-white poster of Annie Oakley in a fancy cowgirl costume with a smoking Colt .45

in each hand graced the wall behind the old-fashioned soda fountain with round barstools in front of it.

At a small table by a front window, two men sat in chairs across from each other and stared downward, concentrating on a checkerboard.

Belle started to head that way, but she was waylaid by a server with a big smile. She wore cat-eye, rhinestone eyeglasses, and her bright red hair was pulled back in a curly ponytail. She'd squeezed her long-limbed, athletic body into a turquoise tunic matched with hot-pink tights and purple cowgirl boots. She had a yellow pencil stuck in her hair and an order pad clutched in her hand.

"Elsie, good to see you," Rowdy said.

"Ber—"

"Let me introduce you to Belle Tarleton. She took over the Lazy Q."

"Hello," Belle said. "I love the café."

"She's the owner, cook, and chief bottle washer." Rowdy chuckled as he gestured around the room.

"That means I work 24/7 with nary a break," Elsie said.

"I know what you mean. But it's fun, too, isn't it?"

"On good days," Elsie agreed. "On bad days...let's forget them."

"I totally agree," Belle said.

"Belle runs a business, too," Rowdy said. "Maybe you've heard of Lulabelle & You."

Elsie's eyes widened in surprise. "You're *that* Belle Tarleton?"

"On good days." Belle chuckled at continuing the joke. "On bad days, I try to be somebody else."

"How's that working out?" Elsie joined her laughter.

"About how you'd expect."

"I hear you." Elsie cocked her head to the side.

"I wish we had time to eat," Rowdy said, "but we're here to talk with Arn."

"Good luck on that one." Elsie shook her head. "He's playing checkers. And he's serious about his game."

"He might talk with us," Rowdy said. "The Buick Brigade sent us."

"Wow. How'd you get involved with that bunch?"

"They took a liking to Belle."

Elsie gave Belle another look…one of deep respect. "I guess they like your style."

"I don't know," Belle said. "But they did bring me cookies."

"Double wow. Cowboy cookies?"

"Right," Belle said.

"Were you able to name their shapes?"

"Not so as I'd take an oath on it."

"Join the club." Elsie glanced around the room as she checked on her customers. "Tasty though, aren't they?"

"Delicious," Belle agreed. "If I got it right, they're Fernando's favorite."

"I heard that, too." Elsie laughed harder. "Listen, I'd like to stay and chat, but work calls."

"Go ahead," Rowdy said. "We're going to try and snag a moment of Arn's time. Wish us luck."

"Good luck. You'll definitely need it." And Elsie sashayed over to the nearest table with customers.

"She's wonderful," Belle said in a low voice. "Everybody I meet in Wildcat Bluff County is just terrific."

"I hope that includes present company."

She leaned in close. "If you'll take me home soon, I'll show you just how wonderful I think you are."

"It's a date. But first, let's go see Arn."

She didn't know what to expect, but the moment they approached the checkerboard table, one of the cowboys stood up, grabbed his hat from the back of the chair, and quickly left the café. The other one slowly stood up and turned to her. She felt her breath catch in her throat because she wanted him—oh, how she wanted him—in a photo shoot.

He was tall, lithe, muscular, and handsome in the way a ninety-or-so-year-old man should be if he'd lived right, loved right, and worked right...and if he still resided in the Old West. He could've passed for Buffalo Bill Cody in his old photos with the flowing locks of thick, silver hair, a handlebar mustache, and a trimmed beard. He looked at her with lively blue eyes in a strong, tanned face.

"Howdy, ma'am," he said in a deep, rich baritone with that slow, mesmerizing Texas accent. "How may I help you?"

She smiled, and it felt like a silly one because it was a wonder she didn't melt right down into ooze on the floor, even with Rowdy standing right beside her. This man had the "it factor" in spades. And she ought to know, since she looked for it in every single model book that came her way.

"She has a few questions for you," Rowdy said.

Arn held out his hand, all big-boned, rough, and raw... but with long, sensitive fingers. "Arn Thorsen at your service."

"Belle Tarleton. Thank you so much for taking the time to speak with me." She'd suddenly gone formal and knew why—to show respect for him. She put her hand in his big one and felt enveloped in his warmth and appreciation.

He held her hand a moment. Then he gave a slight smile that crinkled the corners of his eyes and let her go.

She definitely wanted him in a photo shoot, if at all possible.

He lifted a hand and motioned to the chair across from him. "Please join me."

She quickly sat down, glancing at the game and then back at him.

"Do you play?" he asked.

"Not today."

"Another time, another place...perhaps."

"I'd enjoy it."

"Good." He glanced up. "Rowdy, uh, right?"

"Yes." Rowdy frowned. "That's exactly right."

"Today anyway." Arn chuckled, as if he'd said something funny.

Rowdy frowned harder.

"Why don't you pull up a chair and join...unless you'd prefer to be with the lovely Elsie."

Rowdy grabbed a chair from a nearby table, turned it around, and sat down with his arms folded across the back in an aggressive manner.

Belle realized she might have been a bit too appreciative of Arn, so she leaned back in her chair to put distance between them.

"Something to drink or eat?" Arn asked.

"Thank you, but no."

"You want to get straight to business. I appreciate a woman with a mind and a will of her own. Shoot." He gave another smile that hinted at extensive knowledge and experience.

She cleared her throat, not sure how to get the ball rolling without losing him from the get-go. He appeared to be a straightforward man, so she'd go with that impression. "It's about the one-room schoolhouse and the memorial grove."

He smiled a bit more, leaning back in his chair. "So…it's finally come to light."

"Yes."

"And your interest?"

"It's a mystery."

"What makes you say that?"

"Well, I guess it's a mystery to me…and some other people."

He stroked his mustache with the forefinger of one hand. "And you want to know what about it?"

"I'd like to know what happened there."

"Fire."

"Yes, I saw it."

"You've been there?"

"Yes…a bit earlier."

Arn glanced at Rowdy and then back at her. "Why?"

"Buick Brigade," Rowdy said.

Arn's right eyebrow shot up. "The ladies of Destiny sent you?"

"They gave her cookies. They sent her pigeon messages. They invited her to Destiny."

Arn grinned, revealing strong white teeth. "Now don't that beat all."

"I'm pretty busy," Belle said, "but I'm taking time to try and deal with their goal…whatever it is."

"Which we're not sure about just yet," Rowdy said.

"The ladies do have their goals…and their ways of achieving them." Arn glanced out the front window and then back again. "It's Christmas, right?"

"We're almost there," Rowdy said. "As usual, we're overworked and behind schedule."

"Drive-in ready to go, I take it?" Arn asked.

"About like always," Rowdy said.

Belle looked from one to the other, wondering what the drive-in had to do with Rowdy. Maybe he volunteered or even worked there during the holiday festivities.

"Samantha likes the place." Arn glanced at Belle. "That's my hell-raiser of a granddaughter. Chip off the old block, most folks say, but I can't see it myself."

"She's one hell of a horsewoman, no two ways about it," Rowdy said.

"It's in the blood." Arn looked at Belle. "Pardon us. We're being rude to discuss someone you've never met."

"That's okay. I'm new to the area."

"But not to the Lone Star State," Arn said. "That's an East Texas accent, if I don't miss my guess."

"You're right." She smiled, liking him better all the time.

"What is it you want to know about the schoolhouse?" Arn asked.

"First and foremost, did anybody survive the fire?" She leaned forward, really wanting to hear his reply.

"Yes." He glanced out the window before he focused on them again. "You'll want to know the details, but they're not mine to give."

"Oh, please, at least tell if—"

"It was before my time."

"But still—"

He held out his hands and turned them palms up. "Out of my hands."

"It's important." She leaned forward, feeling her goal, her

vision slipping away. "Wouldn't it be wonderful if we could turn that beautiful building and grove into a learning center again? I'm willing to do the work...and others will help, too. Maybe even you."

He nodded, rocking in his chair. "So it's come...finally."

"What?"

"An ending—"

"Maybe so, but—"

"And beginning..."

She glanced at Rowdy, who looked as confused as she felt. Why couldn't she just get a straight answer around here? If she ran her business this way, she'd never get anything done.

Arn stood up and held out his hand, palm up.

Rowdy got to his feet and set his chair back in place.

Was the meeting over? She stood up, too, and put her fingers over Arn's palm.

He lifted her fingers to his lips and placed a soft kiss on the back of her hand. "I will be happy to give you everything you desire...once the ladies of Destiny release me from my vows."

"Thank you. I'll talk with them."

"Do that." He plucked his cowboy hat from the back of his chair and walked out of the café.

Belle fell back into her seat.

Rowdy sat down across from her.

She felt like picking up the checkerboard and tossing pieces of black and red onto the floor in frustration. "Is it always this way in Wildcat Bluff County?"

Chapter 29

Belle was tired and discouraged by the time Rowdy drove them back to Lulabelle & You Ranch. Darkness had descended, wrapping the land in soft shadows. She couldn't help but wonder how the schoolhouse looked at night. Was it eerie? Was it sad? Or was it simply sleepy? She still felt the lingering effects of her visit there… part good, part bad.

Rowdy stopped his pickup on the circular drive near the front door where a warm, yellow light on the porch welcomed them. "Do you want me to come inside or go home?"

"Please come inside. I don't want to be alone tonight."

"I don't want to leave you either." He turned off the engine, and quiet surrounded them.

"It was kind of a rough day, wasn't it?"

"Yeah," he said.

"I wish Arn had told us more about the fire."

"He gave us the best news of all."

"Survivors. I'm so happy somebody escaped the schoolhouse."

"It's a relief." He glanced at her. "If you want to learn more, you'll need to contact the Buick Brigade."

"I know." She sighed. "If I could do it, I'd use a homing pigeon."

He chuckled softly. "That's for later. Right now, let's go inside. It's already getting chilly in here."

As they walked up to the porch, she saw a gift bag nestled up against the front door. "What's that?"

"Let me check it before you touch it."

"Do you think the shingle thieves left me something dangerous?" She started to laugh at the absurdity of the idea and then stopped because she didn't know what might come at her next.

"No. I'm just being cautious."

While he picked up the bag, she opened the front door. Once inside, she locked it securely behind them.

He looked inside the bag, grinned, and handed it to her.

"What is it?"

"See for yourself."

"Let's go into the kitchen." She walked in there, flipped on an overhead light, and then set her purse and the bag on the table.

She liked the gift bag because it had a pretty red-and-blue-bandana motif, which she thought was a great idea. She parted the green tissue paper and pulled out a T-shirt. She smiled at the sight of "Fernando the Wonder Bull" emblazoned across the front. She checked the little attached card and read, "Welcome to Wildcat Bluff County…xoxo, Storm, Fernando, and Daisy Sue (in absentia)."

"You have to admit that girl has style," Rowdy said as he looked at the gift.

"She's just got it all." Belle felt the T-shirt's soft fabric, considering the design and thought behind it. "Sharp and savvy."

"I'm glad Storm welcomed you to the county." He reached out and cupped Belle's chin. "I wish more people had done it."

"It's okay. In this day and age, it's not so important anymore."

"Friendliness is always important."

"That's true. We strive for it at Lulabelle & You." She tucked the T-shirt back into its bag. "Anyway, I do believe there's an ulterior motive behind this gift."

He laughed. "No doubt."

She laughed harder, releasing pent-up tension and feeling better about the day. "I really will give a Fernando and Daisy Sue line some thought."

"It might work."

"And it'd be fun."

"Yeah." He glanced around the kitchen. "Anything to eat?"

"I'm hungry, too."

"I could run to the Chuckwagon Café and bring something back."

"I wish we'd eaten at the Bluebonnet, but I didn't want us to get distracted there."

"We'll go back sometime…maybe when we go to the drive-in."

"Perfect." She walked over to the refrigerator, opened the door, and looked inside. "We can make sandwiches."

"Don't go to the trouble."

"No trouble." She picked up mustard and mayonnaise jars and carried them over to the table. As she set them down, her cell phone rang.

"Do you want take it or call back after we eat?" he asked.

"I'd better take it now. Who knows what I might need to deal with?"

"Right."

She slipped her phone out of her purse, checked to see who was calling, and gave Rowdy a big grin. "Kemp Lander!"

Rowdy gave a thumbs-up and leaned closer.

"Kemp, good to hear from you." She punched speakerphone so Rowdy could hear the conversation.

"Got news," Kemp said.

"Wonderful. Please tell me that you'll be back with Daisy Sue tomorrow."

"No can do."

"What?" She felt deflated at those words and braced for what would come next.

"Well…there's a glitch in our plans."

"I don't like the sound of it."

"That cousin of mine…well, I finally found him holed up with a new girlfriend. That's why I lost track of him. He kept dropping out of sight at her place in between rodeos."

"And he didn't tell anyone where he was?"

"Not likely," Kemp said with a smile.

"Okay." She could see that was a dead-end, so she moved on. "Where did he put Daisy Sue?"

"He didn't."

"What do you mean?"

"He never picked her up," Kemp said.

"Why?"

"Like I said, he met this cowgirl at a bar about that time. Truth of the matter, he didn't remember much of anything for several days…by then, he decided to get back on the rodeo circuit, but he kept getting distracted with the new love of his life."

"Why didn't he tell you?"

"Well…he was partying and rodeoing."

"That explains it?"

"For *that* cousin, it does," Kemp said. "For us, the cow is still missing."

"What!" Belle was fast losing her cool. "Are you telling me that you have absolutely no idea where Daisy Sue is right now?"

"That's about the size of it."

"Rustlers snatched Fernando last year." Rowdy leaned toward the phone. "Do you suppose that's what happened to her?"

"Doubt it," Kemp said. "They hadn't been working the area. No cut fences. Open gates. No nothing like that."

Belle felt sick at her stomach. "Of all the cows in all the pastures, why does the one and only Daisy Sue have to be the missing cow?"

"Don't know," Kemp said. "I'm sorry, but I told you that before, and it hasn't helped one iota."

"What will I tell Storm?" Belle asked. "She'll be heartbroken."

"The truth," Rowdy said. "It's always better to know than not to know."

"It just makes no sense." She pulled out the T-shirt, looking at it, thinking about "Fernando and Daisy Sue" on a clothing line, and wishing she could go back in time to change the current outcome. But she hadn't even been here then.

"You're telling me," Kemp said. "Look, I've got another couple of ideas about Daisy Sue's whereabouts that might work out, but first…and I'm embarrassed to ask for some time off…but Aunt Dotty has the whole family in a snit about Lester. I'm the only one he'll ever listen to, so it's got to be me to get him out of the hands of that 'black widow hussy,' as Aunt Dotty calls her."

"What?" Belle couldn't believe her ears. "Are you trying to lose your job?"

"I'm trying not to lose my family. We're talking about *that* cousin and saving him from a fate worse than death, as Aunt Dotty says...although I doubt Lester would agree."

"But what about Daisy Sue?"

"I'm between a rock and hard place," Kemp said. "Like I said, I haven't forgotten my main job here, but...well, Lester...just let me get him home to his mama and all will be well."

"How long?" She couldn't back out now because Kemp knew better than anyone how to find the missing cow since he'd been on the hunt so long.

"Not sure...that cowgirl's got her hooks in deep."

"We must find Daisy Sue before Christmas."

"I'm on it. I'll find that cow one way or another," Kemp said. "My job's on the line. My reputation's on the line. My self-respect is on the line. And by the time I'm done, Lester is going to owe me for the rest of his miserable life."

"I guess there's not much else I can say except stay in touch." She just shook her head.

"Will do."

"If you need any help, let me know," Rowdy said.

"Thanks." Kemp cleared his throat. "If there's not anything else—"

"Just Daisy Sue. I do appreciate your hard work, but please, please get her home." Belle clicked off, dropped her phone in her purse, and looked at Rowdy. "Can you believe it?"

"Maybe we should call in the Buick Brigade."

"Maybe so. I'm sure fresh out of ideas."

"It'll be all right…somehow, some way." He pulled her into his arms and hugged her close.

She held him tightly, wondering how she'd ever gotten along without him. He was so much a part of her life now that she couldn't imagine going back to the city and living as before. And then a thought struck her…he was in her world, but she wasn't in his world. She didn't actually know very much about him. She knew his friends, yes, but family and home, no. It was a chilling thought. Who was this man who'd come to mean so much to her?

"If rustlers didn't get Daisy Sue, we'll find her," he said. "She's got an ID, so she's traceable. I'll check with the American Angus Association tomorrow and see if there's any news about her."

"Thank you." She took a deep breath, wondering if she wasn't letting the day slant her emotions. She'd always trusted her gut with people, and she'd always been right. She had no reason to change that view now just because Rowdy was slow in sharing his personal world with her. They hadn't known each other that long. Time was on their side.

"Always." He hugged her harder.

"I just want Daisy Sue safely back home so she can be reunited with Fernando and Storm."

"That's what everybody wants." He set her back and looked into her eyes. "Let's get something to eat. Everything looks better on a full stomach."

She nodded in agreement then reached up and gently stroked down his cheek, feeling stubble from the long, long day. If she hadn't already fallen for him, she'd be all in right about now.

"Maybe sandwiches aren't right. I think something warm would suit us better."

"That sounds good. Soup?"

"Yeah." He walked over to the cabinets. "Where do you keep the cans?"

"Pantry."

He opened that door and looked inside. "Vegetable isn't right. How about chicken noodle?"

"Comfort food, you mean."

He glanced back at her. "It's been that kind of day, hasn't it?"

"Absolutely."

"If you'll sit at the table, I'll heat up the soup, pour it into mugs, and bring it over there."

"I won't argue with you." She suddenly felt really tired and wanted nothing more than to rest for a little bit. "You're making it easy for me."

He glanced back her. "That's my job…for the moment. Sit."

She pulled out a chair and did exactly that, thinking she could easily get used to being pampered by this big, strong cowboy.

A little later, she sat by his side at the table, eating soup, looking out the window where darkness reigned supreme, and saying nothing at all. It felt easy, companionable, as if they were the only two people in the world. It felt good, comfortable, as if they belonged together in this time and place. It felt right, preferable, as if everything in their lives had led to this pivotal moment.

He downed the last of his soup, then turned to look at her with a serious expression on his face.

"What is it?"

"You know what I said about the truth?"

"Yes." She set down her spoon, no longer feeling hungry because this sounded serious…and not in a good way.

"I guess you've wondered about me."

"Yes."

"I guess I've been pretty private about my personal life."

"Yes."

"It's not about you."

"No?"

"I mean, it is, but it isn't."

"Yes?"

"It's nothing bad…I mean, about me."

"Good," she said.

"It's good, but it's bad, too."

"Maybe we should go to bed and forget where this is going."

"I'd tell you everything…I will tell you everything…I can't tell you everything, at least not right now."

"You do realize you're not making sense."

"I know it." He stood up abruptly, knocking his chair over backward. "Hell, I'm going about this all wrong."

"Whatever it is, it's okay."

"No, it's not." He jerked up the chair, pushed it back into place, grabbed their mugs, and walked into the kitchen.

"Let me clean up. You cooked." She stood, feeling her gut churn and wishing she hadn't eaten anything.

"I've got it." He turned on the faucet and got busy.

She picked up a dish towel and dried the first mug.

"Whatever it is, I'll understand. Don't we know each other well enough for that by now? Don't you trust me enough?"

"I trust you. You have more integrity in your little fingertips than most..." He thrust the other clean mug at her.

"I wish—" She started to dry it, taking a deep breath.

"You wish?" He walked away from her and looked out the front window, presenting his back, as if to delay or stop the conversation.

She quietly put the mugs, spoons, and saucepan back in the cabinets.

He turned around, crossed his arms over his chest, and stared at her. "What am I going to do?"

"Love me?"

"If I loved you any less, I'd be okay." He threw his arms wide. "But this, this—"

"It's been a long, hard, emotional day." She walked toward him. "We don't need this right now. *You* don't need it."

He ran a hand across his stubble, covering up his mouth as if to keep the words he didn't want to say inside.

She gently took that hand in her own and pressed a soft kiss to his palm. "Come with me. I'll make it all better."

She led him out of the kitchen, down the hall, and into her bedroom, where the bed was still unmade—cover thrown back, sheets rumbled, pillow half over the edge, and the scent of lavender in the air. She switched on the soft light of the lamp on the nightstand and then maneuvered him until he stood with his back to the bed. She gently pushed his shoulders, knowing she couldn't move his rock-solid body but also well aware that he'd let her have her way.

He sat down, but he looked as if he might bolt at any moment.

"It's been a rough day for us." She picked up his foot and pulled off his boot, using both hands. "You pampered me with food. Now let me pamper you."

"Belle, you don't need to do anything." He spoke in a rough sandpaper whisper as if anything louder would jar the intimacy of the moment.

"I want to take care of you." She tossed his boot in a corner and then picked up his other foot and did the exact same thing. "You take care of me all the time. Let me return the favor."

"You know I can't say no to you."

"I know."

He gave her a little half smile before he lay back full-length on the mattress and flung his arms out to each side. "Go ahead. Have your way with me. I won't fight you."

She chuckled low in her throat. "I didn't think you would." And she slowly...oh, so very slowly began to strip him.

She started with his big, shiny, metallic belt buckle with the multicolored crystals gleaming in the light. She unhooked it and then undid the first button of his Wranglers so that she could see his cotton briefs underneath. She chuckled at the sight.

"Are you wearing red?"

"I thought two could play that game."

"You're a very bad boy."

"I'm trying... How am I doing?"

"Good. Real good."

"I better try harder...if I'm going to be bad."

"Harder? I'm not sure that's possible." She stroked down the zipper of his jeans, feeling the hard, hot length so ready for her.

He groaned, pushing up against her hand. "You're playing a dangerous game."

"Am I?"

She clutched his hard bulge through the fabric, watching his face as he reacted to her touch, seeing that he was quickly losing control. She felt a strictly feminine surge of power and pleasure at the sight. He needed her as much as she needed him...and they needed each other—particularly this night of all nights. They needed to share the renewal and continuity of life after what they'd experienced in the one-room schoolhouse. And she was the one to make it happen.

She let her hand drift upward, unsnapping one pearl button after another as she slowly revealed the hard muscles of his chest to his stomach, with the little trail of short hair that ran downward to disappear into his jeans. He was just so beautiful...perfect for a photo shoot, but she'd never share by putting him out there for other women to see. He was hers—all hers—and she'd keep him that way.

She followed her hands with her mouth, kissing, licking, nibbling all the way up his chest past his throat to his lips, where she lingered as she stoked their passion higher and higher. When he returned her kiss, she felt their dormant flames burst into a raging inferno of fire. Abruptly, she didn't want to play anymore. She was too needy, too desperate to be joined with him in the best way possible.

She turned aside, jerked open the nightstand drawer, and selected a condom. She ripped the wrapper off and turned back to him.

He raised his head. "I don't need to do anything, do I?"

"Do you mind too much being used?"

"Use me all you want...make me your toy."

She knelt over him, knees to each side of his hips, and unzipped his jeans, letting his hard length spring out. She took just a moment to appreciate him and then slipped on the condom. He was ready for her...and she was more than ready for him.

And then she remembered she was still wearing clothes, even her cowgirl boots. No time now to undress, even if she'd wanted to do it. Instead, she simply unzipped her own jeans, pulled them down, along with her thong, and positioned herself over him.

"I hope you're not disappointed," she said. "I believe this is going to be really quick."

"Quicker the better." His voice sounded strained as he uttered those few words.

She lowered her body, felt him fill her, and sighed in relief, excitement, and eagerness. And then she began to move, up and down, building the extreme tension, the growing connection, the exciting road to paradise.

"Can't take it any longer." He groaned, grabbed her hips, and thrust into her, upping the rhythm, the power, the intensity.

She rode him, staying with him all the way as they reached out together, caught the fever together, and soared to the highest of heights together...and hung there together as one.

"A cowgirl with a golden heart," he whispered in a husky voice as he continued his poem. "Daytime. Nighttime. *All* time."

Chapter 30

Rowdy sat in a chair at Wildcat Hall with his back to the wall in a defensive position because he was ready to square off with anybody who gave him trouble. He glared down the row of tables that had been pushed together and now contained drinks, pens, pads, and notebooks. Hedy, Bert, Morning Glory, Mac, Craig, Fern, Slade, and Ivy, representing the committees for Christmas in the Country, Christmas at the Sure-Shot Drive-In, and Wildcat Hall's Honky-Tonk Christmas, were all there…and at the moment they were giving him uneasy looks.

They were two weeks out from the three big events, but that's not what was on his mind that afternoon. Either he'd get his way, or he was out of there—for good and forever. He wore a blue sweatshirt with a big Lulabelle & You logo emblazoned on the front with his Wranglers and boots, so that alone should give them a clue about his state of mind.

At the ranch, Belle was plugging along with setting up more and more of her business there…and he was flat-out helping her. He was installing the flagstone patio in back of the house, and it was looking good. Even more important, it made her happy, and what made her happy made him happy.

There was still no word about Daisy Sue, but Storm had been over for a visit, bringing samples of what she'd created for Fernando's image. She and Belle had put their heads together, and there was no telling what they'd eventually come up with. He could hardly wait to find out, but he knew it'd be sharp and sassy like the two of them.

Belle hadn't had time to visit the Buick Brigade about the one-room schoolhouse yet, but she wanted to go before Christmas. Time was running out, but he'd make sure they got there because the schoolhouse was important not only to her but to the community.

Hedy looked up at him, sharp brown eyes missing nothing. "Bert Two, you called this meeting, so you might as well get on with it."

"I think we're wrong...and I think we ought to be ashamed of ourselves." He took a deep breath. "And don't call me Bert Two. I'm Rowdy now."

"Oh my." Hedy glanced from him to Morning Glory. "He is het up today."

"No, I'm not." He tamped down on his unhappiness because he felt more sad than angry.

Morning Glory leaned forward, long necklaces dangling around her neck chiming softly together. "You've come to chastise us, haven't you?"

"I'll be the first to admit I'm unlucky. That's why I drew the short straw on this deal with Belle Tarleton."

"We all agreed it was for the best to keep ideas like hers out of our county," Bert said gently. "We're talking big media, lines of vehicles, weekenders, and who knows what all."

"That's right," Hedy agreed. "We invite folks here for our festivals several times a year so they can enjoy our Old West world...and we enjoy our visitors, too."

"Belle wants hoards to be here year-round," Mac said. "I don't even know how the infrastructure could handle them."

"I understand your concern." Rowdy backed off a bit because he realized they hadn't had the chance to get to know Belle the way he had over the past several weeks. "I felt it, too."

"And now?" Hedy asked, pointing at his sweatshirt.

"She's reevaluating her original idea."

"Really?" Fern leaned forward with a smile on her face. "Would it have anything to do with Sure-Shot?"

"What do you mean?" Slade looked up from doodling on a pad of paper.

"None of us understood that she didn't plan to establish a dude ranch, although that's not a bad idea." Rowdy looked around the group. "She wanted to expand the ranch into a learning center so city folks, particularly kids, could experience a working ranch, but her bigger goal was to expand it into a learning center for the creative arts."

"Oh." Morning Glory's eyes opened wide. "But I thought the ranch was going to be a promotional tool for her Western wear line."

"She's a celebrity through Lulabelle & You. That means that lots of folks, like youngsters, reach out to her for support and information."

"Like Storm." Slade gave a sharp nod. "She can't stop talking about Belle and all she's learning and all their plans. I've never seen her so inspired by anyone...and I'm her favorite uncle."

"You're her *only* uncle." Fern patted his hand, chuckling at the old family joke.

"She's generous," Rowdy said. "She has a dream of

helping others, and she can do that through Lulabelle & You. I'm not saying she won't use the ranch to promote her business, but that can help our community, too."

Slade pointed at the sweatshirt. "I see she's made a believer out of you."

"I've spent enough time with her to understand that her heart is in the right place." He looked around the group again. "And our hearts haven't been."

"That's a harsh assessment," Bert said.

"Dad, I'm ashamed to say I was ever part of trying to stop her."

"Are we that far off the mark?" Bert asked.

"You met her. What do you think?"

"I like her."

"I like her, too," Hedy said. "But that doesn't mean she can't do Wildcat Bluff County harm."

"Are you saying you think we should have let her have her head and do whatever she wants in our county?" Morning Glory asked.

"I'm saying she's as strong-willed as any of us here, and she's going to do what she's going to do no matter what we say, do, or want."

"I don't understand," Ivy said. "When I arrived here, not knowing what I was doing and being from the city, everyone went out of their way to help me. What's different with Belle Tarleton?"

Rowdy stayed quiet, watching, waiting, as silence descended on the room and they looked from one to the other, evaluating her words.

"You're right, Ivy, that's who we've always been," Hedy finally said.

"That's who we are." Morning Glory nodded in agreement.

"What's so different about Belle?" Rowdy asked.

Hedy took a deep breath as she glanced down the tables. "Maybe she didn't need us."

"Maybe she appeared too high-powered for us," Bert added.

"Maybe she flat-out scared us with her big-city ways and big honking ideas." Morning Glory picked up her necklaces and ran her fingers up and down them.

"We've always been a little island of our own here," Slade said. "It worked for our ancestors. It works for us."

"But times change." Ivy looked right at Rowdy. "If we're willing to change, is she willing to change?"

"Good point," Hedy said in agreement.

"She's already changed." Rowdy smiled at the group, proud they were coming around to his point of view.

"How do you mean?" Morning Glory asked.

"For one thing, the Buick Brigade decided to intervene in her life. And mine."

Everyone around the table nodded, as if they'd been there, done that.

"I'll say it again." Fern tapped a forefinger on the tabletop. "Sure-Shot."

"What do you mean?" Bert asked. "Bert...I mean, Rowdy, what do we have to do with Sure-Shot except our drive-in?"

"I bought this small piece of property because it came up for sale and it connected my ranch with Sure-Shot," Craig said. "I'd been busy, so I hadn't even bothered to look at it until I was driving around with Fern looking for another dance hall."

"It's special." Fern took up the story. "Over a hundred years ago there was a one-room schoolhouse on the property."

"I'd never heard of it before," Morning Glory said. "Neither had Hedy."

"And that's odd," Hedy said. "You'd think it would have been in our county's history or at least handed down as a legend."

"Is it intact?" Bert asked.

"Yes. It's in good shape," Rowdy said. "Belle and I were there not so long ago."

"Why?" Mac asked.

"Buick Brigade." Rowdy glanced around the group. "Y'all understand."

"Right," Hedy agreed. "Are you saying they reached out to Belle, instead of to one of us, about this one-room schoolhouse?"

"I'm a newcomer here," Mac said. "Is that so strange?"

"If it wasn't the Buick Brigade, I'd say yes," Morning Glory said. "In this case, I'd say they want something done or discovered or—"

"What did you find?" Bert asked.

"There'd been a fire."

"Oh no," Hedy said. "And there wouldn't have been Wildcat Bluff Fire-Rescue to save them."

"The building is still intact, and it's a beautiful structure," Rowdy said. "But I think there was death there because someone built a memorial grove around the building so it was lost to sight."

"And memory," Morning Glory said.

"We still don't know what happened, do we?" Fern

clasped Craig's hand. "We were hoping you and Belle would solve the puzzle."

"We talked to Arn of the Crazy Eight," Rowdy said. "He told us not everyone died in the fire, but it was the Buick Brigade's story to tell."

"What did they say?" Fern asked.

"We haven't talked with them yet. Belle's busy with her business. I'm installing a patio for her."

"So, you are doing more work there," Bert said.

Rowdy glanced around the group. "I'm telling you flat-out right now that I'm pulling out of our arrangement. It's wrong. It was bad from the get-go. And we should make amends somehow."

"Does she know about you...I mean, your name and all?" Hedy asked in a gentle tone.

Rowdy looked down at the table. "No. I've got to tell her, but I just haven't found the way yet."

"Son, it's obvious you're developing strong feelings for her. You'd better tell her before she finds out the wrong way."

"I know."

"Bert...uh, Rowdy, you're right." Hedy knocked with her knuckles on top of the table. "We overreacted to the news of Belle Tarleton with Lulabelle & You descending on our community with a bunch of cockamamie ideas."

"I agree," Morning Glory said. "And we turned lower than a snake's belly. That's not like us...not like us at all."

"I agree, too," Slade said. "Belle is good for my niece... and that means she can be good for the county."

"Okay. I agree. But how do we make amends and help her?" Bert asked.

"First, stop getting in her way at her ranch. I've already

done that. Second, we're too busy with Christmas to do much of anything else. But—"

"What?" Fern leaned toward him.

"It's about the schoolhouse." Rowdy looked around the group. "Belle is full of ideas. As far as I can tell, they're good ones."

"Out with it," Morning Glory said.

"She'd liked to reopen the schoolhouse. I guess to sort of heal the memory…and turn it into a learning center for the arts like she'd had in mind on her ranch," Rowdy said. "Of course, Craig owns the property…and we don't know the whole story about the fire, so it may not even be a good or feasible idea. I mean, it'd be a big investment, money, time, energy. The place is basic at best."

"I like the idea," Craig said. "Fern and I, we've kind of been haunted by the grove and the schoolhouse."

"That's right," Fern agreed. "I'd like to lift the sadness there and replace it with happiness. And creativity."

"I adore the idea," Morning Glory said. "I can't wait to see the building."

"It's a small, beautiful Victorian structure. You'll love it," Fern said.

"It's just what our creative community needs." Morning Glory grinned with excitement.

Hedy nodded in agreement. "However…if this involves the Buick Brigade, and it sounds like it does, we make no move without their approval. They might know something that makes going forward, even if we decide to do it, not a good idea."

"Absolutely." Morning Glory looked at Rowdy. "I take it they'll probably only share information with Belle."

"And maybe me."

"Okay," Hedy said. "That means you're off one project and on to the next one."

Rowdy glanced around the group again. "I just want to be clear that there'll be no more interference in Belle's life. Right?"

"Right," Morning Glory agreed. "I regret our misguided actions."

"Well, it worked," Rowdy said. "She's not going to have her Christmas party."

"I feel bad about that," Ivy said. "But I guess there's so much else going on there's not really time for it anyway."

"That's what I told her," Rowdy said.

"We need to make it up to her." Bert squeezed Hedy's hand as he turned to her. "Don't we?"

"We will, dear," Hedy said. "But it'd be best for all involved, particularly Rowdy, that she never know—"

"How does he morph from Rowdy back to Bert Two?" Morning Glory clutched the chains around her neck in agitation. "If she'd gone away like we'd planned, she'd never need to know, but now..."

Rowdy groaned and shook his head.

"Son, you need to 'fess up. And the sooner the better," Bert said.

"I guess we'll all be in hot water with her soon." Slade looked disappointed at the idea. "And just when we'd decided she was a keeper."

"Okay," Rowdy said. "I'm glad we're all in agreement about Belle."

"Tell her what she needs to know but no more." Hedy gave him a gentle smile. "It's the right thing to do."

"Yeah." Rowdy glanced down at his sweatshirt and rubbed his fingertips over the logo. "I get the short straw again, don't I?"

"Yes, I'm afraid you do," Hedy said.

"I really am the unluckiest cowboy in the county."

Chapter 31

Okay, Belle admitted to herself. She was running around, rushing around, tying up loose ends, unraveling others—not make work but focused work—in an effort to keep Rowdy from telling her what she didn't want to hear.

It was bad. She knew it was bad from the way she'd catch him looking at her with sadness in his eyes, as if he was close to the point of losing her forever. When he made love to her, it was with such intensity, such love, such passion that it might have been the very last time. It didn't make sense. Then again, nothing had made much sense since she'd arrived in Wildcat Bluff County...and yet, in an odd way, everything made more sense than it ever had before in her life.

Still, maybe she should just pull up stakes and head back to the city...or put her plans into action in East Texas near her family. But there was Rowdy. Storm. The Buick Brigade. The one-room schoolhouse. And Daisy Sue. How many threads would she leave dangling if she left now? And...and she'd grown accustomed to the place, put down roots, felt at home here in a way she never had anywhere else in the world. Still, she was a practical businesswoman. Sometimes things just didn't work out and you moved on to what did work.

If she lost Rowdy, would she stay? Could she stay, knowing she'd run into him here and there, knowing she'd eventually see him with another woman, knowing he'd never be back to Lulabelle & You Ranch? She felt heartsick at the thought, and yet…

She couldn't make a final decision, not before Christmas anyway. Maybe she could put off whatever Rowdy had to tell her until after the holidays so she could enjoy the time in Wildcat Bluff County. Just ten days until all the big events…surely everything would remain stable until then.

She typed another email, fielded several phone calls, made notes on the summer line, and approved the next marketing campaign from her office that was still more warehouse than magazine layout for a CEO's perfect working hideaway. She didn't care. It'd all come together in time. She just had to keep meeting deadlines and avoiding Rowdy's news. If she could hold all that together, then she'd happily get through Christmas. If not, well…she wasn't going there.

By late afternoon, she was feeling pretty good about everything, even Rowdy. She was surely overthinking the situation. He was there for her, either working on her patio, pleasuring her in bed, or making suggestions for her life. She helped him here and there, but she still didn't know enough about his life to be there for him like he was for her.

He was busy, just as she was. He was finishing up her patio or disappearing to work on the upcoming Christmas events in the county. Now he was moving forward with astonishing speed at her home. Of course, the shingles were still in front awaiting their final destination, but she'd sort of gotten used to them being there…at least the ones that hadn't been stolen.

She decided to take a break and see if Homer and Aristotle were flying around outside surveying their territory. She walked into the kitchen, poured a cup of coffee, and headed for the back door. She stopped, cocked her head to one side, and listened. Had she heard something out front? The heater was running, so most sounds were muffled, but still… There, she heard it again. She'd better check. It was still daylight, so she could see what was going on, if anything.

She sipped coffee, feeling it warm and energize her before she set down her mug. She walked to the front door, opened it, and looked outside. She didn't see anything move, but she hadn't really expected to, so that wasn't a surprise. She walked onto the porch, enjoying the cool, crisp air, and then ventured farther outside, gazing down the hill toward Wildcat Road. A red truck roared down the highway before being lost to sight.

She heard the sound of wings and glanced upward. Homer and Aristotle gracefully circled overhead before they quickly descended to land on a shingle stack that was right beside the circular driveway. She didn't remember shingles being that close to the drive, but in all the confusion, it wasn't too surprising that she didn't remember everything's location.

When Homer and Aristotle cooed and began to clean their wing feathers with quick swipes of their beaks, she walked over to them. They were so beautiful in the sunlight, all glossy and sleek and iridescent. She had a sudden, sad thought. If she left the ranch, she'd leave them behind because this was their home of homes. She didn't like the idea of leaving them at all.

She stroked the top of Homer's head with the tip of one finger, and then she did the same thing with Aristotle.

They cooed in response, appearing as happy as she felt. She smiled in pleasure, enjoying them. For now, she wanted nothing more complicated in her life than to hang out with two beautiful birds on a lovely winter day in North Texas.

And then she noticed a small piece of paper under Homer's foot. It wasn't a pigeon-gram but a blue-lined piece obviously torn from a small notebook like construction workers carried in their breast pockets for notes. It hadn't been there earlier in the day. In fact—she stepped back to get a better look at the shingle stack—those shingles hadn't been there either. What was going on in her front yard? Had Rowdy ordered replacements and had them delivered today?

She grabbed the note, but it'd been duct-taped to the shingles, so it ripped loose, leaving behind one corner. The paper was wrinkled, as if it'd been sweated on or rained on or dropped in a bathtub, but it didn't matter because it was a message. She read, "Ladies say return. Merry Xmas."

She looked from the note to the shingles to the note again, and then she glanced all around the area. Did this mean the thieves were no longer thieves but Santa in disguise? Maybe in this county if you didn't have the funds for gifts you simple stole something and returned it at Christmastime. She just shook her head at the thought.

Homer cooed, flew over, and landed on her hand. He beaked one edge of the note, ripped it loose, and then gave her a knowing look with one dark eye.

"Are you telling me…ladies…Destiny…the Buick Brigade somehow or other persuaded the thieves to return my shingles?"

Homer tore off another bit of paper, appearing quite pleased with himself.

"That's some kind of power."

She set Homer on her shoulder, and then Aristotle flew up and landed on her other shoulder. She tapped the paper with her fingernail, considering the situation. She guessed she shouldn't look a gift horse in the mouth, but still it seemed more than a little on the odd side. And yet she was glad to have her shingles back, or at least the ones that hadn't been used as projectiles in that mad chase down Wildcat Road.

While she and the pigeons contemplated the return of the shingles, she saw a pickup turn under the ranch sign, rattle over the cattle guard, and chug its way up her lane. Rowdy was back...

He parked near the returned shingles, got out, and walked over to her. "What's going on?"

She pointed at the shingles and then raised the note so he'd notice it.

"You're kidding me." He laughed, shaking his head as he glanced from her to the shingles and back again. "You look as if you've just stepped out of a fairy tale with a bird on each shoulder and a gift on your front lawn."

"I'm not sure it's a gift if it was yours in the first place." She held out the note. "Better have a look."

He took it, read it, and simply shook his head. "The Buick Brigade strikes again."

"Homer and Aristotle seem to think so, too."

"I guess they'd know." He knocked his knuckles against the top of the shingle stack. "What do you want to do about it?"

"Roof? Maybe the sooner the better?"

"We'll get to it."

"I like the patio."

"Good." He walked away from her and looked out over the pastures. "I'm making progress now, but I can only do so much during the holidays."

"I know. It's okay."

"I wish you weren't so understanding about the situation."

"I could be more understanding if I knew the situation."

He glanced back at her and then quickly looked away. "Belle, it's just that…I'm trying to do the right thing here."

She held back a sigh. If he didn't want to go there, she didn't want to go there. "Maybe we ought to call Sheriff Calhoun. There's no point in him hunting down thieves if they aren't thieves anymore."

"Yeah." Rowdy jerked out his phone. "I'll do it."

She couldn't help but think he'd do about anything to keep from talking to her. But so be it. She just wanted to get through Christmas without a blowup, so it suited her fine, or it would've if it didn't worry her.

"Sheriff, I'm here at Belle's ranch." Rowdy glanced at her as he punched speakerphone. "Shingles again."

"What! Again?" Sheriff Calhoun hollered in an irritated voice.

"They returned them."

Sheriff Calhoun laughed, loud and long. "Buick Brigade."

"What do they have to do with shingles?" Rowdy asked.

"Stuff's getting returned all over the county."

"Who's doing it?"

"I'm betting the Everett brothers. They're troublemakers, but basically good-hearted wild ones. And they've got mothers, grandmothers, great-grandmothers just like everybody else."

"So?" Rowdy asked.

"It's Christmas. A word or two in the right ears by the ladies of Destiny could make a big difference."

"If they hadn't snatched Belle's shingles, they might have gotten away with the other stuff," Rowdy said thoughtfully.

"Maybe. Maybe not," Sheriff Calhoun said. "Bottom line, Belle, do you want to withdraw your complaint?"

"Yes, I do." Belle walked over to Rowdy so she was closer to the phone. "It's Christmas. I want everyone to have as wonderful a holiday as possible."

"Thanks," Sheriff Calhoun said. "That's the way it ought to be, particularly here in Wildcat Bluff County."

"But if they pull something like that again..." Rowdy tapped his fingertips on top of the shingle stack.

"Right," Sheriff Calhoun agreed. "Hopefully, this run-in with the Buick Brigade will turn their lives around."

"I wouldn't doubt it," Belle said. "They do seem to have a way of getting things done."

Sheriff Calhoun chuckled again. "If I could hire them, well...I'd probably be out of a job."

Belle smiled, thinking he could very well be right.

"Anything else?" Sheriff Calhoun asked.

"That's all," Belle said. "And Sheriff, please have a very Merry Christmas."

"Thank you. Same to you."

Rowdy clicked off and tucked his phone back in his pocket. "Well, that's that."

"After our wild ride chasing them down the road with shingles coming at us hard and fast, this seems sort of anticlimactic," Belle said.

Rowdy shook his head. "Isn't that what you want? Things nice and quiet and easy."

"That's the theory." She looked at Homer and then Aristotle. "But when you work for the Buick Brigade, I suppose you take it as you get it."

He laughed harder. "Are we working for the ladies of Destiny now?"

"I'm honestly beginning to think Lulabelle & You is simply a sideline until I solve whatever it is they want me to solve." She hesitated, glancing around again. "And I don't even know how I came to this point."

"Nobody ever does."

She smiled, shaking her head. "At the very least, you have to admit it's just flat-out interesting to know them."

"Yeah…at the very least." He looked at the pigeons. "Do you think it's about time we went to see the ladies again?"

"I can't get the schoolhouse off my mind. It's so lovely and yet so tragic. That fire. It's as if hot embers are still smoldering in that building just waiting to reignite."

He nodded, obviously catching her meaning because he'd been there with her.

"You're a firefighter. If a fire extinguisher won't work, you'd use anything and everything in your firefighting equipment to extinguish that blaze forever, wouldn't you?"

He gave her a slow smile that spread from his lips to his eyes. "That's easy to answer. Yes."

"Okay. We're in agreement. Maybe it's not any normal kind of firefighting, but it's still what firefighters do. They're first—and maybe last—responders. They save. They heal. They give hope."

"We do our best." He grew quiet. "Sometimes it's not enough. Sometimes it's just right."

"Let's make this just right."

And with those words, she heard the flutter of wings again. She looked to her right shoulder. Homer perched there. She looked to her left shoulder. Aristotle perched there. She looked into the sky and saw a pigeon circling lower and lower until he descended to the returned shingle stack.

"Speaking of the Buick Brigade," Rowdy said. "Looks like you've got incoming mail."

By now, she wasn't even too surprised because things had started to move fast. She walked over to the new bird, slowly reached out so as not to startle him, and extracted the pigeon-gram.

She rolled it open and read out loud, "Students require a teacher. News awaits you. Socrates is home."

"Hello, Socrates," she said. "Welcome home."

Socrates flew over to Rowdy, perched on his shoulder, and started to preen his feathers.

"Friend of yours?" Belle no longer felt amazed at the sight, but she was still impressed at the wonderful bond between people and birds.

"Yeah." He stroked a fingertip down Socrates's back. "I bet he's glad to be home with his friends."

"At this rate, we may need to enlarge their coop."

"It'll do for now."

"I hope so. I don't know when we'd get time for another project."

"Busy, huh?"

She just shook her head. "Like I'm the only one."

"Belle," he said, turning serious. "About all this house business and—"

All three pigeons suddenly took to wing, swooping

around Belle's head and then Rowdy's before they took off for the barn.

"What was that?" Belle asked.

"Goodbye, I guess."

"I suppose we weren't taking care of business."

"The Buick Brigade's business."

"What other kind would the pigeons think important?"

"Nothing that I can think of."

"Me either," Belle said.

"It's kind of late to start out for Destiny right now."

"Too late." She turned back toward the house, but he didn't follow her, so she glanced at him. "Rowdy?"

He looked at the house, the barn, the road and then back at her. "I need to go take care of something. I'll see you in the morning."

And he left her standing there, all alone.

Chapter 32

"Dad, I love Belle." Rowdy sat in a rocking chair on the veranda the next morning at Holloway Farm & Ranch. He turned a mug of coffee around and around in his hands.

"I thought as much." Bert held his own mug of coffee, not drinking, just staring. "Did you tell her what you've been doing at her ranch?"

"No. I'm scared that if I tell her, I'll lose her."

"You can't let it drag on."

"She thinks I'm a good, honest man."

"You're my son. I raised you to be a good, honest man. And you're exactly that man."

"Maybe I was, but I'm not anymore."

"Nothing's changed."

"Everything's changed," Rowdy said.

"This whole thing with Lulabelle & You Ranch wasn't your idea. You'd never have done it if you hadn't drawn the short straw."

"I know…but it doesn't change the fact I went along with it."

"True." Bert took a sip of coffee as he looked out over the land. "What can I do to help?"

"You're listening to me. That always helps."

"We share our troubles."

"True."

"Your mother…now that was a rough patch. Sickness is hard no matter which way you turn."

"We got each other through it."

"Woman trouble." Bert sighed. "Now that's the worst. A man can only control it so far."

"And we're used to being in control of our lives, our land, our cattle…you name it."

"But not our women." Bert sipped coffee again. "We like strong."

"Belle's strong."

"That's what you've got to count on now. She's smart and strong…and she has a kind heart."

"What if she tosses me out the door and goes back to Dallas? What would I do?"

"You know damn well what you'd do." Bert glanced at his son with a gleam in his eyes. "You'd go after her, and you'd find a way to bring her home."

Rowdy nodded, turning his mug around in his hands again. "If nothing else, we Holloways are persistent, aren't we?"

"How else do you think I finally persuaded Hedy Murray, the most independent and cantankerous woman on this green Earth, to give me a chance? Persistence and, well…enough love to last a lifetime."

"I've got both. And they're all for Belle Tarleton."

"You got the guts. Go for it."

Rowdy set his mug down and then stood up. "Right now I'm taking her to see the Buick Brigade."

"Ah, the lovely ladies of Destiny. Maybe they'll throw a bit of fairy dust your way and change your luck."

"I could sure use some good luck."

"Couldn't we all."

"After Destiny, I'll find a way to tell Belle the truth, come hell or high water."

"That's my boy." Bert stood up and gave Rowdy a big bear hug. "Love. That's what life is all about. Nothing else is worth a hoot without it."

"Thanks, Dad."

He walked down to his pickup where he'd parked in front. And it was his *regular* truck. He was done with the rattletrap that wasn't safe enough or good enough for Belle. It was fine out in the back pasture, but out on the highway he didn't trust it. Anyway, he'd had enough of his disguise. He was back to wearing a pearl-snap shirt, pressed Wranglers, his favorite rodeo buckle, and his python boots. Life didn't get much better than when you were comfortable in your own skin...with your own, well-earned name.

He sat down inside, pulled on his seat belt, and started the engine. He appreciated the growl of the one-ton engine because it meant he had the power to haul plenty, if and when he needed to on the ranch. And Belle would be safe inside this vehicle with him driving it. Above all, he wanted her safe.

He hit Wildcat Road and headed for Lulabelle & You Ranch. He had to break the habit of trying to stay out of trouble so he didn't set off his bad luck. It hadn't worked in the past, so why would it now? He was headed toward a collision with Belle, and he was ready to get it over with.

If she loved him, she'd understand...or come to understand after he'd explained the situation. If she didn't, she could use it as an excuse to break up with him. Maybe she'd break up with the whole county and go back to the big city. If she did that, well...he was strong enough to live with a broken heart, if that's what it finally came to, but he had no intention of going there.

By the time he reached the turnoff for Belle's ranch, he had his feet under him in a way he hadn't since he'd agreed to the deception and met Belle. He realized now that the entire debacle had been so wrong for him, so against his personal principles that he'd been living a lie for weeks and it was eating him up inside. No more. He'd moved past being Bert Two, but he wasn't a weak-willed Rowdy either. If you were going to be a cowboy poet and every other thing it took to run a honking-big ranch, you better have a will of iron.

He drove under the Lulabelle & You Ranch sign, over the cattle guard, and up the lane to the circular drive. Plenty of shingle stacks now. And someday they'd be on top of the roof instead of on the ground. In the meantime, he wasn't going to let their location worry him. He'd about completed the patio in back, and Belle could start using it right away.

He was surprised to see her waiting on the porch. She must be anxious to get to Destiny and find her answers. He'd be glad to learn what actually happened in that fire, too. She walked toward him with a little spring in her step, looking fine like she always did in her own personal line of Western wear and cowgirl boots. She'd tied a red bandana around her throat so she looked a little jaunty with her green sweater and black skinny jeans... The sight made him hungry all over again.

She opened the door, hopped inside, set her black purse on the floorboard, and gave him a big grin.

"Looks like somebody's excited about their trip to Destiny." He said the words, but he was really focused on her lips because she'd painted them red to go with her bandana, and all that did was remind him of that time in the shower when she'd worn nothing but red silk and pink skin. That particular memory still had the power to stoke his fire.

"Oh yes...and I got a good night's sleep."

"No interruptions?" He glanced at her before he headed back toward the road, suddenly realizing how the very idea of another man in her bed affected him. He could easily pound something.

"A certain guy I know wasn't there, so no interruptions at all."

"Good."

"Good?"

"I'm glad you got a good night's sleep."

"Thanks." She reached over and squeezed his arm. "I hope you did, too."

"I did."

"I missed you."

"Missed you, too." He realized he'd gone all stilted in his words because he was trying to get over that image of another guy.

"So...am I to assume we're expected in Destiny?"

"I wouldn't bet against it."

"Doris again?"

"We'll head there first," he said. "If that's not the right house, she'll tell us where to go."

"Okay." Belle clutched her hands together in her lap. "To tell you the truth, I'm a little tense about today."

"Why?"

"So much rides on what we learn about the schoolhouse fire."

"It doesn't have to, not really," he said.

"What do you mean?"

"We could go forward with your plans no matter what we learn or don't learn."

"I guess that's true, if Craig was onboard." She glanced at Rowdy. "But I don't think that'd be right."

"Maybe not, but it's an idea."

"Thanks. We'll see how it goes."

He continued down the highway, letting the whine of tires on pavement muffled by the vehicle set the tone. He was quiet. She was quiet. He figured they were both gathering their thoughts for the coming meeting. He hoped they'd learn something useful, but no one could ever be sure with the ladies.

When he reached the top of the cliff overlooking the Red River, he turned west and followed the two-lane road into Destiny. Nothing had changed on Main Street. The four three-story Victorian homes still stood side by side on large lots. The painted ladies were as pretty as ever with their bright colors. On the other side of the street, the five single-story buildings with Western false fronts painted white continued to promote their business with hand-carved, hand-painted signs that hung above the boardwalk under a connecting portico. On either side of the businesses, twelve small, single-story farmhouses in pastel colors with peaked roofs still spread out, six to each side.

He made a U-turn, drove back down the street, and parked in front of the Victorian house painted fuchsia with purple trim to accent its wraparound porch, octagonal turret room, ornamental trim, and multi-peaked roof. A wide entry staircase with an elaborately carved handrail led up to Doris, who stood on the portico under the purple gingerbread-laced edge of roof. Next to her stood Louise, Blondel, and Ada.

"The Buick Brigade is out in force today." He glanced over at Belle. "I bet they have news for us."

"I hope so." She gave him an excited smile. "Let's go see them."

He quickly rounded the front of his truck, opened the door, and helped Belle down, ever mindful that their deportment was being watched and judged by the discerning ladies. He held out his elbow, and Belle tucked her hand in the crook of his arm.

When they reached the stairs, he saw that the ladies wore their usual colorful sweaters, knee-length skirts, and low-heeled shoes. Today, they'd added luminous white pearl necklaces to accent their clothes.

"We're so happy you could make it," Doris said. "Please join us in the parlor for tea."

Rowdy groaned quietly as he walked up the stairs with Belle because he'd been in that parlor before and there wasn't hardly room to move for the delicate furniture and gewgaws on every available surface with scarves and tablecloths and such covering about everything. But he said nothing as he followed all of them inside the shadowy hall with dark-wood paneling and into a brighter room with lace curtains over windows with maroon-velvet drapes.

He stood back until the four ladies were seated on delicate Queen Anne love seats made of gilded wood with maroon-velvet upholstery. A small table between the settees held a tray with the same delicate china teapot in a violet-flower pattern and six matching teacups with saucers that Doris had used the last time they were there...plus a plate stacked high with misshapen cowboy cookies.

He figured the two fragile-looking chairs that had been left empty on either end of the tray belonged to Belle and him. Belle sat down in one while he took the other.

"How kind of you to join us today," Doris said.

"We're happy to be here," Belle replied with a smile.

Doris picked up the teapot, poured liquid into all the cups, and handed them around the group.

Rowdy withheld another groan because the cup and saucer in his hands were a disaster waiting to happen, so he sat still and held steady…until he could escape the house.

"We understand you made a little trip to Sure-Shot recently," Blondel said with a raised eyebrow.

"Yes, we did." Belle glanced at Rowdy.

"We made an interesting discovery near the town." He realized Belle wanted him to help out with the story, although he'd have preferred to let her take center stage.

"There's a one-room schoolhouse in a memorial grove." Belle took a sip of tea. "But sadly, we could see there had been a fire."

"And no firefighters to call," he added.

"Indeed." Louise sipped tea.

"What do you think of the building?" Blondel asked.

"It's beautiful," Belle said. "In fact, it reminds me of your four lovely homes right here in Destiny."

"And well it should," Doris said.

He waited for more explanation. When it wasn't forthcoming, he cleared his throat and hazarded a drink of tea. It was black and bitter, and he wished he'd never touched it.

"Perhaps the same architect?" Belle asked.

"Exactly." Doris smiled at Belle as if she were an exceptionally good student.

"We found hats, small hats, that had been used to put out the fire," Belle said.

Doris glanced at her friends and received nods in reply. "It's an old story."

"And a sad one," Blondel added.

"For that reason, our families preferred to let it rest in peace," Louise said.

"And never speak of it again." Ada shook her head in dismay.

"Your arrival, Belle Tarleton, brought the past to life," Doris said.

"Me?" Belle appeared astonished at the news.

"Yes, indeed," Blondel agreed. "You see, my ancestor was named Belle, too."

"Really?" Belle smiled at the group.

"And my ancestor was named Bertram." Doris looked straight at Rowdy.

He went on alert, not knowing where this was headed now.

"How interesting. I just met Bert Holloway at his ranch. His name is Bertram, too, isn't it?" Belle said.

"Yes, indeed." Blondel glanced at Rowdy. "And so we knew the time was right..."

"To bring the past into the present..." Louise said.

"And share the knowledge..." Ada said.

"That lights the way," Doris said.

"That's all well and good." Belle looked from one lady to the other. "But it doesn't explain much."

Rowdy almost dropped his cup and saucer. Nobody talked to the Buick Brigade straight like that. He stiffened in anticipation of being kicked out the front door.

A peal of laughter erupted from Doris.

Blondel clapped her hands in delight.

Louise gave a little smile.

Ada reached for a cookie.

He couldn't believe it. Was Belle actually going to get away with challenging the ladies?

"We knew you were a lady after our own hearts," Blondel said. "And that is why you have received our blessing to..."

"Reopen the one-room schoolhouse." Doris looked at the group in triumph.

"She doesn't own it." Rowdy clamped his mouth shut but too late. His words hung heavy in the room.

"Small matter," Ada said. "The current owner will make it available for use by deed or rental."

"I did think it would make a wonderful center for the arts in our community, but there is the expense of making it usable again." Belle glanced at him because that was exactly what he'd told her earlier.

"Wildcat Bluff County will make it happen," Blondel said.

He wasn't so sure of that, but he kept his mouth shut because the ladies usually made stuff work, one way or another.

"Thank you," Belle said. "I love the idea, but I still would like to know what happened after the fire."

"Did I mention that my lovely Belle was the teacher there?" Blondel asked.

"No." Belle leaned forward. "Please tell me about the students. Did they survive the fire?"

"Yes, indeed," Blondel said. "And yet, even after all this time, I am so very sad to tell you that our dear Belle perished in the fire...but not until she saved every single one of her pupils."

"I'm happy to know about the children." Belle glanced at Rowdy and shook her head. "But I'm so sorry about your Belle."

"Why the memorial grove?" He leaned forward with interest.

"That is my story to tell," Doris said. "Bertram was engaged to Belle. They were to be married on Christmas Day, but the fire occurred on Christmas Eve."

"Oh, that's tragic." Belle put a hand to her heart.

"And so your ancestor built the grove in her honor." Rowdy glanced at Belle. "I can understand. I'd do it, too."

"Love is the greatest gift of all," Doris said. "Bertram never married...and he wore her blackened locket with their photographs in it until his dying day."

Belle bowed her head and sniffed back tears. "I'm honored you would entrust such a sacred memory to me."

Rowdy couldn't help but wonder how they'd kept such a poignant tale secret all these years. Fortunately, they hadn't mentioned that his name was Bertram, but they'd made it clear, at least to him, that they included him in this story with Belle.

"Christmas is upon us," Louise said.

"It is time for all to be right in the world," Blondel said.

"Wildcat Bluff County is ready for what it once lost," Ada said.

"With the return of our Belle and Bertram," Doris said.

Rowdy stood up, set down his cup and saucer, and then held out his hand to Belle. He'd better get them out of there before the ladies accidentally, or on purpose, revealed his true identity before he'd had a chance to tell Belle himself.

She got up, too, looking confused at his abruptness.

"Ladies, it's been a pleasure, as always," he said. "I appreciate your story, but I'm not sure it has much to do with me…or Belle."

All four ladies rose to their feet in unison with sweet smiles on their faces.

"Our story is not really the point," Blondel said. "We simply shared it—in secret—with the two of you because we have been inspired to heal the past."

"We want to see the schoolhouse put to good use again," Doris said. "And we do hope the two of you will spearhead that process."

"We're both really busy," Rowdy said as he held out his elbow to Belle. He needed to get them out of there before they spent the rest of their lives working for the Buick Brigade.

"We understand, dear heart," Louise said.

"Yes, indeed," Blondel said.

"Time is on your side," Ada said.

"Patience is a virtue," Doris said. "When the time is right, the schoolhouse will once again be of service to our community."

"Thank you for everything." Belle tucked her fingers around Rowdy's arm. "We'll see what we can do about reopening the schoolhouse."

"Don't bother to see us out." He headed for the door and then looked back. "It would make a fine center for the arts."

Chapter 33

"I think there must have been a lot of tragedy in the lives of the Buick Brigade's families over the years." Belle spoke quietly, breaking the silence as Rowdy drove hard and fast out of Destiny toward Wildcat Bluff, as if he were trying to outdistance a looming personal tragedy.

"At least the kids got out of the schoolhouse alive," he said.

"The other Belle was heroic, wasn't she?"

"That's the thing with firefighters…first responders… folks who put their lives on the line for others."

"What?"

"They don't know they're heroic or brave or any other name you want to put to their actions. They simply do what they do because it's important for their loved ones, their community…for life itself."

"Do you think the Buick Brigade is sort of like a group of first responders? They see a need and respond, no matter the personal cost or how others view them?" she asked.

"I'd never thought of them that way before, but I can see it now."

"Sometimes people who've known tragedy become very kind to others…thoughtful, sincere, protective. Don't you think?"

"Yeah. And if you're thinking what I'm thinking, their families came west and settled in Destiny after something or someone sent them reeling away from danger, tragedy, loss, or it forced them out…no way to know. And their descendants still watch and protect," he said.

"It'd explain the ladies, wouldn't it?"

"In one way, yes, but in other ways…they're in a world all their own, one they control and manage."

"I like them."

"They like you."

"And you."

He slowed down as he neared Wildcat Bluff and then glanced over at her. "That stuff about Belle and Bertram…"

"Yes?"

"What do you think?"

"It was a lot to take in. "

"Do you believe them?"

"What!" She turned to look at him in surprise. "It never entered my mind not to believe them."

"I know. Still, you might trust too much."

"Trust?" She swiveled in her seat to focus on him. "I'm a hard-headed businesswoman. I make informed decisions based on the information at hand."

"What if the information isn't correct?"

She felt that old uneasiness with him rise up and grab her. She shivered at the feeling. "I go with my gut."

"What does your gut tell you about the Buick Brigade?"

"Truth. If their story hadn't fit with what we'd observed at the schoolhouse, then my reaction would have been very different. Wouldn't yours?"

"Yeah. I agree. If it'd gone down any other way, I'd have been out of there in a flash. But their reputation also precedes them. That influenced me, too."

"You've never known them to lie, is that it?"

"Right," he said. "Sometimes people lie for good reasons."

"Social lies?"

"Yes. And lies that protect others."

She took a deep breath. Here it came, finally. He'd been lying to her. Would the truth hurt as badly as she thought it might? They didn't have to go there, not yet, not after such an emotional visit in Destiny.

"Belle, I—"

"What do you think about taking on the schoolhouse and turning it into an arts center?"

He gave a deep sigh, glanced at her and then looked back at the road. "You don't have to go there…*we* don't have to do it. Craig owns the property. You can do whatever you want to do on Lulabelle & You Ranch. Maybe that's where you should concentrate your time, energy, and money."

"That makes practical sense, doesn't it?"

"Yes."

"Sometimes life just requires you to take a chance. Maybe you get lucky, maybe you don't."

"Don't count on good luck with me."

She felt her heart go out to him at his words. "I've had enough of your bad luck. I agree with the Buick Brigade. By the time we're said and done, you're going to be the luckiest cowboy in the county."

He laughed out loud, glancing over at her. "If I've got you *and* the ladies of Destiny in my corner, how can I be anything except lucky?"

"Exactly." And she joined his laughter.

"Seriously, though," he said. "The one-room schoolhouse

should be a community project. It'd bring folks together, from youngsters to oldsters and everybody in between."

"I agree."

"I just don't want you to think you need to take on this project alone...if it's even possible."

"I won't."

"And Christmas comes first."

"Right."

"We're almost back to your ranch. It's been a long day."

"True."

"Why don't I drop you off, get out of your hair, and let us both take care of some business?"

"Sounds good, as long as you come back later."

"How could I stay away?"

Rowdy turned off Wildcat Road and drove over the cattle guard and up to the front of the house. A black pickup was parked on the circle drive, so he nosed in behind it and turned off his engine.

"Who's that?" he asked.

"Looks like Kemp's truck." She unhooked her seat belt. "Let's find out if he has news about Daisy Sue."

She grabbed her purse, got out of the truck, and hurried up to the porch. No Kemp in sight. She looked over her shoulder. Rowdy was glancing around the area, too. They looked at each other and shrugged, so she just unlocked the front door, set her purse on the entry table, and walked back to him.

"Hey, folks!" Kemp called as he rounded the side of the house. "Patio looks good. I could use one at my place."

"Thanks," Rowdy said.

"You taking orders for more patios?"

"No," Rowdy said. "That's my limit."

Kemp chuckled as he walked over to them.

"Well?" She put her hands on her hips in frustration. Why was he talking about patios when he knew they were anxious for news?

Kemp nodded, shrugging. "Daisy Sue, huh?"

"Yes." She leaned toward him. "And what about your cousin?"

Kemp shook his head. "Lester's back home, but he's one unhappy cowboy. I don't know how long Aunt Dotty can keep him pinned down on the ranch, but I'm out of that mess for good."

"And you're back to work?" Belle asked.

"Absolutely."

"With news about Daisy Sue?"

"Yep. Here's my best guess."

"Guess?" she asked.

"I talked with the other cowboys here on the ranch."

"And?" She moved closer to him.

"We discussed the Daisy Sue situation up one side and down the other."

"Your conclusion?"

"She must be at your family's ranch in East Texas."

"What?" Belle fell back a step. "That's too simple. And how could she possibly have ended up there?"

"It was before your time here. A load of cattle from your ranch went to that ranch."

"Okay." She nodded, quickly thinking that it'd make sense for her brothers to move cattle between two ranches. "But what would that have to do with Daisy Sue?"

"Far as we can figure, those cowboys must've picked her

up at the same time as the other cows, loaded her up, and hauled her away."

"Did you contact them yet?" Rowdy asked.

"No." Kemp tipped his cowboy hat back on his head, rubbed his forehead, and tugged the hat down again.

"That's not Kemp's job. I'll do it." She caught an odd look on Rowdy's face but dismissed it in the heat of the moment.

"Hate to say it, but Daisy Sue might've been sold by your family," Kemp said. "Good breeding stock like her—"

"Don't even go there." She shuddered at the idea.

"You could still track her," Rowdy said. "She's registered, so she can't completely disappear."

"She has so far." Belle looked at the ground, the sky, the house, trying to think how she'd gotten into this mess. Of course, if she'd stayed in Dallas, nothing of this would have happened to her. She glanced at Rowdy, realizing that if she hadn't come here she'd never have met her own personal cowboy.

"What do you want me to do?" Kemp asked.

"For now, go on back to your regular work," she said. "I'm sure you're way behind on stuff."

"You know it."

"I'll call my brothers and see if they can find her."

"Okay," Kemp said. "If you need me to run over to East Texas, let me know. By now, I want that cow back here as bad as anybody."

"Maybe not as much as Storm and Fernando...but we're all with you on this one." She just shook her head because she still hadn't found Daisy Sue.

"I doubt it'll take them long to check tattoos or ear tags," Rowdy said.

"Lot of cattle on that ranch, but it's doable." Kemp looked at Belle. "Right sorry about the mix-up. What with that cousin of mine and all, it's just been a flat-out mess."

She smiled, shaking her head. "You're right. A mess. But at least we now have another way to go. Thanks for all your help."

"Anytime." He tipped his hat and then headed for his truck.

As she watched Kemp drive away, Rowdy's phone rang.

"Fire station." He gave her a serious look as he answered his cell, engaging the speakerphone. "Hedy, what's up?"

"Need you down here pronto. I'm sending two boosters to a barn fire in the northern part of the county."

"Arson? Accident?"

"Don't know yet."

"I'm at Belle's. I'll be there as quick as I can."

"Thanks." And Hedy was gone.

He turned to Belle. "Got to go."

"Stay safe."

He squeezed her fingers. "Will do. Why don't you call your brothers while I'm gone? If you can wait, I'll bring back Chuckwagon when I'm done."

"Thanks. I'll wait up for you." She went up on tiptoes and planted a soft kiss on his cheek.

He quickly stalked away, got in his truck, and drove down the hill.

She watched until she couldn't see him anymore. Then she walked inside, leaving the front door unlocked for his return. She slipped her phone out of her purse before she plopped down on the sofa in her living room. She stared at the fireplace for a moment. She could use a nice, warm, cozy fire...a controlled one, for sure, but she didn't know if she had any firewood. She probably didn't. Maybe Rowdy could get some for her. And she stopped her thoughts right there. She was coming to rely on him too much. He could be gone in an instant...just like Daisy Sue.

She punched Ty's number on speed dial. Tyrone was her youngest brother and the most available in a time of crisis. He'd get the loss of Daisy Sue as an iconic symbol of cows everywhere. Her other brothers... Well, they were of a more practical bent.

"Hey, Sweetie," Ty said, using his favorite endearment for her.

"Hey yourself." She smiled at just the sound of his voice. "How're you doing?"

"Fair to middlin'."

"Good."

"You?"

"I guess I wouldn't call if I didn't have a problem, would I?"

"That's about the size of it."

She exhaled on a sigh. "I'm here at my new-and-improving Lulabelle & You Ranch."

"How's it going?"

"Slowly."

"You need me to come over and speed things up?" He chuckled low in his throat, as if the idea of busting heads or using brass knuckles held a certain appeal to a cowboy like him.

"Don't you dare. I have enough trouble without my big brothers... Let's just say I'm taking care of business fine and dandy."

"If you are, why do you need me?"

"I don't suppose you've been following this whole Fernando and Daisy Sue fiasco online, have you?"

He laughed harder. "Yeah. How'd you get Lulabelle & You entangled in that reality show?"

"Oh my…oh my…oh my goodness, don't you ever let Storm Steele hear you say something like that."

"Reality show?"

"She'd do it. She'd do it in a heartbeat. And it'd work. That girl is an entrepreneur in diapers. Wait till she gets into training pants. It hardly bears thinking on."

"Sounds like somebody I watched growing up."

"I don't know anything about that."

"And that sounds like a lot of admiration," he said.

"Well, yes, but the reason I called—"

"You're making friends, aren't you?"

"Yes, I guess so. It's an interesting community."

"We always thought so." He cleared his throat. "Anybody special?"

"Well, there's this guy named Rowdy…"

"Rowdy who?"

"Uh…just Rowdy."

"Who's his family?"

"Uh, don't know."

"How'd you meet him?"

"He's doing some work here at the house," she said.

"Handyman?"

"Construction."

"Cowboy?"

"He's got a small place."

"You been there?"

"No."

"Belle, you know I've always looked out for you."

"I know where you're going, so don't do it."

"If you don't know his last name or his family or his home, what do you know about him?"

"He's kind and considerate and—"

"He's a guy...of course he's all that until—"

"I told you not to go there."

"Okay. I just don't want you to get hurt."

"I'm a big girl. If I need to, I can pull up my big-girl panties."

"I know. I just don't want you to have to do it," he said. "Anyway, did you get a chance to meet Bert Two Holloway yet?"

"No. I met his dad and Hedy Murray on the Holloway ranch, but Bert Two wasn't there."

"I wish you'd find time to meet him. I think you'd like him a lot."

"I'm sort of hooked on Rowdy right now."

"I hear you. Still, if you need a shoulder to cry on later, I'm here for you."

"Thanks." She stared at the fireplace. She really could use a nice, warm, cozy fire—one to share with Rowdy.

"But I got us off track, didn't I?"

"Right. Let's back up to Fernando and Daisy Sue."

"Okay."

"You've read or seen or heard that she's missing from my ranch."

"Yep. That's not bad publicity. I figured you had her stashed somewhere till folks lost interest and you unwrapped her like a Christmas present to start up the interest again."

"I wouldn't do something like that."

"Some marketing folks would do it in a heartbeat," he said.

"Never. It's too painful for Storm and Fernando."

"Wait a minute…if you don't have Daisy Sue, where is she?"

"That's my problem. She really is missing."

"You're kidding me."

"No, I'm not." She took a deep breath. "That's why I'm calling you. Kemp Lander, my foreman…remember y'all hired him."

"Yeah. Sound guy."

"He's been looking for her all this time."

"He finally found her?"

"No…but he thinks she might have been picked up with that load of cattle y'all transported from here to our ranch there," she said.

"Why would he think that?"

"We can't find her anywhere else."

"That was right before you got there and took over, wasn't it?"

"Yes."

"Let me think back," he said.

"Please tell me you didn't sell that load."

"I don't know. We don't watch over the day-to-day operations. I'll need to talk with our head honcho and get back to you."

"I'll send her AAA registration number."

"Good."

"We need to find her as soon as possible. Storm is getting more anxious all the time."

"I'd like to meet that little girl sometime."

"All I can say is you ought to be careful or she'll try to sell you a T-shirt or signed photograph or corral you into some type of business."

He laughed. "Is that what she did to you?"

"She really thinks a Fernando and Daisy Sue line of Western wear would sell like hot cakes."

"Now there's a girl after your own heart, isn't she?"

"Yeah. She's adorable."

"I've got to tell you, you're fitting in there a lot better than I thought possible."

"It's taken a while, but I like the people and the community…and it's just a really fine county."

"I'm glad it's working for you. For now, I'll get right on the Daisy Sue situation."

"Thanks."

"And if you need me to come over and knock a few heads together, just let me know."

"Appreciate the support, as always."

"Bye, Sweetie."

When he was gone, she sat there a moment, feeling a little lonely, a little blue, and yet knowing her connection with her family was deep and strong and unbreakable… much like the way she felt about Rowdy.

Chapter 34

After touching base with Ty, Belle took a quick shower to wash away the day while she waited for Rowdy.

She slipped into a soft blue sweatshirt and sweatpants... and nothing else. Clean and sweet-smelling, she returned to the living room. She sat down on the sofa, wishing she was watching a crackling blaze in the fireplace while she snuggled into Rowdy's warmth.

She'd accomplished a lot that day. Kemp was back, and there might actually be a lead on Daisy Sue. She'd learned that all of the children had survived the schoolhouse fire, even if the teacher hadn't made it out alive. And then there was the tender, touching, yet sad tale of the other Belle and her Bertram.

Belle had developed a great appreciation for the strong friendship between the ladies of Destiny as well as for the obvious deep love between Bert and Hedy, Ivy and Slade, and Fern and Craig as well as all the other loving folks in the county like Sydney and her daughter, Storm. They didn't overlook animals, either, revealing their love for Fernando and Daisy Sue as well as so many others like Homer, Aristotle, and Socrates. They included strangers, too. They did their best to ensure the welfare and happiness of each and every person who came to their community festivals throughout the year.

She didn't doubt for one second that she'd made the

right choice in coming here because what she wanted to do dovetailed so perfectly with what was already being accomplished in Wildcat Bluff County. And then there was Rowdy. How could she have anticipated such generous love?

Now that she was getting things more under control on the ranch, she looked forward to interacting with others in the county. So far, she'd liked everyone she'd met, and she was anxious to do even more with them, particularly when the time came to develop the one-room schoolhouse.

She felt satisfied that she'd done all she could for the moment. Now was the time to catch her breath. She wished Rowdy was with her, but he'd be back soon enough and he'd bring delicious food. She heard her stomach growl at that thought, so she patted it in reassurance that it'd be full pretty quickly.

She hoped all the firefighters were staying safe while fighting the fire. Maybe they could even save the barn. She tried to relax, but with Rowdy and others in possible danger, she felt on edge. She resisted getting up and checking outside for him every few minutes, although that was what she wanted to do.

As night fell, she noticed a chill in the air, so she put her feet up and tucked a pretty Lulabelle & You throw around herself. Life was good…except for the lack of Rowdy. She smiled, thinking of him getting there, thinking of tasty food, thinking of her big bed, thinking of his naked body, thinking…

And then he was there, opening the front door, calling to her, leaving food in the kitchen, and finally, coming to her… wearing a clean Wildcat Bluff Fire-Rescue sweat set.

He smiled in triumph.

"You fought the fire and won?" She tossed aside the throw, jumped to her feet, and hurried over to him.

"That we did. We saved the barn and didn't lose any animals."

"I'm so happy to hear it."

"And nobody suffered an injury."

"That's experience for you."

"It helps."

"Hungry? Thirsty? Tired?"

"Yep." He grinned, holding out a hand to her. "All the time I fought that fire, I knew I'd be coming home to you. It gave me energy and purpose."

She slipped her fingers into his hand. "And I waited for you, knowing you'd soon be with me."

"And that I'd bring food."

She chuckled. "Well, I was anticipating Chuckwagon."

He joined her laughter. "Come on. I cleaned up at the station. Now I'm so hungry I could eat a horse and chase the rider."

She smiled at the old joke as she led him toward the kitchen and the delicious scent of barbecue.

"That food smelled so good on the way here I almost tore into the sack."

"Now that would have been naughty."

"I'm feeling naughty." And he gave her a suggestive grin.

She smiled at his words. "You're almost as satisfying as food."

He grinned bigger. "Give me time and I'll see if I can take care of all your appetites."

"I don't have a single doubt you can." She gave him a

quick hug, enjoying the feel of his hot, hard body, and then walked into the kitchen.

He followed her. "Am I being tossed over for Chuckwagon eats?"

"Don't take it personally. I'm sure many a man has lost out to the aroma of barbecue."

He grinned as he opened the sack and set out two white dinner containers, two drinks, two smaller pie containers, and plasticware with napkins. He pulled out a chair at the table and gestured for her to sit in it.

"You're too kind." She smiled at him as she sat down. "The Buick Brigade would approve of your manners."

"I do my best." He sat down in a chair across the table from her.

She slid a set of everything across to him and then pulled her own dinner and dessert close. She popped open tops and inhaled the delicious aroma. He'd selected sliced-beef sandwiches with sides of potato salad and fried okra. A big wedge of pie beckoned her, so she picked up a fork, cut off the tip, and put it in her mouth. She closed her eyes as the rich, sweet taste of pecan pie melted in her mouth.

"You can't do any better than Slade Steele pies, can you?"

"Absolutely divine."

"He's developed quite the national following for his award-winning pies."

"I can see why." She picked up her sandwich. "If I don't save my pie for dessert, I'll eat the whole slice first."

"Go ahead. You deserve it."

"I do, don't I?" She had another delicious bite.

He watched her as he bit into his sandwich. "You can't get any better barbecue in the state of Texas."

She took a bite of her sandwich and nodded in agreement.

"What'd your brother have to say about Daisy Sue?"

"Ty says it's feasible, so he's going to check tags or tattoos and see if she's on the ranch."

"I sure hope so."

"Me, too." She forked up potato salad and sighed in pleasure. "Just the way I like it. Plenty of mustard."

"Yeah."

She ate with him in silence for a while, enjoying the food, the company, and the satisfaction of a day's good progress.

After a bit, they finished their food, set down their forks, and simply looked at each other. She smiled. He smiled. And they stood up as one, never looking away from each other.

"When I was in her store, Morning Glory gave me something. Do you want to see it?"

He grinned. "Do I?"

"I think you might like it."

"Morning Glory, huh?" He grinned even bigger.

She smiled back. "You know, all the pampering scents and creams and bath products that she makes for her customers."

"Oh yeah."

"Well, this is along those lines, but not quite the same."

"Am I going to enjoy it?"

"I'll let you decide for yourself."

He glanced down at the leftovers and then back at her with a question in his eyes.

"Let's clean up later," she said as she stepped away from the table.

"Where are we going?"

"Where do you think?"

"I hope the bedroom."

"You hoped right."

As she headed that way, she glanced over her shoulder. He was with her. And no wonder… He was eager to see what the legendary Morning Glory had sent their way.

In the bedroom, she tossed throw pillows to the floor, pulled back the cover to expose the sheets, and glanced back at him again. He stood in the doorway simply watching her with a smile on his lips.

"I could get used to this every day of my life," he said.

She froze. He sounded as if he truly meant it.

"Belle, I'm serious." He took several steps into the room. "I'd live here. I'd live anywhere you wanted me to live…as long as I could be with you."

"But Rowdy, it's so soon to get serious. We hardly know each other. We've never met each other's families."

"We know each other. We know what we do to each other. We know what we mean to each other. Does anything else really matter?"

She took a deep breath. This wasn't what she'd planned. She wanted something lighthearted and fun after the seriousness of the day.

"I'm always too soon with you, aren't I?" He raised his hands to either side and then dropped them again. "Don't you think we've been through enough high water together that we know each other pretty well by now?"

"Yes, of course…but if you're talking about moving in together, then—"

"No. That's not what I want."

"But—"

"I want it all with you. I knew it from the first."

"I treasure our time together, but—"

"Marriage. Kids...runny noses, dirty diapers. All of it. I want to share my life with you."

"What about your ranch? My ranch. My business. Your business—whatever it is."

"Do you think we can't have it all?"

"I think we can have it all, but tonight... Tonight I really just want to have sex." She put her hands on her hips, letting him know she was annoyed with so much seriousness at the end of a long, hard day. "Is that too much to ask?"

He grinned, dimple flashing in his cheek. "I thought you'd never ask."

"I'm not sure I'm in the mood now."

"I bet I could get you in the mood." He stalked toward her.

She backed up. "I don't know."

"What if I told you I loved you?"

"You told me that before."

He chuckled as he reached her. "Do you need to hear something new?"

"Yes. You owe it to me now after all that seriousness about moving in together."

"I am serious, but not about that. Like I said, I want it all."

"You're greedy."

"You'd make any man greedy."

She put a fingertip to her lips and wet it with the tip of her tongue as she cocked her head to one side, considering him.

"Are you trying to torment me?" He slipped her fingertip from her mouth and put it between his lips.

When she felt his gentle kiss, she just sort of melted inside. "You're the one tormenting now."

He placed her hand against his chest. "Undress me."

"No."

"No?"

"Strip for me and get on the bed."

He smiled as he snapped open his shirt, revealing hard muscles underneath. "Is this what you want?"

"Yes." She feasted her eyes on him, wanting the play after the serious but realizing she also wanted him to want her, wanted him to want permanent, wanted him to want to be with her forever...and love cascaded over her like the gentlest of rainwater on a soft, summer day until she melted for him alone.

He jerked off his shirt and tossed it aside, revealing his tanned and toned chest. He didn't stop there. And he didn't take his eyes off her as he sat down on the bed and shucked his boots, his jeans, and finally his shorts. Finally he simply sat there watching her watching him...waiting.

"Greedy," she said. "You look very, very greedy."

"That's the way I feel when I see you." He looked her up and down. "Now it's your turn. Strip."

"No."

"No?"

"We're talking about your greed, not mine."

"And so?"

"Lie down on your back...and let me see to your greed."

He smiled, nodded, and lay back, putting his arms above his head and crossing his wrists. "Like this?"

"Perfect. Now don't move."

"I wouldn't dream of it."

She knew he was smiling, thinking he knew what was coming, but she wore a secret little smile of her own because Morning Glory kept a few items hidden behind a counter that she might share or she might not. In this case...Belle pulled open a drawer of the nightstand, lifted out a very special canister, and set it on top.

"What's that?" Rowdy asked.

"You'll see."

She lifted the lid and set it aside, and the sweet scent of honey wafted across the bedroom. She pulled apart the golden strings of a yellow-satin drawstring bag inside the canister to reveal fine white powder. Atop the powder nestled a feather duster about three inches long with a group of feathers attached to a wooden knob. She slipped the tips of the feathers through the dust and turned to him.

"What've you got there?" He narrowed his eyes in suspicion.

"Honey dust."

"Am I supposed to eat it?"

"No." She raised an eyebrow at him. "I am."

And then she stroked the feather duster down his chest and around his nipples, watching them harden in response. She followed the dust with her tongue, lapping at his sensitive skin, tasting him, tasting honey, tasting pleasure.

She moved up his throat, tickling with the feather and following with her tongue until she reached his lips, where she paused to nibble and lick until he grasped her head with both hands and gave her a deep, searing, searching kiss and they both groaned with spiraling desire.

She lifted her head and smiled down at him. "You like?"

"Morning Glory is a genius, but we already knew it."

"Oh yes."

"I thought I was greedy before," he said, "but it was nothing compared to what I am now."

"There's more honey dust."

"There better be." He took the feather duster from her hand and swirled it in honey dust. When he turned back, he stopped and eyed her clothes with a raised eyebrow. "Are you going to strip for me?"

"Maybe. Maybe not."

"I have the honey dust."

"Good point." She stood up, slipped her sweatshirt up and over her head, and then dropped it to the floor, knowing he was watching her every move. She hooked her hands in the waistband of her sweatpants and then slowly slid them down her hips and her legs to the floor. She kicked them away.

He gestured toward the bed with the feather duster, and she lay down exactly as he had before and waited for him to give her what she'd given him. She shivered in anticipation.

When she felt the first light touch of the feather on her breasts, she caught her breath at the erotic sensation, and then he was tickling, teasing, licking, and sending her higher and higher...up and down her body, into her belly button, inside her thighs, even the tips of her toes...and she was grabbing him and holding him and wanting him until she heard him groan deep in his throat.

"I want your honey now." And he tossed the feather across the bed where it rolled out of sight.

She was so ready to give him anything he wanted because

she wanted everything he could give her, too. He spread her legs, knelt between them, kissed her on the lips, and gently eased inside. She grasped his shoulders, pulling him tightly to her, feeling him move harder, faster, deeper as he lifted them to ever greater heights until they flew free, soaring into ecstasy together...with the sweet scent of honey and the sweeter taste of love.

Chapter 35

Life had taken on the magical quality of Christmas that Rowdy enjoyed every year. As he drove down Wildcat Road, he thought about the fact that the county was only two days out from the annual festivities centered in Old Town, Sure-Shot, and Wildcat Hall Park. Out-of-towners were starting to arrive and fill up Twin Oaks B&B, Wildcat Bluff Hotel, Cowboy Cabins, and every other available space for rent. It was fun and exciting, but everybody was running to get last-minute details completed so everything rolled out smoothly for those who came to relax and enjoy the holidays.

Well, not quite everybody was involved in supporting the festivities. At Lulabelle & You Ranch, Belle had created her own little island of holiday happiness. She wasn't involved in the county's affairs, so she was focused on her clothing line, the horses and cattle on the ranch, and the pigeons in her barn. He smiled at another thought. She also put a little focus on him because he spent evenings at her house. She planned to attend the festivities with him, so he planned to wait until after Christmas to tell her anything that might negatively impact her holidays. Maybe it was selfish of him, but he wanted to prolong this special time and share Christmas with her.

He turned off the road, rattled across the cattle guard of Belle's ranch, and drove up to her house. He parked in front on the circle drive. He shook his head in disgust at the shingle stacks. They were a glaring reminder of what he—and others—hadn't done for her, but at least most of them were there. If she had a leak on her roof, there'd have been no question about reroofing her house, but upgrading could wait until they were past the holidays... At least he hoped she saw it that way.

He'd make up for the shingles today because he was arriving with gifts in the back of his one-ton pickup, sort of like Santa Claus with gifts in the back of his sleigh. Horsepower and reindeer-power got the job done.

She knew he was coming, so she opened the front door, raced across the lawn, and threw herself into his arms just as he stepped out of his vehicle. She felt good like she always did...and so right with him.

"Did you bring my gifts like you said?" She grinned at him, excited like a little kid on Christmas morning.

"Look in the back of the truck."

She started to run back there but stopped and looked at him. "You could have waited until Christmas."

"I want you to enjoy my gifts now. Besides, aren't you going to your family's ranch for Christmas dinner?"

"I always do, but this year..."

"Family is important. Tradition is important."

"But we're important, too."

He pressed a soft kiss to the tip of her nose. "Let's table that for today. I want you to have what I made."

"Made?" She opened her hazel eyes wide in excitement.

He clasped her hand and tugged her to the back of his truck.

"Oh my!" She turned and hugged him hard. "You made furniture for my new patio?"

"Remember, I told you I did a little woodworking as a hobby. I hope you like cedar. It's perfect for outdoors."

"It's gorgeous. I love it."

He was pleased with the two chairs, love seat, and table he'd created for her. He lowered the tailgate and hopped up into the bed of his truck. He set each piece on the ground and then picked up a big sack and handed it to her. He leaped back down and closed the tailgate.

"What's in here?" She hugged the sack to her chest. "It feels soft."

"You need cushions for your furniture, don't you?"

"Wonderful! You thought of everything."

"I wanted you to have it all for the holidays."

She peeked into the open sack. "I can hardly believe it. You matched the color of the new trim on my house."

"If I'm going to do something, I do it right."

She gave him a little self-satisfied smile. "Yeah. I can give testimony to that fact."

"And a little honey dust never hurt."

"Helps, you mean."

"Right." He grinned back. "Come on. I'll carry your new furniture around back and set it up."

"I'll help."

He picked up the love seat and headed for the backyard. She kept right up with him, lugging the sack of cushions. When they got there, he set down his piece of furniture near the metal set. The old patio set looked insubstantial, almost whimsical, in comparison.

"Where do you want me to position your new furniture?"

"I'm not sure." She set the big sack on top of the old table.

He checked the flagstone patio under his feet, looking

for any problems that might have occurred since he'd finished installing it. No issues so far, but he didn't expect any because he did meticulous work. He liked the big size of the patio. It stretched the length of the house just outside the long bank of windows, so the patio served as an extension of that room, melding outdoors with indoors.

He was as proud of building the patio as he was of making the furniture. He'd worked hard to bring her vision to life…and he'd succeeded. He realized now that when something was made for someone out of love, it turned out not just beautiful but special as well. He could easily spend a lifetime creating beautiful things for her just to see her face lit up in happiness as it was at this moment. He'd learned that was part of what love was all about.

"Let's center it just outside the windows so when I'm inside I can see how beautiful it looks outside."

"The set is perfect for the patio parties you had in mind, too."

"Yes, well…in time, perhaps."

"We can add a grill or firepit or complete kitchen later, too."

"Sounds wonderful." She walked over, put her arms around him, and nestled against his chest. "You're so good to me. Thank you."

He hugged her close, feeling his heart swell with happiness. He wanted to say they'd make this moment last a lifetime, but he couldn't promise anything yet except that they'd enjoy the festivities together.

She stepped back. "I don't have anything for you… except I could give you some Lulabelle & You promo items. How would you like a Fernando the Wonder Bull sweatshirt?"

He laughed at the idea. "You don't need to get me anything. To see you this happy is more than gift enough."

"That's so sweet, but I'll think of something. I have a little time left."

"Please don't go to any trouble."

"No trouble. It'll be my pleasure."

"Okay," he said. "Let's get the rest of your new furniture back here."

He headed back to his pickup, and she came right along with him...more in a supervisory position than anything. Soon they had the furniture arranged on the patio with the cushions in place. It looked good, even better than he'd imagined when he was making it.

"Rowdy, I love it." She set the crimson-silk-flower holiday arrangement he'd included in the sack in the center of the table and then plopped down in a chair and stroked long fingers across the smooth, varnished tabletop.

He sat down in the other chair. "You're sure you like it?"

She chuckled as she continued to stroke the table. "You're just fishing for compliments."

"Always."

She turned a warm gaze on him. "You'll always get them from me."

He started to answer, but he heard a whir of wings overhead and glanced upward. Homer, Aristotle, and Socrates circled once and then came in for a landing on the tabletop. They cocked their heads, putting one eye on the table and then the other. They walked across the wood, nails tapping out a staccato beat. Finally, they flew to the love seat and perched on the back all in a row...and began to preen their feathers.

Belle grinned at the sight. "Looks like you just received pigeon approval."

"I'm glad. Nothing is worse than pigeon disapproval because—"

She laughed. "Droppings."

"Yeah. They know exactly how to make their displeasure known in a very graphic way."

She laughed harder and then smiled at him, growing quiet as love filled her gaze and spread from her to him.

And in that silence he heard the sound of her cell phone in the house.

"I'd better get that." She stood up. "I set the ringer on high so I'd be sure to hear it."

While she disappeared into the house, he sat there watching the pigeons and the pigeons watching him... wishing the disruption that was her regular life would go away so they could be alone together.

In a moment she ran back outside, holding her phone out to him. "Great news! Ty's on speakerphone so you can hear, too."

"Like I told you," Ty said. "We found Daisy Sue. She's alive and well and definitely pregnant."

"That's wonderful news," Belle said. "I can't wait to tell Storm...and Fernando."

"Well, she's a dirty, muddy mess. I'm not sending her back until she is in show barn–worthy state."

"Nobody here will care how she looks. We all just want her home."

"I care. It's a reflection on our ranches. She's just been out with the herd, so there's nothing wrong with her."

"I'll send Kemp over to get her right away."

"No. I told you. I'm not sending her back till she looks good."

"Okay. When?" Belle asked.

"Tomorrow."

"Fine. Kemp will be there with a trailer early."

"Not too early."

She laughed at their old joke because they both knew he'd be up by five like most ranchers and farmers. "Need your morning coffee first?"

"You know it."

"Ty, really, this is absolutely wonderful news. Daisy Sue will be home in time for Christmas. You've just made a lot of people, including one lonely bull, very happy."

"I regret that we didn't figure it out sooner. It'd have saved folks a lot of worry. Please give the Steele family our apologies."

"Will do."

"And Belle, we want to give not only our apologies but Daisy Sue as well."

"What?"

"Daisy Sue is our Christmas gift to Storm."

"Oh, Ty—"

"Don't you think that's a good idea?"

"I think it's a terrific idea. This way Storm and her family can really take care of Fernando and Daisy Sue."

"Great. Glad that's a done deal." Ty chuckled. "And Belle, I thought you said you hadn't met Bert Two."

Rowdy sat up straight and leaned forward, listening to the conversation harder. Everything had been going so well with Daisy Sue and Storm that he'd relaxed his guard. Now he was suddenly in defensive mode.

"I haven't met him," she said.

"Sure you have."

"I don't know what you're talking about."

"I checked Fernando's website. There's a photo of you standing with Storm and Bert Two in the garden at Wildcat Hall."

"You must be mistaken." She glanced at Rowdy, looking confused at the news. "I've never been with Bert Two."

Rowdy felt a sinking sensation in the pit of his stomach. It'd finally come, that moment when his two lives collided in the worst possible way at the worst possible time. He should've told her. He knew he should've told her. His dad had told him to tell her. And now it was here, hitting him in the face with no retreat possible.

"Well," Ty said, "were you or were you not at Wildcat Hall?"

"Yes, I was there a few weeks ago."

"Okay. That settles the matter. You were there long enough to get caught in a photo with Bert Two."

She focused on Rowdy, cocking her head to one side as she considered him. "Storm wanted her mother to take our picture."

"And Bert Two just happened to be there?"

"No…at least I didn't think so at the time."

Rowdy didn't know what to do. Did he get up and leave? Did he smash her phone before the truth finally hit her? Did he stay and try to explain the unexplainable? He had only one option, and he'd always known it. He just had to suck it up and hope for a Christmas miracle… or that maybe that for once in his life his luck would turn good.

"Belle, you're not making sense. I know Bert Two. He's standing right beside you in that photo."

She stared at Rowdy as tears gathered in her eyes. "That's Rowdy with me."

"What?"

"Rowdy. You know the guy I've been telling you about helping me here at the house. That's Rowdy with me."

"Are you telling me that Bert Two and Rowdy are the same guy?"

"No...that's what you're telling me."

"All I know is that's Bert Two in the photo. Maybe he's taken on an alias I hadn't heard about. Maybe it's a leftover Halloween joke. Maybe it's—"

"Ty, I need to go. Kemp will be over tomorrow to pick up Daisy Sue. Thanks for all your help."

"But, Belle, are you okay?"

"Everything is fine. Not to worry. I'll be in touch later." She flung her phone across the patio where it hit the grass.

"I can explain," Rowdy said.

"I don't think so."

"I love you."

"I don't think so."

"I have a good reason for the deception."

"I don't think so."

She stood up, shaking her head with tears spilling down her cheeks.

He stood up, too, and held out his arms. He wanted to comfort her, comfort them both.

She backed up. "I think you'd better go."

"Not before you hear me out."

"All right. You've got thirty seconds to tell your side of the story."

He swallowed hard. It was bad. Worse than he could've expected, and he'd expected bad. "We can work this out."

"You lied to me. In what world of love is that okay?"

"It's not."

"And still you did it."

"My luck...my bad, bad luck."

"It's not luck. It's choice."

"No, it's not."

"If you won't even accept responsibility for your actions, how can you possibly expect me to believe a word you say?"

"I love you. That's not a lie," he said.

"Hah."

"I didn't want to lie. That's the truth."

"Hah."

"At least accept this truth." He was grasping at straws, but he needed her to at least believe something about him. "I *am* Bertram Holloway. Bert Two to folks around here."

"And the Buick Brigade knew it when they told us about the first Belle and Bertram. That's why the two of us together were so important to their story."

"Yes."

She swiped away the tears on her face. "Rowdy is, what... an alias, a penname, a joke on me...a joke everybody in this county is in on?"

"No. I'm Rowdy now. You made me Rowdy." He wanted to hold her and make everything right so strongly that his teeth ached from the pressure. "I'd always been Dad's sidekick, a chip off the old block. Bert Two. When you're young, that's okay. I'm even known as the unluckiest cowboy in the county."

"I heard."

"I accepted it all, every bit of it as my place in life... until you came along. You accepted me as Rowdy, a footloose cowboy poet who was lucky enough to do anything he wanted to do if he wanted to do it when he wanted to do it. He had no bigger responsibilities than to love you and make you happy."

She swiped at her eyes again.

"I liked that man. I enjoyed being that man. I became that man." He moved closer to her as he realized the truth about his actions. He hadn't even known completely what he was doing until this moment.

She rubbed her nose and looked down at the patio, but she didn't move away from him.

"I wasn't Rowdy until you saw me as that man. You believed in me. You changed my luck. How could I not love you with all my heart?"

She looked back at him, tears glistening in her eyes.

He held his breath, hoping against hope that his words would mean as much to her as they did to him. Maybe hope was the wrong word. Luck. He'd never accept being the unluckiest cowboy in the county ever again.

"I love you, too." She took a deep breath. "And yet I need you to leave now."

"But, Belle, there's so much I want to tell you."

"Not now. Right now my heart is breaking, and I just need to be alone. Please don't make this any harder on me."

"No, I won't do that." He glanced around the patio...at the pigeons, the furniture, the patio. Home. Belle's ranch had come to be home. "If it helps, I'm sorry. I was wrong. I regret it." He felt like crying, too, but he wouldn't, at least not now.

"I'm sorry, too."

"If it's all I'm ever able to give you, please enjoy my Christmas gift. I made it for you with love."

And he walked away, leaving his heart behind.

Chapter 36

Belle was all dressed up and on her way to Steele Trap Ranch. She looked a whole lot better on the outside than she felt on the inside. Lulabelle & You duds could hide a world of sins, but nothing could hide the pain that was tearing her apart after learning that her Rowdy was actually a stranger named Bert Two Holloway. Okay, so they were the same man, but that wasn't the point. She'd been betrayed by him...and for that matter, she'd been betrayed by the entire community since everyone had been in on the deception. If she'd been any further off her estimation of folks here, she'd be in orbit.

Eventually, she'd have to address the issue of Lulabelle & You Ranch, like dumping it as fast as she could and getting back to the city where life and people made a whole lot more sense. But for now, she had to finish what she'd started in Wildcat Bluff County.

She glanced over at Kemp Lander. He'd cleaned up well, too. He wore a red-plaid, pearl-snap Western shirt, pressed Wranglers, a jean jacket, ostrich boots, and a beige cowboy hat. She'd opted for one of her new Western rancher suits in charcoal gray with a pencil skirt, fitted jacket, holiday-green blouse, and black cowgirl boots. All in all, they both understood the importance of the return of Daisy Sue to Fernando. Storm would make sure there were plenty of video and still shots for them to use in cross-promotion later.

Daisy Sue rode in the trailer pulled by Kemp's one-ton truck. By this afternoon, she'd been on the road several hours from East Texas, so she was probably ready to get out and stretch her legs. Fortunately, she'd been primped for her photo shoot. She was all sleek and shiny black with polished hooves.

Belle wished the drive between the two ranches could take a long, long time, but they were next-door neighbors, so there wasn't a chance of that happening. As it was, she took a deep breath and braced herself for the coming confrontation. Not that she was going to say anything. She was born and bred to be polite. Besides, she just wanted to get through today and let it go at that.

She figured quite a few folks would turn up. Maybe even Bert Two aka Rowdy. She could handle it. She'd handled worse, maybe. And she could do it because she knew she'd never see any of them again for the rest of her life. That thought buoyed her spirits. It would help get her through whatever people might say and whatever events Storm had planned for her beloved Angus. And that was that. She'd prefer a deletion of the past few weeks, but she could at least end it with a definite period.

When they rolled under the Steele Trap Ranch sign, she glanced at Kemp, and he glanced at her. They both took a deep breath at about the same time.

"You don't think they're going to chew us out for not finding Daisy Sue sooner, do you?" he asked.

"No...not on camera anyway."

"She's not even their cow. If you want my opinion, they've got their nerve making a big stink about us moving a cow from one ranch to another ranch."

"That's one way of looking at it."

"It's the only way to look at it because it's a fact. That Steele family treats reality pretty loosely."

She took an even deeper breath. She had to get Kemp settled down before they got there. He'd been on a wild goose chase for what must seem like forever, and he had to be ticked off about all the wasted time and effort.

"And that Storm—"

"Kemp, I know this has been an embarrassing fiasco for you. It has been for all of us. I regret it...but you came through in the end and figured it out. We found her. There'll be a bonus in your end-of-the-year check, if that helps out."

"Thanks. It's not the money or the time and effort as it is the sheer off-the-wall, out-of-the-blue strangeness of it... not to mention *that* cousin of mine. I've been a cowboy my whole life, but this business with Fernando and Daisy Sue is something else."

"It's different, I admit. At the same time, Fernando—and now Daisy Sue—is an inspiration for people. He's a hero. And she's the love of his life."

"He's a bull. She's a cow."

"Yes, that's the basic fact just like you're a man and I'm a woman. And yet we become so much more as we live our lives. Wouldn't you agree?"

"Yeah. It's a fact, and I know it well, that every single cow or bull in a herd is different...ornery, smart, tricky, placid, you name it."

"That's so true. As it turns out, Fernando is a smart, loving hero. We don't know about Daisy Sue yet, but she'll be a mother, and that's important."

"Guess it doesn't hurt none for city folks to find out that cattle are a lot like them."

She couldn't keep from smiling at that assessment. "Somehow I don't think that's what they'll get out of it, but you're not far off the mark. Ultimately, I suppose it's all about love."

"That's another whole kettle of fish." He glanced over at her. "Best not go there for peace of mind."

She didn't say it, but she couldn't have agreed more. "Anyway, this can only last so long, and then it'll all be over."

"Sooner the better."

As he drove up toward the barns and corrals, she could see it was going to be a bigger circus than she could've imagined in her wildest dreams. Oscar Leathers and his dog, Tater, were directing traffic to an area of the pasture that had been roped off as a parking lot.

"Would you look at that," Kemp said. "Storm's got the Wildcat Den out in force."

"What's that?"

"Take a look. Wildcat Jack is the guy with long silver hair wearing his trademark fringed buckskin jacket, and beside him is Eden Rafferty. They're DJs for KWCB, our local radio station. It's got a big online audience, so I bet they're live-streaming."

"Oh...well, that's good publicity."

"They're live-streaming, all right. There's Nathan and Ken of Thingamajigs. They're tech."

Belle realized once more how few people she actually knew in the county, but it didn't matter anymore. After this performance, she was out of there for good.

"And there's Storm with the Steele family and Dune

Barrett, her mom's fiancé. Morning Glory and Mac. Hedy and Bert. Fern and Craig. Ivy and Slade. Misty and Trey. Lauren and Kent. Looks like Cole came in from the county dump. And there's, uh, Rowdy."

At that name she felt a shiver run up her spine, but she ruthlessly tamped it down. She'd known that he'd be here. She could live with it because he no longer existed in her world. She wouldn't be able to see him even if she looked directly at him. She felt a little better at that idea, but not much. Still, she must rally and put on a good performance. Lulabelle & You depended on her being professional and in control no matter the circumstances.

"Lots of folks here."

"Go very slowly, not only for the camera but so all those people can get out of the way."

"Where'd they come from?"

"No idea."

"They're wearing Fernando and Daisy Sue sweatshirts."

She looked closer and saw that he was exactly right. Storm probably sold them…and the design was good. Belle got an even better look as the group parted to each side of the road to make way for their pickup and trailer. A shout went up. That's when she realized that this was, indeed, a circus.

"I hope I don't run over anybody."

"We're on camera. Lower your window. Look out and wave as we go by folks." She did exactly that and was rewarded with waves and cheers from the crowd of well-wishers.

"I'm driving. You wave."

"I feel like I'm in a parade and I should be throwing out candy."

"I could use some candy about now. What do you have in mind? Fruit or chocolate?"

"No candy." She gave him a stern look and then went back to waving and smiling as they slowly made their way to the corral.

"If I can't have candy, I deserve hazard pay. The way those folks are darting back and forth across the road, they're lucky I don't wipe them out. And they're taking pictures with their phones and not looking where they're going."

"Please, whatever you do, don't hit anybody or even slightly nudge them."

"And I thought hunting Daisy Sue was bad. I thought getting Lester home was bad. This is about a million times worse. I take back anything good I ever said about the situation."

"I don't think you ever said anything good."

"Well, that's good."

"Please focus on the road. I changed my mind. You'll get candy later."

"Thanks."

She smiled and waved as he slowly drove up to the barn where Storm stood in front of Fernando's corral. She wore her trademark "Fernando the Wonder Bull" sweatshirt with jeans, boots, and red cowgirl hat. Fernando wore a jaunty green cowboy hat between his ears for the occasion. They were surrounded by family and friends, all dressed in Western wear with big smiles on their faces.

Kemp slowly and carefully maneuvered the trailer so Daisy Sue could be led out the back and taken directly to Fernando in his corral.

"Showtime," she said.

"Not for me." He glanced over at her. "I'm done. When you need a ride home, call me and I'll come get you."

"Are you sure you don't want to stay to see Fernando and Daisy Sue reunited?"

"There are some things in life I might not be too sure about. This one's a no-brainer. I'm done and done." He grinned at her. "Let them get her out of the back, and then I'm out of here."

"Thanks...for everything."

"Anytime, boss."

She put a smile on her face and stepped out of the truck. She headed for Storm, but she was waylaid by the radio guy with his tech team in tow. She had no doubt they were live, so she might as well make the most of it.

"Ms. Tarleton, I'm Wildcat Jack of the Wildcat Den. It's a pleasure to meet you."

"Thank you. The pleasure is all mine."

"Now that you've brought Daisy Sue home to Fernando, is there any chance you'll be taking her away again?"

She glanced over at Storm and beckoned her over. They probably only had a few moments to get this right before the big unveil when Storm led Daisy Sue out of the trailer.

Storm hurried over and gave Belle a hug. "Thank you so much," she whispered.

"I'm so happy that Lulabelle & You Ranch could come to the assistance of Fernando the Wonder Bull." Belle looked from Storm to Wildcat Jack as she swiveled into promo mode.

"Fernando and I are grateful for your help." Storm followed Belle's lead and smiled at Wildcat Jack.

"There's a big question on everybody's mind," Wildcat Jack said in his deep voice with his Texas accent.

"What is it?" Storm asked.

"Wildcat Jack already asked me, and I have a ready answer," Belle said. "Daisy Sue will never be returning to Lulabelle & You Ranch because she is now in her permanent new home on Steele Trap Ranch."

"Really?" Storm clapped her hands together in delight.

"Merry Christmas." Belle gestured toward the back of the trailer. "Why don't you lead Daisy Sue to her new home? You'll receive her official American Angus Association papers soon, but as of right now, she can join Fernando on Steele Trap Ranch."

"Thank you!" Storm threw her arms around Belle again in a strong hug and then stepped back with a big smile.

"You heard it here first," Wildcat Jack said. "Daisy Sue is now permanently at home with Fernando. And now, let's watch the happy couple as they are reunited after their long separation."

Belle walked with Storm to the back of the trailer where Slade and Sydney joined them.

"Your generosity has made my daughter very happy," Sydney said. "Thank you so much."

"I'm glad I was able to help," Belle said. She knew she sounded stilted, but she couldn't help but think they were part of the Rowdy deception and were no longer to be trusted with friendship. She felt sad about that fact, but she couldn't ignore reality.

"You really came through for us," Slade said. "We won't forget it."

"I'm happy I could do it." Belle gave them all a smile she

hoped was warmer than it felt to her. "I'm delighted everything has turned out so well."

"Please, let's let Daisy Sue out," Storm said. "Fernando is getting impatient."

"Is she on a lead?" Slade asked.

"Yes," Belle said.

"If you don't mind, I'll take her out of the trailer," Slade said.

"Please do. She belongs to Steele Trap Ranch now." Belle knew her job was basically done here. It was now the Fernando and Daisy Sue show. She stepped back to get out of the way and hit something. She glanced back.

Rowdy stood there with a burning look in his eyes.

"Excuse me," she said formally. "I didn't see you."

"My fault. I came up behind you."

"I won't be staying long." She moved closer to the railing so she had a good view of Slade opening the door to the trailer.

Rowdy followed her. "May I come over later?"

"No."

"We need to talk."

"No."

"You can't just throw away what we've got."

"We've got nothing." She moved away from him again, but he followed her. "Rowdy, please. I'm trying to enjoy the show."

"We make a better one."

"Oh look, Slade's bringing Daisy Sue out now."

As she watched, sunlight glinted on the beautiful cow's sleek coat, and the crowd roared its approval. Storm walked up, gently ran a small hand down Daisy Sue's long nose, and then took the lead from Slade and led the cow toward the corral where Fernando stood, tail switching as he extended his head in her direction, blowing softly through his nostrils.

Slade opened the gate and held it wide. Storm led Daisy Sue into the corral, unclipped the lead, and slowly backed out. Slade closed the gate and put an arm around his niece.

Fernando walked over to Daisy Sue. They touched noses. He licked her face. She licked his face in return. And they slowly walked together away from the noise and people and excitement toward the pasture in back.

"That's the way it ought to be," Rowdy said.

"Sometimes there is no happy ending." Belle quickly strode away from him and caught Kemp before he left so she had a ride home...or at least to her temporary home.

Chapter 37

Belle woke up the next morning to loud noise... scraping, thudding, and hammering above her head on top of her roof. She just lay in bed blinking sleepily. What were the cowboys doing? Maybe they were at the barn and it just sounded like they were on her roof. As soon as she could think straight, she'd get up and do something about it.

She was in a bad enough mood as it was without being subjected to extra irritation. She'd tossed and turned all night, thinking about Rowdy, not thinking about Rowdy. All her thoughts had whirled around him. She'd had enough of it. She was going to her family's ranch that afternoon to celebrate Christmas with them. And that meant leaving Wildcat Bluff County forever.

Yes, she'd miss all the county festivities that started tomorrow, but they wouldn't be fun without Rowdy anyway. She'd enjoy her Christmas vacation in East Texas, get over her cowboy poet, and be back at work in her Dallas office after the New Year celebration. If she felt sad and a little blue, she'd get over it. Hearts didn't break. They just cracked a bit. She'd mend once she was away from the constant reminders of him.

But first, she had to get that awful racket stopped, brew a pot of coffee, pack a bag. And all in that order.

She threw back the covers, put her feet over the edge of her bed, and pushed her hair back from her face. She wouldn't worry much about what she put on, since most anything was too much trouble and not worth the effort. She wouldn't be seeing anybody anyway, unless it was Kemp for a moment. No photo shoots. No parties. No nothing.

She grabbed clean underwear out of a drawer and put it on. She found a green sweatshirt and sweatpants tossed over the back of her chair. Good enough. She pulled those up, over, and on before she slipped into running shoes without socks.

She stumbled out of the bedroom and made it to the kitchen…all the while listening to the horrible racket on her roof. She was going to give those cowboys a piece of her mind right away.

She walked to her front door, threw it open, and stepped onto her front porch. She froze, squinting into the sunlight, trying to make sense of the scene before her. If she hadn't known better, she'd think she'd thrown a party in her sleep and invited half the county. Maybe she should've given her clothes, her makeup, her hair a little more thought.

All sorts of vehicles were parked on her circle drive and on the lawn, from four-wheelers to pickups—big and small—to one-tons with attached trailers. Folks she'd met and folks she'd never seen before were busily filling a dumpster with shingles that others on the roof were scraping off with shingle shovels and sending flying to the ground. Dust swirled in the air. Somebody walked by with a roll of tarpaper. Others hoisted heavy shingle stacks onto broad shoulders, nail guns hanging in holsters attached to belts around their hips, and jogged toward the back of the house.

Who were all these people? Did they take a wrong turn?

Get the wrong address? And the best question of all…why were they roofing her house?

"Belle, good morning!" Hedy zoomed over in her power wheelchair, grinning from ear to ear. "Did we wake you?"

"Uh…yeah."

"Early bird gets the worm and all that."

"What's going on?"

"Can't you see? You're getting a new roof just in time for Christmas!"

"But why now?"

"As to that…well…" Hedy looked down, around, and back at Belle. "I could use a cup of coffee. And a visit. Would you be kind enough to make a pot for us?"

Belle hesitated, not really wanting to talk to anybody this morning, particularly not a powerhouse like Hedy who just happened to be involved with Rowdy's dad.

"You're owed an explanation. And they don't need me out here, so we could go inside."

"I'm not so sure if—"

"Please give me an opportunity to explain things."

She wanted to leave the county, but she didn't want to leave a mess behind her. It'd reflect poorly on her family and maybe even her business. She opened the front door wide enough for Hedy's wheelchair.

Hedy powered into the house.

"If you'll follow me, I'll take you to the kitchen." She sounded formal and knew it, but she didn't believe she was on a friendship basis with anyone in Wildcat Bluff County anymore.

"Thank you."

She led Hedy into her cozy kitchen with its eat-in table.

She pulled out a chair and set it aside so Hedy could roll up to the table.

"Thank you." Hedy positioned her wheelchair at the table and then smiled at Belle.

She tried to return the smile, but it didn't go anywhere. She just wanted to go back to bed and tug the covers over her head to block out all the noise and confusion. Instead, she pulled out the coffee maker.

"Texas pecan coffee okay?"

"Perfect. Nothing better," Hedy said in a cheerful voice.

"Good." She spooned in coffee, poured in water, and started the machine to humming, gurgling, and burping.

"Life isn't always easy or straightforward." Hedy drummed her fingertips on the arm of her wheelchair. "But love really does conquer all."

Belle cringed because she knew just where Hedy was going with a talk about love. Rowdy. She put both hands flat on the countertop, watched dark liquid drip in the coffeepot, and tried to control her reaction.

"I love Bert," Hedy said.

"I'm sure he's a very nice man."

"Bert Two, or Rowdy as he wants to be called now, is like a son to me. He's hurting…and it's our fault."

Belle kept her back to Hedy because she didn't trust her expression not to reveal her total skepticism.

"It's not his fault. It's not your fault."

"Can we just let this go?" Maybe she could persuade Hedy to leave the Rowdy situation alone. "I'm done here. I'll be out of y'all's hair in no time flat."

"Maybe we're so set in our ways or maybe we're so protective of what we've built here over the generations that we've come to distrust outsiders. All your high-flying ideas simply set our teeth on edge."

Belle watched the coffee drip, giving up on diverting Hedy. She'd let her say her piece, and then they'd be done with it.

"I'm here to explain our actions. Like I said, Rowdy isn't to blame. He warned us it wasn't a good idea. He didn't want to do it, but he drew the short straw, and so it fell to him."

Belle wheeled around, finally goaded into action. "What was his job? Seduce me?"

Hedy chuckled softly. "Oh no, that came straight from his heart."

"Right."

"We didn't want to hurt you. We just wanted you to leave. We thought you'd get discouraged and go away if you couldn't get work completed on your house in time for Christmas. Rowdy was our last resort to slow down the process."

"Do you mean to say that's what this has all been about... just keeping the job from getting done?"

"Yes. It's pretty simple really...and not even our brightest idea. You could've brought in a team from Dallas and had the work done in no time."

"I thought about it, but I wanted to be liked in the community."

"We counted on that fact."

Belle just shook her head as she poured two mugs of coffee. She set one in front of Hedy and held the other as she walked over to the window and looked outside at all the activity.

"That's in the past. Done. Over." Hedy sipped coffee. "Now you're liked, admired, appreciated."

"You don't really think it's so easy, do you?"

"No, of course not." Hedy set her mug on the tabletop with a click. "What we did was wrong. As a community, we apologize. We're here to roof your house as a way of making amends and asking you to stay."

"Don't you think it's too little, too late?"

"Nothing is ever too little or too late when so much is at stake. Our county needs you. We need your smarts, your drive, your vision...and your love."

"It's all about trust now."

"If you stay, we'll earn your trust."

Belle held her mug tightly for warmth and support. She was wavering and knew it. She wanted to believe Hedy, but could she afford to do it?

"Another thing," Hedy said. "Your house will soon be ready for your party."

"What party?"

"New Year's Eve. It'll be a good way to start the year. What about a benefit for the one-room schoolhouse renovation? What about we start that transformation right here at Lulabelle & You Ranch? What about you give us a second chance?"

"A second chance?"

"Exactly."

Belle looked into Hedy's earnest brown eyes...and questioned her earlier determination to leave. What if everything Hedy had just said was true? If so, could she walk away from so much promise?

"Never forget the power of love. It doesn't just make the world go 'round, it powers this community." Hedy backed away from the table. "If you can find it in your heart to forgive, please go see Rowdy. He's waiting for you on the patio."

Belle simply stood there as Hedy left her alone...with her jumbled thoughts, with her new dilemma, and with her desire for Rowdy. Did people make mistakes, learn from them, and go forward? Was she a big enough person to accept an apology, particularly one as huge as putting on a new roof, and go forward?

She set her mug down beside Hedy's mug. She needed to see Rowdy before she made any sort of final decision.

She quickly walked through her house to the back door. She stepped onto the beautiful patio he'd made for her, but he wasn't there. Instead, the Buick Brigade lounged on her cedar furniture, appearing quite pleased with themselves as the noisy roofing activity went on around them.

"Belle, please join us," Louise said.

"We brought cowboy cookies." Ada gestured toward a plate heaped high with drunk-looking cookies. "As you can see, I made enough for all the busy bee workers."

Belle smiled, not even surprised at the sight. She should've known this was all part of their master plan. "I don't suppose you lovely ladies had anything to do with my new roof being put on today?"

"Us?" Ada feigned innocence. "We just brought cookies."

"And this." Blondel set a tarnished gold locket on a long chain beside the plate of cookies.

"Is that the other Belle's locket?" Belle put a hand over her heart, feeling it ratchet up with heightened emotion. She quickly sat down because her knees had suddenly grown weak.

"Yes, dear," Blondel said. "Belle's locket has come home...to you."

"Christmas is a time to heal and renew," Doris said. "Bertram will be back from visiting the pigeons soon."

"He needs you," Louise said.

"And you need him," Blondel said.

"Together," Ada said.

The ladies of Destiny rose as one, smiled benignly at Belle, walked across the patio, and disappeared around the side of the house.

Belle simply sat there, feeling almost as if the Buick Brigade had never quite been with her or real at all. Yet the cookies and locket were on her table. And the thud of nail guns hammering shingles continued unabated on her roof.

As she gazed at the locket and listened to the guns, she felt a soft breeze caress her face…and her heart expanded in happiness. If the locket had come home to her, had she come home to Wildcat Bluff County?

She glanced up. And there was Rowdy. He walked toward her with his strong, confident stride. As he grew near, four pigeons flew out of the barn, circled overhead, and disappeared in the direction of the Buick Brigade.

Wait. *Four* pigeons? What was the message of the fourth one? And then she knew. The last pigeon-gram needed only one word. Love. And Rowdy was its messenger.

He stepped onto the patio that he'd built with so much love, looked down at the table he'd created with even more love, and picked up the locket steeped in long-lasting love. He knelt in front of her with hope shining in his eyes.

"If you'll marry me, I'll love and cherish you forever." He held out the locket nestled in his palm.

She clasped his hand…and felt the locket grow warm.

Acknowledgments

Judy Forehand Lewis deserves credit and appreciation for her wonderful book reviews of my Smokin' Hot Cowboys series and her suggestion that it "sounds like Bert Two is about to get a little matchmaking from Hedy and friends!" Exactly right. It's high time Bert Two aka Rowdy found love in his own book.

Once more I set off into the backwoods, took a canoe down the Kiamichi River, and arrived at the red rock enclave of the Williams—Buck-Saw, Hot-Rod, and Reed-the-Steed. A shout-out goes to them for input on pigeons, memorial trees, brush fires, construction, taste-testing cowboy cookies…and to Rod for help with the shingle chase scene.

I attended the delightful production of "Some Enchanted Evening: the Songs of Rodgers & Hammerstein" at Eastern Oklahoma State College in Wilburton, Oklahoma, as a benefit for the music department. Shelley Dennis, actor and writer, gave a great performance while Ruth Askew Brelsford, former professor of theater, made sure the audience was enthralled with the entertainment. They inspired me by their dedication to the arts to create the Wildcat Bluff County Arts Center.

Cathy Dennis Cogburn also inspired me to create Lulabelle & You Western Wear with her clothing designs for Cowboy Threads and jewelry designs for Grace Designs.

Ron Shaw and Roy Shaw are the perfect duo to set

everything right when something breaks or goes wrong at Twin Oaks Ranch. They're also wonderful bluegrass musicians. I appreciate their long-time dedication to the community.

Deputy Sheriff Julie Garriety deserves a big thank-you for her timely arrival when the shingles for my house were stolen…along with fun lunches, great advice, and support for my books.

About the Author

Kim Redford is the bestselling author of Western romance novels. She grew up in Texas with cowboys, cowgirls, horses, cattle, and rodeos. She divides her time between homes in Texas and Oklahoma, where she's a rescue cat wrangler and horseback rider—when she takes a break from her keyboard. Visit her at kimredford.com.

BLUE SKY COWBOY CHRISTMAS

Joanne Kennedy's Blue Sky Cowboys series reminds us that there's really no place like home for the holidays

Weary from a long deployment, Griff Bailey has been dreaming of a quiet Christmas on his father's ranch. But all his hopes of peace are upended when he finds his one-time fling Riley James has moved in.

Riley swore off dark, dangerous men a long time ago, but there's something about Griff she still just can't resist. It'll take a miracle for these two stubborn former lovers to open themselves up again, but isn't that what Christmas is for?

"Full of heart and passion."

—Jodi Thomas, New York Times bestselling author, for Cowboy Fever

HONKY TONK CHRISTMAS

You're in for a rockin' country Christmas with *New York Times* bestselling author Carolyn Brown

Out-of-work journalist Sharlene Waverly is determined to finally write that mystery novel, until she's charmed by the Honky Tonk's stories of romance come true. She decides to write a romance so hot it'll melt the soles off a cowboy's best eel-skin boots, and she finds inspiration in the hot cowboy who's helping her get the Honky Tonk renovated in time for an unforgettable Christmas shindig. With his whiskey-dark eyes, Holt Jackson is the perfect present to find under the mistletoe...

"Makes you believe in Christmas miracles."
—The Romance Studio

For more info about Sourcebooks's books and authors, visit:
sourcebooks.com

THE BEST COWBOY CHRISTMAS EVER

A Garrett Family cowboy from author June Faver will you keep you warm this Christmas

When handsome sheriff Derrick Shelton meets Angelique Guillory and her young daughter at the Garrett family ranch, he is immediately drawn to the woman who seems to desperately need a true family Christmas. Determined to erase the shadows from her eyes, he decides to give her the best holiday she's ever had…

"June Faver has become a must-read author."
—Harlequin Junkie for When to Call a Cowboy

For more info about Sourcebooks's books and authors, visit:
sourcebooks.com

COWBOY CHRISTMAS HOMECOMING

The rugged Texas cowboys of June Faver's Dark Horse Cowboys series are putting it all on the line for love...

Zach Garrett is home from war haunted by PTSD, trying to fit in to what has become an alien world. With the holidays fast approaching, his uncle Big Jim Garrett offers him a place on the family ranch. Zach isn't sure he's up for a noisy, boisterous Garrett Christmas. . .until he meets beautiful Stephanie Gayle, and all his protests go up in flames. . .

"Guaranteed melt-your-heart romance."
—*Romancing the Book*

MISTLETOE IN TEXAS

Bestselling author Kari Lynn Dell invites us to a Texas Rodeo Christmas like no other!

Hank Brookman had all the makings of a top rodeo bullfighter until one accident left him badly injured. Now, after years of self-imposed exile, Hank's back and ready to make amends… starting with the girl his heart can't live without.

Grace McKenna fell for Hank the day they met, but they never saw eye to eye. That's part of why she never told him that their night together resulted in one heck of a surprise. Now that Hank's back, it's time for them to face what's ahead and celebrate the Christmas season rodeo style—together despite the odds.

"This talented writer knows rodeo and sexy cowboys!"
—BJ Daniels, New York Times bestselling author

Also by Kim Redford

Smokin' Hot Cowboys

A Cowboy Firefighter for Christmas
Blazing Hot Cowboy
A Very Cowboy Christmas
Hot for a Cowboy
Cowboy Firefighter Christmas Kiss
Cowboy Firefighter Heat